THE FAMILY

The

FAMILY

David Plante

FARRAR STRAUS GIROUX
New York

PS
3566
L257
F3

6/1978
Soc.

First published by Victor Gollancz Ltd.
First American edition, 1978
Published simultaneously in Canada by
McGraw-Hill Ryerson Ltd., Toronto
Printed in the United States of America

The author gratefully acknowledges the support
of the Arts Council of Great Britain

Library of Congress Cataloging in Publication Data
Plante, David. The family.
I. Title.
PZ4.P714Fam   [PS3566.L257]   813′.5′4   78-4189

to my brother
Donald Plante

There is another Russia.

Gorky, *The Zukovs*

Part One

I

HE, STANDING at the window—

Daniel raised the blind as quietly as possible, held the cord taut, and leaned close to the large dark window. The cold came off the glass like breath on his face. He adjusted his head to see through his reflection out to the street, the street lamp and snow falling through the light about the lamp. Silent wind blew the snow at an angle, and for a moment he thought that gravity had shifted, and he leaned a little to the side. Gravity shifted again and the snow fell in another direction, and suddenly the snow fell in many criss-crossing directions at once, and then with a sudden rush it rose silently slowly upward.

He let the blind come down. Through the open slats he saw a car drive up and stop before the house. It was a grey car, or in the pale light of the street lamp it appeared grey, with round bulging fenders, a bulging hood, and covered with snow. It was like his father's car.

He turned when he heard, behind him, the door to his parents' bedroom open. The furniture appeared immense in the dimness, and he couldn't see the wall out of which the bedroom door opened, just the door now open, and his father in a woollen bathrobe standing before it.

"You're still up?" his father said.

"I heard a car stop outside."

His father's hand was on the door knob. He was standing in the light beaming through from the kitchen, and that light on him isolated him in the darkness. His bathrobe was open at his chest. When his father leaned forward the bathrobe came away from his chest, and Daniel saw underneath to an armpit. He heard his mother say, "Jim." His father went back into the bedroom and closed the door. He did not allow the spring to work the latch but turned the knob, for Daniel saw the outside knob, a crystal knob, turn slowly, as by itself.

In the bathroom, under the soft yellow light, he filled the basin with warm water and lowered his face to the surface. He heard knocking. He shook his hands and opened the door. It was his mother. She had her arms crossed over her breasts. Her hair was all out. She said, in French, "You're not asleep yet?" He said, in English, "I'm going," and passed her as she passed him to go into the bathroom. He stopped, however, to turn round and say, "But you'll wake me early tomorrow." She didn't answer. Her nightgown rode the heavy flesh of her thigh.

At the door to his bedroom he paused. Through the closed door of the bedroom opposite he heard the snoring of his brother Edmond.

He undressed in the chill dark. The inside window was open a little; snow piled up against the frame of the outside storm window. He got into bed quickly and pressed himself to his younger brother Julien, his chest to his brother's back, his knees into the backs of his brother's knees. His brother moved a little, then settled. Daniel lay awake. He heard his mother go back to her bedroom. The headboard of his parents' bed was on the other side of the wall behind him. He heard the springs of the bed as his mother got in, and heard talking, now his mother, now his father.

His mother told him that whenever she couldn't sleep she would in her mind go through the house she was brought up in, room by room. She remembered her mother blackening the kitchen stove, her father winding the kitchen clock, the red light through the isinglass of the coal stove in the living room, the gas lamp over the round dining room table— As though he were years and miles away, Daniel went through the rooms of his own house, a small bungalow with a large columned porch and an attic dormer, in a French Canadian parish in Providence, Rhode Island.

He had two dreams, and he had them simultaneously. In both, he was alone in the house, but in one he was in the back entryway, and he knew that if he didn't lock the door soon enough he would be in danger, and he couldn't lock it, couldn't make the loose lock hold, and the key turned and turned without doing anything; in the other, he was in the front entry, and he knew he must open the door quickly and get out of the house, but he couldn't open it, the lock stuck, the key wouldn't turn.

The parish church bell rang early Mass, clanked. He wondered what the Indians had thought when they first heard a bell ringing in their wilderness. The bell stopped. He remained half asleep, but through his sleep he heard his parents in the kitchen. He heard boots being stamped on in the back entry, and heard rapid voices, then the door shut. He heard a factory whistle. His brother Julien was lying on the far side of the bed, his back to him. He felt he had an inside body which wouldn't be moved no matter how he tried to move his outside arms and legs. His mother opened the door—she did not open or shut doors in a slow, deliberate way, but, first turning the knob, she pressed sideways against the door as if it needed all her thrusting weight and banged it open—and said, "It's time." He hated her. He half opened his eyes to see her close the window, lock it, and turn on the heat in the radiator. She leaned over him and brushed his hair from his forehead with the tips of her fingers. She said, her voice as low as when she had been speaking to her husband, "But you don't have to get up, you know, not yet, unless you really do want to go to Mass. It's cold out. There's a lot of snow." He said, his eyes closed, trying to raise his sinking body, "No, I'll go." She said, "Then you can pray for us."

15

In his underclothes, he rushed from his cold bedroom into the warm bathroom. His mother's stockings were drying on the radiator. His father's bathrobe was hanging on a hook at the back of the door. He put it on. The wool bristled with thousands of fine entangling hairs, and a smell of his father rose from the nap. He was about to run from the bathroom back to his bedroom to dress, wrapped in his father's robe, but now a little shiver passed through him, and he quickly took it off and hung it back on the hook.

He sat on a stool next to the radiator in the kitchen. The heat off the radiator moved the pages of the calendar above, which was turned to MARS 1952. Daniel watched the calendar pages move. A sock dangled from his right hand. He heard the bathroom door open and he turned to see his mother come into the kitchen wearing his father's bathrobe. She sat at the table and buttered a slice of toast, unaware, it seemed to Daniel, of him; then she half turned round to see where he was, and said, "Tu peux me rendre un grand service."

"What?" he asked.

"Offer your Communion for a special intention."

Daniel said, "Yes," and continued to look at his mother. She put jam on her toast and bit into it. Daniel put on his sock and got off the stool. His mother was looking away from him towards the kitchen windows, the outside storm windows opaque with frost through which a gelid colourless light made everything in the kitchen appear blue-grey, that light on her face. She said, "He'll do what he wants." Daniel sat across from her at the table. He held his stockinged feet a little above the cold linoleum. She said, "But you'll miss the beginning of Mass—it won't count."

He said, "I have a little time." He twirled a knife round and round on the bare kitchen table top.

She looked at the kitchen walls. She said, "It took us twenty-five years to pay for this house. If he died, I'd have the house." She paused, watched Daniel slowly twirl the knife, then said, "Daniel, you've got to go."

The snow was up to his shins. He climbed over a bank thrown up by a plough at the side of the road and walked in the street, his boots loose about his shoes. The light was yellow through a yellow-grey sky. Lumps of snow fell from the branches of maple trees and thumped into the drifts below. In the vacant lot next to his house, the little dark wood of thin bleak bare trees was bent in all directions under the white. Daniel imagined he had come to this place from a great distance, to another country abstracted from the snow-covered streets, the telephone poles, the large snow-white tree on a corner, a wide snow-expansive wilderness, very still, where an Indian fur trapper out looking at his traps—

The sloping side streets on the right ended at a river. The river was black against the snow, and small ice floes raced down it. Each section of the river between the rows of tenements seemed to be the same section repeated, until there appeared the corner of a plain two-storey brick building with large grille-covered windows and surrounded by a high iron fence in the midst of woods on the other side of the river. He crossed the next street and saw the front section of the file shop where his father worked, saw its gateway and a black iron grid bridge over the river to the gateway. A group of men who he knew worked in the factory were standing on the bridge, and many were gathered in the factory yard. They were black and grey against the snow, and a thin grey mist rose about them. Daniel paused in mid-street when he heard someone shout, "Hey!", and saw his father step through the open factory doors. The men outside all began, together, to shout his father's name, "Jim Francoeur, Jim Francoeur, Jim Francoeur." At his distance Daniel stood motionless and looked down the street at the men, some of them now laughing, others walking about.

The sacristan was wheeling the catafalque down the centre aisle of the dim grey church. Daniel walked behind him. The black velvet drape over the catafalque was bordered in gold braid and embroidered in gold thread at the top with a great

17

crown of thorns; the gold fringe dragged along the brown linoleum. In his seat, Daniel opened his black missal to Messe pour les défunts.

He followed the Mass in his missal, but from time to time lost his place, arrested by an image, deeper than the words, of a second-storey tenement porch with a clothesline strung between the pillars and snow collected on the line, a garbage can half-buried in a drift of snow, a section of a hard black river between soft white banks, a distant white spindly wood with a wrecked car dumped in it, a black iron bridge, snow-covered water tanks on the snow-covered roof of a long brick building. It seemed to him the images came to him as if to fill out a sense he had that he had forgotten something, and he couldn't recall what it was; the sense, as compelling as it was empty, took on the shape of a porch, a garbage can, a river, a water tank, then a moment later it was empty again; even when the sense was filled with the animated images of his father at the dark open entrance of the factory, it wasn't this he'd forgotten, wasn't this he was trying to recall.

On the way down the aisle (all movements slow in the church; as he approached the altar it appeared to recede from him) he thought, not of what he was to receive, emptying his mind of all other thoughts, but of Indians. He thought of how they called on their namesakes, called on the powers of a black crow, a running deer, a lean wolf when they went out to hunt or to fight, so when they went out they were no longer Indians, they were a black crow, a running deer, a lean wolf; crows, they flew, deer, they were swift, wolves, they were cunning; their black feathers were wings, antlers and hooves grew out of their heads and cleft their feet, their necklaces of wolves' teeth extended their jaws; they were no longer what they had been, they were no longer men.

In his pew again, he knelt, he placed his clasped hands on the edge of the back of the pew before him, he lowered his forehead to his hands, and he closed his eyes. He thought of his mother's special intention. As he didn't know what it was, he could only think of it as a round empty space, an opaque globe, and he tried by the force of his concentration to make that space, that globe, glow with his appeal: he strained his mind to do it, he strained all his body. He was praying for he had no idea what, but what he was praying to have happen must happen; as he pressed his face into his hands it was to suppress a shout to have it happen, a shout out of such longing, such longing to have it happen that it, now happening, fulfilling his mother's intention, might fulfil his as well, because they were, his mother and he, and his mother and father and he, and his mother and father and his six brothers and he, and his mother and father and six brothers and sister-in-law and he, all one, all one world, all longing—

Daniel wanted something to happen. It wasn't in his power to make it happen, but he wanted it to happen with his whole heart and his whole soul. He saw the feather on a woman's hat, the taped temple of the eyeglasses of an old man, a classmate on the other side of the aisle rubbing a finger back and forth across her teeth. No. He must pray, pray for his mother, his father, for his six brothers, those at home and those away from home—

The snow outside made him squint as he descended the steps from the church. He re-crossed, on his way home, the street that went down to the iron bridge and the file shop, and saw the men in the factory yard making a snowman. He watched a man roll a head-size ball across the ground, pick it up and place it on top of the two-ball torso, and the other men pelt the snowman with snowballs.

He crossed the street where his grandmother lived, stopped in the middle. His Aunt Oenone opened the door. His grandmother was sitting, arms crossed, in a rocking chair by the black kitchen coal stove. Oenone said to her, "C'est Daniel," and she said, "Oui, je l' vois." Daniel sat on a chair pushed against a wall.

"I'm coming from Mass," Daniel said in French.

His grandmother couldn't speak English. The only

expression she knew in English was "by and by", which came out "bymby".

Matante Oenone (the "matante" a one-word honorific) sat at the big wooden kitchen table and stretched her arms out on it, but kept her hands raised from it and articulated her fingers as if to display many rings on both hands. She said, "I should have gone too, but I took a laxative," then she said to Daniel, "It was an anniversary Mass for your mémère's younger brother, Polidore, who died a year ago."

"Who was he?" Daniel said.

Matante Oenone said, "Your mémère didn't speak to him when he was alive, and she's not going to speak to him now that he's dead."

The grandmother looked out of the window. Her face appeared without flesh, all bone, and stretched over the bone skin; her cheekbones jutted out as though the muscles beneath them had been cut away, and the deep vertical wrinkles on either side of her face were the scars from the incisions; her black eyes, which were completely round and always half shut, looked as if held in the dark sunken circles of the sockets by skin bruised from rubbing against the bone; they were close to her large nose, which looked too to be made of bone, but cracked at the bridge; her jaw thrust out so far her natural bite might have been that of her upper teeth clenched; her thick hair, white, was pulled away from her high bony forehead and braided into a knot at her nape. She was a quarter Indian.

"What did he die of?" Daniel asked.

Matante Oenone looked at him for a long while, not sure she could tell him, then she said, her fingers suddenly still, "Cancer."

The grandmother moved in her rocking chair.

Matante Oenone kept her fingers still. "Cancer," she said, "just like my poor father."

The grandmother moved again.

"Cancer doesn't forgive," Oenone said.

The grandmother rocked.

20

Matante Oenone raised her hands and pressed the middle fingers to her temples and moved the other fingers. No one spoke. The aunt pressed more and more on her temples and lowered her head, her eyes wide open. The left eye was white with a cataract. Then she raised her head and said, "Well, I offer it up."

Daniel said, "Your eye—"

She said, "It sometimes feels as though it's boiling. I think I know a little what it must be like to be in hell. But they can't offer up their pain, and I can. I didn't sleep all night long. Maybe the devil's in my eye, that eye, and he makes the pain so great to try to force me to plead with him to take it away. But I don't plead, I won't. I accept. I say, 'Thank you, devil, because all the suffering you send me I can offer up to my Jesus.' It helped my poor father, I know it did, to be able to offer up his cancer. I helped him do that. I was there with him, offering up my own father with his cancer."

Daniel squirmed in the wool-lined heat of his coat.

Matante Oenone said, "When I was a novice in the convent, they said I wouldn't make a good nun, they said that I didn't know enough about life, that only a woman who knows about life makes a good nun, so I had to leave. Well, I got married to a rotter, a drunkard, who spent more nights with the sluts in South Providence than with me. He'd come back at any hour, any time, I never knew when, drunk, and I'd take him in, I had to. You don't think I had a lot to offer up then! I saw my eldest little girl die in her crib of starvation. She went all blue and suddenly grew, her arms and legs grew so long they reached out of the crib. I saw it. My husband came home that night, and when I showed him the baby dead in the crib he leaned over, and he was so drunk he threw up all over it. I saw him die too. He died of cancer too. He came back to me to die. He had a horrible death. The cancer came out all over him. His skin was like the bark of a tree, with blood and pus running in the cracks. I never abandoned him—"

Oenone gave to the incidents of her life the form of little epics handed down, not from generation to generation, but from visit to visit. The grandmother said to Daniel, to interrupt her, "Your father came by this morning on his way to work."

Matante Oenone said, "He asked me to say a prayer to give him strength, but I had to tell him I couldn't. He'll have to depend on all his own strength to do what he wants. I won't help him."

The grandmother said to Daniel, "You tell him I wrote a prayer for him—"

"You'd support him in anything," Oenone said to her mother. The grandmother said nothing. Oenone again pressed the tips of her middle fingers to her temples and closed her eyes. After a moment she looked at Daniel, who would be more compassionate than her mother. (Oenone once told Daniel that as a child, because their parents never brought the children toys, Daniel's father, older than she, had made her a doll's house; one morning Oenone couldn't find the house, and asked her mother where it was, and the mother said, "You left it in the middle of the floor so I burnt it," and Oenone saw, under the round burner on the top of the coal stove, raised because the house had been too big to fit entirely into the stove, the roof go up in flames.) She said, "I've got to bathe my eye." She went into the pantry, came back with a basin and a dish towel. She spread the towel on the table, placed the basin on it, then went into her bedroom just off the kitchen and came out with a bottle. She sat and poured water into the basin. She took off her glasses, dipped the index and middle fingers of her right hand into the water, shook them, and very slowly and very delicately touched the lids of her closed eyes.

The grandmother used the baptismal name of Daniel's father, not his nickname Jim. "Arsace knows what he's doing."

Oenone talked with her dripping fingers pressed to her eye. "He doesn't know. If he knew, he'd stay with the union.

Doesn't he know he's a *worker* in the factory, not the owner? Doesn't he know the union is on *his* side, is fighting for him? It's not reasonable. It doesn't make any sense what he's doing, crossing the picket line." "Picket line" was in English. Matante was shouting. "You'll see where his stubbornness will get him—"

"They'll lose their jobs," the grandmother said. "Arsace knows what he's doing."

"If he only looked, he'd see that it's to make sure he keeps his job that the union is striking. They'll win, those men. And you'll see, they won't push Arsace out for not being one of them. He won't lose his job, but it won't be because of his stubbornness, it'll be because of the union after all—"

The grandmother uncrossed her arms and slowly got up from the rocking chair. She went into her bedroom off the living room, an angle of which (the arm of an overstuffed chair with a doily, the corner of a mirror reflecting a crucifix) Daniel could see from his chair in the kitchen, and came out with a square wooden box. She sat in the rocking chair again, put the box on her knees and opened it. She poked around in it. She asked Daniel, "Will you be taking his lunch to him?"

"Yes," Daniel said.

"Give him this."

Daniel got up to take it. It was a worn scapular tied round with a thin strip of dry palm. He put it in his pocket.

Then Matante Oenone said, "Well, tell him I'll say a prayer for him." Daniel thought she meant later, but she stood, swung her large right arm out in front as far as it could go and brought it back, with various looping movements of her wrist, to her forehead, to her breast, to her shoulders, and bowed with each point of the traced cross, and held the bow, her hands pressed between her breasts, to pray, "Ô mon Jésus—"

Daniel lowered his head. He couldn't pray, and he couldn't hear his grandmother pray. He heard Oenone fart. Daniel held his breath. His aunt finished her prayer.

Oenone opened the door for him to leave. She said to her mother, "How my poor father would have liked to see all his grandchildren. If he could come back, even for an hour—" The grandmother said, "No. I wouldn't want him on this earth again. He worked too hard. We work too hard to die to want to come back."

The morning had gone darker. Daniel found his mother, changed into her housedress and apron, washing the gas stove. The burners on the stove rattled. He sat at the kitchen table with his brother Julien to have breakfast before they went to school. The door to his brother Edmond's room, which he could see from the kitchen, was open; he had left for work. The sounds the mother made were very loud, as the silence of the kitchen was insulated from outside sound by the snow. Daniel poured himself a glass of milk. There were times, Daniel knew, when his mother could be as hard, as metallic as the stove; cleaning the stove, she slammed the oven door, rolled out and shoved back the grill, took off and banged on the burners.

He collected his books together, waited for Julien to stamp his boots on over his shoes and tuck his trousers into his boots. He knew that he should simply say goodbye to his mother from a distance, saw that now she would say, if he approached her to kiss her, that she didn't have time. But Julien, his boots squeaking, went to her and she bent so he could kiss her. Julien picked up his books from a chair and followed Daniel out.

They didn't speak. Daniel walked ahead and now and then turned to see if his younger brother was behind; he sometimes saw his brother standing with his back to him, looking the other way. Snow began to fall through the soft grey cold air. When Julien hung back too long Daniel told him to come on, but that was all he said. They passed in front of an empty bare lot in the centre of which, grey-black and jagged above the smooth snow, was a jutting ledge; the ledge had been a buffer to the wind, and before it was an exposed patch of dry, brown-yellow, crumpled grass. Daniel walked on, but he felt his brother wasn't behind him, and he looked back to see Julien standing on that patch of ground, facing the ledge. Daniel watched him go to the edge of the patch, reach down with his mittened hands for snow, pat it into a ball, and hurl it up at the ledge. Then, as always silent, he rejoined Daniel.

They separated in the parish school yard. Alone, Daniel snapped off small icicles from the edge of a low sill. Mère Supérieure came out, pushing open the two black doors of the school's entrance, and rang a heavy bell held in both hands, so her white arms jerked out of the wide black sleeves and Daniel saw, beyond the false inner sleeves which were like long black gloves cut off at the wrists, the white undersides of her forearms. The students in the yard formed ranks. Daniel joined the assembling ranks of his class, girls and boys in two rows according to height, and they, being the eighth grade, marched in first, in total silence.

He was not able to listen as the teacher of the first half of the day, Mère St Joseph de Nazareth, taught the first class of the day, which was catechism. It was in French. His book was open on his desk but he looked out of the window. He didn't really see the window, he was aware of a grey plane surrounded by a cold but soft white glow. He was startled when a bird appeared in that abstraction and bounced about in all directions until its sharp beak was pointing at him. He heard the sharp voice of Mère St Joseph de Nazareth say in French, "That bird is the devil, don't look at it." Daniel turned to her so quickly it was as though her stark grey face, pinched together by its fluted white wimple, had appeared behind the window, not that he had turned to her. He listened to Mère St Joseph.

Because Christ was God, He had to have suffered more than any human being had ever suffered, had to have suffered as only God could suffer. The false gods of all other religions, the nun said, did not suffer, and many non-Catholics thought Catholicism was strange because its God suffered— And it *was* strange, Daniel thought, that his

Saviour should have suffered as much as Mère St Joseph made Him suffer. His suffering passed beyond all suffering, was worse than being burned or cut, was worse even than the sufferings of the missionaries who, because they were Catholics, were tortured by the Indians, their bodies hung up with fish hooks through their muscles, red-hot tomahawk heads pressed against their bodies and hung round their necks, deep incisions made all over their bodies and the cuts opened and stuffed with grease-soaked moss and set aflame —this was nothing compared to Christ's suffering. Christ wanted to, had to, suffer, and He did it for us, for us at each Mass, day after day after day, for ever and ever, in all parts of the world, and as there was never a moment when a Mass wasn't being said somewhere in the world there wasn't a moment when He wasn't suffering: the blood burning through with sweat, the crown of thorns with the biggest thorns possible which stuck into His eyes and brain, the carrying of the cross, the rough splintering edge of which sawed through the muscles of His shoulder, the nailing to the cross with long rusty nails, the first attempts failing because the weight of His body pulled the nails through the flesh between the bones in His palms, so He fell forward, and had to be nailed through the wrists. And, Mère St Joseph de Nazareth said, raising her voice, His worse suffering, a suffering not depicted on any crucifix, was that He had to hang on the cross for three hours, not covered by a loin cloth, but *nu*, suffering His passionate shame. And while He hung there the devil came to Him with one last grotesque temptation: not to suffer, to renounce His suffering, to abstract Himself, by a simple act of inattention, from His suffering, never to suffer again.

The radiator hissed steam. Daniel glanced at the window. There were four sparrows on the ledge.

During the boys' lunch at home, the mother, silent, cleaned the cupboards of the pantry. When they were putting on their coats to go, she gave Daniel a brown bag, their father's lunch. Daniel held the bag away from him and stared at his mother. "What's the matter?" she asked. He couldn't say he didn't want to take the lunch to his father. "Nothing," he said.

They stopped at the iron bridge, where men still stood about in the snow, a grey trampled slush they from time to time kicked in clods over the edge into the rushing black water. Daniel pushed his brother's shoulder, but Julien wouldn't cross the bridge. Daniel ran across by himself, across the yard, and through the factory entrance.

It was almost church-quiet inside but for a distant shrill hum and a steady *tac tac tac*, the noise of two or three machines. He found his father by a wide high window with a semicircular transom. The transom was pushed a little open and the many-paned window looked as if it had been painted a semi-transparent yellow, so the brush marks showed. The light through it, falling on the father and his machine, was pale yellow, and in the great empty space of the shop floor, in which all the machines were still—except for his father's and those of two men working at the far end—the father, in his overalls, did look as though he were in a kind of church, a spare grey-yellow church with the iron beams and struts exposed, and it smelled of dust and grease. The father switched off his machine, the shop floor fell quieter.

Daniel handed his father the brown paper bag and watched him take out a sandwich, unwrap it, take three bites, chew carefully, and swallow. He asked, "How is your mother?" This way both father and mother had of asking the sons about "your father" and "your mother" put the one asking at a slight distance from the other, as though "your mother" might not necessarily be "my wife" or "your father" "my husband"—it was perhaps the only formula they could find, unable for some reason to accept the informality of "your ma", "your dad", or even "ma", "dad". Daniel said, "She didn't say anything." "Nothing?" the father asked. "She said she wondered what we'd have for supper." "I see." Daniel waited. His father ate the sandwich.

27

He said, "You tell her everything's going to be all right." Daniel raised and lowered his head. "And where's Julien?" the father asked. "He wouldn't come in," Daniel said. "Why?" Daniel shrugged his shoulders. The father smiled a little.

The long light from the windows fell across the rows of still machines and along the bare floor boards of the spaces between the rows. Daniel lingered a little, walking up and down the rows. His father was quietly eating, the other men had stopped their machines to eat. Daniel's attention expanded in the silence, taking in details in the pale yellow light he hadn't seen before: that the supporting frames of some of the machines were decorated with iron scrolls, or that a strut against the ceiling, though painted so often they were almost obliterated, was embossed with a vine and flowers, that a pillar had a capital of large petals. In this unfamiliar shop, his father was leaning against the bench, turned towards the large yellow window as if he were looking through it.

He had a sharp jaw, a straight nose, black eyes, a strong lean body; in him, and just visible beneath his outward body, there was, always tensed but still, a stark Indian brave.

Daniel recalled the scapular. He dug it out of his coat pocket and brought it to his father. "Mémère told me to give you this."

His father looked at it and stuffed it into a shirt pocket under the bib of his overalls.

Daniel, after a moment, asked, "Why does Mémère keep bottles of water in her room?"

"That's water she collects on the day the waters are blessed."

"Who blesses the water?"

"God does."

After school, in the kitchen reading, Daniel waited for the back entry storm door to open and close, the inner entry door to open and close, and the knob of the kitchen door to turn slowly.

The mother, in the pantry, stopped peeling potatoes, took off her apron, and went into the bathroom to wash her face, comb her hair, and make up with powder, rouge, lipstick. Daniel saw her stand before the bathroom basin and stare at herself in the mirror. She came into the kitchen. She sat at the table while Daniel continued to read in the rocking chair. He closed his book and held the place with a finger to give her the chance to talk if she wanted, but perhaps she had been looking past him when he thought, glancing up from his reading, that she'd been looking at him. He finally said, "He said everything would be all right." The fresh red lipstick and rouge and powder set her face. She did look at him, and she appeared to be a little surprised by his appearance. Her mouth, her eyes, her face opened in a smile. She said, "You remembered my special intention."

Julien came into the kitchen from the front room. He said, "My father is coming home."

"How do you know?" the mother asked.

He said, "I saw him through the window walking down the street."

The father would use his car to drive to church on Sunday, to visit his mother or relatives, but not to go to work.

The mother stood. She said to Julien, "Ouvre la porte pour ton père."

Julien left the kitchen door open, opened the inner door to the entry, and left the storm door till he could see, through the small frosted window at the top of the door, his father's cap. Daniel was standing by his mother at the kitchen door. He saw his father come in, saw him slowly take off his rubbers, come up the few steps to the kitchen, take off his cap at the threshold, step in and kiss his wife (who made a jerky movement towards him), then hand her his rolled-up overalls, carefully take off his heavy coat and hang it in his closet behind the rocking chair—all these actions, for their quotidian regularity if for nothing more, of greater importance

29

than anything that might have happened. He sat in his rocking chair, unlaced his shoes, took them off, put on his slippers, and said, "Well, the strike is over. They got what they wanted, the union, but it doesn't concern me. I've been made a foreman."

When Edmond, a printer, and the only one of the five older sons to live at home, came in from work, his father said nothing to him.

At the supper table, the mother said to Edmond, frowning, "Your father has been made a foreman." Edmond's eyes dilated, staring at his father, and he said, "Gee whiz." His father was eating his soup. Edmond said, again, "Gee whiz," and picked up his spoon the way a child would, his fist clutched round the handle, and said, looking at his mother, "How about the old man."

The father said, "I remember my first job. I was seven or eight. I spent the whole day cleaning used bricks, knocking the old cement off them, piling them in a neat wall. After a whole day of that the old geezer I was doing the job for said to me, 'What do you want—ten cents or a bunch of bananas?' I said, 'Neither,' and leaned my shoulder against the brick wall and pushed with all my weight until it crashed, then walked away."

Edmond got up from the table before the others finished.

His mother said to him, "There was a letter for you."

Edmond stood still, his face stark. "A letter?"

"It's on the top of the icebox."

Edmond didn't move, as if, when he reached for the letter, he'd find there wasn't one there. He went for it slowly, reached slowly for it, and held it out before him. He stared, not at it, it seemed, but through it. He said, "It's from my buddy Bobby." He took the letter into the front room.

The father, mother, the boys were getting up from the table when Edmond came back into the kitchen. The letter was sticking out of the pocket of his old khaki Army shirt. He said, starkly, "He still says I should go on down to

30

Kentucky. He said I should drive right on down there in my car."

His mother said, "Yes," but his father nothing.

Edmond went to his room to change his Army shirt for a red and white checked wool shirt. In the kitchen, he put on his coat, then he left the house.

The father went into the bathroom to read his paper. The mother, at the pantry sink, washed the dishes. Daniel dried. Above the long low smooth-edged sink was a window and from the window was a view at the back of the house of bare white maple trees and a street going down to a hill, called Violet Hill, towards which the white sun in a grey sky was descending. The mother was agitating the water in the dishpan with a soap strainer to make suds. The dishpan was a round metal basin from which most of the grey and black mottled enamel had been chipped or worn off. It was a kind of centre to the life of the family; it had been bought when the mother and father were furnishing their new house, was older, the mother said, than any of the seven sons, and it was always with an indefinite but vivid sadness that Daniel saw his mother yet again take out the dishpan from beneath the sink, place it in the sink, fill it with hot water, make suds, and, as she was doing now, drop the glasses in and immerse her hands to wash. She rinsed the glasses and put them on the rack as if Daniel wasn't there. Outside the window Violet Hill was blue-grey, and above it the pale sun sank in the dark grey clouds. Beneath the window, on the other side of the narrow yard, was a tall old grey wood fence. Where the fence met a corner at the sidewalk there was a brick post with a white stone ball on top, and the top of the ball was layered with a hemisphere of snow.

The yard below was in darkness, the fence, the car, the garbage cans visible only by a dim grey glow from the snow. Daniel said to his mother, "Look!" She raised her eyes from the dishpan; if she saw what he wanted her to see she didn't say, but Daniel had got her attention, and, as though his getting her attention was for her a point of sudden resolution, she said, standing straight for a moment, "Well, he knows what he's doing." She threw her shoulders back, bit her lower lip for a moment, and looked at Daniel and asked, with a deliberate attentiveness and clarity of voice, "Look at what?"

He had wanted to ask her to look at the sun, but with her attention fixed on him, he couldn't. He said, "No, nothing." He put down the dish towel. "I've got to go to the bathroom." "Your father's in there," she said. "I've got to go," he said. "He'll say you always want to go when he's in the bathroom." He went to the bathroom door and knocked. "Dad," he said, "I've got to use the toilet." "Yes," his father said. Daniel jogged up and down. "I mean really, right away."

He heard a window open, then the toilet flushed, then the toilet seat slammed. "Dad." He heard the window close. The father unlocked the door, opened it, and came out in a billow of smoke. His lips were drawn tight; he looked hard at Daniel. The mother came, drying her hands on a dish towel.

Daniel said, "I can hardly see inside for the smoke. I won't be able to find the toilet." The mother said to the father, "If you're going to smoke, Jim, smoke wherever you like. This is your house as much as mine. You don't have to hide in the bathroom." The father said, "But I wasn't smoking!" "Look at the smoke!" the mother said. The father went to his rocking chair to finish reading his newspaper.

The house went dark. They listened to the radio in darkness in the front room. Between programmes the radio hummed, and in the humming were faint voices speaking foreign languages.

II

IN BED ALONE on Saturday morning, Daniel stared at the
blue roses in the wallpaper of his bedroom. His body was the
body of another person, and he held that person motionless
against him, while he himself lay still, hardly breathing,
staring out. Then, suddenly, he jumped out of bed into the
cold.

In Edmond's room, the mother was making his bed.
Daniel watched her smooth out the sheets, very wrinkled,
of the narrow bed Edmond had slept in. There were three
other made-up beds in the small room.

He asked, "Where is Dad?"

"In the cellar. He's putting order in his workbench."

Daniel went down. His father had, in a corner of the
cellar, a large heavy workbench with four drawers for tools.
One of the drawers was filled with files. He had all kinds,
from thin fine files to huge coarse files with big wooden
handles. Julien was with him at the workbench. The four
large drawers were open, the top piled with oiled tools and
disassembled lathes and vices and small motors, large gears
and flywheels and shafts—parts of machinery which the
father had collected over years, perhaps imagining he would
one day have enough for a small factory of his own in the
cellar, the product most certainly a tool—and while Daniel
sat on the tool chest by the workbench and watched, Julien
handed tools from the top of the bench to his father, who put
them in special compartmented sliding trays.

Daniel stood, looked at the tool chest he had been sitting

33

on, a battered, paint-spattered chest that had belonged to his father's father, who had been a carpenter, and he opened the heavy lid. A smell of grease rose up. He looked through the old planes and hand drills and stamps for simulating wood grain, looked among them as if to find something. He found plumbs and plumb lines, rolled-up cord and blue chalk, rulers and spirit levels.

His father said, "I'm trying to put order here, tsi gars, and you're making disorder there."

Daniel closed the chest. He looked at his father reassembling the wooden parts of the model of a big industrial tool, a precision grinder. He left his father and Julien to go to another part of the cellar where, in a corner, were pushed together high-backed chairs on a big oak table, a massive sideboard, a glass-fronted cabinet, an old stove and an older icebox, his mother's mother's furniture.

Daniel recalled his grandmother in his and Julien's room; at night she moaned, and she often called for the bed pan. Daniel one day shouted, "The old witch!"

He went upstairs and wandered about the house looking for his mother. He found her making hers and his father's bed. He said, "I'll help you," and stood on the side opposite her, wedged between the bed and a cedar chest. She threw out a sheet. He grabbed it. They stretched it across the bed.

She said, "Whenever I was giving birth, Dr Dalande stood at the foot of the bed, your father at the head, and I'd hold your father's hand. I'd say, 'I can't go through this again, I can't.' He always promised I wouldn't. Son after son came. The doctor said, again and again, 'It's a son.' I'd say, 'Well' is he normal, Doctor, does he have all his fingers and toes?, The doctor'd say, 'You have nothing to worry about, you two, your babies are perfect.' I would keep hold of your father."

A little shiver passed through Daniel as his hand smoothed out the wrinkles.

"Son after son came," she said. "All seven of you perfect."

34

He wandered to his own room. The bed was made, he lay across it. A heavy warm liquid seemed to rise and ebb, rise and ebb in him. He placed his hands on his chest as if to feel the rise and ebb.

He went out into the kitchen, where, now, his mother was making out the Saturday shopping list at a corner of the table. One elbow was resting on the table and she was resting her forehead in her hand; the other hand held a pencil stub above a scrap of paper. She looked as though she were trying to balance an impossible equation. She said to Daniel, "You tell me what we should have."

"A big ham," he said.

She made a face. "I'm sick of ham."

"Pork chops," he said.

She said, "Cooked how?"

"On the grill."

"That'd get the grill all greasy and dirty." She let her pencil fall on to the paper. "No, I can't think. It's the same thing over and over again. We never have a change. Your father doesn't like to try anything different. I'm tired of it all, aren't you?"

Daniel didn't have a chance to answer. His father, followed by Julien, came into the kitchen and stood by the door. Daniel remained in his father's rocking chair, rocking, and he looked at the floor. He felt his father looking at him, and he thought: he wouldn't get up and give him the chair. His mother said, "Give the rocking chair to your father." Daniel got up. His father sat. Daniel sat next to Julien at the table, across from their mother.

She said, "Sometimes I think I wouldn't mind moving out of this house. We've lived here for more than twenty-five years, almost thirty. Sometimes I think I wouldn't mind a change. We worked hard for it, I know. Your father did. And I know it's well built, and you can't get a solid house like this any more, but I wonder if we're going to be here until we die—" She said to her husband, "What do you think, Jim? Will we?"

He said, "Well, I will."

The mother said to Daniel, "You see, he won't move."

The father said, "Now that's enough, ma p'tite fille."

She said, "But I live here too, and I don't have much of a say about the house, about staying or moving. I guess we're lucky to have a house at all, so many don't—"

The father stopped rocking and said, "Now cut it out."

She looked at him for a moment. Daniel waited. She suddenly got up, swiftly went to the rocking chair, put her arms round her husband's head and leaned down and kissed his forehead.

She let him go and the father rocked. The mother went back to the table, sat, picked up the pencil stub, and wrote out the shopping list.

Edmond came in, his face bright from the cold, and said, "I've been down town. I bought a lot of hillbilly records." Daniel and Julien followed him into the living room where, on the huge combination radio-phonograph, he played the hillbilly records. The twanging nasal repetitive music was to Daniel, as it was to Edmond, the music of a far country. Edmond said, "I'm going down to Kentucky, I really am, to join my old Army buddy Bobby down there."

The father, Edmond, the two boys dug the Dodge out of the snow drifts in the back yard. Once they got it out in the street, they linked snow chains about the back wheels. The mother watched them through one of the frosted kitchen windows; the white frost round the edges of the window, diminishing towards the centre of the window into a dark hole, made her head appear as though it were detached from a body, and floated in the inside darkness.

In the afternoon the father and the two boys drove to the shop of the eldest son, Richard; it was one floor of an abandoned textile mill on the same river as the file shop, but in the midst of a sagging clapboard slum. The thick boards of the shop floor were unpainted, splintered, warped, some loose, all with wide cracks between and bolt holes through them, so Daniel saw beneath them to a layer of dust and bits of broken brick, old yellow rumpled newspapers and brown paper bags, rusty screws and nails and rats' droppings, and no doubt masses of old rotting tangled threads, scraps of cloth, shattered parts of shuttles and looms. In a far corner was a grey mass of what must have been worm-eaten raw cotton.

Richard's back was to the entrance. He was working. The father and Julien went up to him. Daniel hung back from his father and Julien to look out of a window—dirty, the broken panes taped—at the river where the rusted chassis of two cars, one following the other, looked as though driven by ghosts who, watching the black river swiftly flow past them, imagined that though dead still they were moving. It was cold inside. Daniel wandered to where Richard, his father and Julien were standing. As he approached, Richard, who was the only other son to have like him blue eyes and light brown hair as their mother did, grabbed his younger brother by the back of the neck, brought him stumbling to him, and pressed his face into his shoulder. "How's it going?" he asked. He released Daniel, who after he regained his balance said, "All right."

The father said, "Don't let us stop you from working." Richard immediately got back to work. With a large electric drill he was drilling fine holes in small tubes of steel. After he did a few, the father said, "How about letting me have a go at that?" Richard stepped away. The father drilled the holes as though he didn't care how he did it, his ease matter-of-fact evidence of his skill. Thin coils of steel rose out of each cube as the drill sank into it. (Studying them, Daniel wondered why it was always what was irrelevant that interested him—why wasn't he as interested in knowing what the block of steel was going to be used for as he was in those fine spiralling coils?)

While his father was working, Richard asked, "Has anything happened at the file shop?"

The father jerked a thumb back over a shoulder as to indicate someone behind him and spoke out of the side of his mouth, "They've made the old man a foreman."

37

Richard simply stared at him; the father's hand was on the lever of the drill press and the drill spun with a screech above a block of steel, but he didn't press the handle down. Richard said with a sad voice, "Come on, shut off the drill, and let's sit down at my desk." The father didn't move, so Richard reached to switch off the electricity. But instead of leading the way to his desk he stood before his father with a continuing look of sadness, and finally raised his hands and put them on his father's shoulders and said, "I'm happy for you, I really am," then turned away.

The father tapped his two younger sons on the shoulder to make them come also, and followed Richard to what, with no other definition of the space but the old desk which might have been left behind in the mill as rubbish, was his office. Richard sat at his desk, his father sat before it, the boys stood by their father. Richard rested his arms on papers and circulars and said, "Now tell me."

The father hunched his shoulders, he stuck out his chin. He said, "Your old man did what he thought was right." Richard lowered his head a little. The father said, "Maybe he's stubborn, but his work means a lot to him." Richard stared at him. The father stated blankly, "He held out against the union. He went it alone." Richard said, "I see."

The father didn't say anything more. He reached out for a paper on the desk and held it up. It was a circular advertising the precision grinder, Richard's invention; the photograph showed the grinder on a black background, below it, in pink letters, FRANCOEUR MFG. CO., INC. PROVIDENCE, RHODE ISLAND, and above, also in pink, the company's emblem, a grinding wheel with wings. The father asked, "How're they selling?"

Richard asked, "The grinders?" The father remained silent. "Let's not talk about the grinders now," Richard said, "not with your news. You haven't told me anything." The father said, "So they're not selling." "Yes, they are," Richard said.

The father looked around as at a shop floor crowded with

machines producing parts which would be assembled into thousands of precision surface grinders to fill the many orders that arrived every day by mail on his son's desk. "You'll have a shop," he said.

Richard scratched the eczema on his hands, the eczema he had got years before in the service. He said, "I never realized before that we're poor."

The father said nothing.

Richard said, "Neither did I realize before something funny, that because I'm poor I can't do the work I want to do. You know, Dad, I'm not really interested in money. I'm interested in doing my work, in making those grinders. They're good grinders, I know they are. It's not the demand that's missing, it's the supply. I've been working seven days a week, a good fifteen hours a day. I can't supply. What's missing is the money, enough money. It's stupid, I know, but I had never thought of my work, my own work, my own private work and money together till just these past few days. I thought I could work enough to make the money I need to work—"

"You couldn't hire anyone?"

"I couldn't afford to. Even if I was paid immediately for the deliveries we've made, I couldn't afford to continue to work, never mind hire someone to help, never mind take my wife to a restaurant. Maybe I'm not a businessman, as no one in our family is, but I don't want to be a businessman, I want to do my work, not anyone else's. It still seems to me a very simple thing to want."

"So," the father said flatly.

"I've got on my desk fifteen orders, but I've gone bankrupt."

The father sat silent for a moment, then asked, "What will you do?"

"I'll do what's always done to small businesses. I'm letting myself be bought by a bigger company. They'll take over, and I'll work for them. I'll be a designer. It'll mean moving the household out of Providence."

The father got up. Richard got up too, came round the desk to stand by his father, and said, "I'll pay you back everything you put in, Dad. I'll pay you back with interest."

The father turned his black eyes on Richard and held them on him for a long time before he got up and buttoned his heavy coat. "You couldn't pay me back," he said.

Richard half turned away, then turned back quickly. He held his hand out and said, "You're a better man than I am. You could have made it work out right." His hand at the top button of his coat, the father, immobile for a second, looked at Richard, then he reached out, stiffly shook Richard's hand, and quickly released it.

Richard looked away. He rubbed the red backs of his hands.

His father said, "Your eczema is bad again."

"I sometimes wish that because of it I could get discharged from work as I got discharged from the Army."

The father took a step away.

Richard said, "Do you remember, just after I got married to Chuckie, and we were living at home with you and Ma, when I was working in the factory and going to mechanical-drawing classes every evening to learn to draw the precision gauges I had in my head? I'd come home with the drawings and show them to you. You'd say, 'Yes, yes.'"

In the car Daniel thought of the skeleton cars he had seen in the river and, watching the banks of snow pass, he imagined he and his brother and father in the silent car were in fact still and the snow banks were moving.

His mother, at the kitchen table, was writing letters.

His father said, "I should have known."

"What?" she asked.

"He's losing the shop," he said. She raised her hands, a pen in one, and said nothing. He went into his room.

The mother put her arms over the letter paper. She said to Daniel, "Your father's never thought that Richard's serious about work."

"Why?"

40

"I don't know. I remember, though, once, a few days before he was taken into the service, he came home drunk one night. He was nineteen. He had gifts for us. He laughed, showing the gifts to us. Your father didn't laugh. I couldn't either. Richard always thought he wasn't serious, not as serious as his father. He'd left high school when he was sixteen. Your father didn't object to that, but he objected to his drinking. He wanted to throw Richard out. I said, 'No, let me take care of this.' I sent your father to bed. I gave Richard a cup of coffee, then I sent him to bed. He woke up his brothers, who'd been asleep a long time. The next morning, that was Saturday, I took Richard into the front room to be alone with him and I said, 'You and your friends went up to Boston last night to the Old Howard burlesque.' Richard said, 'No, honest.' I said, 'I'm sure you went.' 'How are you sure?' he said. 'I have a feeling,' I said. I couldn't help smiling. He smiled too. He said, 'You're a bit of a witch.' I said, I hoped severely, though I could see my tone of voice made Richard wince because, as serious as I was trying to be, he knew I could never really be serious, and he too, he knew I wanted to ask him about the Old Howard, I said, 'Listen, I won't—your father and I won't—stand for this again. I'll do what he wanted to do last night if it happens again. I'll throw you out. I don't care if you have to sleep in the street. We won't tolerate anything from any one of you that gives us a bad name.' " She looked at Daniel for a moment. "And you remember that too." She looked down. "Anyway, his hangover went on into the afternoon and he stayed in, which he didn't do often, I can tell you. Then my brother Louis came in to visit. He knew he could visit as long as he wasn't drunk, but whenever Louis did visit he used the bathroom a lot, and every time he got out of the bathroom the level of the rubbing alcohol was lower. That afternoon he came a little drunk, and he was slurring his words. Every time he came out of the bathroom he was drunker. I didn't know what to do. Your father went down to the cellar. Then Louis left. I was alone with

Richard. I wondered if I should use Louis as a lesson to him, but something stopped me, maybe because I knew I couldn't be serious, not like your father, and I said, 'You know, Louis's the best of my brothers.' Richard's eyes filled. Mine filled."

She looked up at the window and all at once appeared to remember something she had forgotten. She said, "I think I'll clean the attic."

"Now?" he asked.

"I want to get rid of some junk."

They put on extra sweaters against the cold in the un-heated attic and, Daniel first, they climbed the ladder, which rose through her hanging dresses in her closet, to the trap-door he opened. He helped her up into the dim chill slanted space stacked with dusty boxes and newspaper-wrapped bundles.

She and Daniel piled in a clear space near the trapdoor things she pulled out of boxes, tore out of the newspapers: babies' clothes, babies' shoes, a drying frame with hundreds of pins for stretching and holding taut starched lace curtains, signed photos of silent-screen movie stars. She said, "I think we need your father to take this all down."

Daniel went for him. He was in the cellar, sitting on a broken chair by the furnace, smoking. He threw the cigarette into the open furnace when he saw Daniel.

"She's cleaning the attic," Daniel said. He made a face.

Daniel wandered about the packed boxes while his parents worked. He opened the flaps and looked inside. His mother had collected together and put into cartons the belongings of the family that were no longer in use, of her mother and father, of her husband and herself, of the sons after they left for the services, for college, and placed these cartons in the attic. She added to the cartons whatever was left behind by the sons each time they came home on furlough or holidays: Army socks, collar stays, ties, books.

A smell of dust rose up to Daniel's face when he opened a box which contained some of his father's belongings. He pulled out a pair of dumb-bells. He found many dull straight razors and badly nicked razor strops, a pair of tempered steel figure skates and a manual on making circles and large but delicate designs of overlapping circles on the ice, old hernia trusses, a pair of pointed shoes with buttons on the sides, an old slim pin-striped suit with a narrow high-buttoned vest, and a pamphlet on physical fitness, which Daniel opened to the photograph of a muscular man hefting a boulder. He raised his two sweaters, stuck the booklet under the waist of his dungarees, and pulled the sweaters over it.

His mother said, "Daniel!"

"Yes, yes," he answered.

He opened Edmond's box. It had very little in it: comic books, a cap pistol, holy pictures of Christ as a young man, jigsaw puzzles, a partial plate of false teeth, a fountain pen, Army shirts and ties, and an elastic-bound pack of letters written to his parents when he was in the Army which Daniel lifted out.

His mother said, "We're going down now. You can help with the rest." He wasn't sure she was talking to him. With Edmond's letters, he went to her. His father was filling a brown bag with many pairs of infants' shoes. She asked Daniel, "What are those?" "Old letters," he said. "Throw them there," she said, and pointed to a heap of letters on the floor. "What are they?" Daniel asked. "They're letters I wrote to Richard and Albert during the war. I used to write them each a letter a day. They saved them all and brought them back home in their duffle bags, and I put them up here, and now I'm throwing them away." "Why?" "Who cares?" she said. "Maybe—" "No," she said. "Throw those on the pile." Daniel dropped Edmond's letters on top of the others; they slid and caused a little avalanche of envelopes.

In the grey afternoon, Daniel tried to nap, but he couldn't fall asleep. His mind had itself become a body somehow aware of itself, of its skin and hair, and he could not break the awareness enough to sink away from his mind-body into sleep. He got up.

43

He found his mother at the kitchen table, again writing letters. She asked him if he'd like to read the two letters she'd already written. While he read, read as if in darkness, she finished a third. The letters were to his brothers away from home, in Korea, in Cambridge, Massachusetts, in Miami, Florida, and each one was different except for the sentence, "Your father would like me to tell you, his good news. He has been made foreman, at the file shop. We are, all, very happy for him." The sentence, read three times, the only variation the placing of commas, did not at all account for what the father had done; it struck Daniel that his mother didn't understand.

He said nothing about the letters. He wanted to be with his father. He asked where he was. "He's in the cellar," the mother said.

There was only one light on in the cellar, so Daniel couldn't immediately see what his father was doing. With Julien standing by him at his workbench and watching, he was chopping with a small axe at what appeared to be frail wooden boxes, then he carried the bits of wrecked box to the furnace. The door of it was open, and the wavering light from inside made his father, Julien beside him, bright red, as he threw the bits in—when, with a roar, the father and Julien were turned bright yellow. The father watched whatever he'd put into the furnace burn away before he went back to his workbench to continue to chop.

At this workbench, the father and his oldest son Richard had worked together, night after night, under the low yellow light of the hanging bare bulb, on a wooden model of the precision surface grinder Richard had designed, which would be able to grind to .0001 of an inch, and which Richard wanted to manufacture. Richard gave his father the wooden model. It was this he was now breaking up to burn. He had almost finished.

At supper, Edmond spoke with a French Canadian accent he'd picked up during the afternoon at the ice-cream parlour near the church. Neither his mother nor father spoke English

44

with a French Canadian accent. Edmond switched accents easily. Daniel had once heard him speaking to the blind Polish wife of the Italian next door, who had lost her way trying to get into her yard and, her hands searching the air for contact, fallen into the hedge of the Francoeurs' yard; Edmond helped her out, shouting in case her blindness obliterated her hearing as well, "Is she broke all the bones?" He said now to his parents, "Mr Dufresne, he told me, he said, your father put on a good show, they were all talking about it, there. They asked me, hey, what's he going to do with all the money, there? I said, you ask him. They laughed. They're all right, you know. They said, why don't your father and mother ever come in here and have an ice-cream soda with us? Why don't you go to the ice-cream parlour some time, there? Jeez, you never go anywhere. I'll take you. I'll treat you to a nice ice-cream soda, there. They're really nice, you know, there, the people. Jeez, they're all from the parish, there." But as his parents didn't respond, Edmond stopped.

Daniel was the last to have his bath. It took him a long time. After it, instead of joining his parents, Edmond and Julien in the front room where they were listening to the radio, he went into his bedroom and quietly closed his door. He opened the drawer of the bureau that was for his personal belongings. He looked over the contents: a flat square of polished steel, a fine glass tube, an empty perfume bottle, a fragment of fringe, a tassel, the small dried skull of a squirrel. (What he saved, as if he had by putting everything together in his drawer and closing it created some small closed fiction, he had done out of some strange compulsion to save objects which suggested to him more than what they in fact were, but, once put away, a strange revulsion towards the collection made him, at times, tip everything in the drawer into the wastepaper basket, because, all in a jumble, they suggested to him more than he could take in, a thick, an almost sickening plethora of private ideas and feelings.) He felt a slight vibration in his stomach. He lifted the edge of the newspaper lining his drawer and saw the corner of the little physical-fitness book he had found in his father's box in the attic. He thought he would look at it quickly, then put it back; he lifted it out carefully by grasping the corner with only the tips of his thumb and index finger. He sat on his bed and studied the cover. The title, *Promotion & Conservation of Health, Strength & Mental Energy*, by Lionel Strongfort, was entwined in billowing ribbons. He opened it. The pamphlet started with Lionel Strongfort's creed—"I believe in the divine right of every being to possess a body that is strong and beautiful and radiant with energy"—and on the page opposite the creed was a photograph of him wearing briefs and a pair of Roman sandals and standing on a Turkish rug. With a sense of something he must put off, Daniel read, straining his interest in a way that would put the something far off, the creed, the foreword, the introduction, the text. The introduction was by Lord Douglas, Marquess of Queensberry, and the text, by Strongfort, was dogmatic about improving the fitness, the vigour, the symmetry of the body. Then Daniel read,

Parents ought to have their sons take up the practice of Strongfort to develop that manliness, that courage, that moral fibre and strength of purpose that would lead them onward and upward and prevent the very existence of degenerative influences. The realization of the effects of pernicious [Daniel didn't know the meaning of that word] habits and their results on posterity has made human eugenics [nor did he know that one] one of the most vital subjects of the day, and it is safe to say that the time is not far distant when marriage under the circumstances will be a crime. A casual observation of the statistics of idiots, degenerates, deformed children, show beyond dispute a few of the terrible results of such deplorable habits, and the asylums are filled with victims who have become enslaved, and, in most cases, through no fault of their own.

Daniel knew he must put the book away, must not look at it. He heard the murmuring radio from the living room. He tried to visualize the suffering body of Christ, tried to raise Him from the great depth beneath the words which his eyes kept slipping back to look at. He wouldn't appear, and there appeared instead, with an involuntary turn of the page from text to photograph, the body of a man. He imagined all the photographs of Strongfort were separate men, standing, posing, lifting weights in his bedroom. He wanted himself to be an intimate of that strange race. He took off his bathrobe and stood before the large mirror over his bureau to look from the photographs at himself flexing his muscles, standing with an arm raised as to throw a javelin, taking the position of discus thrower, gladiator, archer, the poses of classical sculpture. But there was something more naked about the photographs than his body; it seemed to him the nakedness of the man in the photograph had to do with more than skin, more than chest and thighs. The man was publicly naked. He studied all the photographs and he studied himself. He tried, flexing and positioning his body, to see in it that manliness, that courage, that moral fibre and strength of purpose that would lead him onward and upward. He wanted to go onward and upward. If he couldn't pray to Christ to help him, he could pray to the photographs of Lionel Strongfort to help him, to help him to undress his body to a naked body that was more naked than his private physical body. He wanted that naked body, the body made powerful by the black and white image of it. Standing before the mirror, he studied the muscles of the legs, the large strong feet, the ankles; he studied the muscles of the thighs, the hollows at the sides of the buttocks, the abdomen, the chest, the shoulders. He felt throughout him small, shocking sensations as of a compulsion to reach out and grab something, but there was nothing to grab. He ran the tip of his index finger over the photograph. What he wanted, what he wanted! He thought: Ah Dieu, ah Dieu! Then this happened: beyond the picture of Lionel Strongfort in the pose of

47

a gladiator, the sword and the shield removed for the fullness of the body in its pose, he saw Lionel Strongfort, the beautiful Lionel Strongfort, hanging nailed to a cross, and he was without the figleaf to hide that part of him which, exposed, caused him shame so passionate the part, for the sheer passion, began to rise. All of Daniel's body revolted against what he saw; he vaguely wanted to vomit. He closed the book. He wouldn't allow himself to touch himself, to touch that part of himself which of itself, as if it had hundreds, thousands of small deaths and resurrections, had risen in the air. He sat on the edge of the bed. He squeezed his risen part between his legs. He opened the book again and laid it across his legs. He couldn't help it. He would become weak, would lose all his teeth and hair, would lose all his power, would become an idiot, would die, but he couldn't help it. He would commit a mortal sin, he would be impenetrable to grace, he would go to hell, he would find himself abandoned and beyond hope, but he couldn't help it. He squeezed his legs together. He thought: If Christ had resurrected in His body, and now was bodily in heaven, then His body, because it was His body, was also the body of God, or at least a third of God, and it had, because it was God's body, to be even more beautiful than the body of Lionel Strongfort, and why, why, why couldn't he, why was it condemning to, want the body of God? He wanted it. He wanted to have seen Christ hanging naked on the cross, he wanted to have touched His bloody hot ankle, he wanted to have helped take that long loose-limbed body down from the cross and held it in his arms while others spread a sheet on the ground, wanted to have put the body down and wrapped it in the clinging sheet through which the remaining steaming wetness of the body would slowly penetrate. How could he stop? He opened his legs. His released erection jolted the thin book, made it jump up and fall away. Ah Dieu, ah Dieu, he said almost out loud, and, bending double, he grabbed his cock in both his hands at the moment his brother Julien came into the room. Daniel didn't move, looked down, but

48

at an outer rim of vision saw Julien go to the bureau and open his drawer and, as though Daniel hadn't been there, leave the room, closing the door with a slam behind him. Daniel couldn't help himself. Not even the entrance of his brother into his most private world, making that world all at once utterly public, could make him stop and dress; perhaps that his private act was made public made Daniel, for the very fact that he imagined he was being watched by others, more helpless in what he was doing; perhaps, in his self-enclosed privacy, all his greatest longings had to do with a wide, a world-wide, an all-involving public; perhaps his longing was for some totally exposed public body, a naked body, placed in the midst of the world, and everyone would look at that body in wonder at its nakedness, in awe at its beauty, its fitness, its vigour, its symmetry, in love for its total, total mystery, and it was to that body, that body, that he was making love. He couldn't help it.

He felt he had killed himself. He wiped himself with a handkerchief which he then stuffed under his pillow. He put on his underwear, turned off the light, and got into bed. He wanted to be asleep before his brother came in, but he couldn't sleep waiting for Julien to come into the room. He listened to the voices of the radio which would not clarify into words.

When Julien did come in, Daniel's body went rigid. He did not open his eyes, but the sounds Julien made were as loud as they would be if he were matter-of-factly undressing in the room by himself. Julien got into his side of the bed and immediately, his breathing changing from one breath to another, fell asleep. Daniel felt a great distance from him; he imagined that if he stretched out an arm as far as it would go his hand would reach through space, and wouldn't touch his brother. He tried to force himself to sleep. He couldn't. He slowly moved his body towards his brother, so slowly he wouldn't himself be aware of his movements but would suddenly, as in sleep, find himself in contact with his brother's body. Julien woke just enough to turn his body

49

away from Daniel to settle close to him, Daniel's arm about his waist, and Daniel fell asleep.

On Sunday morning, Daniel, who was dressed for Mass, sat on the edge of Edmond's bed and listened to him talk with a drawl about Kentucky, where Edmond had never been, and Daniel also looked at the way his brother had rolled up the sleeves of his undershirt to make them high and tight about his arms, at the black beard growing through his soft skin, at his clothes thrown on a chair by the bed. Their father came into the room, and Daniel rose and Edmond quickly got out of bed.

While Edmond dressed, Daniel studied, on his brother's bureau, placed in the middle of a lace cloth that was like an altar runner, a painted plaster statue of Christ as a boy, his features very small and pointed, wearing a short red tunic, his legs and feet bare, and holding at his sides three large spikes in one hand and a hammer in the other. Propped about the base of the statue were holy pictures of the young Christ sawing wood, planing planks, driving nails into beams. Edmond came up behind him to look, too, at the array on his little altar to the youthful Christ. Edmond reached out for the statue, raised it, so the holy pictures dropped flat, and held the statue close to his chest for a moment before he replaced it and carefully replaced the pictures around its base.

Daniel went in Edmond's car to church, the others in the father's car.

He asked, "What will you do when you go to Kentucky?"

"Well, I won't be doing what I do here."

"Kentucky is different?"

Edmond didn't answer; he hadn't been to Kentucky.

Daniel and Julien knelt between their mother and father at Mass, Daniel next to his mother, Julien next to his father. Edmond knelt on the other side of the mother, the first to have got in the pew; the father was, as always, last. Both parents were saying their rosaries. The mother's rosary, which had a silver chain and beads of blue crystal, she had taken out of her mother's dead hands before the coffin lid was closed; she rubbed each bead between her thumb and index finger. Daniel looked from his mother's hands to the altar. The altar appeared very far, and he could not bring it into focus enough to see what stage the curé had reached in the Mass. His distant sense of the Mass was that it had been going on for hours. His back ached. He looked at his mother. She wasn't looking at the altar either. Her lips were moving with her prayers, and her eyes seemed to be staring at what she was praying for. The sight of his mother, appearing, it seemed to Daniel, all at once beside him, made him still. Her face, her cheeks and forehead, were clear, open, bright. It was as if the head of a little girl were just beneath and showed through her skin, as if, in some sudden clarity, openness, brightness, the face of a girl, her face as a girl, were revealed, and she was, while praying, unaware that she had become fourteen years old. Daniel stared at her deeply. He thought: And did she know, at fourteen, what she would have endured by the age of fifty? Daniel imagined himself, suddenly capable of reversing and arresting time, preserving her as she was at fourteen, protecting her from her older brother, from her mother and father, from growing older, from sex and falling in love, from having to work, from marriage and childbirth, from age. A year older, and she would be destroyed; she must remain as she was in this moment, and Daniel must keep her as she was in this moment. He imagined taking that little girl in his arms and pressing her to him. He wanted to save his mother; he wanted to save her, if he could, but how could he? Her lips moving, she turned to Daniel and looked at him. Daniel looked back at her, tried, with the beaming force of his love, to communicate to her that he would, if no one else would, protect her, but her innocence was so total she couldn't take in anything more from him than that he was distracted from the Mass, and she looked back at the altar to indicate that he, too, should look there and pay attention. He tried to, but he continued to feel that his mother, kneeling beside him, was a fourteen-year-old girl, unprotected, and he was terrified of what might happen to her.

M. le curé left the altar to go to the pulpit, and the congregation sat. The curé spoke as if his throat and tongue were covered with sores. Daniel wanted to get out. His body, which he pressed against the back of the pew, was struggling against the imposed stillness to rise up. He heard the sermon as in bursts of sound.

It was in French. The curé never spoke English. He made the students of the parish sing, "Ô Canada! terre de nos aïeux," whenever he came into the classrooms to give, each month, the report cards.

"We know, we should know, that when Jesus Christ ascended into Heaven, He ascended bodily and stood before His Father. Now the Love of the Father is brilliant, and the Light of that Love casts the Shadow of the Body of the Son down and across our earth. That living Shadow, as true as His true Body, is the Holy Roman Catholic Church. We are ourselves, we who make up that Church, the Shadow of the Body of Christ, we ourselves make up the Mystical Body of Christ on earth. *We are* the Body of Christ here." He paused. "The body has many parts, and all the parts work together. The feet stand firmly on the ground and the legs become rigid when the arms reach down and the hands take up a heavy weight to lift it, and the neck passes the instructions from the head to let the members know where the great weight should be put down." He paused again and stared with his black eyes. "Look at your hands, look at your fingers. As truly as those hands and those fingers exist, there exist the hands and fingers of the Church. The Church also has a neck, a head. Do we know which parts of the Body we make up?" Daniel tried, tried as hard as he could, to keep his mind from visualizing, with grotesque accuracy, the dark, complex part of the vast recumbent body which he knew the curé would never appoint anyone to make up, but without which the body could not be complete. "What parts do we, we in this church, in this parish of Notre Dame de Lourdes, we who are workers, what parts do we compose? I asked you to look at your hands and fingers. What parts of the body do most for the life of the body, feed it, clothe it, work to give it a home and a bed? Could it survive without hands? Just try to imagine a body without hands trying to dress, to eat, or work a machine. The body of the Church would be as helpless. You, you the workers, are the hands and the fingers of the Church. You, who work with your hands, are the hands of Christ. No matter what your work is—hammering nails, sawing wood—" there he made a gesture as though the occupation occurred to him out of the air and he grasped it—"making files—you are working not only for yourself, but for the whole body. And if you don't—" The curé suddenly shouted; everyone's shoulders jolted a little. "When you do not work in and for the Body of Christ, you work for nothing!" He lowered his voice. "To be with Him is what we must all long for, and those who devote themselves to His Mystical Body here will, after the Last Judgement, be with Him in His Body." He raised his hands. "Then, once again about these bones our flesh, once again in our heads these eyes, ears, this nose and this mouth—but all glorified, all glorified in the Body of Christ, the Great and Resurrected and Adorable Body of Christ."

Daniel's body seemed to him to try for a moment to expand outward.

The father waited till he was in the vestibule to put on his overcoat. He, his wife, Edmond, the boys, stood by a holy water font, out of the way of gathered parishioners. Daniel saw, through the opening and closing doors, that snow was falling; beyond the falling grey snow was grey packed snow on the church grounds. From where he stood, he could not see anything but snow, and he imagined that the church was isolated in a great wilderness of snow, the snow drifted across wide plains, piled on fields of low scrub bushes, filling the cracks of jagged ledges and the low long ridges of glacial

53

rock. He imagined that parishioners had come long ways, and would have to go back long ways. He saw the side door of the vestibule open and M. le curé come in, his soutane a vivid black. Immediately, some parishioners grouped round him. His small white head, with black eyes that appeared completely round because of the dark circles about them, was like a skull.

The curé said a few words to those about him, then, Daniel noted, looked with his black circular eyes directly at them, at himself, his brothers, his mother, his father. Daniel didn't have to indicate to his father that the curé was staring at them; the father, knowing that the stare was a summons, went towards him. The parishioners about the curé retreated. The mother took the hands of Daniel and Julien and drew them closer to her sides. When the father came back, he said, "He wants to see me later." The mother asked, "What about?" The father shrugged his shoulders. Only the children in the vestibule moved. As the father led his family through them to the door, a man broke out of his still silence as if he had just decided to, and, raising his hand in a kind of salute, said, "How's it going, Jim?" Daniel was tense with fear as his father searched the face of the man as though he couldn't recall him and was trying to place him— he was in fact a well-known man in the parish, Mr Labrie, who owned the gas station—then smiled, raised his hand in a similar salute, and said, "It's getting better." It was a formal political gesture, as of a political candidate starting his campaign.

Edmond went from the church to the ice-cream parlour.

Though the father usually took off his tie and unbuttoned his collar on coming home from Mass, this morning he kept his tie on, his collar buttoned, when he sat to read the papers. They were all in the living room. The inside air was as grey as the outside; it seemed that snow might fall inside as it was lightly falling outside. Like a politician who knew just what sudden shock he wanted to produce and, though this he kept to himself, why, the father held the newspaper out and

54

turned to the back pages of small advertisements, folded it in two, then again in two, and, holding it up, said, as if the announcement were meant for many people, a whole crowd, "Well, girlie, if you want another house, we'll get it for you."

The newspaper the mother read was a New York tabloid. Its news was limited to the domestic: baby beatings, rape, murder, fires. She closed it and frowned. "Another house?"

"We'll have a house in the country. We'll have a big house, big enough to take us all, all the boys, their wives, their children."

She stood, not quite sure where she would go, while the father read out the brief descriptions of houses. She felt a little lost. She went into the kitchen. She stared at the kettle. She turned the gas on under it. The water inside raged. The father came into the kitchen, his head stuck out on his neck to look for her.

He asked, "What's the matter?"

She said, "I'm waiting for the water to boil violently to make a cup of tea."

He said, "Will you bring it into the front room?"

She said, "I'll have it here at the kitchen table."

He put his hands, clenched into fists, on his hips, and watched her. She had her hand on the handle of the kettle. He raised one hand and combed his fingers through his hair, again and again, from his forehead to the back of his head. "Now tell me what it is," he said.

She stared at the kettle. Steam was rising from the spout.

He insisted, "What is it?"

She said, "I don't know."

"You must know," he said.

"Keep your voice down," she said.

"I want to know what's wrong."

She tightened her grip on the handle of the kettle. She clenched her teeth for a moment. "I don't know."

Again, he ran his fingers through his hair, this time quickly, repeatedly. "Look, girlie—"

She suddenly shouted, "No!"

He tried to hold her.

She broke away.

He went back into the living room. Daniel and Julien were standing, silent. He sat, picked up the newspaper, the sports section, which he was not interested in, and held it up to read. The mother burst into the room.

"I can't stand it any more!" she shouted. "I can't take it, not any more!"

The father's voice was sharp. "Now stop it."

"I try to be a good wife. I try to do everything you want from me."

"Stop it."

"What do you want? What do you want?"

He stared at her. His face looked as if he were tasting his own sour vomit that had risen to his mouth. He said nothing. Julien left the room. Daniel began to tremble.

"You never tell me! You do what you want! You never discuss what you do with me! *I want to know!*"

The father was now staring at the floor; he appeared as if he couldn't spit his vomit out, and had to swallow it.

Daniel stood between his mother and his father. He felt his body shaking. His father reached out for him and pulled him to him. Standing between his father's legs, crouched, his father's arms about him, his head against his father's shoulder, his trembling gave way to dry heaves. He clung to his father's hard dark body which smelled of greased metal. His mother was shouting. He didn't hear what she was shouting. The shouts shocked him again and again. His father was patting his back. He couldn't stop his heaving. It seemed to him he could see, from a great height, himself, and though he looked the same he was not sure who he was, he was someone he didn't know, a person so different from him he might do things he, Daniel Francoeur, would never do. With a sob that was a sudden scream, that person closed his eyes, clenched his arms about the father, and kissed him, his own jaw rubbing against the father's rough though clean-shaven jaw, on the neck under his ear. The father clutched him, began to rock him back and forth, saying, "Tais-toi, tsi gars, tais-toi, tais-toi, tsi gars." The mother had stopped shouting. She stood above her husband and son.

The outside doors opened and slammed, and Edmond came into the living room, his overcoat on. His eyes widened. "Not again! I stop at the ice-cream parlour for one vanilla ice-cream soda and to chew the rag a bit, and I come home to find this! Not again!" He was carrying a glove in each hand; he threw them down; they slapped the floor one after another. "I thought this had finished between you two! I thought you'd grown up, were too old for these arguments! Are you going to start all over again? Are they? Can't we have some kind of final peace in this house?" His parents didn't answer. Edmond shouted, "The sooner I can get away from here and get down to Kentucky the better, as far as I'm concerned."

"You've been saying that for a year," the mother said, and left the room.

The father released Daniel. Daniel's chest was heaving. He sat on the couch. The father remained where he was, sitting on the edge of the armchair. Edmond, with a grunt, which was both an added unarticulated reprimand in case it was needed and an unarticulated last word, took off his overcoat, threw it on the back of a chair, picked up a paper from the floor and sat to read it.

The dinner was formalized by polite requests to have the bread, butter, salt passed. The quiet about the table seemed to Daniel a great empty space. It was almost, in its spaciousness, the quiet he felt in church before the lights went on and Mass began. Whatever tension there was now was, he thought, the tension of the quiet, and it annoyed him, as, initially, did the lights coming on in the church and the priest entering, when Edmond, completely unaware of the tense but wide quiet, suddenly started to recount conversations he'd had at the ice-cream parlour. No one took him up. The mother from time to time would say distractedly, "Is that right?" but she was not listening. Edmond slammed his fork down; it made the others at the table jump a little. He said, "Well, if this is the way it's going to be—!"

Edmond went into his room and closed the door. The quiet inside settled like fog. Outside the clouds opened, and sunlight fell in thin flashing layers. The mother looked out of the living room window. The father lay on the couch. Daniel and Julien were sitting each in an armchair. The mother turned into the living room. Her voice seemed to echo a little in the quiet when she said: "We should go out."

The father didn't respond.

"The boys should get out," she said; "they never go anywhere, see anything, outside the house and the parish."

The father closed his eyes.

Her voice strained; it was as if she were talking against a great indrawing desire to lie down also, lie on the floor and close her eyes. "If you don't want to, I'll take them out. They've got to see a little of the outside world."

The father placed a forearm over his forehead. "Do as you like," he said.

She put on her scarf, her coat, her boots, her gloves. The air outside was bright, cold, still. She and the boys walked to a bus stop. She walked slowly, anticipating perhaps that Jim would call her back before she had gone too far.

Downtown, they had to change from their bus to another which, cold, almost empty, the large dark windows on one side reflecting the dusty sunlit windows on the other, took them out of the city. They got out at the large gates of a park. The bars of the iron gates were thick white icicles, the large shrubs on the right and left of the entrance were piles of snow sagging and slipping with their own weight, the plaque on one of the gateposts, ROGER WILLIAMS PARK, was green ice.

The mother didn't know where to take her youngest sons. They wandered about the shovelled paths, under bare white branches. At times they walked through small woods, the black trunks rising out of the clear smooth snow, the high thin upper branches moving in an unheard wind; on the snow were imprints of claws, and the sky was a livid purple behind the black trees. In the distance, in a snowy field, was a small wooden house with a large chimney and a thick naked wistaria vine knotted about the roof. They went, not so much out of interest as for some place to go to, towards the house. When Daniel and Julien followed their mother through the narrow doorway into the house, Daniel was thinking, instead of Betsy Williams's house, of the surrounding snow.

They looked at the spinning wheel by the brick fireplace, the dark highly polished furniture, the hand-hewn floor boards. They climbed a small twisted staircase to a small barren cordoned-off room with a bedstead. Daniel kept looking out the little many-paned distorting windows at the snow. The purple-grey shadows were lengthening on it. He tried to imagine, behind him, the strange former life in the house.

The wet snow creaked under their feet as they walked from the old house to the park's museum, yellow brick, with windows lit yellow. The main hall, at the top of the internal stairs, had at its centre a glass case. A young man, wearing a peaked hat and earmuffs, was standing by it. There was no one else. The mother, Daniel, Julien went to the other side of the case.

In the bright cube was a delicate model of the Galaxy. The sun was a light bulb, and the planets, with their moons, were on long wires which vibrated a little as they rotated the planets slowly round the sun, the moons slowly round the planets. The tiny moons were white, the planets mottled green and blue, red and grey.

The mother moved on. They passed a gigantic seashell on a plinth and went into a side room. It was a room filled with Indian artifacts in long glass cases. The mother walked ahead, hardly looking. The boys followed, looking closely at tomahawks, wampum belts, beadwork, quill-decorated medicine bags with dangling feathers, long pipes, bows and arrows, oars, and a large birch-bark canoe on top of one of the cases.

59

The mother came up to the boys leaning over a case which contained, in miniature, the huts and immobile figures of an Indian encampment. She said, "Your father didn't tell me, before we were married, that he had Indian blood."

Julien asked, "Wouldn't you have loved him?"

She smiled.

The boys continued to study the little encampment, in which tiny men, red-brown and with long black hair, crouched about a fire, and a woman, carrying a bark tray against her tiny naked breasts, was advancing towards them.

They walked the paths out of the park, and Daniel, as much to talk to his mother to bring her out of her continuing silence as to know, asked her, "Did Dad ever know his Indian grandmother?"

His mother said, "No, he never saw her."

"Can Mémère speak any of the language?"

"No, I don't think so."

They had to wait a long time for a bus. The cold from the ice rose, making their legs ache. No one else joined them at the bus stop. Julien asked his mother if she was sure there was a bus. She didn't answer, but it was clear she was trying to control her fear as the cold rose and the dark descended so swiftly passing cars put on their parking lights. She stared up the avenue at the oncoming cars, searching for the bus. She would always be lonely, always vulnerable, whenever she exercised her own will; if she did exercise it, she did so alone, and, alone, she was frightened. Daniel, and Julien too, felt her fear as though it were a dark cold emanating from her, from her dark, her cold. She leaned to look further up the avenue. As if he were frightened she might take a step into the rushing traffic, Julien reached for her hand; she turned round to him; he didn't let go of her hand.

They found the house empty, with no lights on. The mother looked in all the rooms, lighting lights, followed by Daniel and Julien. Daniel said, "Maybe he's gone to Mémère's house." The mother sat in the rocking chair in

60

the kitchen; she rocked as if she were shaking herself. Julien said, "Maybe he's in the cellar." She ceased rocking, then, after a moment, rose and went down, leaving the kitchen and cellar doors open. Daniel and Julien remained in the kitchen, Daniel heard her voice, "Please come upstairs, please come up, please don't stay here. I'm asking you, please—" There was a long pause, then Daniel heard footsteps on the cellar stairs, and he drew back when his father, at first view twice his size, his head and hands enormous, stopped at the kitchen door and looked round before entering. He went immediately to his bedroom and closed the door. The mother again sat in the rocking chair, and, as before, shook, rather than rocked, herself. Then she was still for a while. After a short time, she rose and went into the bedroom.

When the father came out of the bedroom, he was dressed for visiting the curé. He carefully combed his hair at the bathroom mirror. He said to Daniel and Julien, "Why don't you get your jackets on and come to the presbytère with me?"

Their coats unbuckled and unbuttoned, their caps in their hands, they stood on either side of their father who, his overcoat on his knees, sat across from the curé. The curé had one elbow on the arm of his wooden chair, and leaned his temple against three fingers; the tips of his thin fingers appeared to sink into the white wrinkles they made. He said, "You of course must know what you're doing—"

"Yes," the father said.

"I hope that you are thinking of more than yourself. I hope that you are at least keeping in mind your wife and sons—"

"I do," the father said, quickly.

The curé took his hand away from his temple; the wrinkles remained. "I didn't ask you here to tell you of your social duties, your duties towards your fellow workmen, towards your parish, towards your Church—" He stopped for a moment. "What I want is simply this: to tell you, in case you're not aware of it, that you've taken a risk."

The father nodded his head.

"What do you want?" the curé asked.

The father stared at him; his jaw was set.

"You're going against all that is most natural to you, don't you see?—against the very heart your life and your family's life depend on, the heart of a worker. Do you want to take that risk?"

The father tapped his chest with his index finger.

The curé raised his hand. "Never mind, never mind you," he said. "What I'm thinking of is more important than you, to have here a Syndicat catholique—"

The father said, "I've no reason to interfere if they don't interfere with me."

"You might have got their full protection if you'd stayed with them."

"I didn't want their protection."

"No," the curé said. He stood. The father stood. The curé asked,

"You're a Republican, aren't you?"

"Yes."

"What has the Republican Party ever done for the workers?"

The father remained silent.

The curé said, "You'll be getting more money."

"Yes. I'm going to buy a big house in the country, in the woods, on a lake."

Daniel, that night, dreamed of his parents' closets, of his mother's closet in his parents' bedroom, a large closet lit by a small window with coloured panes, so the light streaming inside was yellow and violet on her dresses, among which he stood, enveloped by the dangling skirts and a powdery smell of talcum, and of his father's closet, off the kitchen, just behind the rocking chair, where he stood in darkness, stood still among old shoes and clothes that were rough and gave off a sharp metallic smell, which was, maybe, the essential smell of the family, and he dreamed, as he was able to have two dreams at the same time, of both closets at once.

After Mass the following Sunday, the curé, standing by one of the outside doors of the vestibule, touched the father on the elbow as he passed, stopping him to ask, with stark brevity, if he would help organize a pre-Lenten soirée to raise money for the church. The father immediately said yes. Perhaps the curé knew that Arsace Francoeur would see the soirée for what it was intended: not for amusement, but for fund-raising.

~~~~~~

NOTRE-DAME DE LOURDES, PROVIDENCE, R. I.

SOIREE DU BON VIEUX TEMPS

Mascarade   .:.   Danse   .:.   Lunch

Samedi soir, le 9 mars 1953, à 8 heures

Salle de l'école

Don: $1.00

~~~~~~

The father reserved a ticket for his family as if it were a ticket to the Presidential ball which automatically followed the successful campaign. Daniel examined the ticket, and said to his father, "If it's taking place in the evening, how can lunch be served?" The father said nothing. Daniel turned the card over.

Compliments of

Modeste Vanasse Funeral Home

1240 Charles Avenue

Providence, R. I.

The school hall, the basement in which the soirée was held, was lined on both sides, under pipes running the length of the walls, with folding chairs, and on the rows of folding chairs were old women. Old card tables, borrowed from the parish French Club, were set up on the bare unpolished wooden floor, and at them large round-shouldered people were playing whist. The mother, Daniel and Julien sat at a card table, but didn't play whist.

Daniel glanced across to the back of the hall where Edmond, just outside the entrance, was talking to the janitor, who was just inside. He realized that whenever he looked at his brother a little shock of strangeness passed through him. Edmond was talking through the doorway to the school janitor as if, out of everyone there, it was only the janitor he could talk to. He could talk in the same way with the fat boy who worked at the gasoline station, with the old man who sat in a corner of the cobbler's shop and polished shoes, with a crippled man who sold newspapers outside the church on Sunday morning. Edmond, among them, got along with them, got along with those people who, most familiar in the parish, were most strange to Daniel. Daniel stared at him, then at a few of his classmates silently pitching pennies against a wall, then at a woman in a large picture hat sitting alone, then at an empty root-beer bottle on the floor, then at his mother.

She was staring past him, and he turned to see, at the opposite end of the school hall, on the stage, his father at a little table selling raffle tickets. He put the stub ends into a large drum, which had a crank. He appeared very busy. The curé was also on the stage, at the back, behind the father, standing among tall empty wicker flower baskets; two old severe bonnes femmes de la paroisse were on either side of him, talking, but he looked out from them, out into the hall, frowning.

Daniel left his mother and brother and walked towards the exit to go to the toilet. He passed the old women sitting in a long row along the side of the hall, under the pipes. He felt they were looking at him. Not one of them was smiling, and only a few were talking. Their mouths were turned down at the corners; they had chin hair; their arms were fat and loose-fleshed, and they kept them folded. Daniel walked at a distance from them, imagining they would emit a smell. A sudden, surprising to him, hatred for them rose up in him; he hated them, and he could separate himself from his hatred only enough to wonder why, all at once, he should hate so their mouths, their heavy chins, their arms. When he found one woman staring hard at him as though he had done something wrong, he imagined time had for a moment run backward, and that the woman's face had caused, retroactively, his sudden hatred. He stared back hard at the woman; she stared through him, out at the whist players. He knew that his family had never been a family of any importance in the parish; they had, as a family, always been considered by the central families as somewhat outcast, as, perhaps, a family with strong physical markings of Indian blood— which his family didn't have—would be outcasts, would come to the church, would receive first Communion, would be confirmed, with the others, would take part in a church social occasion, but would never enter the inner church, receive the secret sacraments, be invited to the private parties of those who believed their inner church, their secret sacraments, their private parties were of the true religion; it was the religion of those old women.

Before leaving the hall he looked back at the stage, where his father was now cranking the drum to mix the raffle tickets. Everyone had stopped playing whist to watch. Julien had been called up to stick his hand through a little door that would be opened in the side of the drum and to choose the first ticket stub. Daniel concentrated on his father. As with a rush of blood from his body, he thought, almost said: No, no.

Daniel left the hall before the first raffle ticket was drawn. He used the toilet, but didn't go back into the hall. He stood just outside by a pile of crates of empty soda bottles with bent drinking straws sticking out of the bottles. He heard his father call out numbers. He thought suddenly: Yes. He heard his father shout, above the voices, "One hundred and twenty-eight!"

Daniel turned. Outside a dark basement window he saw

a white face looking in, a little boy's face. The boy stared at him. It seemed to Daniel that that face presented him with everything he didn't understand. It didn't wince or smile. He wanted to ask it questions which, he knew, it wouldn't respond to; not only what it longed for, but why, for what incomprehensible reasons, did it long for what it didn't have?

He returned to the school hall. His mother and Julien were not at their card table. He saw Julien first, at a far corner of the hall, facing outward from between his mother and father. They were standing before the curé, whose high white forehead moved between their heads. Daniel stayed back. He saw his father's and mother's bodies sway a little, now one in one direction, one in the other, now together. He saw the curé raise his right hand. It seemed to Daniel that the curé was marrying them, and Julien was the witness of the small stark ceremony. The mother all at once reached out and put her hand under the father's left arm; he pressed his arm against his side and put his right hand ov er hers.

The car was a car of black ice. Daniel could see, in the pale light of the street lamps, his breath steam about his face. The snow chains clanked. Daniel closed his eyes for a moment.

After a while he asked, "Are we really going to get a house in the country?"

The father said, "Yes."

"And when will we buy the other house?"

"We'll start looking as soon as it gets warmer. We'll drive round the country looking at houses."

Daniel felt his nerves slowly go slack.

III

ARSACE LOUIS PYLADE Francoeur was born 8 November
1898 in St. Barthélemi, near Trois Rivières, province of
Quebec, Canada. He was taken by his parents to Providence,
Rhode Island, U.S.A., when he was two, to the French
Canadian parish of Notre Dame de Lourdes. The parents
had, on arrival, fourteen cents.

Arsace as a child often said, "J'aime ça," and was nick-
named Jim. Only his mother continued to call him Arsace.
He became naturalized at twenty-one; his parents never did.
He had thirteen brothers and sisters. Most of them were
dead. His favourite was a little brother, named André, who
died when he was two.

Aricie Melanie Atalie Lajoie was born in 1902, in Providence, Rhode Island. Her family on both sides had been in
the United States for generations, since the English dispersed
the French from Acadia in 1755.

Aricie was called Reena. She was one of twelve children.
She went to the parish grammar school, then to a public
high school; she left in the first year of high school because
her mother forced her to wear an old-fashioned blue bloomer
gym costume. Her first job, during World War I, was to
examine brass mortar shells for defects; she and other girls
and a few men whose parents had managed to keep them out
of the service lifted the large shells from crates, one at a time,
and held each one up to the light from the tall dirty windows
of the warehouse to look through the small hole at the firing
end, turning the shell round slowly, to look for any fine

cracks. Her second job was as a telephone operator. Whenever, years after, she gave a number over the telephone, she said the number as she had been taught to say it as an operator; woe-on-e, tah-who-o, ni-u-o-ni-ne.

She was from the northern part of the parish, he from the southern part.

The southern part was all tenements, three-storey tenements with porches at each storey, and it was solid Canuck. The curé never paid social visits to the houses in the northern part, but was often at homes in the southern part. The French Club was in the southern part. The grandmother, Arsace's mother, with most of her children, six remaining from the fourteen, lived on the southern side.

The church was between the northern and southern sides.

When Reena and Jim looked for a house to buy, they looked in the northern part. The northern side was made up of clapboard bungalows with porches, called piazzas, along unpaved sidewalks with weeds growing at the curb, and overlapped with three other parishes: the Irish, the Polish and the Italian. Jim and Reena bought a house on a corner across from Italians, with a blind Polish woman married to an Italian on one side and a big Irish family in a big house on the opposite corner, but their house was, to them, in the French parish.

Jim and Reena Francoeur were married in 1923. They had seven sons: Richard, born in 1924; Albert, born in 1925; Edmond, born in 1927; Philip, born five years later, 1932; André, 1933; Daniel, seven years later, 1940; Julien, born in 1942.

Daniel and Julien stacked the large storm windows at a slant against the side of the house and looked down into them; they reflected Daniel and the blue sky to deeper and deeper levels and when he moved one way blazed with multiple suns, or when he moved the other way revealed weeds growing at the cinder-block foundation of the house and the white clapboard which appeared at a great distance.

The air penetrated the window screens with the smells of the spring-green hedge, the maple trees, the house, the tangle of wild roses separating the yard from the lot next.

The mother was at the kitchen table, a newspaper spread open before her and on the newspaper a round pedestal mirror, a glass of water with a comb stuck in it (tiny bubbles effervesced from the teeth of the comb), a china box, the flower-painted lid to the side, filled with hairpins, a hairnet. Looking in the mirror, she separated clumps of hair, combed the hair through with the dripping comb, twisted the hair round and round, coiled it tightly against her skull, and fixed it with pins she first opened with her teeth. She had done up half her head. Her skull showed white between the separated clumps. The hair on the other half of her head she'd combed down straight. Her exposed ears, her nose and chin appeared large and very white. The soft flesh of her face was at points pulled in and it seemed attached, like upholstery, at these points to the skull, under her chin, under her ear lobes, just to either side of her mouth. Daniel watched his mother. Julien was polishing his shoes. The father was reading an old magazine. The mother was taking a long time to put up her hair. She parted the remaining half head of hair from the top to her ear, and, looking not at the mirror but as though at an aura about it, subdivided the hair over her temple into equal squares.

Daniel wondered why he should be studying his mother as an example of how a woman, at a certain time in a certain culture, did up her hair, in the same way he would if he could go back in time and place, study how an Egyptian woman shaved her head and prepared her wig.

In the midst of her hair-pinning, the mother lowered her comb, her other hand holding a clump of hair, and said: "I just had a feeling that Albert will be coming home."

The father, Julien following as if attached to his father's back, went out to go to the hardware store to buy nails.

The mother said to Daniel, "And yet I wonder how Albert can want to come home." She rolled up her hair and stuck a pin through it. "You know," she said, "your father didn't want him to go into the Marines. He told him that if he did go off against his will he'd never speak to him again. Albert said to me, he said, he couldn't understand the reasons for your father's not wanting him to go. I said, 'I don't understand either.' He said he had to go. There was a war on. He went downtown and signed. When it came time for him to leave the house, I stood between him and his father, and I didn't know which one I should turn to. I knew that if Albert did go out, did close the door, your father would keep his vow. Then Albert turned round, and he said, 'So long, Dad,' but your father got up from the rocker and went into the other room. I watched Albert open the outside door to the entry, go out, close it. I had to close the kitchen door. I hurried into the living room and stood at the front window. I saw Albert climb the street, and saw him stop, look round, and take a handkerchief from his pocket and wipe his eyes. A week or so after, the clothes he wore when he left were sent back squashed in a small box. I unpacked them. I put them in the attic."

"And when he came home—," Daniel said.

"When he came home, at first I didn't recognize him. I ran to the door to open it. His hair was short, his face was brown and gaunt, his Adam's apple looked very big. He smiled and hugged me. While Albert sat at the kitchen table and talked to me, your father rocked in his rocking chair and read his paper. Albert kept his chin drawn in, his neck rigid, even when he spoke. He said to me, he said, 'Dad could have taught them one or two things about dedication and discipline.' Your father lowered his newspaper and told him, 'The Marine Corps has got to enforce dedication and discipline if the war's going to be won.' Albert smiled at him and said, 'Yes, that's right, Dad.' Your father told him everything about the Marine Corps." She wound strands of hair around a finger and pinned them into a curl. "Well, when I was alone having tea with him while your father was at work, he told me what he'd been through in his basic training. He'd say, 'I was on the firing range, and was told to get down low, my bum was sticking up, so I tried to dig myself into the ground, but the Sarge shouted that my bum was still too high, so he, a big strapper, maybe two hundred pounds, came and sat on me, and you know what he said?' I didn't know what to say. 'He said, the Sarge, "You remember this, you remember you were born in a gutter, your mother was a gutter whore, and you ain't going to get higher than that. You're low, and you better never forget how low you are."' I said, 'Albert!' 'You don't have any right to be shocked,' he said to me, 'that's the way it is, and that's the way it's got to be—' I couldn't tell him I didn't want to hear any more. I said, 'But how can they treat any young man like that? Don't they realize they're the sons of mothers?' Albert shouted, he even frightened me a little, 'When you're out there fighting, woman, you don't have a mother!' He said that to me—" She tied a kerchief about her pin-curled hair.

When she and her husband, with Julien, went out to do the Saturday shopping, Daniel, alone, wandered through the house. He opened the flap of the desk in the living room to search through the pigeonholes; he raised the lid of the cedar chest in his parents' room to look through the old clothes, first Communion suits, fringed satin pillowcases with Marine Corps emblems on one side and poems to Mother on the other, a bolt of blue silk; he opened his mother's closet and looked through the boxes of rags she kept under her hanging clothes; he pushed his mother's hanging clothes aside and very quietly, as though someone might be in the house and listening to him, climbed the ladder to the attic trapdoor and pushed it open.

Later as he helped his mother unpack the shopping from the big brown bags in the pantry, Daniel asked, "Do you really think Albert will come?"

"Yes."

"Why don't we take the Japanese things he's sent that you put in the attic and put them around so he'll see them?"

"Put them where?"

"Around the living room."

Albert arrived without letting them know beforehand. He arrived after they had gone to bed. Daniel heard the doorbell—the front doorbell—in his sleep, and, without waking fully, he heard footsteps, heard doors, heard his parents' voices, and heard as if he were dreaming it the familiar but unfamiliar voice of Albert, at once soft and guttural, saying, "Well, look at this." Daniel woke up and listened, but didn't go out. He lay in bed and imagined his brother in the living room, with his parents, among the Japanese objects. Then he heard Edmond's door bang open and Edmond shout, "Well, gee whiz!"

Albert had been away so long, Daniel could imagine him only as in a photograph, as in the photographs kept without order in a box in a drawer in the family desk, and which jumbled his career in the Marines: a photograph of him with his pilot's helmet on, the chin strap unbuckled, standing by an open cockpit, of him standing at attention but alone in lieutenant's dress whites (which he would wash himself, then soak, with his gloves on to do the job, in a mixture of water and white shoe polish, so the uniform and the gloves dried to a matt but brilliant white, and in the photograph it appeared to glow like ectoplasm), of him at boot camp lined up with others of his regiment or sitting apart from them, his collar buttoned and his tie firmly knotted and tucked into his shirt, while they leaned towards one another with bottles of beer, their shirts undone, laughing, of him receiving his wings, of him standing in a doorway, the creases of his major's uniform straight and rigid, his visor shadowing his face, a swagger stick under his arm.

Daniel heard Albert say, "Dad, congratulations." Daniel fell back to sleep to the sound of wind through the dark spindly wood in the lot outside the open bedroom window.

The house in the morning was vibrant with silence. The

mother warned Daniel and Julien not to make noise, but the rattle of a knife on the table or the splash of water in the bathroom basin jarred. They turned to the bedroom door when it opened, but Edmond came out, in his work clothes, and quietly left. Albert was sleeping behind the closed door, but, because Daniel hadn't yet seen him, he was remote, he was near and remote, he was in the house and he was far from it, in his old bedroom and in the unknown places he had been in the past ten years, and perhaps if Daniel quietly opened the door he would find, not the familiar bedroom of his older brothers, but a room with straw mats, sliding screens, dim and still and empty but for Albert sleeping on the floor.

When he got back from school for lunch, Albert was still asleep. Daniel and Julien sat on kitchen chairs and looked at the bedroom door beyond the kitchen alcove. They saw the handle turn and the door open, and they jumped up. Both were motionless for an instant, then Daniel rushed towards the opening door and put his arms round a figure he hadn't made out was his older brother, who, in a cloud of sleep, drew back as if he were being attacked, so Daniel lost his balance and half fell against him; Albert put his hands on Daniel's shoulders both to rebalance and embrace him, and held him for a moment. Even after Daniel stood away and Albert smiled at him, his gaunt, unshaven face retained the surprise of his younger brother's attack. Daniel looked back at his brother Julien, who stood by his chair and simply stared at Albert until Albert turned to him and said: "Hey, come here and let me give you a punch on the nose," and Julien smiled.

Albert wore green fatigue trousers, a white undershirt, straw sandals held on by straps between his big and next toes. He stretched his clenched hands high, shook his head, and sat to a cup his mother had put on the table. Daniel watched him with the attention of someone trying to see in his very clothes a man who was his brother, and therefore accessible to him, and yet a stranger. The green fatigue trousers were Marine Corps trousers, were clothes he wore in the big dark severe house of the Marine Corps, where every article of clothing, every shoelace and pin was very strictly assigned to a special military duty. The trousers and, too, the tight white undershirt, the sleeves stretched by Albert's brown upper arms, were worn for duties Daniel knew nothing about, duties that had to do with war.

Albert's body had been formed by war. It was a tight, hard, muscular body, and it had endured the unimaginable, lately in Korea and earlier in Guam, in the Philippines, in—but the family didn't really know. After he drank his cup of tea and lit a cigarette, he turned to Daniel and Julien and, moving his chair out from the table and pushing the narrow sleeves of his undershirt up to expose his shoulders, said, "Come on, both of you, either side," and Daniel and Julien, taking their positions—this was done every time he came home; if he thought it was a ritual expected of him by Daniel and Julien, Daniel at least would have liked to say he didn't want to do it, but then maybe Albert expected it of him—clenched their fists and waited for Albert, a little slouched in the chair, to say, "Now hit me hard," and the two younger brothers bashed their fists into his biceps, while Albert, rocking back and forth from the impact and laughing, said, "Harder! Harder! You're not hitting hard enough!" Daniel and Julien had to stop punching because it was time for them to leave for afternoon school. They put on their jackets slowly. Albert said, "I'll be here when you get back." But they stood at the door. Albert pulled Julien's cap down so it covered his eyes, but instead of doing the same to Daniel he grabbed him by the back of the neck as if to pull him down and drew him to him, and Daniel's face hit the side of his chest, and he breathed in the metallic smell before he stepped back and, without looking at Albert, turned to leave. In war, Albert had gone so far his body was different from anyone else's.

Back again, he found Albert sitting as he had been at the kitchen table, the tea cup before him, but dressed now in a long blue Japanese robe with Japanese characters on each breast and tied at the waist with a black belt. The robe was open and showed a yellow-white chest; his brown-red neck rose from a sharp line as if he were wearing an undershirt in every way transparent but for a pale yellow, and his real colour was the dark of his neck, face, arms. He had had a shower. His short stiff black hair was wet. Water was running from a temple down the side of his face like sweat. The mother sat at the opposite side of the table, a cup before her. The kitchen windows were open; leaves of the big maple tree brushed against the screens. Albert kept rubbing his eyes, as though he hadn't yet woken. Julien went into his bedroom and closed the door. Daniel sat at the table next to his mother. Dressed for it, Albert was talking about Japan. He might have come all the way back home to talk about it.

The very small island of Japan floated just an inch above the table. Albert said, often, "How charming, how charming it is." It was a very strange expression to come from him. It was as if he were in speaking about Japan speaking Japanese. "Ah, and the charming girls," Albert said. His mother said, "I don't think I'll ever get to Japan, but you've sent so much of it here maybe I don't need to go." There was silence from Albert. "Don't you want to look over what you sent?" she asked. He said yes, but he didn't move. It was as if the Japanese were all around him now, and he couldn't leave them, as much out of politeness towards them as an excited appreciation for, he said, "their charm, their charm". "They giggle, you know, in such delightful ways, the girls. And they'll make a flower out of a napkin and hold it out to you and laugh, and you think, how adorable! How adorable when one of them, just like that, recites a pretty poem and everyone else listens." He looked out of the window.

His mother asked, "Would you marry one of them, Al?"

He slammed his open palm on the table. "But I'm not talking about *marrying* any of them!"

"Oh," she said. She blinked. "Well, wouldn't it be nice

75

if they came here, and you could show them your way of life—"

He didn't pick this up. He appeared to her alone, as if all the Japanese had quickly left.

She immediately said, "Come and look at the things you've sent. I've put a lot of them around, but they're all yours."

He followed her into the living room where, on the top of the piano, were glass cases in which, on lacquered stands, small delicate thin women, their faces porcelain white, their kimonos open at their feet as if they were stepping to reveal the kimonos' pastel linings, were arrested in positions of surprise at all at once discovering where they were. The mother said, "Perhaps I should have left everything in the attic, where it'd be safer—" Albert didn't reply; he hardly looked at what he'd bought in another country and sent home in huge teakwood crates. The living room was crowded with objects: a large lamp of translucent rice paper into which leaves and grasses had been pressed, a round glass tray showing flowers and butterflies, framed wood-block prints of moons and wistaria or willows, lacquer trays and bowls, small many-drawered chests, each drawer opened by a silk tassel, many fans strewn on all flat surfaces, left by the party of Japanese who'd all gone so quickly and forgotten their fans. Albert didn't appear to be interested.

She said, "You've been so generous. So much—"

He waved his hand. "Never mind that," he said. He looked about. "I thought you might be interested. I thought, too, the kids might learn a little about another country." Daniel, who had hung back, advanced as if called, but Albert seemed as little aware of him as he was of the lamps and trays and bowls and fans. He sucked at his teeth, running his tongue back and forth across them.

For Daniel, these foreign objects defined some clear, almost visible space, shaped like no other space he knew, and jumbled together outside that clear, simple space were the worn linoleum with its pattern of large blue flowers, the big lumpy armchairs, the radiator, the crooked floor lamp, the sockets and plugs and wires, the litter of old magazines and newspapers; he was aware, he knew, of these familiar objects only because of the displacing strange ones, and he stared at a glass ashtray on a circular lace doily.

"Some day you'll have a house of your own, and you can fill it with all this—," the mother said.

"And what would I do with a house of my own?" Albert asked.

They went back into the kitchen. She asked Daniel to go to the cellar for potatoes, and she peeled them on a newspaper at the table. He sat across from her at the table and watched her.

He said suddenly, "But if I got a house one day, it sure as hell wouldn't be around here."

"No." Her voice was flat. "Don't you ever want a family, Al?"

Albert moved a little. "I've thought about it."

"The right one hasn't come along, has she?"

He said, "Ma, why have your solutions to all problems always been so banal?"

She looked at him, a muddy knife in one hand, a muddy potato in the other.

"Is it because you're not really interested?"

"I—"

He cut her off. "No, never mind, it doesn't matter."

"But I—," she said.

He said, "Never mind. I'm the one who's banal."

"I don't know what you mean," she said.

He pointed to himself. He said, "Look, woman, both you and I know I'm a load of shit."

She put the knife and the potato down. "Albert!"

"Don't get motherly on me now," he said.

She was stunned. "But, Albert!"

"All right," he said.

Her eyes shifted about him. She said, "You're so intelligent, you've done so much, you've been to so many places—"

77

"I'm stupid," he said, "I haven't done anything, and I haven't been anywhere."

She looked at her hands. They were smeared with dirt, and she thought of diaper mess on them. She wiped them on her apron. She said, "You shouldn't have come back if you're not happy here. You should stay in Japan. You should find someone who'd take over, some woman, maybe a Japanese girl—"

"No woman would have me," he said.

She placed her hands flat on the table. "That's not true."

He shook his head; he seemed to be trying to shake off his annoyance with her. "Of course it's true."

"But it isn't. If you found someone who was used to your Marine Corps ways, if she was a woman Marine—"

He smiled a little. "You really want to marry me off. But no, no woman would take it."

She stood. She lifted the pan in which the white potatoes bobbed in the black water. Instead of leaving the table, however, she asked, "You're strong, Albert, but don't you ever want a woman, someone who'll take care of you?"

He stopped rubbing his eyes and looked at her. Then he all at once shouted. The water in the pan splashed. "Haven't I? Woman, what do you think I'm made of?"

She remained still.

He said, "What kind of life do you think I've been living all these years? Do you think I don't have any blood? How could I fight a war if I didn't have blood? But let me tell you—and this is no credit to me, I couldn't have done it on my own, without the help of Christ himself—I've never given in, I swear, woman, I've never given in. I keep the laws, I keep the commandments. I'll tell you, once, out in the Philippines, I went with some buddies to a whorehouse, a straw shack, where a mother was pimping for her daughter, a big fat flat-faced woman with black teeth, and I waited in a room while my buddies, each in turn, went in to the daughter, and the mother said to me, 'What's the matter, you don't want to too, is there something wrong with you?' and I had to stand not only against what I felt knowing that a girl was waiting for me in the other room with her legs open, but the humiliation that that fat black-mouthed woman caused me, in myself and in front of my buddies. I waited for my buddies, and left with them. I spent days and days afterwards thinking I should go back. But I didn't. I didn't give in. I swear I didn't."

His mother put the pan of potatoes on the table. She asked, "What's wrong with your eyes?"

He said, "I don't know."

"Haven't you been to a doctor?"

"Yes. I was told there's nothing wrong with them."

"Why do you keep rubbing them?"

"They hurt."

"When did they begin to hurt?"

"About six months ago, in Korea. When the doctor told me there was nothing wrong with them, I made up my mind that there wasn't, and that I'd get over it. I told myself every night, every morning, that I'd get over it, and that I must stop rubbing my eyes."

"And you can't stop."

"They still hurt," he said.

She picked up the pan and looked at the potatoes for a while.

"They told me to take two months' leave, they told me to come home."

"Oh."

Albert stared at her, and as he did the muscles of his face, Daniel saw, contracted as with a sudden wince. His mother raised her eyes to him, and his face contorted again and he smiled. He said, "Hey, Ma—"

She said nothing.

"It's good to be home," he said. He kept his smile.

She smiled a little.

"Listen, I've got a joke to tell you."

Her smile increased.

"Come on, put the potatoes down, sit here, and I'll tell you. It's about—"

She half laughed. "Later," she said, "later."

"Before Dad gets back," he said.

Daniel was left with Albert. Daniel shifted in his chair. Albert studied him for a moment, then abruptly asked, "Have you thought what branch of the service you want to go into, lad?" Daniel simply looked at him. "Stay out of the Marine Corps." Daniel looked at him with the silent wonder of why he should have to make a choice at all, and Albert said, "You do realize, don't you, that you owe two years to your country." He hadn't known, and suddenly imagined his brother commanding him, shouting, raging at him, "Your mother was a gutter whore, you were born in the gutter, and don't forget it," and Daniel, who never once had had to obey his brother—in fact, the mother had made it a law of the family that the older brothers should never dictate to the younger—would have to submit. Daniel said, "I don't know." He thought he saw Albert's mouth twist up a little; but Albert said nothing.

The potatoes were boiling when the father came in. He was followed by Mr Girard.

Georgie Girard lived in an adjacent street. He claimed to be—he had calculated it—a twenty-second cousin of Jim Francoeur. He had low, soft cheeks. He worked at the file shop, often stopped by the house in the morning on his way to work to walk to the shop with Jim, and often walked back with him in the evening. That Jim had been made a foreman and that Georgie was a machine operator and had been a striker made no difference to Georgie, though to Jim it made these differences: Georgie appeared to him a little shorter than before, a little more stunted, a little dimmer.

Mr Girard extracted three long cigars from his shirt pocket; he offered one to Albert, who accepted, one to Jim, who held up his hand to decline, and lit up one himself. He said, "The wife and kids can wait a bit." He and his wife had nine children. He said to Albert, "I bet you had some tough times over there."

Jim Francoeur watched his son shake his head. Jim raised himself up to a greater height in his rocking chair by pressing against the arms and lifting himself a little. He said, for his son, "They asked for volunteers to bomb China and Albert was one to go."

Albert frowned. He could only look at his father. For a moment his face appeared to Albert as closed in its ignorance as that of a Korean dishwasher from the officers' mess squatting at the edge of the runway and watching Albert get into his plane, without any idea why Albert was in his country, and perhaps thinking Albert was about to go off beyond the Yalu to drop bombs on China.

The father, smiling, stared at Albert. Georgie too, puffing his cigar, stared at Albert.

The mother, standing at the pantry door, watched the three men. She wanted to exclaim, "Jim, no!" but she thought Albert would somehow be angry with her if she did deny what his father had said. She thought that Albert would make those bombs verbal and attack the whole of China from where he sat, making his father's statement in some way true. He could not attack his father.

Albert said, "Mr Girard, people as ugly as I am aren't really allowed to drop bombs, otherwise my mug would frighten the poor bastards away before the bomb reached the ground, and there'd be no one there to bomb. The Chinese, you see, are very sensitive to beauty."

Mr Girard laughed. The father's smile broadened. The mother thought: But you're not ugly!

As soon as Georgie Girard left, the father untied and took off his shoes, put his slippers on, placed his shoes in his closet (everything he did was so plotted out it seemed to Daniel that it would take volumes to work out all the intricacies of the plot) and again sat in his rocker. He held the arms of the chair and waited for Albert to speak, as if now they could speak. Albert took the cigar from his mouth, leaned towards his father with a pack of cigarettes, one cigarette tapped out. His father took the cigarette, reached in his trousers pocket, having to lift one leg and twist his body a little, for a match book, and lit it. The mother, at the stove, looked away.

Albert said, "Well, how is it being a foreman?"

The father drew his lips in a long straight line. He held the arms of the rocker, his elbows out, his shoulders raised high, his head held up and to the side, motionless, the thin long line of his lips expressive of some power taken entirely for granted. Albert didn't care about his life, and his father cared very much for his life—the father would have never volunteered for any war—but the father could, like Albert, risk everything with a sudden dark movement by stepping past a line of men, as Albert had sworn an oath: both acts the consequences of which they'd not at all thought out.

"It's a job," the father finally said.

Albert said, "Maybe you'll have your own shop one day, Dad."

"No, I don't think so. It takes too much. Too much money. I've given up the idea of ever having a shop of my own. I'll continue to work for the file shop. I've been there since I was fourteen. I'm fifty-four. That's forty years."

"Do you think it'll last?"

"The shop?"

"Won't the union destroy it?"

His father frowned a little. "No."

Albert said, "I'm warning you, Dad. If I were you I'd fight the union in every way I could."

Albert's level but strict advice came from someone who seemed to know, and the father listened with the attention of someone who knew nothing about the stock market listening to a man, not a stockbroker, who had some access to the market floor. He nodded and said, "I'm not worried about the union. They're only a bunch of men. The shop'll go on."

"Well—," Albert said.

Jim Francoeur said, "I'll tell you, I've seen a lot. Management thinks of work in terms of profit and loss, and maybe it's management's forcing their terms on the workers that makes workers have to get together to fight for themselves, and to think of their work as profit and loss. I'm not for the boss, I'm not for the union. I've worked in the shop all my life. I'm working, as I've always worked, for the shop—"

There was a sound of heavy steps on the back entry stairs, the door opened, and Edmond stood on the threshold, his black staring eyes wide enough, it seemed, to take in the entire kitchen. Those in the kitchen turned to him, and he knew they were watching him. Daniel saw behind his eyes that he was letting them wait a moment. Then he smiled, a large smile, stepped into the kitchen, put his green tin lunch box on the table, held out his arms to Albert, and said, "My brother!" Albert got up, his hand held out, though he leaned a little back, and Edmond grabbed his hand and his elbow. "My older brother Al," he said.

"But you saw him last night," his mother said.

"It'd be good to see my brother every day like this," Edmond said.

Albert said, "You're all right, Ed."

Edmond let go. He took off his jacket. Albert sat again where he had been sitting, at the end of the table. Edmond's smile went.

He said, "You're sitting at my place."

"Oh, Edmond," the mother said.

"No. I'm the oldest one living at home. When Al left the house he gave me the right to sit at the end of the table. I sit there."

Albert smiled. "I could always pull rank on you."

"Not here, not in this house, you can't."

"But I'm prettier than you are."

"No you're not."

Albert got up.

Edmond looked at the chair for a moment and said, "Well, hell, you can sit there."

"No," Albert said. "No, that's your place."

Edmond sat and smiled. He said, "It's good to be home."

"You had a tough day at work?" Albert asked.

Edmond worked for a little business in Providence which printed name cards, handouts, leaflets, menus.

"Yeah," he said.

"Tell me about it," Albert said.

"Well, if *I* were running that place—"

The mother said, "The potatoes are done."

While they ate the potatoes and slices of meat loaf, she said, "We've been looking at ads in the paper for a house in the country to buy."

Albert didn't look at her, but at his father. "What's this?"

The father looked at the mother.

She said, "Your father thought it'd be a good idea."

"A house in the country?" Albert said. "What made you decide on that?"

"We have the money now," the father said.

"But there are many things you can do with money. Why buy a house in the country?"

The father was hesitant; he wasn't sure of Albert. "We need a big house."

"What do you kids think?"

Silent, they stared at Albert; it seemed the final decision was up to him.

The father said, "It'd be for the family."

Albert asked Julien, "What would you do in a house in the country in the summer?"

Julien's face was dark with seriousness. "I'd play."

"And you, Daniel?"

"It'd be different," he said, and swallowed what felt like a hard potato.

Edmond began, "Well—"

Albert said, "Then we'd better have one. But it'll have to be a big one."

"Yes," the father said.

"You haven't seen any yet?"

"Not yet."

84

"It's getting on in the year, isn't it? We're into May already. We want it for this year, don't we?"

"I thought we'd get one by and by."

"We'll have to find one soon."

"I was thinking of looking next Sunday."

Edmond put his fork down on his empty plate, got up and went into the living room, from where a moment later radio voices sounded.

To the father, the outside world, the world Albert inhabited, the world he had travelled in, met many people in, ate and slept in, did not exist. When Albert spoke to the father on his return, after no matter how long an absence, they discussed the church, the parish, local politics, the local set-up of the Republican Party. They did after supper.

The father took another of Albert's cigarettes. He lit it. With the smoke, he said, with a straightforward officiousness, an officiousness that in some way pleased Albert, "Well, your old man has put in his bid for District Representative in the November elections. He thought it was about time to try again, fifteen years after his defeat in the '38 elections."

Albert suddenly whistled. He became, for the father, a crowd. The father reached out and pointed a finger towards the window, over which a shade was drawn.

"*They've* been in so long, they can't see what they're doing. Someone else has to step in, someone who can see from the outside." He bunched his fingers up and hit himself again and again in the middle of the chest. "It's no disadvantage to have been on the outside for so long. I've been outside, looking in, and I've seen what's been going on, not only in the district but the city, the state. I've been looking into a dirty, badly kept, run-down house, and I see that a big cleaning, a new caretaker, a complete redecoration is what's needed!"

Albert hesitated. He wondered how much his father knew of the political situation of the district, never mind the country; he wondered how much his father knew about the process of government, state or federal.

He said, "You get into politics, Dad, you get in and clean out our churches, our schools, our shops, our houses."

Albert all at once rose. He walked to the door to the pantry, across the kitchen to the broom closet, to a chair, then to the door to the back entry. He stopped at the door and, facing it, his back to his father, he smashed the side of his fist against the door jamb. He said, "And what am I doing here?" He looked round at his father.

His father had stopped rocking; his mother, with Daniel and Julien on either side of her, was at the pantry door, staring at him.

Albert bared his teeth. "I should be out there fighting. I think of the war in the Pacific almost with nostalgia. I could almost weep when I think of a Marine fighting. I think of Marines throwing grenades into the little openings of underground foxholes to blast those goddamn Japs from out of the earth, and I feel: that's how you get rid of shit—"

His mother said, "Albert!"

He didn't say anything for a moment, then with a clear matter-of-factness he said, "Does it upset you, Ma, when I talk about war? Do you know anything about it?"

She didn't move.

"You know, if a commanding officer issues an order in the jungle that no prisoners are to be taken, you shoot them, one after the other, in the back of the head. If you hate the Japs enough, you're going to try to kill them even after they're dead, you're going to cut them up because just killing them outright isn't enough. And you may even want a token of your hatred. You may go around yanking gold teeth out of their mouths to keep them, to remind yourself how much you hated those sons-of-bitches."

The father's features were set firm with the expression of his having known it all, somehow, long before, and he was even nodding his head. The mother, however, said, "But, Albert, you love the Japs." The father breathed in deeply and out.

Albert said, with a greater, a more even matter-of-factness:

86

"I had a dog for a while in the Philippines, a mangy mongrel puppy, which I found by a heap of stones that'd once been the entrance to a Jap bunker. It'd belonged to a Jap, I suppose. I pulled it away. It was weak with hunger, but it wouldn't leave that heap of stones. I picked it up and took it away. The first thing I did to it, before giving it even a drink of water, was to beat it. I beat it with a stick. I beat it and beat it. It tried to run away. I kept beating it. Finally, it lay down, it looked at me. I put water and steamed rice in front of it. It jumped up. I beat it. It lay, looking at the food, looking at me. It wouldn't move till I said, Get it! and it wolfed down the rice, lapped up the water. I beat it before every meal. Whenever anyone came near it, I beat it. I got that dog to hate me, but it was terrified of me, too. It did everything I commanded, it had to or it would be beaten. I had to keep it tied. But I was waiting to release it on a Jap—"

The mother didn't speak, though her mouth was open and her face twisted to the side.

Albert ran his tongue along his upper and lower gums. He rubbed his eyes with his knuckles. He lowered his hands. He looked about. He blinked. He said, "Hey, Ma." Her jaw twisted to the other side. He smiled at her. "You know what I think about it all, about the whole business of war?" He continued to smile, but the smile was forced up into his cheeks and his chin was thrust out. The muscles of his face were strained. He retained the smile, raised a leg, and farted. "That's what I think about it." He suddenly laughed. "Mais comme il pue!" He waved his hands.

The mother all at once laughed, grabbed a dish towel from Julien and waved it about. The father, smiling thinly, rocked and watched his wife flap the dish towel where Albert, pointing, indicated the smell remained, under his chair, under the table. Albert farted again. The mother's laughter rose. She shook the towel all around Albert, who said, in French, "The curé will smell that one." The mother put her hand to her mouth and, laughing more, said between her fingers, "C'est un péché mortel." Albert pushed his chair out from the table to give himself room for a bigger fart. The mother's laughter made her false teeth loose; she kept her hand to her mouth to hold them in place.

"Come on, Ma, I haven't heard you in a long time," Albert said.

"Albert!" she shouted. She looked at her husband, whose lips were still drawn in the long thin smile. Her body began to shake with silent laughter as she pressed it back with her hand. Her face was red.

Albert clapped his hands once. "Come on, Ma."

She put her hands on the edge of the table, the dish towel hanging from one hand, and leaned forward. She was trying to keep her mouth closed, as much from the fear of losing her teeth as the shame of laughing out loud. She released, like a stream of small hard bubbles, five distinct poops. Her body shook more with silent laughter, though now her mouth was wide open; there was too much laughter for her throat to release it, so it was released through her shoulders, breasts, thighs; she couldn't catch her breath, and she stamped her feet. Albert, bent over, guffawed. The father's smile was drawn into a straighter, thinner smile. The mother sat, her body still heaving.

She was all at once having fun. She looked about as if to find someone else who could, by joining, keep up the fun. She passed by her husband, passed by Julien standing against the stove. She saw Daniel sitting on the stool by the radiator, and, knowing he wouldn't join in any more than her husband or Julien, she wanted to knock him from where he sat with his feet together on the rung of the stool, his knees pressed together, his hands loosely folded on his knees, his lips pursed, his eyes looking above her at the ceiling light, and she said, trying to laugh, "You know, Daniel never farts? I've never heard him." "Then he can't be human," Albert said. "Sometimes I don't think he is," the mother said; "at least, he never makes a sound." "Then he's the worst kind of pooper, he's a silent pooper, the kind who, in church, poops, then makes a face and looks around at others in the pew." "Et comme il pue!" the mother said. Albert and the mother laughed. Albert said, holding his nose, "The pew pues." They both laughed again. The mother said, "Daniel doesn't think it's funny. He never thinks anything is funny. He not only never farts, he doesn't have a sense of humour." She looked at Daniel, who stared back at her. As a matter of fact, he did strain to fart silently, and he didn't, he knew, have a sense of humour. She said, "Look at him. Il est fâché. Il va broyer du noir." Daniel switched his stare to Albert and the two brothers looked at one another. Albert said to him, "If you were out in the world, you'd be ashamed to have us with you, wouldn't you? You think no one farts out there?" Daniel's irises, hard with concentrated anger, became suddenly unfocused. He looked at the floor. He was aware of the way he was sitting, and changed his position to try to sit naturally. He wanted to get up and leave, but that, he knew, he couldn't do naturally, and he saw himself walking across the floor with exaggerated swinging loose-limbed movements. He heard Albert say: "Mom, how about having a cup of tea?"

She was a little disappointed by the change in subject: from farts to tea.

Albert said, "And look, Mom, let's not have any of your chipped mugs and tea bags. Didn't I send you a tea set from Japan?"

"You sent about seven," the mother said.

"Then take one out. Let's have our tea as it should be had."

Edmond, when called, said he didn't want any tea, he wanted to listen to the radio.

Daniel, with the use of the stool, took down a tea set from a high shelf in the pantry—a small, seashell grey, delicate pot, small, thin, handle-less, seashell grey cups. Albert took over the making of the tea; he rinsed the pot out with hot water, broke open a tea bag into it, poured in more steaming water. He placed the pot in a circle of cups and let the tea steep. Everyone watched him. When Julien said, "I want sugar and milk in my tea," Albert replied, "You're in Japan, now, and there you don't have sugar and milk in your tea." He poured out the tea, handed the cups about. The father took his, but immediately placed it on a corner of the table and left it. The mother sipped hers, and said (which had it been repeated would have annoyed Albert for its affectation; it was, as it was, an acceptable affectation, because formal), "This is much better than tea-bag tea." Julien, like his father, put his cup down and left it. Daniel held the cup up with the tips of the fingers of both hands and took quick bitter sips. Albert sat back.

The theme music of a radio programme sounded very far away.

"You know," Albert said, not to Daniel but in Daniel's direction, "you can be on a crowded, noisy street in Tokyo, pushed and pulled from all sides, and all you have to do to get away from the street, as though you were able to step a thousand miles away from it in one step, is to step into a teahouse." He now looked at Daniel. "You'll like it, I'm sure. You'll go there some day." He drank his tea. He said, "There are some teahouses in Japan from which you can see the sun set. I've been with Japanese friends. As the sun sets everyone stops talking and looks, and everyone is silent till long after the sun has gone down." Albert rubbed his eyes.

The silence in the kitchen was the silence that followed a Japanese sunset. It was a sad silence to Daniel, a silence that made him, for some reason, nostalgic for other places, other times which he could not relive, could not go back to; but as he was young, and had been nowhere, his nostalgia could not have been real. He said, "I'll have more tea." But Albert didn't hear. If he was feeling nostalgic, his nostalgia had to be real, because he had known different times, different places. He was, now, in Japan. But he was, in Japan, thinking about something else. He raised his head and said: "You know what'll really save the world?"

The family looked at him.

"Prayer," he said.

The family continued to look at him, all their faces, as always when listening to him, open with attention, but also, like open skies, a little clouded. The father scratched his head. The mother got up to clear away the tea things, and asked Daniel and Julien if they didn't have homework. Albert arrested them all, however, by saying, his voice suddenly raised, "What are we doing sitting around having tea? We should be praying for the world." The mother didn't look at him, continued to look at her husband, but said, "You're right, Al. You're right. Isn't he right, Jim?" Jim nodded his head. "Yes, he's right."

Julien said, "I'm going to bed."

Albert stared at him. "You'd better join us, boy."

Julien simply stared back. "No," he said, "I'm going to go to bed."

"I'm telling you you'd better pray," Albert said, but he was half smiling.

Julien again said, "No," and went into his bedroom and closed the door.

When Albert stood, the others stood.

The nuns at school, once inspired to bring devotion to the Virgin into the homes of the pupils, fitted into a small wooden box with a handle, like the blue satin-lined coffin of an infant, the statue of Our Lady (Our Lady of Fatima, which given that the parish was called Our Lady of Lourdes, might have made the nuns wonder if they were causing a conflict between at least two of the manifestations of the Virgin, for finding her as Our Lady of Fatima more open to appeal than Our Lady of Lourdes) which, along with the formula for the prayers and a votive lamp, was taken home, in turns, by each pupil for family devotion; when Daniel's turn came, he carried the box home with a sense of anticipated failure, because he knew his family wouldn't pray at it, opened like a shrine on the table. The mother had examined the statue, had said they *should* pray, but to the father the statue hadn't even been an object of special attention. Now, Albert was bringing prayer into the family as he had brought Japan and the war. They all knew how to pray, but praying in the family, everyone on knees before chairs in the living room, was as strange as it would have been if they'd been saying their prayers in a Shinto temple, or about a military chaplain in a jungle clearing.

Edmond had to shut off the radio. He knelt by it.

They would say all the mysteries. Albert asked the father to lead. With a hoarse voice, the father recited the first half of each of Je vous salue Marie and Notre Père, Albert and the others completing them. Daniel, kneeling with his back towards them, said his prayers in silence; he didn't want to be there, he wished he could be like his brother Julien and refuse; his silent praying was almost in defiance of the full-voiced prayers of Albert and, at Albert's side, his mother, who, though kneeling there and praying only because of Albert, might, for the carrying force with which she prayed, herself have thought of and insisted on the family praying. She was showing Albert how deeply she could and did, after all, agree with him.

Before each rosary the father announced the mysteries—joyeux, douloureux, glorieux—and at the beginning of each dizaine he paused to indicate each single mystery and its intention; Joyeux: l'Annonciation, pour l'humilité; la Visitation, pour la charité; la Nativité de Jésus, pour la pauvreté; la Présentation, pour l'obéissance; Jésus au Temple, pour la piété; Douloureux: L'Agonie au Jardin, pour la contrition; la Flagellation, pour pureté (a mystery Daniel was sure Albert meditated upon with fervour; he felt during this mystery very close to Albert without Albert knowing); le Couronnement d'épines, pour la force; le Portement de la Croix, pour la patience (his mother, Daniel knew, would be praying especially for patience); le Crucifiment, pour le renoncement (yes, Daniel wanted to renounce himself, to renounce himself totally); Glorieux: la Résurrection, pour la foi; l'Ascension, pour l'espérance; la Descente du Saint-Esprit, pour l'amour; l'Assomption, pour le bonheur éternel; le Couronnement de Marie, pour la dévotion à Marie.

Was the family aware, while praying, that they were going through all the mysteries of earth and its surrounding heaven? Were they aware that those divine mysteries were meant, by their power, to infuse the earth with transforming virtue, to save the world?

Daniel's knees and back ached by the final dizaine. The repeated prayers had set up a movement of sound which reduced the prayers themselves to sound; he hadn't been reciting out loud, so the prayers repeated in his mind set up a rhythm without sound, and he couldn't think outside it; he let the rhythm in him and the repeated sounds outside him carry him to the end.

They rose to their feet. The mother said to Daniel, "You weren't praying out loud."

"I wasn't praying to you," Daniel said.

Albert said, "You should have prayed out loud. You should have prayed with us, not by yourself."

Daniel cowered a little. "Does it make a difference?"

"It makes a great difference. We're appealing to God together, not singly."

Daniel had never heard that; he didn't know what Albert meant. The mother said, winding her rosary round her fingers, "Well, that was wonderful!" She would have been shocked by anyone telling her—as Albert, looking at her for a second, might in a flash have told her—that she was faking. She said again, "It was wonderful." Albert said nothing; neither did the father. Edmond turned the radio on.

His parents watched Albert walk from room to room, pick up magazines and put them down, open and close desk drawers, look in the fridge. Then he again sat at the kitchen table. He smoked. Albert wanted to know in detail about everyone in the family. He listened with fixed and silent attention as the mother brought forth each member of the family. She thought he was examining them, and she described them as to defend them: Richard was doing *very* well, he was *merging* with a bigger business in Massachusetts, and though they would be moving out of Rhode Island they wouldn't be moving *too* far (she talked about Richard knowing Albert had invested a thousand dollars in Richard's business, but she also knew that Albert had never thought of the investment as anything but an outright gift); Edmond was so happy with his new car (Albert had helped Edmond to buy the car) and he still talked of going down to Kentucky; Philip, the son in Cambridge, Massachusetts, was doing *very very* well, he'd be graduating summa cum laude, and he'd be so pleased to know Albert would be there (Albert had paid to send Philip to M.I.T., had, years before, when Philip was a senior in high school, and he, Albert, was a captain home on leave, said to Philip, "Ma tells me your marks get better and better, lad. Let's have a look at your report card," and the family watched as Philip presented the report card to Albert, who looked it over and said, "Lad, with all A's, any college will take you, so which one do you choose?", and Philip chose the Massachusetts Institute of Technology; Philip, the first in the family, not only to go to college but to graduate from high school, went to Cambridge; Albert sent to the father a monthly check for tuition and expenses and the father deposited the money in his account and sent his own checks to Philip); André, in Miami, was doing very *well* studying singing, he sang in the chorus of university productions of operas, and sent photographs of himself on stage, one in Spanish costume, another in a satin suit with knee breeches and long white stockings and buckled shoes—

Out in Korea, Albert had thought he would come back to a square, simple house, a house created for him in the long lines of a perspective made clear to him by his distance: the house of a man of God, the house of a man honoured by his wife and sons, the house of a family which converged—as the simple clear sightlines of the perspective, originating at points spread out on the horizon behind him, converged at the horizon before him into a house with a single central

94

point—in their devotion to God. The house was not a house of its own making, it was created not of wooden beams, clapboard and shingle but of long rays of grace. He had been, from his distance, moved by the small white bungalow he remembered at a crossroads—

The father said, "I think it's time to go to bed."

For a while before falling asleep, Daniel heard the footsteps of his brother Albert wandering about the kitchen, the bathroom, the den, the living room.

Up early the next morning, Albert sat at the kitchen table and rubbed his eyes. His face was very gaunt, the muscles of his cheeks and jaw knotted. His mother was careful not to talk to him. She walked about lightly, as though he were still asleep and she did not want to wake him. Daniel and Julien sat silently and ate their breakfast. The morning outside was bright; the mother opened the kitchen windows.

The inside of the house, had, from the night before, remained starkly purged of all smallness. The mother wondered if Albert would think her small if she sat by a window to breathe in the clear air, made so clear by the great dense moist dark green maple trees round the house. She saw the postman walking under the trees. He had a small box in his hand. She heard footsteps on the porch, and the clank of the letter slot. She went quickly, and quickly unwrapped the little package. It contained, in a green box, a small bouquet of dried flowers tied round with a ribbon. The card read: "Everyone in the frat was given flowers for his girlfriend, but as you're the only girlfriend I have, I'm sending them to you. PHIL." She took the flowers out; she looked at them for a long time, turning the bouquet round and round. The fine small dried blossoms vibrated on thin stems. That she should have got them from Philip, who never showed any emotion but anger, much less sent gifts, made the flowers vivid with an intention she tried to take in by taking in, one by one, the flowers themselves: pale red, straw yellow. She might have been, suddenly, a diminutive bride with a diminutive wedding bouquet, wondering, standing alone in the front hall just before she was to leave the house to go to the church, how many children she would have, and all at once thinking, with a soft giving way in her body, so she felt weak and had to lean against the door: I'll have seven sons. The little bouquet in her hand might have come not only from Philip but, for that one moment, from them all, all of them reaching back to her, seven hands holding it out to her, a bride who did not even know how seven sons would be produced. She squeezed the dry bouquet. She wanted to show it to someone. Then it occurred to her that it would perhaps make Albert angry. She stood away from the door. She looked at the flowers a while longer, then placed them back in the narrow box. She heard Daniel say, "What is it, Ma?" She placed the lid over the box. She thought she might first go to her room and put the box in a drawer. She took off the lid, however, to look again. She didn't think, she suddenly felt: she'd show them to Albert. She went out to the kitchen, the open box held out, and simply said, "Look." His gaunt face lowered to look; he reached out, a smoking cigarette between his fingers, to take the box. The mother drew back. He smiled. He took the bouquet out of the box and held it up. He said, "Aren't they pretty." He read the card. He said, "We're faithful suitors, Ma."

IV

THE BUMPY DIRT road led to a wind-shaken clump of blueberry bushes at the edge of the lake, curved sharply to the
right and led into more shaking bushes at the lake's shore,
again swerved to the right into more bushes and scrub pine,
and then in a sharp curve round them to a straight road
through tall pines, the black smooth trunks bare, the thin
high branches thrashing. Beyond the pines on the right rose
a bank of dry pine needles and ferns and up the steep bank
the spaced, straight trunks of thinner pines, and between the
pines along the left side of the road the lake appeared black,
was broken into sharp small waves as on a river, the opposite
shore a bank of trees in the mist. The car rocked over the
ruts and water-filled holes.

From the back seat, the boys on either side of her, the
mother said, "We're lost." Albert was driving. The father
was sitting next to him. "We'll go to the end," Albert said.
"But we'll end up in the water," the mother said. She kept
glancing at, then turning away from, the black water of the
lake. "We'll drive to the end," Albert repeated. The father
said, half to Albert, half to his wife, "There's no room to
turn around."

Low branches scraped against the side of the car. The
road narrowed, always following the edge of the lake, at
times sinking below the level of the lake, so the moving
water looked as if it would at moments flood over them,
but was held back by the rows of wild bushes, and at
times the road rose at a tilt over a bank so they were high

97

enough above the water to see long weeds streaming in it.

The car came to a big rock covered with poison ivy, and Albert stopped. Perhaps they were lost. They didn't speak, but looked out of the rolled-up, misted windows at the woods around them.

Albert shut the motor off and got out. A smell of wet leaves and pine swelled through the car. The mother asked the father to slam the door quickly. They watched Albert outside, pushing away the bushes to get behind the car. From the rear window, their heads turned round, they saw him walking slowly down the road, which was overgrown with weeds, some crushed by the car tires. He was looking from left to right. He disappeared behind trees and bushes. Those in the car simply stared out. Mist was rising in the woods.

When Albert came back it was as if from a solo reconnaissance mission in the woods, and in the car they waited for what he had discovered. He said, starting the motor, "We should have kept right when we came to the fork."

"I didn't notice a fork," the mother said.

Albert backed up slowly, backed round a curve, backed up a stretch of rutted road lined on either side with high thick bushes, and stopped at a gap in the bushes and turned into it.

The car jolted a little when a front wheel rose over and crashed from a jutting rock, then, sinking into the weeds and grass covering the road, it rolled smoothly down the long narrow road, dense woods on one side, the flat exposed river-lake on the other. At the far end of the road, surrounded by gigantic pine trees, was the roof and the high stone side of a house.

The road continued, but they stopped just below the house, which was three storeys high, a garage at ground level, built of timber and fieldstone, and set into the side of a pine- and birch-covered hill. All the windows were blank. Weeds grew close about the walls. They looked at it from the car. They sat for a long while looking through the closed windows. It was as if they didn't want to get out, unsure that this was the house they had made an appointment to see, and, too, the outside was unfamiliar. They heard, overhead, the high resonant *caw-caw* of a bird. The big stark house was on the right; on their left was the lake and, between two scrub pines, a small grey weatherbeaten listing dock, a tire tied to it, and a half-sunken boat attached to it by a rusted chain. The black *caw-caw*ing bird flew low over the black lake, then up.

Albert opened the car door. The others followed. They stayed together feeling the pebbles and twigs through their soles as they walked over the strange ground. They walked slowly up the continuing road that curved round the edge of the hill into which the house was built, to another side of the house, a long low side, half brown-stained timber, half stone, with large many-paned windows and an entrance under its own small pointed portico, and a wide, overgrown lawn, birch trees bending over it, sloping away from the house to a stone wall which followed the curve of the drive, and beyond the drive a steep drop to another, vaster part of the lake, an expanse of water below them that stretched so far across, the other shore was lost in cloud; dark clouds rolled just above the surface of the water and down the lake. The wind behind them pulled them in the direction of the clouds, pulled them out over the open water, out into the low sky. This larger part of the lake was separated from the narrower, river-like lake by a long thin island covered with pines, and connected to the headland by a broken bridge made of railway ties and rotting planks. A current, thick with swaying weeds, ran about the bridge, from the large lake into the smaller, and ducks were going in and out of the railway ties and planks half fallen into the water. There was a path down the steep bank to a stone and earth jetty against which lake waves rose and fell, rose and fell.

They turned back to the house. The hill into which it was built was a small peninsula, water on three sides, the island just out of reach of the longest point of the peninsula. Pines and oaks rose above the roof and wide stone chimney. They continued up the drive to the back of the house, on this side one storey high, with a long screened-in porch; wet leaves were stuck to the screens through which the thin wind screeched. They looked through the screens. They looked through low windows into the dark, empty interior.

The mother asked, "Do you think this is the right house?"

Albert looked at his watch.

They walked over the shaggy lawn, among the birch trees. The great lake was obscured by clouds, and the island rose out of the moving mists. They stood among the birches.

Rain fell. It spotted the water. Albert suddenly ran to the car to get inside. By the time the others came water was sheeting in thin folds down the windows. They sat in a slightly steamy silence. The rain fell more heavily, shattering against the windshield. Albert said after a while, staring out, "I hate rain." It streamed through the pines, ran in rivulets down the drive. The mother wondered if she should suggest, again, that they might be at the wrong house. Albert said, "Maybe we've made a mistake." The mother said, "Let's at least wait for the rain to stop a little." Albert turned his head suddenly to look behind; he had seen in the rear-view mirror a car advancing through the rain.

The car stopped behind and a man, turning up the lapels of his jacket, stepped out and ran towards their car. Albert lowered the window. Rain splashed on the wide brim of the man's fedora. He said he would open the side door to the garage and they could run in. He ran back to his car and opened the door to a woman with a small hat and a coat with a fur collar, who hurried in high heels first to the house, he close behind.

The electricity was not on. They followed the owner and his wife up a dark flight of stairs into the house.

The house was built on different levels, so there were steps and stairs everywhere. Empty, the rooms appeared huge. The inside air was dim, cold, damp. There were dry leaves and twigs on the bare floors, as if wind had pressed them through the stone walls, through the shut windows. A green-grey light beamed palely about the stark, rain-wet windows. Their footsteps rang as they walked from room to room, up and down steps, upstairs to the bedrooms, in and out of closets, into the low attic, unsure, inside, how the large asymmetrical house was laid out about them, not quite sure how to get from the kitchen to the living room, from a downstairs back room with a balcony porch to the downstairs bathroom. It was a house with many corners, doors, cubbyholes. They separated, went in and out of rooms alone, met in the back hall, the screened-in porch off the large living room, in a linen closet. The father examined the ceilings, the walls; he tapped the length of thin cracks in the plaster. He questioned the owner, who stood with his wife in the kitchen and flipped the keys, tied together with a string, over and over in his hand.

Daniel, alone in a large empty room, heard footsteps about him, heard voices. He couldn't imagine the footsteps as the footsteps of his family actually inhabiting the house. He heard the owner speaking, and went quickly to hear more clearly. The man was giving a short talk. The house had been designed and built by himself, he'd gathered together building material from the land (the stones had been taken from the side of the hill when it was being dug out for the foundations, grey and white boulders; the mantelpiece of the fireplace was cut from a huge oak tree that had to be sawed down to make space) or from old houses and mills for miles around which he knew were being demolished (the narrow windows were made with pegs, not nails, and were from an old house just outside the nearest village, which was called Greenville; the beams, the floor boards, the large many-paned windows at the front of the house were from an old textile mill by a river; the inside doors were from an old schoolhouse; the panelling in the living room from a small village hall blown down in a hurricane) and had built the house in stages, so it was as though many houses had been built one into another, all at different levels, as he decided to expand. The mantelpiece, floor boards, windows, doors, panelling were examined carefully after the little talk, as if they were still more parts of trees, an old house, mill, school, village hall than they were parts of the house they were in.

The father looked at Albert, who nodded once, and the father stepped towards the man.

He didn't tell the man and his wife that he liked the house, or even that he wanted it. He started by saying, "I'd like to know if the terms of the sale are amendable." The man said, "How much will we knock off?" The father stared at him for a moment. Perhaps because his English was not his first language, was a language learned in a French school and taught by French nuns, whenever the father encountered a man whose first language was idiomatic English, like this man, a momentary uncertainty made him think the man was speaking properly, and he, the father, was not. The father searched in his mind for an idiom. He said, "By how much would you be prepared to slash the figure quoted?" (The figure quoted was twenty-two thousand dollars.) The man said, twisting the keys on their string, "You want a straight answer?" "I'd like to know," the father said. Albert stepped towards the man and his father as if to interpose. The man said, "Twenty thousand." The father's face remained expressionless. Albert's look pressed him to accept now, but the father said, "I'll telephone you by seven o'clock," and held out his hand to shake at least on this. "In the evening?" the man asked. "In the morning," the father said.

In the car, driving back to Providence, they talked.

The mother said, "Twenty thousand dollars?"

"It seems reasonable to me," Albert said.

"But we don't have twenty thousand dollars," she said.

"We'll mortgage the house in the city," her husband said.

The mother said, "It took us twenty-five years to pay off the bank loan on that house, and that was only seven thousand dollars."

"I know," the husband said.

"It's all we have," the wife said.

"I'm making a good salary now. We'll pay off the mortgage very fast."

Whenever in the past she'd said she wanted to leave the house in the city, she'd said it knowing he wouldn't take any action on what she wanted, and she realized she'd kept saying she wanted to leave because she knew he wouldn't move; now he was about to take the city house away from her by mortgaging it for another house she couldn't believe would ever be theirs, which wouldn't be a home, and she wondered if she had made him do this, if she had after all forced him to do something he really didn't want to do. He didn't take risks.

"You leave it to me," he said.

"I remember when we were scraping together quarters, making up enough to pay off the interest, never mind the mortgage itself, and what a relief when we finally did pay it all off."

Albert said, "You don't seem to want Dad to buy the house."

"No—"

"You shouldn't try to stop him from doing what he wants to do."

Her voice rose, "Stop him?"

The father said, "Assez, Assez."

The mother stared at the backs of the heads of the two men in the front seat as if to make them see her. "I've never tried to stop him from doing anything! He has always done exactly what he wanted!"

"Assez, assez," the father insisted.

She sank back. She withdrew into her thinking as she withdrew into the back of the car. But, after a while, she couldn't stop herself from asking her husband, "Have I ever stopped you from doing anything you wanted?"

He didn't turn round to her. "No, you never have."

"Never," she said.

She said it as much to Albert as to her husband. Her husband would never defend her against Albert, against any of her sons, who all, she thought, went quickly to the defence of their father. They thought he could never do anything wrong, would be on his side if he decided to sell the city house outright to invest the money in a pile of old rusty pipes. And if she wanted to, say, get a job as a telephone operator, or get a licence to drive a car, or even smoke, all of which her husband would disapprove of, would any of her sons say: You should do what you want? No, she thought, not one.

She didn't have a mind of her own, as she didn't really have a house of her own. Whenever she went into Mrs Girard's house, where the family was bigger than hers but where there were more girls than boys, she was struck always by the arrangements of flowers in vases before mirrors, of views through bedroom doors of skirted dressing tables stacked with boxes of powder and bottles of perfume, of silk underpants and stockings and bras drying on racks in the bathroom, of the ironing board draped with dresses to be ironed. Didn't she come home from Pauline Girard's with the feeling that her house was a stark masculine house, in which there were no flowers in vases, in which her boxes of powder and perfume were pushed to a corner of her bureau, in which she tried to hide her underpants and bra, and all her ironing was men's shirts? If she put a little rug down by the toilet, it'd be quickly stained by urine; if she hung bright curtains in the kitchen, they'd soon be brown with cigarette smoke; heavy car keys scratched polished surfaces, large dirty hands blackened towels, big unwiped shoes left footprints on the floor.

A moment later she thought: I'd probably always be fighting with daughters, and I never fight with my sons.

When they got back to the house in Providence she looked about her masculine house, and, tired, thought: What will happen if it's lost?

She said, while they were eating, "The law seems unfair. I mean, to parents. You have to bring up your children. You're supposed to be responsible till they're twenty-one. Isn't that right? Why isn't there a law that children should be responsible for their parents after they're, well, over sixty-five? If your father and I got, say, five dollars a week from each of you—well, how much is that? Seven times five. Thirty-five dollars a week. We could live on that if we had to. Shouldn't the children take care of their parents after the parents have taken care of them? But they don't, do they, and parents can't expect it—"

"We wouldn't abandon you," Albert said.

"Well, we couldn't expect anything. You all have to do what you want to do. We don't have the right to stop you. We've never stopped you, any of you, from doing just what you wanted. You all leave, and when you leave, it's for good. Only Edmond stays. That country house seems very big for a family that isn't really together any more. It's been eleven years since we've all been together in the same place. You all go your different ways. That's the way it is, and your father and I just have to accept it, and manage on our own—"

"Don't worry about it," Albert said.

"No, I'm not worried. I can't be worried. I have to learn to accept." Eating, she fell silent, then after a while she raised her head and said, "You know, I'd rather die than not have a house of my own, than be a dependent on my sons."

The father glanced at Albert, who was about to speak; the glance stopped him.

"I couldn't be a burden to my children. I'd go to a state home before I'd move in with any of my children. Sometimes I think, well, maybe they wouldn't mind if I stayed in their attic—" She laughed. "They could bring me soup once a day in a wooden bowl with a wooden spoon. But no. I put it out of my mind right away, staying with them. I'd die in the street first."

Julien said, "That's crazy. You won't die in the street."

"You never can tell," she said. The father ate quickly. The mother ate slowly. She said, "Not that I'd mind dying."

105

"Ah non—!" the father said.

"No, I'm not being morbid, honest. We shouldn't mind, should we, Albert? Haven't you said that? Isn't it better to die than to live? Shouldn't we want to die?"

The father couldn't deny that that was what Albert, who spoke as with the authority of a theologian on such matters, had insisted on; but Albert, putting his fork down and looking at his mother, didn't insist now.

She said, smiling, "We won't need any kind of house after we're dead. And after we're all dead, we'll all be together. Isn't that so? Just think of it, Jim. We think, now, we're all separated, but there we'll all be together. We'll be there, you and I, and looking out, we'll say, 'Here comes Richard, he's come back. And look, there's Albert coming. And here comes Edmond. And there are Philip and André. And oh, there are the kids coming, too, Daniel and Julien. And here we are, all of us.' "

Albert stared.

After supper Daniel helped his mother clear the table, and dried the dishes as she washed. She said, "I wish your father would let me get a job."

"Why?" he asked.

"To have it. To get out. To get out of the house."

He half listened.

"Once, he let me. But that was during the Depression."

"Yes," he said.

"Well, Philip and André were babies. I used to go out in the yard with them to watch them play. Neighbours stopped to talk to me over the hedge. We always talked about the Depression. Once Nora Dionne stopped. I knew Nora from Our Lady of Lourdes, Nora was married, had two boys. Her husband, like your father, was bringing home about seven dollars a week. She said she could get me a job as a waitress in a catering concern, Mr Hardy's Catering, where she had a job. Your father let me go because we needed the money. He was doing odd jobs, repairing, painting houses. I wore a black dress with a white collar and cuffs and a small white semi-circular apron. I was thin then. The first time I served was at a formal wedding. I was serving soup. I didn't notice a woman who moved her arms a lot while she talked. Her arms flew up, hit the tray, and sent a bowl of soup pouring down her back. Mr Hardy had to pay for her dress, but I earned fourteen dollars. Another time I served in a private house where the people were Irish. You know how the Irish are. The house was a mess. You could see shoes under the beds. A teenager followed me around, tried to touch me, and even when I said, 'Look, I'm a mother of five children,' he still followed me. Mr Hardy had to tell him, 'Leave her alone or I'll give you a sock on the jaw.' He said, 'She's beautiful.' After it was over Mr Hardy came up to Nora and me and asked us if we wanted to do more that day. Well, we said yes. We took a ferry. It was a party of just men. While I was serving a fat man reached down and pinched my leg. 'What's the matter with you?' I said. But I didn't want to say too much or I'd lose the tips. And when that was over, Mr Hardy asked us if we wanted to do more. Well, it was late, but we went anyway. It was a party of French people in Woonsocket. They were thrilled when I went to them with the clam chowder and asked, 'Est-ce que vous en voulez encore?' 'Ah, vous parlez français,' they said. I made quite a hit there. When Nora finally left me off at the corner it was seven-thirty. And still another time—" She paused. "Is this boring you?"

"No, no," he said.

"Another time," she said, "we went to a stag party at the Elks. One man asked me my name. 'Marie,' I said. I always wished my real name was Marie. He called me over a while after and he was holding a ten-dollar bill crumpled in his hand. 'See this?' he said. 'Here, I'm just shaking hands with you.' And he slipped the ten-dollar bill into my hand. After a while I went back to him. 'I can't take this,' I said. 'You've probably got a wife and a child and a home, and they need the money.' 'No,' he said, 'I'm not married. Keep it.' Then he said, 'I'd like to see you after this. I've got a car.' I didn't say yes or no. I sneaked out the back way with Nora before the party was over."

She looked out of the window at Violet Hill, which was violet in the evening light.

"Nora came to the house once with her two boys. Some one of my boys was eating an apple. 'Oh, let me have a bite of apple,' she said, 'I don't have any food in the house.' 'Nora,' I said, 'how awful.' So I gave her children some apples. One day, while we were working, she came up to me and said, 'Two men are going to wait for us behind the Post Office after. They've got a car.' 'Nora,' I said, 'what do you think I am?' 'Oh, what's the matter with a little fun?' she said. Mr Hardy brought me home. He asked me, 'Do you go out with Nora?' 'No,' I said, 'it's purely business.' 'I'm glad,' he said. Then she did something that made me stop catering. 'I've got two men to take us home,' she said, 'they said they'd take us straight home.' I got into the back seat with her. 'You're going past where I live,' I said. 'Oh, we're just going on an errand,' one of the men said. They were Italians. One was a big fat thing, greasy and old. They drove out to a house in the country. There were loads of little Italian children playing in the dirt round the house. 'I'm not going in,' I said. 'Why?' Nora asked. 'There's nothing wrong. Look at the little kids.' So I got out of the car and went in. A big fat Italian woman lifted a mat from the centre of the floor. Beneath was a trapdoor. She opened the trapdoor and went down. When she came up she had a bottle in her hand. This was during Prohibition. 'If you're going to drink that,' I said to them, 'you won't be fit to take me home. And if we get into an accident—me with five children to take care of—Nora, I want to go home. What kind of a woman do you think I am? *Take me home.* If you don't I'll start walking right away.' 'All right,' she said. On the way, she sat in the front seat with the younger one, and he wasn't driving with his two hands on the wheel. The fat one sat in the back with me. He tried to put his arm round me. 'Stop the car,' I said. 'I'll get out right now. You take your arm off me.' 'What a mope,' he said. We went past Nora's house and I said, 'Nora, aren't you getting out at your house?' 'No,' she said, 'I'm not getting out.' 'Turn in here,' I said, 'and stop.' I got out. 'You pig,' I said to Nora. I told your father. When I think of it now, I get afraid." She tipped out the dishwater from the pan into the sink.

V

THE MOTHER WAS alone. She walked about the house, from room to room. She thought: The house feels big. She sat in the living room. The house felt big and it felt a little strange, as if it were not hers, though she had lived in it for so many years. She wished Albert were there, and waited for Daniel and Julien to come home from school. The house felt big, she thought, but it was small, and she wondered how they had managed to sleep in it, all seven sons and her husband and herself. She stood. It seemed to her she momentarily forgot what her work in the house was. At the doorway to the kitchen, she heard the outside back door open and slam, then steps in the entry, then the kitchen door opened, and her body lightly jumped.

She rushed towards André as he rushed towards her, her hands held to her breasts, his arms out wide. His gesture was as if to encompass an enormous woman, so when he threw his arms around her he almost touched his elbows with his hands behind her back. He pressed his face into the side of her neck and held her tightly. Her hands were crushed against her breasts. She tried to pat his chest, but she could hardly move her hands. He drew away, drew far enough away to look at her fully, then embraced her again, and pressed her folded arms against her ribs. He said, "Ah, Ma!" His bearded chin was digging into her neck.

He stepped away, his arms out wide, and looked at her. She said, "You're the best-looking of them all." He laughed. He said, "I get my looks from you." "You're dark like your father," she said, which as she said it she thought was somehow not a compliment; she said, "He's a handsome man." André, his arms still held out, turned about to look at the kitchen, and said, "How often I thought about this house while in Miami."

She prepared him soup while he sat at the table. From the darkness around his eyes, darkness which made his eyes larger, the lids with long lashes sag, she saw that he was very tired, but he kept up the talk.

He said, "Don't tell M. Lambert" (the choirmaster of the church) "that I'm back if you see him." (There was little chance that she would.) "Because he'll want me to sing in the choir while I'm here, and though I know I should, I honestly don't feel up to it." He touched his throat.

Daniel and Julien came in. André didn't get up, but his voice strode out like a body, a voice that was in fact larger, stronger, more forceful than André was physically—he was thin, and his long fingers were poised on their tips on the table top—and met Daniel and Julien just as they came through the door. They almost stepped back. They both went quickly towards the table and sat at the far end from André and watched him.

He asked them, "And *how* is the old parish grammar school? *How* is Mère St Épiphane?"

"Fine," Daniel said.

"She had such a sweet voice, such a fine sweet voice, such a fine sweet instrument, and she said to me, she said, 'Don't ever forget, no matter what or where you sing, you're singing for God, it's only singing for God that will make your singing beautiful.' I'd like to see her after all these years, and yet how could I tell her that I've given up singing—"

The mother had raised the pot of soup from the stove, and she held it in air. "You've given up singing?"

"My sinuses are too bad."

"There's nothing that can be done?"

"I've been to a doctor, the best nasal specialist in Florida, and he said he couldn't guarantee an operation would make me sing less nasally."

"And you no longer sing?"

He threw up his hands. "Oh, I sing. I've always sung and I'll always sing. But I've given up studying singing."

"What will you do?"

"I've switched to business administration."

"Business administration?"

"You know, work in business," he said, "like advertising, promotion, sales—"

"What made you switch to that?"

"I thought it was the most practical move to make."

"Get into business?"

He pinched the end of his nose and shook it as if to unblock it.

"Yes."

"And you're not disappointed?"

"About not being a singer?"

"I thought opera was your passion."

He said, "Well, Mama, I can't live on passion, can I?"

She poured out the soup into a bowl and brought the bowl to him. "I suppose not."

André bared his teeth by drawing his lips back and dipped his head as he spoke. She had seen this very expression of severity on Albert, and she was momentarily surprised to see it on André, as if Albert's skull appeared in André's face, but what she was seeing, she realized, was the skull of the family. It reassured her, but it also frightened her a little. "I'll tell you," he said, "I'm not about to sacrifice my life to any passion. Maybe I could go on, could get into opera, if I had the operation on my sinuses and continued to study voice. I'm already as good as the next person, I know that. But of course you've got to be better than the next person. You've got to be damn, really *damn*, really fantastically *damn* good. Even then, there's no way of being sure you'll make it. You could sacrifice half your life to making it, making it *big*, really *big*, really fantastically *big*, only to realize that for years you've been imagining yourself stage centre, singing 'Vesti la Giubba', while you're still in the chorus. But, you know, I realized this about myself: I'm not the kind of person who takes risks."

The mother thought, Albert, who was so strict, might have said that, said that he would never allow himself to take risks (he said that every time he got into his airplane he checked the controls twice over to be sure), but when André, who wasn't in any way strict, said it, she wondered if Albert didn't in fact take risks all the time. She didn't understand her sons. It seemed to her that André's very extravagance was a great risk, a risk, if of nothing more, of what people would think of him.

She said, "You wouldn't be taking a risk studying business administration?"

"Oh, it's much safer." André scooped up the soup with the soup spoon, raised it quickly to about the level of his chin, held it for a moment, seemed to shake it, then, with an elegant movement as of turning the spoon over in a complete loop without any soup spilling from it, brought it to his pursed lips. He exclaimed, "Mama, ça c'est la vrai bonne soupe."

She said, "I opened a can."

"You know just when it's hot, and not too hot."

But André, before finishing his soup, rose. "I left my bags in the back entry," he said, and went out for them, followed by Daniel and Julien, whose sudden offers to help were really their sudden interest in those bags. They dragged the heaviest, an old army duffle bag that had belonged to one of the older brothers, up the stairs into the kitchen. André came up behind carrying a large portfolio. The boys waited for him to open the big bag, but he pushed the half-finished bowl of soup aside to make room on the table and he placed the portfolio flat, untied it, and slowly opened it, removed a sheet of tissue paper, and, the tissue paper hanging like a veil held at its corners by the tips of his fingers, he stepped back, his head a little to the side, to examine what he had uncovered; it was a painting. He drew back more from it to examine it, but the mother and the boys stepped near and leaned over to look at it, and he said, "Paintings should be seen from a distance."

They stared at it from an oblique distance.

It was a painting done from one of a few photographs of Richard's children which the mother had sent to André in Florida. He had chosen a photograph of the only girl so far born into their family, Geneviève, Richard's second child, who was three. André pulled the photograph out of a pocket in the portfolio so it and the painting could be compared. It was of Geneviève, black and white, in a wide ruffled dress with a ribbon around her waist, patent leather pumps, a wide, startled-looking ribbon in her long banana-curled hair, a ball in her hand. Whoever had taken the photograph of her had been much taller than she, had photographed from above, so she, looking up into the camera, was curiously foreshortened against the flat plane of the ground, and appeared to be not a child but a stunted adult. The shadow of the cameraman, arms raised, was thrown at a diagonal before her. It was perhaps the confusion of perspectives which interested André in the photograph. Beside the photograph, enlarging it and vivifying it with colour, was the painting.

The mother said, "Well, you've got the eyes right, but the mouth goes up too much on one side, so she looks as if she's twitching."

"Do we have any old frames?" André asked.

The mother stepped away. "In the attic."

Julien, too, stepped away.

Daniel remained next to André. He looked at the painting as though it were on special exhibition. He had never seen an oil painting in its painted reality, but he thought he knew how to look at a painting. That it was a painting of a member of the family didn't matter; it didn't even matter, he thought, that she looked like a midget dressed up like a little girl. He looked for something else, which he was sure must be there. He must find it, he thought, to extract it, to show it to André, because the secret of the painting was not André's, though he had painted it, but Daniel's to extract, and the awareness of the secret made the painting his. He could, he thought, so easily have reached out and smeared the painting with his fingers.

André had tried to give Geneviève three dimensions, but Geneviève appeared very flat. Daniel studied the flatness of Geneviève. He strained his mind. He thought: two dimensions could not exist in reality, as the true, the secret, subject of the painting could not exist in reality. Daniel stared at the remarkable square. He might have asked his brother, "What does it mean?" because it *had* to mean something, and what it meant had to be abstract. Perhaps his brother wouldn't have understood the question, wouldn't have thought there was anything behind the picture of Geneviève to consider. And yet, for Daniel, everything was behind. The more he stared at the painting the more sure he was that he did know more about it than his brother. Daniel wished he had painted it. He wished he had been able to show it as his painting. André was exhibiting it in the full confidence that it was *damn* good—perhaps a really *damn* good, perhaps a really fantastically *damn* good—painting, and Daniel saw it as such, saw that, as painted by his brother, it was equal to the paintings of those greats whose works he had never seen (except for those reproduced in the art magazines André had subscribed to) but which stood, dimension beyond dimension beyond dimension, as if all the painting of the world were stacked up and seen all together, for all of art. He would, he felt, see more in, understand more, those works than the painters themselves, because they weren't aware that their works contained secrets. André said, "I got the eyes right, but the mouth goes up too much on one side, so she looks as if she's twitching." He picked the painting up carefully and said, "Let's go up into the attic to find a frame for it."

"You'll make a mess up there," the mother said.

"No, I promise."

"But you said you were very tired."

Daniel, who knew the attic well, pointed out to him a large box that contained frames. He chose a large plaster-moulded gilt frame. It had in it a brown photograph of a man with a high round collar and hair parted in the middle, whose shoulders and chest faded into a brown aura. André quickly removed the picture before testing the frame for size, and found his painting too big. He studied the painting and the frame, and said, "I'll have to crop the picture." He took the painting down to the kitchen, Daniel the empty frame.

The mother said, "Pépère was in that frame!"

André laughed. "He doesn't mind." He made measurements, cut his painting so Geneviève was no longer in the middle but down towards a corner, carefully placed it in the frame, tacked it in, held it up by the wire, and said, "Now, where shall we hang it?"

"Wherever you like," the mother said.

He hung it in the living room.

While André slept, she thought: she was never able to be simple enough when she spoke to Albert, and when she spoke to André she was never able to be extravagant enough. And yet, they were both her sons. She could not recall bringing them up differently, but they were different from one another. The difference, which she could not account for, left her thinking: how could her sons, so different from one another, feel that they belonged to the same house? They did. They all, she knew, got on together. She had made a law that they would, that they must; but it was they who made the law hold, and they who would have been shocked by any one of them not abiding by the law. She hadn't ever heard any of her mature sons say anything but praise about the others. She knew that as extravagant as André would be in his greeting of Albert (he'd shake both his hands simultaneously and repeat, until it was a little like an aria in an opera which consisted of but one phrase repeated over and over and over with variation, "It's great to see you, it's so great to see you, it's grand to see you") and as simple as Albert's would be (his arms being shaken up and down, he'd smile a little and say, "How's it going?") André would not think Albert cold, and Albert would not think André mannered. It was she, at times standing back from her sons, who, to herself, would say, Albert is so severe, or, André is so extreme, she seeing differences in them of which they themselves seemed unaware, much less critical. She thought again: but as different as they were, why did she at times feel close to one, at times close to the other, or uncertain with one, uncertain with another? Leaning out of a bedroom window, she was pinning laundry to a line and pulling the cord through the squeaking pulley so the sheets and pillowcases, shirts and underwear rose out over the back yard like sails being hauled up and, like sails, billowed out in the spring breeze—an unoriginal image, not the mother but Daniel, standing by the window and handing her the clothespins, imagined. She looked at Daniel for a moment as she took a clothespin from him, and saw him as someone about whom she knew nothing. She suddenly felt—she didn't know why—that she didn't want him to be there. She said, "Don't you want to go out with your brother Julien?"

"I don't mind staying here," he said.

"You go out. Go on."

He reluctantly put the pins on the window sill and turned away.

After supper, in the front room, André took his painting from the wall and propped it on the seat of a big armchair with doilies, so the public, his father, his brothers Albert and Edmond, could see it in the light of a floor lamp. The mother and the boys stood back.

André said, "Well, I'd like to know what you all think about it."

The mother suddenly giggled, but disguised her giggle by clearing her throat. The father said, his face stark, "That's a beautiful picture, that's a very beautiful picture, tsi gars." Daniel and his mother glanced at one another, and she giggled again, and tried to transform the giggle into a little cough. Daniel bit his lips.

The mother might have thought that André was like her, but perhaps André, who laughed a lot, who was never dark, who was always elaborately active, shared not her humour but the seriousness of the father.

André said to his father, "You're a great guy, Dad."

Edmond said, "Hey, an artist in the family, isn't that something—"

The mother said, "Well, artists don't make any money, and you've always got to pay your bills—"

Albert, whose chin was drawn in, said nothing, but later he said to André, "Look, I hope you've always known that if you're in need of financial help, you can always come to me. How are you making out?"

"I'll be working in the Adirondacks this summer to make enough for next year."

"You wouldn't prefer to take the summer off, and just paint?"

André's voice was very low. "Al, I appreciate your generosity. You know, I've never felt that in helping Philip through M.I.T. you were wasting your money. He's a great, he's a really great, he's a fantastically great brother. And I never felt, I swear, that because he was helped, help was owed to me. And I'll tell you why I never felt it, and why, too, I can't accept your generosity—because I can't accept, because I never have, because, you see, like Mama, I must know that I'm independent."

That the mother was independent surprised Albert.

"I've got to know that what I've done I've done myself, whatever it is. I want to do a lot. I want to do so much. But I want to do it on my own."

"All right," Albert said.

The mother alone with André, after everyone else had gone to bed, drawing him into a small dim circle of confidentiality in the way she might have said, "I'm pregnant again," said, "Your father's buying a house in the country," and he asked, "Why didn't he mention it?" She didn't know what to answer. "Is it a secret?" he asked. "No, no," she said. "He probably forgot." "Forgot?" She was holding him by the arm; she let go. He said, "Well, it'll be a good investment." "Yes," she said. He reached out and held her arms.

The next morning, André telephoned old friends from the opera group he'd belonged to when he lived in Providence. From the way he talked with them—for long voluble periods, even though most of them were at work in jobs that had nothing to do with singing—he might have made the trip back to be near them rather than his family; he and they belonged, Daniel knew, to a world as closed to Daniel and as rich as the locked blue case in which André kept the powder, grease paint, eye shadow, eyebrow pencils he used to make himself up for performances in the chorus. Daniel heard his next older brother, separated from him by seven years, say to someone, "I can't talk about it now."

André said to his mother, "I'm going out tonight."

"I thought you would," she said.

"I've got to go to a costume party." It was as though he said, "It's essential that I go to this political meeting."

He went out in the family car, came back with a large square box, a large flat box, bags. Daniel followed him into the room André shared with his older brothers. André put the packages in the bottom of the closet and closed the closet door. The bedroom was warm, and on the pale flowered wallpaper across from the window was an oblong of light. Daniel watched André open his drawer in the bureau, watched him take out his make-up kit, watched him find a little key among many keys on a chain and open the box, which had a mirror on the inside of the lid that reflected light on the ceiling; when André looked into the mirror, the light was reflected on his face.

He asked Daniel, "Do you want me to make you up?"

Daniel sat motionless on a chair, his eyes closed, his head pushed back. André was smearing his cheeks, his forehead, his chin and neck with grease paint, and Daniel tried to keep his head stock still under his brother's jabbing fingers. Whatever André did, no matter how extravagant, he did with professionalism; that made the extravagance a practicality. Daniel knew that André was practising on him. He winced when he felt the eye pencil dig into the corner of an eye, and André said, "You'll have to be still if you want me to do a good job." Daniel couldn't keep his eyes shut tight because André wouldn't have been able to outline the lids; he saw light flashes, and once opened his eyes to see André standing back, his pencil raised in one hand, his head tilted to one side, studying him. He watched André open a little round metal box, rub the tip of a finger into blue paste, and watched the blue-tipped finger advance towards his right eye. He watched him open another little round metal box, and this time rub the tip of another finger into red paste, which went to his lips. Daniel knew that when he looked at himself in the mirror he wouldn't recognize himself; when he rose from the chair and went out into the kitchen, not only would no one know him, he would know no one, and nothing anyone thought about him, as nothing he'd thought about himself, would be right. André, with a large brownish puff, powdered Daniel's face, stood back, studied him, pencilled more about his eyes. He put the cap on the pencil and said, "There," and Daniel moved to get up. André said, "Where're you going?" Daniel said, "I thought you were finished. I was going to look in the mirror." "You don't want to do that," André said. "Why?" Daniel asked. His lips and eyes were gummy with make-up. "Because you shouldn't, that's why," André said. "Oh," Daniel said. He remained seated, his body slack, and watched André open a large jar of white cold cream; he spread a gob over Daniel's face and wiped the streaked make-up off with tissues.

André, in the late afternoon, closed himself in his room to prepare for the party. From time to time, he dashed from the bedroom into the bathroom, wearing a bathrobe wide open at the neck, and his face each time was different: white with small red lips, yellow brown with the corners of his eyes extending sharply to his temples, pale yellow with large blue circles around his eyes. He once appeared wearing a bulbous black wig stuck with dagger-like pins with jewelled heads, and he had drawn wisps of hair down the sides of his cheeks. Daniel sat in the kitchen where he could see him whenever he came out. André could do what Daniel couldn't, because getting dressed up was a part of André's profession. Why, with no excuse to make it practical, did Daniel went to get dressed up too? He had no reason to except for a soft deep desire to appear in strange clothes that had nothing to do with their lives. The father sat in his rocking chair and read his evening papers, and Albert, on a chair near, was simply looking at his father. The mother was in the pantry. André suddenly appeared from the bedroom as Madama Butterfly. Edmond and Julien came in from the living room to see.

The father said, his eyes wide, "You've really done a job!"

Albert said, getting up, "Can I give you a few pointers?"

"Sure."

"A Japanese woman in a kimono walks in a special way—" Albert stood beside André. "She walks in a pigeon-toed way, like this." Albert stuck his behind out a little and took a few short steps.

Daniel stood by his mother at the pantry door, and both stared.

When André went out, got into the car and drove off, she said, "But what if he's stopped by the police?"

VI

AT THE MASSACHUSETTS border: Daniel, who sat next to his mother in the back seat of the car, thought I've been outside the parish, outside the city limits of Providence, and now I'm outside Rhode Island.

André sat next to Edmond in the front seat and talked about his friends in Miami, a Jewish family especially, to whom he said he had become a kind of adopted son. They treated him like a son, he said, by making sure he ate enough (they invited him often to supper, always to Sunday dinner) and had enough money (they paid him for little jobs, like cutting the lawn or trimming shrubbery) and by letting him use their pool whenever he wanted and by going to all the opera performances he took part in. It was they who got him a job in a resort lodge in the Adirondack mountains for the summer, and they who had advised him, for his own good, to take up business administration. The mother, who appeared not to be listening as she continued to stare out the window, said, "We're not good parents, are we?"

André turned quickly to her.

"We've never done for you, or for any of our sons, really, what that Jewish family did for you."

André stared at her, surprised.

"We've never been to one performance where you've sung, haven't encouraged you in your singing, we don't send you money, we didn't even have a special meal to celebrate your coming home. You have to find all that outside the family, and I don't blame you."

André said, his face still open with surprise, "But you've given me everything I want."

"What have we given you?"

André turned away, looked out the windshield.

"I'm glad you feel so close to those people," the mother said, "feel like a son to them. They'll be a better family to you than we've been. You, and all your brothers, have to make families for yourselves outside our family, because we've hardly got a family, because what do we do for our sons? It's as though we don't care."

"Oh, I know you care, " André said.

"We don't show it though, do we?"

André said nothing.

Edmond said, "Well, I know my old Army buddy Bobby's mother and father are waiting for me in Kentucky, and once I get down there I'll be, I know I will, a second son to them. Bobby even wrote me that, he wrote me in his letter, 'Mom and Dad ask how you are, Mom says you better get used to rattlesnake meat, because that's all we eat down here, ha! ha!' I wrote back, I wrote back to him in my letter, 'You tell Mom and Dad their second son is waiting for a big meal of rattlesnake meat, ha! ha!' I wrote it just like that."

Daniel, who had been looking out of the window and only half listening, said, "Ma."

The mother said to André, "And what do we have?"

Daniel said, "Ma, Momma."

She continued to speak to André. "You couldn't live at home. There's nothing for you. I know that. We don't read, or go to museums, or listen to music. But there are people outside who do, and of course now you—no, you always did —have more in common with them. You know, I wonder why it is that all my sons, almost all, always had more in common with outside people than the inside family, even when they didn't know anyone outside."

Again, Daniel said, "Momma."

André said, looking at the hood of the car in the bright sunlight, "But—"

She said, "Only one thing—no matter whose son you are, you must be a good son, and I mean that."

Daniel said again, "Momma", and this time touched her knee.

The car was passing a long low even hill, and on the top of the hill were four large oak trees; the green-grey hill and the dark trees seemed to turn as the car passed and the sun flashed through the branches.

"What?" the mother said.

Daniel was pointing. "See the pretty scenery."

Immediately, André, in a lilting high voice, repeated, "Oh, see the pretty scenery!"

Daniel's inside body drew away from contact with his outside body.

André repeated, laughing, "Oh, oh, see the pretty scenery."

They were now passing another low hill half bulldozed into deep ruts, and the roots of trees stuck out of the ruts, and huge ragged slabs of glacial rock were raised above the bare earth. The mother too laughed.

In the outskirts of Boston, Edmond took a wrong turn. He stopped by an old man standing on a corner and asked for directions to Commonwealth Avenue. To everyone in the car, all listening carefully, the man was a foreigner who, speaking the street names of Boston, was speaking a foreign language, whose knowledge of the layout of the foreign city was the knowledge of a foreign culture. The man's voice was as thin, as fine as he was. He said, "I daren't tell you to turn left, as you'll come straightaway into a one-way street," and that "daren't" and that "straightaway" Daniel heard himself say, repeating the man's words to himself. Edmond turned left. André said, "But he told us not to turn left." "I know, I know," Edmond said, "but I think I know my way now." The next person he stopped to ask, a short fat unshaven man, said, "Well, you got to turn right round right away." Edmond asked, "Turn right round right away?" Edmond turned right.

They came across Commonwealth Avenue by chance. André spotted the long blue sign nailed high among the wires on an electricity pole. They were looking for 128, but the house numbers were in the thousands, the houses huge, clapboard, with big porches with fancy cut-out railings, turrets, high pointed gabled roofs, and they all seemed to be sagging; the hedges before them shook with the traffic.

Once into the traffic, the yellow Massachusetts number plates (those of Rhode Island were black and white) flicked past like cards dealt out in a very fast game of poker, and Edmond, not used to the game, couldn't get his hand in order; he remained stopped when he should have started, started when he should have remained stopped. A strip separated one lane from the other, and the traffic flashed by in the opposite direction, in the other lane, and on the strip between the two, clanking down tracks, appeared a bright orange trolley going in their direction. It rattled past them, and Daniel looked at the people in it. The pack of cars, in which the orange trolley was a kind of enormous, very wild joker, which at crossings held up traffic in any way it wanted, got thicker and thicker. Heat waves quivered off the hoods and roofs. Daniel sat close to his half-open window. Another trolley passed, and this one, its back appearing suddenly to tip up, slid down into a subway, and Daniel rose from his seat to see where it had gone. They passed a big intersection, and the houses were brick, rows of brick town houses on either side of the avenue, with large windows, stone stairways, iron fences, and rising above the houses from both the sidewalks and the strip down the centre of the avenue, which now had no tracks and was green, were the delicate green branches of tall elms.

Many of the windows of the houses were wide open. People were sitting on the sills of some, or leaning out, talking to people on the sidewalk below. There were groups of young people sitting on the stone stairs, some with pillows, and people were lounging on the benches or lying on the grass of the mall. Daniel, sweating in his suit and tie in a car from Rhode Island, stared out on a race he'd never seen before.

His eyes slightly unfocused, he saw, standing together on a stoop, before a wide-open door, five or six college students, some young men, some young women, wearing shorts or torn-off trousers, T-shirts or sweatshirts with the sleeves pushed up above the elbows, and all turned towards a a centre, and all leaning a little towards the centre. That centre was a round soft sensitive secret in the air equidistant from them all, visible to them, invisible to Daniel, but he could imagine it glowing, the light from it illuminating their incredible bodies. He thought, in the car, that it would be impossible for him to be among them, and when Edmond said, "There's a space, we'll park there," he didn't believe that when he got out of the car he'd be among them.

André rang the bell of Philip's fraternity house, where the father and Albert and Julien, who had driven up separately in the old Dodge, and Richard, who was to come in his own car from western Massachusetts, and those in Edmond's coupé were all to meet. André's mother and brothers held back, and when the door was opened by a woman in a black dress, they stepped back as André stepped forward. They followed André into the large greyish-white panelled hall, and into a sitting room, brownish white, also panelled, the high ceiling edged with moulding and in the centre of the ceiling a large oval medallion from which a chandelier hung, its prisms amber from cigarette smoke. The father, Albert, Julien were sitting in big leather armchairs. They were waiting for Philip to get dressed. The father was sitting far back in his chair, his legs crossed, as if he owned the house. The mother sat on the edge of another chair, a visitor who would quickly rise the moment the owner of the house came in. Daniel went to the broad bay windows, from which narrow wooden inside shutters were folded back, and through the dirty windows he saw a large magnolia tree with two white blossoms, each blossom of only three petals. He stood still for a moment, and a feeling came over him in his stillness that he, in this house, looking out of the window, was someone else, that he had in an instant become someone who lived in this house, who had lived in it, perhaps, when it had been a private house, a hundred years before. He might have been someone his own age who had been born in the house, upstairs in a large bedroom, who had like Daniel stood in this very bay, the sunlight not penetrating the glass but simply illuminating it so, though the glass was bright, the bay was dim. Like that someone else, he stepped closer to the window to look beyond the magnolia, to see any people passing, and the parquet squeaked as it would have squeaked for that someone else. His mother called him and he turned round. He saw Richard coming into the room, and Richard with a quiet formality leaned and kissed his mother on the cheek, shook his father's hand. The brothers stood on an oriental carpet by the large white marble fireplace with a great mirror above the mantel. Then Philip came in, in a dark brown suit, and the father stood. Philip leaned to kiss his mother, shook hands with his father, with Richard, with Albert, who put his hand on Philip's shoulder while Philip held his hand, smiling widely, for a long time, with Edmond, with André, with Daniel and Julien. Philip said, "I've ordered coffee for us," and the woman in the black dress came in with a tray on which were cups and saucers, spoons, silver sugar bowl and cream pitcher and coffee pot. She put the tray down on a low table before the mother, who began to pour, and the woman left. The stillness Daniel had felt before he now felt come over them all, and he imagined their stillness was the stillness of a photograph they were themselves, maybe years later, in another place, studying. Another group came into the room —a fraternity brother and his parents—and the stillness of the family was broken. Julien spilled his coffee.

Philip, who had, like an engineer, planned the day, asked them if they wanted to see his room. He'd first have to go upstairs to ask if it was all right if his mother came too, as women weren't allowed above the ground floor, and, he said, "the guys may be wandering around up there without so much as a pocket to put a handkerchief in," which, Daniel quickly took in, must have been a common saying in the fraternity house. While he was out of the room, the family moved about a little uneasily. Philip came down to say it was all right, the guys would keep to their rooms if they weren't decent.

The mother said, "I'm not allowed into the upstairs of a house full of boys—it seems strange."

They climbed the wide staircase with a curving banister. Daniel heard doors slam, but there were a couple of fraternity brothers, in khaki trousers and T-shirts, standing at the top of the stairs and talking to one another. Philip raised his hand at them as he passed, followed by the long line of his family, but he didn't introduce them. The mother hurried past them. The family followed Philip up a second flight to his room. They were all just able to get into the room, and Philip, who sensed that his parents, if not his brothers, wanted to be cut off from the fraternity as much as the fraternity would want to be cut off from the family, closed the door. The room had a desk and a narrow bed and a window that looked out over a narrow overgrown garden. Above the desk he had hung the paddle he'd made at his father's workbench for his initiation into the fraternity, an initiation he had had to keep a secret. Above the door, because this was a Catholic fraternity, there was a crucifix. That crucifix was the only totem in the house which the family, from the parents' point of view, could refer to itself; the mother stared at it for a moment as to focus on something familiar in this strange house. It was not a house for parents, and the mother was more sensitive to this than the father; it was not a house for parents, and neither was it a house for blood brothers, as she felt that none of the young men she'd seen in it, who lived in it, had parents, had brothers. The mother, who sat on the edge of the bed, looked up at Philip, who, tall, lean, a broken nose from playing football the only irregularity in his clear even face, leaned against the desk, piles of books behind him, and she thought: There's more that's similar between Philip and his fraternity brothers now than between Philip and us.

She said, "I didn't write to thank you for the flowers."

"What flowers?" he asked.

"The little bunch of dried flowers you sent me."

He might have realized, more than she, why she had brought up the flowers now, and he said, folding his arms and smiling a little, "Ah, les fleurs sèches—"

They all continued to speak in the language of the family.

Daniel didn't want to hear it, much less speak in it. He tried to listen to the sounds of the house; doors opening and closing, thudding footsteps, toilets flushed, showers running, towels being slapped, music, voices raised to be heard from one room to another. Women were not allowed where he, Daniel, was. And yet even though he had a right to be there, because he was male, when it came to him that he had to pee, he couldn't bring himself to ask Philip where the toilet was, frightened he might encounter fraternity members in the bathroom, shaving, showering. And if he got lost in the house and couldn't find the toilet he wouldn't have been able to make himself ask a fraternity member where it was. And when Philip said, "Well, we can go. I'll show you a little bit of the Public Garden and the Common," Daniel, used now to being in the room with the crucifix, was frightened to open the door, was frightened that, walking along the corridor, a fraternity brother who hadn't been aware that Philip had a room filled with visitors, and above all that one of them was a woman, might step out of the room naked. And when he was walking with Julien behind the others as they filed down the corridor, he saw a door at the other end open, and there was a young man, a towel wrapped about his waist and held by one hand, his face, neck, broad chest boiled red; he motioned to Philip, and Philip left his family to go to speak with him. Daniel felt a slight sweat break out on his palms. He watched Philip and his fraternity brother talk, leaning towards one another, the fraternity brother making small gestures with his free hand. Daniel thought: Philip is more a brother to that unknown college student than he is a brother to me, as they had perhaps been initiated together and shared that secret.

They stopped, just inside the gates of the Public Garden, to look up at the green equestrian statue of George Washington, and then went round the twisted paths where they stopped to look at the beds of flowers. Daniel looked beyond the flowers at people sitting and lying on the deep green grass under the high trees. He felt as light as if he were in sun-filled water, and the sounds, the low voices, unaccountable clicks and thuds, were amplified but distorted as under water. He was also as disoriented as he would be under shoreless water.

The mother and father, arm in arm, walked surrounded by sons. Richard, the eldest, walked beside his parents, and his pace it seemed was slower than theirs to slow them down, to make them as he might have said, "go easy", as he had to tell himself often to slow down, to go easy. He scratched the eczema on the backs of his hands and looked at his watch to make sure there was enough time so they could go easy, and the slight anxiety that there might not be, that they would have to rush, made him slow his pace down more, as though he could, by slowing himself and them down, slow down time, and all the while, in a low, soft voice, he kept telling his parents they should enjoy themselves now, should just relax and take everything in; whenever Philip stopped to point out something Richard stopped longest and breathed in as to breathe clouds, trees, the whole garden in.

As they were leaving the garden, Daniel shaded his eyes and looked up at the statue of George Washington again, and, the sun flaring all round the horse's raised hoof, he suddenly thought: there is a secret in this city, there is a secret, and it is that, it is the discovery of that, which will make happen what I want to happen. I know it, I know it. He was excited, he was excited and frightened by his excitement; he didn't know what it was. He thought: he would live in this foreign city.

At the fraternity house Philip collected his cap and gown in a large flat box. Daniel used the toilet after his brothers set a precedent. They walked slowly over a long bridge across the Charles River, the wide blue-brown water widening out to their right into a great basin on which listing sailboats were tacking, and beyond was the brick city of Boston rising to the blazing gold dome of the State House. Daniel stopped to look, then ran to catch up with the others.

He thought as they walked: they *were* in another country, and he and his family, because they were foreign, could be taken, not for a family from a small grey parish in Providence, but a family from anywhere. He felt as he did, he knew, because he was a foreigner, because his well-dressed family were all foreigners. He thought, his mind constantly pulsing with ideas he half understood: it's only for the foreigners that everything is possible, that everything is promised, it is only the foreigners who can have everything. He wanted more than ever to be foreign, wanted his family to be foreign, foreign to la paroisse de Notre Dame de Lourdes à Providence, Rhode Island. It was not that he wanted to have been from Boston; he wanted to have been from nowhere. Edmond ran ahead with his camera to photograph them walking towards him. Daniel felt somehow near to the secret, near enough to sense that the secret itself was unplaceable, was, like some hubless hub, wherever anyone designated it to be; here, now, he thought, centred on the round lens of Edmond's camera, was the hub of the universe.

They followed Philip across a field, patched with grass and bare earth, to a huge tent. Through an open flap in the tent people were filing in. The air inside the tent was hot, yellow, the patches of grass grey, the patches of earth kicked up into dust. The tent was crowded; many seats were reserved. Philip found them a row of seats towards the back, then left them. Daniel looked up into the steep sagging tent, held up by giant poles, and he felt both inside something and outside. After a long while, someone began to speak, but the family couldn't see him.

Daniel felt his body sweating beneath his suit. The heat made him feel sleepy, and his sight, as his hearing, seemed to go in and out, now seeing, now hearing, then seeing, hearing nothing. He half closed his eyes. His mind, too, went in and out, and in his mind he saw, he heard, for sudden moments, the magnolia tree outside the fraternity bay window, the silver coffee pot, the dirty chandelier, the staircase with the curved banister, the two fraternity brothers talking on the landing, the fraternity brother who wore a towel appearing at the end of a corridor. His mind kept expanding what he had seen and heard in the fraternity as if to expose something he knew was there, but which, the moment it was expanded enough for him really to see it, hear it, contracted.

He looked at the people around him, sitting stiffly on the small wooden folding chairs while a voice droned on over the heads, amplified by loudspeakers attached to the posts that held up the tent; their faces, like the voice, went in and out. He noticed a man and woman sitting three rows before him; she didn't have a hat on, her short hair was iron grey, the planes of her face were sharp and clear, he wore a light blue suit with a white shirt, his hair grey, his face, too, sharp and clear, as though some sharpness and clarity of their minds had sharpened and clarified their faces, and they were leaning forward, listening attentively. Daniel knew that no one in his family was listening. That man and woman were listening with the attention of people who knew that what they heard was important. Daniel knew only that a government man from Washington, who had been given an honorary degree, was speaking, and all he could see of him was a large black honorary hat, while his thin-edged voice rose and fell. Daniel tried to listen, but he couldn't understand. The man was speaking a language he hardly understood, from which he could grasp articles and conjunctions and pronouns and all the individual verbs and nouns, but he didn't understand it all together. If he understood anything, it was set phrases, "which is not to say that" or "neither, of course, should we consider that the direct opposite", but the phrases were disconnected. That couple did understand; they more than understood, they were, in their sharp, clear minds, considering what they heard. He wondered where they came from. He thought, by their physical sharpness and clarity, that they must have lived near the ocean, but that was all he could imagine. He wondered what kind of house they lived in, what rooms, what furniture. He couldn't imagine. Would they, if they turned round, be able on sight to tell what kind of house Daniel and his family lived in? They would probably be able to place Daniel and his family in all their particulars, while Daniel could see them only against a background as general as the ocean. He looked at other people; he could not place any of them either, could not see them in rooms, in the midst of furniture. They went out of focus, into a long oblong blur, and he held them in that blur. He thought: he knew too much about his family, knew so much; he knew as much, perhaps, as there was to know; their lives were lives of small daily particulars, and they never went beyond the particulars. Foreigners, he thought, live in worlds that don't have particulars, live in vast, sharp, clear, general worlds. If he thought of the fraternity house, if he thought of the bodies of those college students living on Commonwealth Avenue, he thought not of particulars but of something that wouldn't allow itself to be thought of as a particular: some sense, some sense as positive but as elusive as the sense he had of his own body, some sense the very idea of the initiation evoked in him, that the unfocused idea of the bodies of the college students evoked in him. That sense was the secret he felt, and had felt since he arrived in this foreign city. It was a large globe in his chest. The secret was in the abstract, not in particulars. His mind again expanded about the couple listening to the address. They had both raised their long hands to their chins. Daniel too raised his hand to his chin. He must, he thought, pay attention. What was being said was important. He must understand. But he could pay attention only through the couple, between whom he tried to imagine himself sitting, a sudden son, listening, understanding. He heard the speaker say, "until such day as pingpong balls are thought of as weapons", and he saw the couple lower their hands and laugh, and he too laughed, and the moment he did he turned and looked, as if he had been expecting it, right into the eyes of André staring hard at him. He had laughed, he knew, out of shame and pretension. He was a fool.

Names were being called out. He heard, "Philip Francoeur." He saw his mother reach out to grasp her husband's hands and laugh, and he too laughed, and the moment he and he, his head raised as though he could see his son over the thousands of heads before him, smiled.

Daniel thought: Philip has graduated into the general world.

Philip found them later, outside the tent, in the milling crowd. He was wearing his gown, carrying his tasselled mortarboard. Edmond made him stand back and put his cap on to take a picture of him. He took many pictures.

The seven sons lined up, by age, for a picture. The mother took it. It was a picture that would be reproduced and given to all aunts and uncles, married cousins, neighbours: Richard, a cigarette in his hand, turned a little to the side, his hair thin, his eyes half closed against the glare, then Albert, his suit perfectly tailored and pressed, bunched up because of his hands in his pockets, stepping, one foot before the other, as if away, frowning, then Edmond, his hands too in his pockets, his warm, almost sad smile concentrated outwards with his smile, then in the middle Philip, the tallest, in his gown, carrying his cap, his jaw set, staring with a fixed severity, then André stepping, it appeared, forward, the waves of his hair broken, his mouth a little open, then Daniel, his eyes shut, standing with his arms hanging on either side of him, his light suit wrinkled, his tie knotted with what he had thought a fashionably big knot, then Julien, shorter, his suit wrinkled too, his hair parted crookedly, he too with his eyes closed, smiling, no one could have said at what.

One of them might have thought: what did they think of one another? They didn't really think about one another. If they did they thought indirectly, in terms of something outside them, of an idea, which was not an idea that originated in them, an idea as round as the lens of the camera the mother held to snap their picture: that they should love one another. The father stood by her side, looking away; he glanced quickly from time to time at the line-up of his sons.

VII

ALBERT WAS LEANING against the wall, under the kitchen
clock, Philip was eating at the table, his back to Albert,
André was sitting across the table from Philip, his chair
turned away from the table, Daniel rocked lightly in the
rocking chair, Julien was on the kitchen stool, the mother,
with two wrapped loaves held against her waist, stood by
the open kitchen door, and in the doorway was the parish
baker.

The baker said, "C'n'est pas vrai, plus ça change— Moi
j'ai vu des changements dans la paroisse, et c'n'est plus
pareil, c'est différent, et ça sera encore plus différent—"

The outside door opened. The mother and sons leaned to
see beyond the baker, who turned around to look also. The
mother glanced at the clock to see if the baker had been
there for so many hours it was time for her husband to come
home, and even when she saw it was still before noon, her
sense of time, regulated after thirty years by her husband's
leaving for and coming back from work, tried of itself to
rearrange the time to make her suddenly see the baker as
out of time and not her husband, who was coming up the
entry stairs; and yet another part of her, her sense, perhaps,
of place, of the kitchen in the morning with green cool light
when it was entirely her kitchen, when the table, the chairs
had a special morning stillness that her sons, sitting, standing
quietly, hadn't disturbed, knew that the presence of her
husband in this place was wrong. She exclaimed, "Jim!"
The baker didn't move out of the way, but stood facing the

father; he might have taken over the house and was not going to let him pass until he explained to him why he had come home when he should be at work. But the father simply looked at him, and the baker stepped to one side. The father stepped into the kitchen, not sure, it seemed, how to walk or where he should go; he raised his feet high when he stepped, as if he were walking in water.

He said in English, "I've been fired."

No one spoke or moved.

He said, "They fired me."

The baker frowned and asked, "Quoi?"

The father said, again in English, "I've been laid off."

None of his family spoke or moved. The baker asked, "Who fired you?"

After a long moment the father touched his head and said, "The old man did."

The baker narrowed his eyes, "Why?"

The father opened and closed his mouth a number of times and made a face, as he often did, as of having tasted vomit; he looked at the baker. Albert stood away from the wall, about to say, "Dad, come into the other room," where the baker wouldn't go with them, but the father, though he stared at the baker with an expression of bitterness, answered him. "They're cutting back."

The baker didn't understand. He put his weight on one leg, thrust the other leg towards the father. The father turned away.

"Jim!" his wife said.

He said to her, "It's finished." He walked past his sons and went out of the kitchen to his bedroom.

The baker said, "Well, that's what happens, there, if you don't just keep quiet, there."

The mother and sons stared at him, and the baker left.

The mother looked from her sons to the doorway through which her husband had passed to go to their bedroom, then to her sons again, not sure, it seemed, if she should stay with them or go to her husband. Her face set hard and she left them, went through the doorway, and they heard her call, "Jim." There was no answer. She called again, "Jim." If he answered, they didn't hear him. They heard her open the bedroom door and close it behind her.

André asked, "Is there anything we can do?"

After a while, Julien went into the living room to sit near the father and mother's door.

André rose and went to the room he shared with his older brothers. From the bureau top he picked up the opera score to study it as he had that morning. He looked at the grey cover: a design of fluted columns on either side, a sagging drape tied to and hanging with deep folds between the columns, and the title in large letters below. He flipped through the yellowish pages. He put the score down on a chair and looked out of the window.

His brother Philip came in. André turned to him. Philip came to the window, stood by André, looked out at the small bare yard with weeds growing along the fence.

He said, "I can't do anything."

"No," André said, "I guess not."

Albert said from the doorway, "He has to work it out for himself."

The two younger brothers looked round to him, and André saw, past him, the mother, followed by Julien and Daniel. They all came into the room. The mother closed the door, then she sat on the bed.

Philip asked, "How is he?"

"He won't speak," she said.

"You couldn't get him to talk?"

"No." She looked up at Philip.

"He said nothing at all?" André asked.

"He said he was grateful he hadn't signed a mortgage on this house. We've still got a house to live in."

"I never understood why he wanted the house in the country," Albert said.

"No." She waited for a moment. She suddenly asked, "What will happen now that he doesn't have his work? He's never not worked. Will he lie there, day after day, and do nothing? Even during the Depression, when there was only two days a week at the file shop, he went out to look every day for more work. He did house repairs, painting, reshingling. Now—" Her eyes widened.

André put his hands on her shoulders. "Don't be frightened." They heard a knock on the closed bedroom door. They remained still. Albert opened the door. The father looked in. He said, "I'll be all right."

They sat round the kitchen table to eat bowls of soup. His wife and sons watched him, but no one spoke to him. He ate silently, and when he finished he said, "He told me, the old man, that it couldn't be helped. The shop is losing money. They have to cut back."

"And they can't fire anyone in the union," the mother said.

The father didn't take her up. "They had to let me go," he said.

Again, the sons said nothing, but stared at their father. It was as if, though they knew he had never drunk a glass of beer in his life, he were drunk, and they were not sure what he would do in his drunkenness. He appeared to be trying to sustain an immense sobriety.

Albert thought: their father was, and always had been, above consolation; nothing had ever happened to him that they knew of which made him go to them for their support, for their understanding, and they on their own didn't know how to give him their support or understanding. The father wasn't now talking to his wife any more than he was talking to his sons; and he wasn't talking about himself, he was talking, with a strained but vast impersonality, about someone else, at a great distance.

The mother watched her sons follow their father with their eyes as he walked about the kitchen, worried, it seemed, that he would all at once fall over. She got up and approached him. He stopped, he said, "I think I'll go down to the cellar."

Daniel and Julien, at a sign from the mother behind his back that they should go down with him, stared at him while, at his bench, he opened drawer after drawer and took out the files, from the fine files to the large coarse files, and piled them on the top of the bench. His elbows went in and out, and his shoulders, the back of his head, his back were, it appeared, concentrated on his work, a job he had been asked to do which was urgent but which he, in his slow, intentional way, was doing as he knew it should be done. The files were sorted out, examined, laid side by side. He took them in batches to the barrels of cinders and ashes from the furnace, and thrust them in, not looking twice, and went back to his bench for more. He threw out all his files, then shut the drawers and turned and leaned against the bench for a moment.

He very slowly climbed the stairs to the kitchen. As soon as he opened the kitchen door, Albert, who had been sitting in the rocking chair, got up to give him the chair. The father lowered himself into the chair with the same muscle tensions it would have required to get up from the rocker. Albert left the kitchen. André and Philip, who had been talking to the mother in the pantry, went silent.

Through the window, the father saw Georgie Girard walk past the house on his way home from work.

Julien stood by the rocker and asked, "What will you do?"

"I've got to find a job, tsi gars."

No one slept that night.

Albert, in the very early morning, heard his father cough in the kitchen. He got out of bed, put on a robe, and went out. He saw his father, dressed in his suit, sitting in his rocking chair.

He asked, from across the kitchen, "Where're you going?"

"I'm waiting till there's a little more light out, then I'll go out."

"Where's Mom?"

"She finally fell asleep. I didn't wake her."

"Where will you go?"

"I wrote down a few textile mills that want men."

"Do you want me to drive you?"

"No."

Only half the father's face was visible, the half towards the window, through which there came a pale grey glow. Albert approached his father to sit on the chair across from him; close to, he saw on the grey side of the father's face terror as set as stone, and Albert didn't sit, he stood above him.

"I came out to use the bathroom," he said.

Jim Francoeur didn't take a bus, he walked into the city of Providence. As he walked under a subway bridge a lighted train passed overhead. The city was deserted in the grey morning light. He saw a bus, still lit up inside, pass him with a number of passengers, then a truck at a corner from which two men were throwing down bundles of newspapers, then a man with a briefcase got out of a parked car. The office buildings were brightening with rising sunlight. He walked through the city and along the cobbled edge of the Providence River. His mind wandered, and he sometimes wondered what he was doing walking by a rusted corrugated-iron fence or a derelict wharf. The river became a narrow, cobble-lined canal, and bottles and broken crates floated in the scum. He found the textile mill. Three men were before him.

He sat, trembling a little as with cold, in a small room, chairs pushed around thin, tongue-and-groove board partitions with a high narrow window at the top of one wall, giving not on to the outside but into the shop. The three men were on one side of the room, talking to one another. He sat on the other side, leaning over, his elbows on his knees, his hands tightly clasped together. A man came to the door and called out the first man to have arrived. The others stopped talking. Jim Francoeur looked away. After a while, the man came to call the second. Jim Francoeur glanced at the remaining man across the small space, then looked at the floor. The other man was called out. Jim Francoeur rose slowly and walked to the middle of the room. He felt his body shaking, he heard, from the other side of the partition, machines clacking, voices. He thought he heard a voice approaching. He hurried so he wouldn't encounter the man who'd called the others for interviews, and left the room and the mill. He walked fast over the cobbles.

He walked back into Providence. He had the small advertisements for jobs in other mills in his pocket. He walked slowly in the heat. He walked up the steep hill to the State House, its great white dome floating in the wavering heat that rose from the green lawn. He stopped at Smith Street. Traffic raced past him. He thought, Where will I go?

His sister Oenone opened the door to his mother's when he knocked. Oenone asked, shading her eyes as against blazing light, "What is it?" "I want to see my mother," he said in French. "She's in bed," Oenone said, "like always." He went into her bedroom.

She was propped up on pillows. Her cheekbones stood out sharp. Her closed eyes were black pits. Her hair was drawn back in a thick braid, but the braid was loose, and hair was wild about her face. He knew she was not sleeping. Her features were tense with the fixed concentration of her pain, a concentration meant to keep the pain in one place. Her son sat on a chair by the bed and she opened her eyes and without turning her head looked at him. She immediately said, in French, "But it's a weekday today, isn't it?"

"Yes."

"Why aren't you at work?"

"They showed me the door," he said.

Oenone, who had been standing at the door, came into the room. "It's what I told you, didn't I? Didn't I tell you the end would be like this?"

"What happened?" his mother said. She didn't move her head or eyes while she listened. "And where will you find another job?" she asked.

"I don't know."

She said, "Oenone, take some paper and a pencil."

Oenone opened a drawer in a bureau and drew out a

small pad, a pencil stub, and a spool of thread. The mother said to her son, "I can't go to church any more, so I can't offer Masses, and I can't pray very well." She said to Oenone, "Write this for me: 'I offer up everything for Arsace to find work.'" "No, no," he said, and got up from the chair to go out of the room. "Yes," she said. He stood by the door as Oenone wrote at the very edge of the paper, folded the edge back, tore it off, and rolled the thin strip into a tight roll, then tied it round with thread and hung the small scroll about the neck of the painted statue of St Joseph which stood, a lily in one hand, on the top of the bureau.

She closed her eyes, and opened them as he was leaving to ask, "And the other house, the house in the country?" He shook his head.

His wife met him at the door. He said, "No, nothing. They all found out I've got a hernia. None of them would hire me."

She said, "I was thinking about you all day."

"I walked around a lot."

When the three elder sons came into the kitchen, the mother announced, "They wouldn't take him because of his hernia."

Albert said, "You should have had that operated on a long time ago, Dad."

The father didn't answer him.

André said, "What happened?"

"It's as your mother said, and if it hadn't been for the hernia, they wouldn't have had me because I'm too old."

Philip asked, "What jobs did you apply for?"

The father sat back in the chair. He stared at his sons standing above him.

"Let him be," the mother said.

Julien said, "But he's got to get a job."

"Go on," she said.

They did leave him. He sat not in his rocker but on a kitchen chair, his back to the window.

In bed with his wife, he said, "I think I'll go see my mother tomorrow morning."

"Before you go out to look for a job?"

"I'll take the boys to see her too," he said.

She said, "But your mother is dying."

He looked at her from the pillow.

The boys stood at the foot of the bed. Their father sat by the bed, and, leaning close, was whispering to their grandmother. They didn't hear what he said. Daniel looked closely at his grandmother, Julien ran one finger of his right hand back and forth over the back of his left hand, and didn't look. Her head was pressed far back into the pillows, her mouth was partly open and her long lower jaw moved a little from side to side. A thin moan rose it seemed from her entire body, over and over. Her eyes, the irises half visible, appeared to cross, and for a second before they crossed she looked down to the foot of the bed where her grandsons were, then she looked, or tried to look, towards her son, and she whispered something to him. The father said, "Julien, viens ici." Julien went to stand by his father, but kept his eyes to the floor. "Your mémère wants you to put your hands on her head," he said. Julien raised his hands, palms up, and looked at them; he lowered them. "You don't want to do it?" the father asked in English. He shook his head. "It'll help her," the father said. "I don't want to," Julien said. "You won't do it for me?" the father asked. "If I put my hands on her head," Julien answered, "what good would that do for you?" "If it helped her, it would help me." The father was about to take hold of his arms and extend his hands to his grandmother's head. Julien drew away and his grandmother, who seemed all at once to go blind and reach out in darkness to grab something, grabbed his wrist and yanked him towards her as he yanked away, and said, holding his extended wrist, "I'll come back to you." The father, his hands about Julien's upper arms, pulled him away with

144

such force the grandmother's hold was broken, and the father pushed Julien behind him. The father kept Julien behind him and motioned to Daniel with three fingers to come. They left the bedroom quickly. The father was breathing through his mouth; he appeared not to want to breathe the air in the house. The grandmother was saying, in a quiet but penetratingly clear voice, "Je n' peux rien voir, je n' peux rien voir, je n' peux rien voir."

The mother was standing with Philip and Albert in the back yard. She said, "If I were my mother, I'd have flowers all over the yard. I'll plant morning glories on the lattice. That'll hide the garbage cans even better."

"Something should be done to the yard," Philip said. "It's as scruffy as a barnyard in rural Canada."

"I wish someone would build on the lot next. The weeds keep coming over."

"If it weren't for the weeds, we'd have no green at all. And the house needs painting."

"Your father doesn't seem to care about things like that, the way things look. I give up. I can't be after him all the time."

Albert said, "He's good at repairing houses. Maybe he should try to get a job repairing houses."

"Yes," she said; then after a pause, "I don't think he wants to find a job, though."

"Come on," Albert said, "he's not a little weakling that he can't go out and find work."

"No. I always felt safe with your father because he was so strong." She looked into the little wood of the lot behind their yard. "I'm frightened that he doesn't want to work. And yet he'll be worried about money."

"Oh, money!" Philip said.

"There's no need to worry about that," Albert said.

"Well," she said, "there's enough around now that you don't have to worry about it, but we know—"

"Do you worry about money?" Philip asked.

"We've got a house to keep up."

Albert said, "Don't worry about that."

She stared at him. "You don't, none of you, know what it is not to have money."

"No," Albert said.

"Dad will find a job," Philip said.

"I don't know," she said. "I know he'll never find another job like the job in the file shop, one that'll be his life. And yet he's got to live. And what will he live for if he doesn't have his work?"

The two sons said nothing.

"Not for his family. His family has all gone different ways. And not for me."

"Would he ever think that?" Philip asked.

"I don't know. He must feel it. Whenever he goes to his mother, I know he feels there's something missing here, and he feels he can get it from her. He gets it. She's stronger than I am. He's like her." She again looked into the little wood of thin trees and weeds. "He told me once—"

"What?" Albert said.

"It was when he was living with his mother. He had an accident at the file shop. His mother was blackening the stove when he came in from work. She asked 'What's wrong with your hand?' 'I got a sliver of steel in it,' he said. She said, 'Well, it should be removed,' and she cut it out. That's their Indian stoicism. But in the morning his arm was stiff. He couldn't bend his elbow. During work at his machine, his arm swelled, and when he got home his mother made him soak it in boiling water mixed with the water she keeps in her bedroom. His father came in from work and said, 'You should have that arm looked at,' but his mother said, 'It'll be all right.' Well, he's like his mother, but he said, 'Maybe I'd better go to the hospital.' He walked to the hospital. He wouldn't take the bus. A doctor pressed his arm, from the wrist to the shoulder, and said, 'You're twenty-four hours too late.' He said, 'No, I'll die with my arm on.' He couldn't put his coat sleeve on, and had to hold his arm against his chest and button his coat with his left hand. He

146

went to Dr Dalande's. Dr Dalande said, 'You're a day late.' 'I won't have it cut off,' he said. 'Why didn't your mother send you sooner?' the doctor asked him, and he said, 'She thought it would be all right.' Dr Dalande said, 'I'll see what I can do.' He cut a wedge of flesh out of his palm and starting at his shoulder stroked down, hard, again and again, to his hands, and pus poured out of the wound. The doctor squeezed his arm till he couldn't get any more pus out of it. Then he capped long thin rods with antiseptic pads and held the arm rigid and forced the rods through the wound up into his arm. The doctor said, 'You'll have to come back tomorrow, you'll have to keep coming back. Go home,' he said, 'get your mother to boil water and soak your arm in it, as hot as you can stand it, and soak your arm in it for fifteen minutes, every hour, day and night. And make sure she uses just water.' His father came in while he was soaking his arm in water so hot his arm was bright red. His father said, 'It doesn't hurt?' He shook his head. He asked his father, 'Could you do me a favour? Could you go to the file shop and say I'll be back in three days?' His father said, 'Your arm won't be cured in three days.' He said, 'Tell them three days.' His mother said, 'Tell them a week.' His arm was reduced to skin and bone. Dr Dalande told him to buy a pair of dumb-bells and exercise his muscles. The dumb-bells are in the attic now. When he told me this, it happened not long before I met him, I asked him, 'Did you get any compensation from the file shop?' 'Compensation?' he said. 'But it was my fault.' Do you see?" she asked.

"Yes," Albert said.

"And," she said, "if something happened in the family—" But she saw Albert look beyond her, and she turned to see her husband coming round the corner of the house. She said to him, "Your mother—"

He lowered his head and put his hand on it.

"What do you think it is?" she asked.

"It's in her brain."

"What?"

147

"A cancer."

"She might still have something done if she'd get a doctor to look at her," Philip said. "She's stubborn—"

"No," he said, "no. Le cancer ne pardonne pas, jamais."

"You're not going out today to look for work?" his wife asked.

He said nothing. He reached down to pick up a large rusty nail from the ground. The telephone rang in the house. A moment later André appeared like a ghost at the screened window above them. He said, "Dad."

The father narrowed his eyes to look up.

"That was Matante Claudine. She was phoning from the bakery. She said Mémère is calling you."

He said, "I've got to go. I've got to go to my mother."

"I'll go with you," Albert said.

"No," he said.

He threw the nail down.

As if he were dead and could only read lips, his younger sister Claudine, opening the door, formed the words, in English, but didn't speak, "The curé is here." He held back and, also in English, silently enunciated, "Didn't she want to see me?" "She was calling for you." "And now?" "She was calling for our father a little while ago."

The bedroom blind was drawn, but the window behind the blind was open, so a hot breeze flapped it a little and the bottom edge scraped against the sill while the crocheted pull at the end of the pull cord rose and fell. Sunlight flared round the blind and at times, when the breeze blew it in, a bright white wedge of light flashed through the dim room, and the candle flame on a small table by the bed disappeared in the brightness, then, when the blind settled, took shape, throwing not light but a smell of melting wax. The curé was giving extreme unction to his mother. Standing by the window, near the wall, was the deaf sister, Juliette, now in light, now in shade because of the moving blind. (She lived with Claudine. Claudine, because in speaking to her sister she had to project her words with exaggerated expansions and contortions of her lips, but not necessarily with any volume, and always in English—for Juliette had been taught at a school for the deaf in Providence where Claudine had taken her, though the mother disapproved, and Juliette, taught to lip-read English but not French, was never able to communicate with her mother—spoke to everyone in the same way she spoke to Juliette, and the silent, emphatic way she spoke gave everything she said the importance of a great intimacy or suppressed danger.) Their brother, Eurybate, was on the other side of the bed, his rosary dangling from his hands, his lips hardly moving. Oenone led the prayers. While leading, her rosary swaying in one hand, Oenone leaned over the bed to help the curé with the other hand by exposing those parts of her mother's body to be anointed with oil. The mother was lying in a rigid arch, her head pressed far back, her eyes wide open and staring, it seemed, at the headboard behind her, and she was rocking, rocking up and down, so the bed shook and the blankets were bunched up and twisted. Arsace stood behind and to the side of the curé. The curé, in his surplice and the purple stole which showed at the back of his neck, moved back and forth from a little table at the side of the bed with a lit candle and a small case on it to the mother, and murmured in a voice a little higher than the voices reciting the rosary. Arsace clasped his hands together at his waist. Oenone, with slow, arabesque movements of her hand, lowered the blanket and sheet to her mother's shoulders, raised her arms so the hands lay out on the confused blanket, unbuttoned the three top buttons of her mother's flannel nightdress and folded the flaps back to reveal grey-white flesh, drew up the blanket and sheet from the bottom of the bed to expose her mother's feet tangled in the undersheet, and all the while the mother was rocking, as if her body were oscillating from the waves of a loud but deep inside sound that would not break out of her. Arsace stared at her hands, her forearms, her throat where the flesh was stretched to her raised, jutting chin, the skin of her chest. He had never seen his mother's body so exposed. He stared at her feet. He had never seen her feet bare. The soles were rounded, the toes were twisted, yellow, the big toes as if broken. Her feet were shaking. The curé anointed them.

The curé removed the stole from about his neck and kissed it as he turned away from the mother. He looked at Arsace as if he hadn't known he was there. He left the bedroom without looking at the mother, as he had completed the sacrament, and Arsace followed him.

They stood in the kitchen. The curé removed his surplice, folded it over his arm, and pursed his lips again and again, and when he opened them not his voice but, it seemed, the one-o'clock file shop whistle blasted out. The curé closed his mouth. The blast continued. The curé looked out of the open kitchen window. After a while he glanced at Arsace, then away.

Arsace said, "Vous avez voulu parler avec moi?"

The curé said, "À c't' heure, non—"

Arsace waited.

Then the curé said, "What will you do now for work?"

Arsace said, "But my mother's dying now."

"Your mother wanted to die."

"She said to me, 'We work to die.'"

"Yes, yes," the curé said. "And I pray for us all to die quickly." He paused. He asked, "Do you want me to talk to anyone in the union—"

"No," Arsace said, "no."

Oenone came out with the curé's case. He took it from her and left.

The brothers and sisters grouped close about their mother's bed. Oenone performed her duties as if she had long prepared in her mind the rituals; her voice, with a driving force in the repetitions—"Je vous salue, Marie—Je vous salue, Marie—Je vous salue, Marie—Je vous salue, Marie" and "Notre Père, qui est aux cieux—Notre Père, qui est aux cieux"—carried the other voices even when the other voices lapsed, kept up a rhythm in keeping with the continuing jerky rocking of the mother. Arsace leaned a little against the high footboard. Oenone had not re-covered the mother's feet. He wanted to cover them, but he couldn't bring himself to reach to draw the blanket over. Her head was jerking from side to side. She said, "Enfin, enfin, enfin." Those who had been kneeling rose; they stood nearer to the bed. They heard through the clear afternoon the high strident voices of two women speaking to one another on the sidewalk two storeys below:

"Ah non, c'n'est pas vrai, c'n'est pas possible!"

"Et je te dis oui, je te dis oui, c'est vrai."

"Et sa mère, sa mère, que pense-t-elle de cette histoire?"

The mother said, "Enfin, enfin," her mouth sliding from side to side, her tongue loose.

Oenone, making the sign of the cross, said, "Cœur agonisant de Jésus, ayez pitié de ma mère qui meurt."

Then the mother's body twisted up on to its side. Her eyes were still open wide, and Arsace thought they were staring directly at him. Her sons and daughters went rigid. Arsace's younger brother Eurybate suddenly broke away and, "I'm going for Dr Dalande." Oenine shouted, "O Jésus, nous vous supplions d'accepter nos souffrances—" Claudine shut the window, Juliette stood where she had been, her hands over her ears, and didn't move.

When Eurybate came back with the doctor the mother was still twisted on her side, and soft loose flesh in her throat, as it sounded, clacked with her deep breathing. Arsace and his sisters, turned in odd directions, were motionless. Dr Dalande looked into her eyes. He said, "She won't come back." Oenone asked, "Where is she?" The doctor didn't answer. He said to Arsace, "There's nothing I can do for her, but then, she wouldn't have wanted me to do anything." "She knew what she was doing?" Arsace said. The doctor sighed. "You're the oldest, aren't you? You'd better get in touch with Modeste Vanasse." "Now?" The doctor glanced at the mother. "Soon. You take care of that. I'll take care of other things." Arsace walked with the doctor to the door and opened it for him, but he stood in the way and asked, "There's no way of communicating with her?" "No, none," the doctor said. "She wanted to tell me something," Arsace said. The doctor said, "She may yet, from another world." Arsace shook his head violently. "Oh no," he said, and quickly moved to let the doctor go out, but the doctor, just outside the door, turned back. "You don't know if she was taking anything she herself concocted, do you?" "I don't," Arsace said. "Maybe Oenone would know," the doctor said. Arsace called his sister. The doctor asked her. She said, "No, nothing but water." The doctor sighed and left. Arsace went back into the bedroom with Oenone. His mother's eyes had been closed by the doctor.

He went to see the undertaker and came back. The doctor came every hour. Arsace stood by the bed for hours, sat in the kitchen, in his mother's rocking chair, for hours. The mother didn't move. She was hardly in this world; she was breathing in this world, but she was thinking, she was feeling, in an unknown world. The wedge of sunlight that from time to time had penetrated the room when the blind was blown out had become, the window again opened in the hot room, a wedge of light from the street light. Arsace went from the bedroom to the kitchen, from the kitchen to the bedroom. He wasn't able to sit or stand in one place, and he finally said to his brother that he must go back to his family. He felt strange, he felt that he didn't have a body.

Daniel, falling asleep, heard his parents in their bed talking; they sounded very remote.

He suddenly woke. The window in his room was wide open, and he heard a light breeze sloughing through the screen, and, beyond, the moving leaves of the little wood in the vacant lot. He lay still, his eyes open, but he didn't look at the window, he stared at the ceiling where a faint grey light was spreading. His brother Julien was sleeping soundlessly beside him. He had woken tense, and his body, as his mind expanded out and out, contracted in and in. He wouldn't look at the window, but it was as if he were staring at it. Then he heard, outside, a dark deep voice say as in a loud whisper, "Hey," and his tense body began immediately to tremble. His ears became enormous as he listened for more; he felt his contracted body suddenly become enormous too, sweating, and all at once, his body shocked into violent movement by the movement of his hand reaching as though by itself above his head, he began to hit the headboard, hit it and hit it, as hard as he could, and to shout. He was reassured by the hitting and shouting, felt that he could hit anything, shout through anything. The light was lit, and his father came into the room in his bathrobe. Daniel stopped shouting, he looked at his knuckles, which were bleeding.

His father said, his face pale: "What is it?"

"There was someone outside the window."

The father went to the window.

"No, there's no one."

"I heard someone."

"What did you hear?"

"I heard him say, 'Hey'."

Julien sat up.

"Did you hear?" the father asked him.

"No, I was asleep."

"It sounded like a man?" the father asked Daniel.

Daniel shivered. He felt very cold. "Yes."

"It was nothing."

"No, no!" Daniel exclaimed. He stared at his father.

"Go into bed with your mother," the father told Julien, who got up quickly and went out. Daniel lay rigid. His father shut off the light, took off his bathrobe, and got into bed with him. Daniel lay stock still and closed his eyes. His smarting knuckles, the cold surface of his skin, seemed to him on a great periphery, and spread out to a greater and greater periphery as he, behind his closed eyes, felt darkness swell and swell out, out as from a point behind his forehead, and at that point he sensed a fine pulse. As from a vast distance he heard his father say: "Tu m'écoutes?"

"Oui."

"C'n'était personne."

"Oui."

He felt his body draw back from going into the funeral parlour, the first night of the wake, though his mother said his mémère would look as if she were calmly sleeping; he hung back behind his elder brothers, who went to a niche filled with carnations and gladioli, flanked by two candles in red glass, with a prie-dieu before it. Albert and Philip knelt, André stood behind them, to pray. André turned round to him and motioned him to come, and he saw over the top of the prie-dieu, in a clear concentrated light like the clearest daylight, his grandmother lying in a casket, her face covered as by a thin film of pink wax, her hands crossed over a satin counterpane drawn up to above her waist, and a rosary twisted about her fingers. She did not look as though she were sleeping; but it did not seem possible, either, that she would suddenly open her eyes and speak.

Here, before the body, he was not frightened. He stared hard at his grandmother's face. His mind strained to think something. He stared at her hands. Her dead body was more impenetrable to his thinking than it would be if it were alive, so impenetrable he couldn't be interested, as if, in its immense stillness, there were nothing in it to interest him. But when Philip rose from the prie-dieu, Daniel knelt in his place to look more closely at the body of his grandmother. He rubbed the scabs on his knuckles with his clasped fingers.

Julien was in bed. Julien refused to go to any of the three nights of the wake. He moved away from Daniel when Daniel got into bed. Daniel lay still. Again, he woke after sleeping, he had no idea how long after; he woke, his body woke, to the awareness that there was someone outside the window. He didn't move. He was sure the someone was watching him, was sure that if he turned his head to the side a little he'd see a face behind the screen. He moved his hand very very slowly under the blanket so no one could see, drew it along his side and raised it towards his head, and when he got it shoulder high, with a burst he slammed it against the headboard, slammed his other hand against it also, and shouted. The knocking and the shouting were, in his mind, like sharp explosive flashes of light, and when the light did come on in the room he thought it might have been in his mind.

He heard Julien say, with a moan, "Not again." His mother came to the bed, a sweater pulled about her shoulders, her nightgown twisted about her. She took Daniel's hands in hers. They were bleeding. She went out and quickly came back with a wet face cloth.

She said, "You didn't have to shout or knock so loud. We would have heard you."

Daniel didn't say there had been anyone at the window. He knew there hadn't been. His pulse was beating hard. His mother raised his limp arms, wiped the backs of his hands, and placed them on either side of him. He let her.

She said, "You've got to control yourself, you're too old."

Daniel didn't respond.

She added, "If it happens again, knock gently, we're right there, right on the other side of the wall, we'll hear, we won't leave you alone. But don't shout. Your father is very tired. He can't come. And you're too old."

His mother turned off the light and closed the bedroom door behind her when she left. Daniel lay still in the darkness. He heard his brother Julien breathing, not asleep. Daniel slid closer to his brother, and put his arms around him to hold his body.

Richard came to the last night of the wake. He went up to his father, whose back was to him, and touched him lightly on the arm. The father turned. Richard opened his arms and held his father's arms, grasping his elbows, and looked at him silently till his eyes filled with tears, and he said, "How strong you are." The father patted Richard's upper arms, nervously opened and closed his mouth, and looked elsewhere. The mother rose from a chair at the back

155

of the parlour, followed by Daniel who'd been sitting next to her, to go to them. Richard hugged her, holding her head against his. When he stepped back, he had to wipe the tears from his face with the palms of his hands. He said, "I haven't greeted Mémère yet," and, with his father and mother on either side, leaving Daniel in the middle of the floor, he went to the prie-dieu. All the while he prayed Richard kept his hands on his cheeks.

When he got up he went to Daniel and grabbed him, turned him round so Daniel's back was to him, and squeezed his head in the crook of his arm. He released him but kept his hands on his shoulders, and said after a moment, "I somehow always wished that you wouldn't ever have to see anyone dead. Isn't that strange?"

"I don't know," Daniel said numbly.

"Maybe because I think you're like me. Do you think that's it? We're the only two brothers with blue eyes."

Daniel smiled at him.

Richard said, "If it were up to me, you'd never see any death or war or anything bad or—" He took his hands from Daniel's shoulders. "But it's not up to me, is it?"

Albert, Philip and André came towards them.

Daniel saw his brother Edmond, apart, watch his brothers talking together. Edmond looked from them to his aunt Oenone, whose eyes were shaded by the green visor she wore to protect them from lights, however dim, and who, the moment Edmond turned to her, threw up her large arms and shouted, "O ma pauvre mère." Edmond rushed to her, but she pushed past him, fell to her knees, not on the prie-dieu, on the floor, and shouted, "O ma pauvre mère, o ma pauvre mère—"

Towards the back of the funeral parlour, standing next to her husband, the mother was looking towards Oenone and smiling. She felt her husband's hand tighten about her arm, and she thought he was going to lead her to the coffin to pray, but he swung her round to him so she almost lost her balance and pulled her so tightly to him she cried out.

156

Everyone turned to them. The sons saw their father's face, over their mother's shoulder, staring out, his eyes wide. She was trying both to draw back from him and pat him on his shoulder. He suddenly let go of her. The sons saw him go to the entrance of the parlour as if he were going to leave, but he stood there, one hand against the door jamb, his back to the parlour. They saw the mother sit and look down.

Daniel woke with a thin shudder, all at once, ejected from one world into another where he felt that he was floating. He felt the bed was floating, the room was floating, the house was floating. He listened to his breathing.

He and his five older brothers were given soft grey gloves by the undertaker. They were the pallbearers. They carried the casket from the foyer of the church after Mass down two long flights of stone stairs to the hearse. Edmond sobbed at the top of the second flight of stairs.

In the graveyard, they placed the casket across straps slung over a trench. Daniel noticed a crank for lowering the casket on the straps. By the trench was a pile of earth and clumps of grass. The undertaker and his assistant placed the flowers over the casket while the curé stood at the head, in his surplice, sunlight flashing on the shaken hyssop, and not water but splashes of light seemed to spray out from it into the heap of flowers. Suddenly this fear came over Daniel: he thought the undertaker was going to turn the little crank and the casket would sink away under the flowers into the trench. He thought: his grandmother's body was in there. He saw, lying on the other side of the pile of earth, two spades. A sudden terror came over him that his grandmother would break out, would smash through the coffin lid, unrecognizably transformed, and he wanted her to be lowered quickly, quickly into the grave, wanted her to be buried deeply, deeply. He stepped away. He had the gloves on still. The undertaker called him. He took the gloves off as he saw his brothers take theirs off, and like his brothers he threw them on the carnations and gladioli. The curé stepped away before the casket was lowered into the earth. Jim Francoeur followed behind him, and Daniel hurried after his father.

The curé walked hard ahead, then, by a large tree, he stopped, looked back, and the father stopped, too, before he went to him.

The curé said, "I want to tell you now that I never knew about the union—"

Jim Francoeur frowned. "What's that?"

The curé stared at him. "That they insisted you be fired."

The flesh of the father's face appeared to draw back tight and reveal his skull.

"You know as a bench operator you couldn't have been dismissed, because you'd have been protected by the union laws," the curé said. "Management made you a foreman in order to fire you."

The father said, "I didn't know."

The curé touched his biretta and walked away.

Daniel stood by his father, who didn't move until his mother and brothers came up, and they walked out of the cemetery.

In the house they sat, the father and mother and sons, in the living room, sat in silence. Daniel stared at the wide trouser legs, the creases, the pointed cuffs just touching the laced shoes. The father sat on the edge of his armchair and didn't look at any of them.

"Dad," Albert said, "this may not be the right time, but we thought, as we're all together, and it'll probably be a long time before we'll be together again, that we should speak all together. We've discussed it among ourselves, and we all want to buy you and Mom that house in the country."

The father stared at him, or beyond him.

"We feel it's the least we can do," Richard said.

"Oh!" the mother exclaimed, raising her hands together and touching her chin.

André said, "We'll give as much as we can, each of us."

Philip said, "You might as well have it, Dad."

Edmond said, "Well, Dad, you've got what you wanted. Isn't that something?"

"Jim," the mother said.

"Yes," he said.

Albert said, "I'm afraid, though, this house will have to be mortgaged, as before, and we'll guarantee monthly payments—"

The father looked at the mother.

She said, her face beaming, "Oh, Jim—"

Her husband said to her, "You're not worried?"

Her face went a little stern. "We're not signing over our house, are we?"

"No," he said.

She looked at her sons, looked at them, it seemed, all together, though they were sitting and standing about her in different parts of the room. She said, "What you're doing for your father, I can't tell you, what you're doing—" She bit her lip, turned to her husband and after a moment said, "We suffered so much to bring them into the world, to bring them up, and now, you see, they're blessing us, all our suffering has come to this blessing."

The father didn't go out to look for a job. Whenever the mother asked Albert, alone with him for a moment, "What's going to happen?" Albert answered, "Let him be, let him be." The mother frowned.

The father sat for hours in his rocking chair. Albert, day after day, tried to engage him in talk. The father would respond with "yes", or twice over, "yes, yes", the single yes a negative, the double a positive, but he wouldn't be engaged.

On a hot afternoon, two men from the bank came. Albert answered the door, and didn't ask them in. They had come to take photographs of the house. Albert went out into the street with them, and from the other side of the street one man held a little camera to his eye and photographed the white bungalow behind a hedge. Afterwards, Albert shook hands with them on the sidewalk and came in.

His father didn't ask him what the men had wanted. Albert said to him, "Dad, I don't want you to think for a moment that we're forcing the other house on you." The father, in his rocking chair, said, "Yes." Albert sat on a kitchen chair across from him. "Don't you think we should discuss the business?" "Yes," his father said. Albert remained silent, and a while later he got up. He found his mother in her bedroom, putting clean underwear and stockings in a drawer. He asked her, "Is there something wrong?" She bit her lip. His father came into the room, went to his armoire, and took out his suit, a tie, a shirt, and put them on the bed. His wife asked him, "Where are you going?" He said, "I'm going to a meeting." "You haven't been in weeks," she said. Albert watched his father begin to unbutton his grey work shirt, then he left the room.

It occurred to Albert that he had not raised his voice in weeks when, at the supper table after his father's return from the meeting, he heard his father, his lips drawn back to bare his teeth, shout, "The house is a mess, it's all a mess, and we've got to put it in order!" His father, he saw, was a fanatic.

The morning Albert left, he took his mother into the pantry and said, "He'll be all right, he has his politics."

"But what about money?" she asked.

Albert handed her money he had been holding folded in his palm.

"No, no," she said.

He said, "I don't need it. I've got too much. All I need money for is cigarettes and brass polish."

The hot evening of the day the country house was bought, the now former owner of the house and his wife came to the Francoeurs' city house, invited by Jim and Reena Francoeur. Because there was no liquor in the house, nor beer, the guests were served tall glasses of sarsaparilla from a tin tray by the mother. Daniel, standing on one side of the armchair his father sat in while his younger brother stood on the other side, watched his parents, both on the edges of their chairs. It was difficult to breathe in the heat of the room; the air seemed to be made up of the prickly mohair of the armchairs and sofa. At one point the mother got up and left the living room, and soon after the father did. Daniel and Julien were left with the guests, who said a few words to them, then lapsed into silence, and, suddenly terrified, Daniel and Julien ran out into the kitchen to find their parents sitting, as if no one else were in the house, at the kitchen table. Daniel knew this wasn't the way guests should be treated, and when he whispered in panic to his mother that she and his father should go back to the living room, the mother looked at him as though he were bothering her at just the wrong moment. She and the father did go back into the living room; Daniel, Julien behind him, stayed in the kitchen and watched the couple rise from their chairs and heard the mother say, "We're not entertainers."

A van came early the day they were to transport the mother's mother's furniture—beds, tables, chairs, bureaus, stove, old Frigidaire, armchairs, a couch—to the lake house.

The mother packed the china, the pots, the cutlery her mother had given her when she broke up housekeeping into cardboard boxes, blankets, towels, sheets into more boxes, clothes into yet more boxes. Daniel and Julien she said must help. The father did nothing. On the kitchen table, to be packed, were rolls of toilet paper, bars of soap, a bucket, more plates and pots, piles of folded sheets, pillowcases, towels. Daniel was putting them into a box on the floor. He rose from the box, and felt a little dizzy. He looked at the things on the table. A strange sensation came over him, a sensation of not knowing where he was; he might have come from a different world into a strange house, as he had gone that day in the park from his world into the strange house of Betsy Williams, to look at it. He looked at his mother, a woman standing at the other side of the table checking a list of what they would need in the country.

He thought: it never occurred to her that what she assumed was essential was essential to them only because of what they were used to. That other cultures did without soap and toilet paper, never mind forks and knives, she would have thought improbable.

And did he want to do without them? he wondered, and then he thought: the knives and forks, blankets and mattresses, stoves and Frigidaires, all that they took for granted, all that made up the elements of their culture, should— He thought: a language could be a person's native language and yet, in that person's awareness of it, a strange language— He thought: should be as strange as copper bed-warmers, round black pots, wooden well buckets, spinning wheels.

Edmond, who had been out, came in with a painted plaster statue of Our Lady of Lourdes. Her robe, as if blown by a gust of wind into furls and folds, was white, her mantle white and edged with gold, she had a blue girdle about her waist, and on each foot a gold rose; over one arm was a long rosary with large white beads. He announced that he had "bought her for the house".

The mother, Edmond, the boys packed the trunks and back seats of the Dodge and Edmond's car. The father was to drive the Dodge, though he said, just when everything was packed, that he had to have a bowel movement as he had taken a laxative. The others waited in the dark hot kitchen. All the windows of the house had been locked, the shades drawn; the house was closed in on itself. The father took a long time. When, finally, he came out of the bathroom, he stood for a minute in the middle of the kitchen floor, as if wondering if he would go.

He drove slowly. Edmond, though impatient, followed him out of Providence, towards the country. They might have been, the cars stuffed with all their belongings— blankets rolled up, a jumble of small boxes, large saucepans, shoes, clothes tied in bundles, pillows, all in a heap, pressed against the rear and back-seat windows—immigrants on their way to another country.

The furniture movers had unloaded the furniture on to the shaggy overgrown lawn, among the birch trees, in front of the house. The mirrors of bureaus reflected the trees, the blue sky.

The father had the keys, and unlocked the big front door. Edmond, with the statue carried in the crook of his arm, said, as the father was about to enter the house, "No, wait," and when the father turned round, Edmond pointed to the statue and said, "She goes in front." The father let him pass, and let the others pass.

VIII

DANIEL AND JULIEN climbed carefully over the tilting, rotting planks of the collapsed bridge to get to the island. Exposed for a few days to the constant sunlight—sunlight which pressed down, with the force of some strange heavy silencing and immobilizing gravity, on their backs, the backs of their necks, their shoulders, and made it difficult for them to move—their bodies, as they wore day after day only bathing suits, were a soft brown. They stood for a long while on the collapsed bridge. Their shadows were cast on to the bright opaque water below, and it was only in their shadows that they could see weeds moving, a still fish. They had to balance themselves along a log, the only remaining part of the bridge on that side, to the shore of the island. Landed, their feet sank into a warm ooze of mud and leaf mould and sponge like massed roots; the sucking holes filled with bubbling water and released a stinking gas. They pushed blueberry bushes aside.

They explored together, two lenses fitting one against the other, Daniel, as the larger outside lens, seeing everything about him—like the patch of low dark green plants at their feet—in wide blurs, Julien, as the smaller inside lens, fixing on details, studying, with a closeness which might, for its concentration, have excluded enthusiasm or emotion of any kind, a clump of small stiff shiny green leaves and red berries which he had pulled from the patch at their feet. Julien put a berry on the end of his tongue. Daniel simply watched him, Julien bit it in two with his front teeth, then chewed it, his face expressionless, even when he said, "It tastes like mint." Daniel chewed a berry. It did taste like mint. Julien chewed a leaf, Daniel did also. He chewed for a few minutes, reducing the leaf to a slimy cud which suddenly gave off the taste of spearmint. They had landed on this wild island with only the vaguest ideas of plants, most of which were to them nameless. They knew what fern was —a large delicate fern grew by a rock near the shore, and beyond more ferns, shooting up like small green fountains in the dimness of the undergrowth—and what moss was—a rotten tree stump, half in the water, was padded with green, green-grey, blue-green moss; they knew what mushrooms were—a frill of brown-red mushrooms grew from the foot of the tree stump—but they knew they couldn't identify the different ferns, mosses, mushrooms, and, as they slowly walked up the hill of the island pushing aside low branches and bushes, they knew they were seeing many of the plants for the first time. Daniel's expansive sight tried to include, include all at once, and he wanted to hurry to the top of the rise to bring in everything together; but Julien hung back, and Daniel hung back with him, both of them tearing off leaves to study them. They gave plants and bushes names with total authority: "snakeroot" to a bush with long thin brown-spotted jagged leaves that gave off a smell of musk, "witch berry" to a high bush with large clusters of very black berries with long red stems, "waxen berries" to a big blunt-leafed bush whose small green granulated berries felt like wax, "skunk cabbage" to a big plant of large furled leaves which, from a distance, radiated a pungent acrid odour. Julien spit out his cud, and Daniel did. Sunlight beamed vertically down through the high branches of intertwining oak, pine, maple. In sunlit spots the ground was hot, and there rose from it a hot smell of parched earth and resin; in shadows, the ground was cold and the smell was of clear air, or water.

They came across an old path through the bushes. Like explorers stumbling on an indication of habitation, they took it with the expectation that it would lead to a small unknown encampment in the woods. It led through a little field of crab grass, round the trunks of very high, very straight pines, to the wreck of a cabin—a pile of boards, sheets of rusted tin, shingles. Grass and plants grew about a circle of ash and charcoal in which were half buried broken bottles. The sunlight beat straight down on the ruined cabin. There had been civilization on the island, but no longer, and Daniel and Julien, poking around the boards with sticks, looked for evidence of what the civilization had been; they found rusted tins, a cartridge shell, an old pair of very rusted scissors. They kept the cartridge shell and scissors, slipped them under the waistbands of their bathing trunks, and went on.

When, turning round, they were unable to see the house or the bridge through the trees, but only sun-shafted woods and below them on either side expanses of dark still water, they wondered if they had gone far enough.

Julien said he thought he'd go back. Daniel wouldn't go on without him. The long hill they had been walking over sloped away, and at the bottom of the slope was a large, dense clump of what they called waxen-berry bush, in fact laurel, and there seemed to be no way through. They didn't move. Noises slowly increased in volume; low insect noises, a lap of water, the sudden high screech of a heat bug. But the noises made Daniel aware of a deeper silence; it was the silence of a person, or people, keeping silent, and he all at once felt they had come into a place where, a moment before, people had been moving about freely and talking, and now, with the intruding presence of the boys, the people had stopped still and become silent, and those people, behind trees, in the waxen-berry clump, floating, perhaps, just beneath the surface of the water, were watching Daniel and Julien, who didn't dare talk, didn't dare move, both of them frightened that any word or sharp gesture might release those people from the tense immobility and silence they kept; then they would appear, and Daniel didn't want them to appear.

166

He had sometimes imagined that if he had been in a cabin in a clearing in the woods with settlers, all of them at windows or chinks with rifles ready, waiting for the Indians to appear from the woods, he would simply open the door and walk out, shouting, "I'm one of you! I'm one of you!" But when the Indians began slowly to advance from among the thick branches and come towards him, their dark bodies greased, their faces slashed with black, and he not able to speak a word of the language, a shiver would pass through him, and he'd try to imagine himself standing firm, perhaps even advancing towards them, but the scene would go dark.

Now, in the unknown woods, he was a little frightened. He whispered that, all right, they should go back, Julien said they should wait a minute, and after the minute said quietly that they should go on into the island.

The laurel clump covered the island from one side to the other, and on either side twisted dead branches dragged in the water. Crouching, Daniel saw a tangle of crooked branches under the laurel. Julien crouched too. Still crouching, he stepped into the bushes, his behind swinging, grabbed branches to support himself, and said they could squeeze through. The branches scratched their bare arms, legs, and chests. It was dank low among the laurel. They came across a duck's nest with two shattered eggs. Inside, they were hidden. They remained there, crouched together. Insects buzzed around them. Daniel's knee, bent as large as and shaped like a skull, was pressed against Julien's knee. They were waiting for something to pass, for the troop of soldiers or the band of braves, he didn't know, as he'd become confused. Daniel noticed that the muscles of Julien's arms and chest were not as formed as his; his body was smooth and soft and a little fat, and the skin bulged round the rusty scissors he had slipped into his bathing suit. Julien raised an arm to clutch a branch over his head and revealed a clear empty armpit. Daniel hated the hair under his own arms, as he hated his pubic hair; and a pimple had erupted on his chest, next to a nipple. Julien's body was, he thought, somehow pure. Daniel drew his knee away from contact with him. Julien seemed not to be aware of him; he pulled the branch down and picked some little green waxy berries to study them more closely.

They continued deeper into the island; the slope descended more and more, the two sides of the island converged more and more, until they had to swing out over the water by grabbing the thin trunks of scrub pine to pass by them, and the two sides finally met at a gap where, for the space of a jump, the big lake and the little lake flowed into one another, and small fish, bluegills, darted back and forth through the canal. Julien, still conscious of his exploration, tried to determine the shape and size of the island so far; he drew an invisible map on the back of his hand, and at invisible points indicated the path, the little field, the ruins of the cabin, the hollow tree, and this gap. They easily jumped the gap, and were on, technically, another island. The second island rose steeply, was higher though narrower than the first and almost barren. Large outcroppings of lichen-covered glacial rock which stuck out everywhere made the island appear as though it were one huge irregular rock covered thinly with earth and ringed, at the water's edge, by gaunt pines and crooked oaks. A faint breeze drew across it smells of water and, it seemed, hay.

On this island they were exposed on all sides, but they were so isolated no one, not Indians or soldiers, could find them, or had ever been there. In a cleft of rocks, among thin bushes, Julien found another duck's nest, with one hatched and one unhatched egg, and stopped to examine it. Daniel went on. He wandered about the bare top of the island, further and further towards the end, so when he looked back he couldn't see Julien. The end of the island sloped down to a pile of boulders and, further out, a chain of boulders which staggered out into the water, and beyond them the little and the big lakes came together in a body of water with waves and a swift-flowing current. Daniel stood on the pile of boulders at the end of the island.

Back at the house, they found Edmond waiting to say goodbye to them. He could not have left without them standing behind the car and waving at him. The mother stood between the two boys, under a pine tree. All three watched Edmond throw his suitcase into the back seat and get into the front to go off on the long trip for which he'd taken all his money out of his savings account and left his job. The mother and the boys waved, silently, as Edmond drove off down the hill for Kentucky, in his metallic green car. Through pine trees, they saw his car stop on the country road, before a curve. The mother said, "He's coming back." His car reversed, and he backed into a clearing between pine trees. The father's grey Dodge appeared round the curve. It passed Edmond's car, and Edmond pulled out and drove on as the Dodge continued up the hill towards the house. The mother and boys went to meet the car. The father stepped out, his shadow extended a long way before him into the late-afternoon light. They looked at his face for an expression that would reveal, before he spoke, that he had found a job. He squinted as he turned to look into the sun, and squinted still when he turned to his wife. She knew, before he kissed her and spoke, that he hadn't found work, though she asked, making the question liltingly incidental, "You weren't able to find anything?" and he answered starkly, "No."

The "No", as closed as his face, caused in Daniel, as it had all the past days, a little shock as of recalling something he had made himself forget. He imagined with sudden impatience that his father hadn't found a job, not because there wasn't one available to him, but because he refused to find one.

The mother said, "Well, maybe tomorrow," and put her arm in his and walked him up the rest of the curved drive to the house.

For the mother it seemed not to make any difference when, after two weeks, the father answered, with as little expression as he'd answered, "No", "Yes", for she took him

169

by the arm as usual and, with the same lightness, said, "When do you begin?"

For Daniel, it was the relief he had been waiting for. It didn't matter to him what his father's job was, it only mattered that he had one. Their supper, that positive evening, was, like the others, eaten in silence, but it was a silence that was, for Daniel, a deep country silence, The father had found a job similar, he said at the end of the meal, to the job he had had during the Depression: reshingling the clapboard of, re-roofing, replacing the roof gutters and drainpipes of, repainting, repairing, outside and in, houses.

He started the following day, and when he returned in the evening his overalls, the backs of his hands, his face and hair were finely spattered with yellow paint and colourless varnish. There was a streak of dry varnish on a shirt sleeve which sawdust had adhered to. The father said nothing about his work, and certainly wouldn't complain. He didn't complain, either, about other things—that, for supper, Reena was preparing sandwiches again, or that Daniel and Julien had not cut the grass as he had asked them to. Reena said he should go into the lake for a swim. He wrinkled his nose. She said she and the boys had been waiting for him to return to go swimming with them. He said, all right. In bathing suits, they walked slowly down a gravel path to the edge of the lake, towels over their arms. Reena's belly swelled the front of her old bathing suit, fat bulged over the stiff bra, and her white legs were riddled with varicose veins. The father's neck and arms were baked red, his shoulders and hairless chest stark white, and his legs, disproportionately thin, it appeared, for his torso, even whiter; his narrow feet were in slippers. Daniel and Julien picked leaves as they went. Uneven stone steps led to a narrow shore of the big lake. It appeared, at this hour, to be overfilled with the light it had been absorbing all day, a heavy, brimming light. Daniel and Julien walked in, hardly disturbing the surface, up to their knees, up to their thighs. They looked round at their parents, who stood ankle deep in the heavy green water, turned a little away from one another. Her knees pressed together, the mother leaned to cup water in her hands and splash it on her shoulders and arms. While the father, as with a sudden movement of impatience, walked further into the water, turned quickly, and sank backwards up to his neck, the mother, calmly, without rippling the water, swam out in another direction, her hands dividing the water before her as she went; both kept their heads above the water. Daniel and Julien sank under. Daniel's underwater gestures were slow, and when he rose up his gestures in the green air were slow too. The heads of his father, mother, Julien were at three points, on either side and directly before him. They were, he thought, together, and yet they were separate. The sunlight over the water began to deepen to a red haze, and deepened more as, silently, they dried themselves. They walked through the air as if walking through water to return to the house, which was under a flood of green red air. The father changed into a clean loose white shirt, which he left unbuttoned and out of his trousers, the trousers light brown. They sat out for their sandwiches at the large picnic table under the oak on the lawn.

The father said he would be late the next day, he had a political meeting in the city.

The mother, while the father was away at night, kept the boys with her. They played cards in a corner of the big living room, away from the large black windows, all the doors locked. It was as if they didn't have a father.

At the time the mother thought her husband would be returning, they went to the balcony overlooking the road to wait, waving mosquitoes away, till they saw the yellow head-lights of the car, shattered into thousands of beams by the branches and bushes, and hurried out to the road to meet him.

During the long bright weekdays, while he was at work, the mother sat on the glider or walked up and down the country road or lay for a little in the sun when it was not too hot, and Daniel felt in her that strange sadness he almost always felt in her when he and Julien sat or walked or lay on the blanket with her. From time to time, sitting or walking or lying out on the lawn on a large rumpled Army blanket, Daniel would watch her: she would stop rocking in the glider, or pause while walking, or lie staring up, and suddenly tears would fill her eyes. He didn't know what the tears were for; if he had asked her if she was sad, she would, he was sure, have said no. In and about the house she didn't seem to need her husband, and in the evenings, in the same room with him, she would sit, her back to him, at a window, and look out at the light on the lake.

One Friday evening, he said, "I saw Georgie Girard on the street today."

"Did you speak to him?"

"Yes," he said, "I invited him and Pauline up Sunday afternoon."

"You invited them?" she asked, as if she didn't want anyone else to come.

"Yes. I thought they might want to see the place."

And Georgie and Pauline, having been given complicated instructions by Jim, stepped out of their car late Sunday afternoon with expressions of amazement that they had arrived; as though they'd been in a maze of rutted, overgrown country roads in which they were sure they were lost, so that coming, as by accident, on the house, or any house, was like suddenly coming on a wood in the tangled streets of the city's downtown. Georgie Girard wore a suit and tie, and Pauline a dark taffeta dress. Jim and Reena advanced to greet them, Jim in his unbuttoned shirt and light slacks, Reena in a pale summer dress. The men shook hands, the two women kissed. They stood motionless.

Jim said, "How about having a look around the place?"

He first showed them the grounds, the little dock, the trees, the curving drive, the lawn, the pine woods behind the house, and indicated the island from a distance, then took them into the house through the garage, and the boiler room, and up and down stairs to rooms sparsely furnished, some completely empty, the shiny wood floors reflecting the windows and the trees in the windows. While Reena and the boys waited outside, where they could hear his voice from time to time through the open windows, Jim guided Georgie and Pauline as if about a house sanctified by a great historical event, saying, every time he opened a door, "And in this room we have—"

Reena finally went to the house to call, "I've made lemonade, and the ice is melting in the glasses."

"Yes, yes," Jim said from upstairs.

She knew he wouldn't come. Upstairs, he would be showing them the attic and giving them a lecture about the roof. She'd annoy him by going up, but she did, and took Pauline by the hand and led her downstairs and out to the lawn. Wooden lawn furniture was placed as about a living room. The settee was under an oak tree, and, across from it, two armchairs were against a clump of birch; between the two armchairs was a small wooden barrel, painted red, and on it a tray of ice-filled glasses and a frosted pitcher of lemonade. Reena drew Pauline down beside her on the settee. The two men came out and sat in the armchairs. The mother asked Daniel to hand round the glasses of lemonade. They spoke in whispers, the sun set.

Pauline asked, from a distance (she was, in fact, Reena's oldest friend; they'd been friends when, Reena sometimes said to her, both were single, and they were still friends now that both were double), "Are you enjoying it here?"

"Oh, I," Reena began, then faltered and simply touched Pauline's arm to bring her closer in some way.

"And Jim?"

"He doesn't say anything."

Pauline sniffed.

"He wanted the house, of course," Reena said. "It was his idea, long before the boys got together to buy it for him—"

"The boys bought it, did they?" Pauline asked.

"We didn't tell you?"

Pauline sniffed again. "Well, when Jim showed us around, he was talking like he bought it himself."

"He didn't mention the boys?"

"No."

"Ah," Reena said. She looked towards her husband. His right leg was crossed and extended over his left, his left hand held a cigarette, his right hand was splayed out on his bare chest over his heart, and he was talking, talking. Georgie, a cigar in his puckered mouth, simply listened. A sadness and pity for her husband spread through her, spread, it seemed, behind her eyes, and as she looked at him he went a little out of focus. She said to Pauline, "Well, of course the house in the city was mortgaged to raise the money, and as it's his house, that one, really he's bought this one—"

Just as Georgie and Pauline were about to get into their car to leave, Jim asked abruptly, "How are things at the file shop?"

"All right," Georgie said.

Then Jim said, making Reena wince, "No one working there, I guess, could expect to have a place like this."

"No, no," Georgie said.

Jim and Reena walked back up the drive in the warm dark, the boys close behind them, and Reena said, "You shouldn't have said that."

Jim frowned, "Said what?"

"About having this place."

"What did I say?"

"Well, it was bragging, and it was a lie, too, because you couldn't afford this place on your income either."

"It's in my name."

"Yes."

"Then it's mine."

"Yes."

"And why shouldn't I want to show it? I don't understand, girlie."

She said nothing more. Daniel thought, and was surprised at the same time by the sudden thought: his father

174

simply did not know how crude he was, or how crude his wife and sons saw him to be, as though he took for granted, like a hard solid block, a way of acting which they, his wife and sons, embarrassed by it, would break down and try to destroy if they found it in themselves; the father would find it strange of them, perhaps, not to show off what they had, not to let everyone know what they had accomplished, not to brag, if that was what showing what one had, talking about what one had accomplished, had to be called. The father talked, talked about himself when with others as though it never occurred to him that he, who talked about himself as though he were another person, could have had another topic of conversation, and, his brow furrowed, his eyes wide, he was always puzzled and mildly annoyed when, later, his wife reprimanded him. When they reached the top of the drive, the mother stopped to look at the dark lake; the boys stayed with her, while the father went on, and in the darkness the screen door clacked. The father could have bragged to his mother if she were alive, and she would not only have accepted the bragging from her son, she would have accepted it as natural. In some world, the world his father belonged to, showing off the house was what anyone who in that world had a large, imposing house would do; in Daniel's mother's world, to have a large, imposing house was somehow to brag, and, ashamed, you never said it was beautiful, you said the roof needs reshingling and the outside wall repainting.

A light came on in the house and was projected to where they stood; Daniel looked round to see his father sitting under a lamp, looking away from the large living-room window, his hands folded against his waist.

Daniel went to the island in moonlight, after Julien and his parents went to bed. Out in the bright night shaking with crickets and frogs, he knew that from every shadow he was being watched. He hurried down to the bridge. The moonlight cast the shadow of the broken bridge on to the water. He thought he might slip off and crash into the water, but

175

once on the island, pushing the blueberry bushes aside, he felt momentarily safe. When he looked up the dark rise of the island, through the dark trees, he was frightened again. He went on.

At a level place surrounded by bushes he stopped. He breathed in deeply, then out. He rubbed his hands up and down his arms, across his chest. Some strained city voice, a voiced memory trying to draw him to another place, to his small room in the city, repeated again and again: Don't, don't. Ah no, ah no, he thought. His body was warm, but he was shivering.

He thought: I've got to urinate. Then thought: No, I don't have to. A vague tension around his lower abdomen strained. He knew it was just an excuse to unzip himself to think, I've got to urinate, but he accepted the excuse and unzipped. His exposed penis made a startling contact with the outside. He held the tip with two fingers, pinching the narrow foreskin a little. He stood for a long while, his mind pressing down on his body to force it to pee. The release came with a sensation of sudden physical abandon, as of throwing himself off a high bank. He heard the stream hissing among leaves. He remained as he was long after the stream was reduced to drops, his exposed penis in contact with the night-time island. He pressed it back and half zipped up.

He had to wash his hands. He went to the edge, where a tree leaned over the lake, and knelt to reach down; his fingers sank into the water and he noiselessly swirled them about.

Withdrawing again among the bushes of the island, he ran his wet fingers up and down each arm in turn. He touched his chest through the thin cloth of his white T-shirt. He thought: No, no.

But he pulled off his clothes quickly, throwing them from him as though he were throwing them off with no intention of finding them again. Immediately his body seemed to expand in the air. He walked among the bushes and they brushed against him, his stomach, thighs, penis, legs, buttocks; he walked among them to have them brush against him, to have them snap against him, to brush and snap against some enclosed inside body, to make it break out in the midst of the warm dark bushes.

The island too was a body. It was, beneath him, a body; the mass of intertwining roots veins, the embedded stones bones, the water trickling through it blood. He felt it heave a little. He thought: Now, fix this moment, fix this moment, the moment when I first make love, this moment of making love to the whole world, the innocent, oh God, oh God, so innocent body of the world.

Matante Oenone came to the lake the day all the waters of the world were blessed by God. The low grey sky floated just above the surface of the grey lake. She changed into a knitted grey bathing suit; her breasts and large nipples and the fat at her waist bulged the knit. She went down to the lake alone. She went out up to her thighs, splashed water to her face, to her breast, held her nose and sank under and remained under the widening rings on the still surface, then rose, came out and carefully dried herself with a towel, not by rubbing, but by pressing the towel against her head, her body, and holding it pressed against her. She carried the towel over an arm and a shoe in each hand, and very slowly walked up the path to the house barefoot as a sacrifice; she winced now and then when she stepped on a sharp pebble or a pinecone, but the sustained expression on her face was that of someone walking on water.

In the evening she and other relatives sat out on the lawn, at a distance from a fire. Daniel stayed a little away from them, as if they formed a ring he didn't want to step into; yet he listened to them talk in their ring, and watched them. The flames of the fire were reflected in Oenone's glasses, and the flames in her glasses would suddenly brighten violently when Julien, alone tending the fire, in a circle of stones, threw a pine branch on it. Matante Oenone was facing relatives—her brother Arsace, her sister-in-law, her nephew

177

Daniel, her sisters Claudine and Juliette (who, deaf, stared at the distant fire), her younger brother Eurybate with his fat wife—and she was telling them, as though it were a story which, though they knew it very well, might in the re-hearing turn out differently, about the death of their mother, about anyone's death. She spoke in French, her voice softly clacking.

"I remember when my father was dying, my mother stood by his bed, she didn't say anything, her expression didn't change. She remembered her mother dying when she was a little girl, and even then she didn't say anything, didn't cry, just watched."

Daniel asked, "How did her mother die?"

"She died of a cancer. The cancer came out all over her body. She never said a word about her suffering, she kept silent, and so did my mother, though she stayed with her till the end. They were strong then, people were. My mother's real mother—no, wait, her father—I can't remember, I think it was maybe her mother—she tore up a big pine tree by the roots to throw it at a bear coming for her because she couldn't find anything else to throw at it. My mother herself used when she was younger to lift the burning range whenever something dropped under it that she wanted to get back. She didn't get burned. She had a cure for burns, too. But Arsace knows more about that than I do—"

They all knew the mother had given to Arsace a prayer for curing burns. He once, years before, at supper, had described to the family having used it, and that was the only time he referred to it: "I was, a young man at the time, passing by a blacksmith's when I heard shouting from inside, and, of course, being an inquisitive young man, I stuck my head in and I saw a lad holding his arm up, which was already blistering bad from a burn, and he was screaming. He didn't move, he just stood there and screamed. I went in, took an old rag, grabbed the lad's arm, pulled it sharply down towards me, wrapped the rag round it, and plunged the arm into a vat of water, and as I did I said a prayer my mother

178

thought" (he always said "thought" for "taught") "me. I took the arm out of the water," (the arm, at this point in the recounting, appeared disembodied, for, as a small influence from French, he often used the depersonalizing article "the" instead of a possessive adjective, and that arm might have been the relic of a saint, belonging now to a religious community which, whenever referring to the relic, said simply, "the arm") "unwrapped the rag, and the arm was as clear and white as a baby's skin". When he had recounted the story, Daniel had not thought anything about it, it had been another brief story his father had told; but, now, it seemed to him to fit into a large, strange context years after he had first heard it.

The father asked Oenone, "Was it on our mother's side or father's side that there was an uncle, or great uncle, who could plough a field without a horse, just by pushing the plough? And he didn't have a brake to his wagon, so whenever he wanted to stop he reached down and grabbed the two front wheels."

"On our mother's side, I think," Oenone said.

Julien threw a branch into the fire. It blazed, crackling, and sparks were blown up and drifted among the dark pine trees. The father was sitting facing the fire; in the sudden rage of light, his body appeared to come out of the darkness, and his arms and forehead were shining.

The father said, "My mother once told me that in Canada, years before she came down to Rhode Island, one early morning she heard scraping at the door, and instead of waking my father she got up and looked out of the window to see what it was—"

Reena, a little removed from the circle, ceased to hear. She thought: they talked of their mother, always their mother, and their father, whom they didn't talk about, didn't matter. She was never comfortable with her in-laws; she had always to make an effort. That she wasn't related to them by blood meant she was only related to them in her and their minds, and, for some reason, the relations between her and them kept breaking down into silence. She withdrew now into silence, thinking to herself: they, her husband and her in-laws, assumed their mother was the centre of their family, and in her family her father was the centre, it was as simple as that.

He said, "—she saw."

Eurybate's fat wife, who was as much outside the blood circle as Arsace's wife, said, "Maybe it was just the milk-man."

Eurybate said, "They didn't have milkmen then."

Claudine enunciated carefully, "I don't believe a word of it."

Oenone said, "Well, I can tell you, my mother saw things we couldn't see. She never said so, at least not to me, but she did. Sometimes when I went into her room, where she'd been praying, I knew she'd been seeing."

She paused. The fire, which appeared to be burning in mid-air, floating in the hot moist night, moved shadows about them while they were still.

Oenone said, "And when she—"

"That's enough," Arsace said, "that's enough."

Woken one night by distant laughter, Daniel lay, eyes open. A soft breeze was seething through the screens of the windows on the three sides of the large room. He slept now in his own room, in his own bed. He got up and, crouching, approached the window, his chin on the level of the sill. He saw firelight flickering through the trees on the island, and someone from there began to sing, a muted, ululating song.

The next morning he went before breakfast to the island. He found the remains of a fire and in the ashes half-burned cigarette packs, crumpled wax paper, and what looked like two long thin white balloons which he picked out of the ash with a stick then dropped back into the ash. About the fire were empty tin cans and beer bottles and cigarette butts crushed into the mulchy earth. He threw whatever was burnable on to the ashes, and collected the bottles and cans in a small heap. It was strange to him to imagine that these objects, so still, had participated in a mad and messy activity. If Indians had camped there, he thought, they, like ghosts, would not have left a trace. He went back to the house for matches and a bag, returned, burned the papers and white balloons, adding twigs and turning over the fire again and again until he was sure everything was reduced to fine ash. He thought he might throw the bottles and cans into the lake, but he'd always know they were there; he put them in the bag and carried them off.

The white mist of an early morning floated above the country road as Jim drove slowly over the ruts without being able to see them, and sometimes the mist rose and he couldn't see ahead to the turnings. The old Dodge rocked or swerved a little when the front wheels dropped into a rut, and he carefully manoeuvred his way out. Round a turning he saw, advancing as slowly towards him as he was advancing towards it, a metallic green coupé. It disappeared into the mist, then reappeared. Jim stopped the car, got out, and stood in the middle of the road to meet Edmond who, when he saw his father, stopped, too, but instead of getting out lowered the window. All his father said was, "You're going to have to back up into a clearing so I can get by, tsi gars, or I'll be late for work." Edmond reversed, and saw his father back in his car, drive by, and Edmond continued through the mist after he had gone.

His mother, too, wasn't surprised to see him. She kissed him and said he must be tired and hungry (he would have expected this; her saying this made a trip away from the family real). She gave him breakfast. He ate with the movements of someone asleep. He said he'd driven from Kentucky non-stop, but that's all he said about it. She saw, by the very fact that he didn't say a word about what had happened to him in Kentucky, not even about the rattlesnake dinner, how dispirited he was, and she knew she must somehow surround his dark, silent disappointment with a bright, noisy family welcoming. She knew she must do it for him, but she felt it was beyond her; she could only make herself say, a little slackly, "The boys will be thrilled that you're home when they wake, they'll want to hear everything." It wasn't enough for Edmond; with the crudity of his father, but crudity inverted from an enormous pride to an enormous humility, he looked up at her from his scrambled eggs and asked, "Did you miss me?" She felt her insides move. "Of course, of course." She tightened her voice. "What kind of parents do you think we are? We missed you very much. We couldn't stop you from going, we wouldn't stop any of our sons from doing what he wanted, but we were sorry when you left, and we're very happy you're back. This is your home as long as you want to stay here." She saw the skin on Edmond's face draw tight. "Don't you ever doubt that," she said firmly, and tried to make her voice even more firm when she added, "You believe me." Edmond appeared to wake up, and asked if he could have two more scrambled eggs.

Before he went upstairs—the mist was billowing against the windows—he said, "I met my father on the road."

"Did you say anything to him?"

"No. He told me to move my car so he could get past."

She smiled a little. "He was worried about being late for work. You can be sure, Edmond, that he's as happy to see you as I am."

Edmond said, "Ma mère et mon père."

"Vas-y, vas-y." She was always a little impatient with Edmond, and now she was also a little sad. "Vas-y," she repeated.

Edmond, in the early afternoon, went out to join Daniel and Julien fishing off the end of the dock with poles Albert had got them. The day was grey, and a thin mist rolled above the still water. Daniel said, "We got your postcard with the picture of Abraham Lincoln's log cabin."

"Yeah," Edmond said, staring into the water.

"Did you really eat rattlesnake meat?"

182

Edmond said, as if none of that—the rattlesnake meat, Abraham Lincoln's log cabin, Kentucky—mattered any more, "Caught any fish?"

"Bluegills we threw back in," Julien said.

"Can I have a try?"

Julien handed him his pole.

Daniel asked, "Didn't you see Bobby Lee?"

"Yeah," Edmond said, and reeled in the line to look at the worm on the hook.

Daniel said to Julien, "Here, take my pole."

"No," Julien answered.

"I don't want to fish."

"No, I don't want it."

Without reeling the line in, Daniel left the pole on the dock, the line hanging straight into the water, and walked away. His body felt disjointed, and he wasn't quite sure where he wanted to go.

The next morning—clear, bright—Julien, at breakfast, said that he was going to pull the half-sunken boat by the dock out of the water and repair it. Edmond and Daniel actually pulled it out while Julien stood on the shore and told them what to do. They managed to turn the rowboat upside down; the slimy bottom was grown over as with fine green soft hair. Julien said to Edmond, "Do you think you could find scrapers in the basement?" and Edmond went. All in bathing suits, they scraped the muck from the bottom of the boat. Edmond's nipples, Daniel noted, were large, unlike anyone else's in the family, and he had prominent hairless soft breasts that shook as he worked, and all the other brothers, and the father, too, had flat hard chests. He smelled, and Daniel wondered if, in the ten days he'd been in Kentucky, he'd had a bath. He wasn't scraping very well, and what he thought he had finished, in a haphazard way, Julien put a finish to, scraping up sodden splinters of wood as well as weed and paint.

The mother came down to where they were working by the lake. She looked at them for a while. Then, as a

183

calculated aside, she said to Edmond, "Now that you're home have you thought of getting your job back?"

Edmond stopped scraping. He said nothing.

"We know, your father and I, that you promised to contribute each month to pay off the mortgage, but we don't expect it. What we think you've got to help with, though, is the daily expenses of running the house, and you've got to get a job for that."

Daniel was as attentive as Edmond. He had never heard his mother speak in this way, never heard her state so flatly what amounted to a law, and he looked at Edmond, whose shoulders suddenly sloped, as though he himself might be standing in his brother's place. The mother had stated the law as Albert had stated the law that he, Daniel, would have to go into the services, and, inevitable to Daniel, fight a war.

Edmond said, "I'll go into the city tomorrow with Dad to see if I can get back on at the printing shop."

"Even if we were rich," the mother said, "I'd insist that all my sons should work. They've got to follow the rules of the house."

"Yes," Edmond repeated.

Daniel thought: it was not only that he had never heard his mother say what she was saying, he hadn't before been aware of a kind of severe intelligence in her; it occurred to Daniel that he would never be able to go to his mother and say, and expect a soft response, I don't want to work, I don't want to go into the Army.

Edmond placed the scraper on the boat and went in. The mother stayed with the boys and said, "I don't want to be boss, I don't, but someone has to be." She put her hand at the back of Julien's clean soft brown neck, and he lowered his head.

Daniel and his mother walked down the road. She said, "I wish I could have kept you all babies, kept you all always at home, but that wasn't possible. Keeping any of you home would be just as impossible." She picked a blueberry and looked at it in the palm of her hand. "You'll be

184

leaving, too," she said, "and I won't be able to keep you."

"No."

"You'll be going to high school, and soon after you'll be going away to college. Do you look forward to that?"

"I guess."

They turned at the bend in the road to walk back to the house.

"Does Dad think we shouldn't go away?" he asked.

"I don't know what he thinks about you," she said.

Daniel sat under an oak at one end of the long green bench, reading, and his mother and his sister-in-law Chuckie sat at the other end, talking. He heard their voices like voices breaking in on the dialogue he heard in his book, and interspersed with the scenes he saw in his book was the scene, before him when he lifted his eyes, of his nephews and nieces splashing in the water. Sometimes water splashed up and across the open page. What he saw and heard in his book and what he saw and heard around him confused; his book raised before him, and he in a very large and lofty room, with long narrow pointed windows at so vast a distance from the black oaken floor they were inaccessible from within, through the trellised panes of which feeble gleams of encrimsoned light made their way to render distinct dark draperies, profuse, comfortless, antique, tattered furniture, many books and musical instruments scattered about, he suddenly found there, bursting in on a wave of water, three screaming children chasing one another in circles and pushing one another over while a fourth child, just able to walk, wept because it was being splashed; or, interrupting the long guitar-accompanied recitation of a verse ("And all with pearl and ruby glowing/ Was the fair palace door,/ Through which came flowing, flowing, flowing/ And sparkling evermore,/ A troop of Echoes whose sweet duty/ Was but to sing—"), he heard a voice shout, "You're out too far, I told you not to go out above your waists," or "Watch out for the baby!" Then, lowering his book, he momentarily saw, among the oak trees whose branches met vaultlike overhead, a black coffin resting on trestles, and heard a distant reverberant clang of iron hitting stone.

Reena looked for her husband. Through the screen door, she heard him and Richard talking together outside in the darkness. She stood inside, just to the side of the screen door, and listened. Richard was telling his father about his work, and Jim, Reena could tell, was listening carefully. She realized that the only time, really, he would listen carefully to his sons was when his sons talked to him about their work and the money they were making. That the work was going well and that they were earning good money was all that mattered to the father; nothing else mattered to him—Richard's marriage, his children, his house—so when, clearing her throat as she opened the screen door and stepped out, she said to them, "I've just been helping Chuckie to get the kids to bed, but they keep kicking off their blankets," Jim said he'd go in and read his paper.

Richard said, "I hoped Chuckie would get a rest here."

"Here or at home, she can't get a rest from the children."

Richard paused. "I guess I'm not a very responsible father."

"You work hard."

"Yes, but, you know, I just don't have the energy to discipline them. And then, when she asks me to belt them, I can't do it, I really can't do it."

She repeated, "You work hard."

"I try."

"Oh, I know you do, up till two and three in the morning over your drawing board, and—"

Chuckie came out, and Richard asked her, "Are they finally asleep?"

"Yes, finally."

The sounds of the crickets and frogs swelled; it was as though they had been creaking and croaking all day through the white heat but were unheard because of the overriding screeching and howling of the children, and were just now audible. After a while Richard got up and left the two women, who said nothing to one another until Reena, not knowing why, said:

"You know, if you and Richard have difficulties between you, I don't want to know about them."

Chuckie said nothing.

"Because I can't take sides, neither with you or with him."

"No," Chuckie said.

Daniel sometimes found his mother wandering about the house from room to room, the furniture turned in odd directions, clothes piled on the floor, cardboard boxes of children's shoes and socks in the middle of the floor, looking, it seemed, for something. He sometimes found her walking up and down the country road. He imagined some black round spot shifting about the family, from one forehead to another, for as long as she looked at one member of the family—Edmond, Julien, her husband, Chuckie, Richard, one of the children—and the round black spot momentarily fixed that one member as the centre of her divided, distracted attention. Daniel saw the dividedness, the distraction, in her staring eyes. She might, at one moment, pick up the one-year-old baby from the floor and hold him very close to her, kissing his forehead, his cheeks, his neck, then in the next moment abruptly put him down on the floor where he would burst out crying. She might at any moment say to her husband, "You never stand up for me," then, turning away and turning back, say, her voice from deep in her throat, "Oh, where would I be without you?" In the afternoons, she went to her bedroom to try to nap, but voices screeched everywhere, like the high white heat made audible. She said to Daniel, "I'm not used to a family any more." She put her hand to her forehead.

Richard and his family left, but the black spot remained, floating about in the great stunned silence and spaciousness. She, for days, followed that spot and wandered about as she had while Richard and his family had been there. The father didn't try to stop her. He let her wander about the grounds as, in the evening after he got home from work, he sat out under the birch trees or, when he got back from a political meeting late in the evening, watched her change from chair to chair in the living room, walking to the fireplace, then to the large window, then to the closed door, between rising from one chair to sitting in another. His expression, as he watched her closely, was of a tense, grim suppression of pain. From the way she would all at once stop, if outside, to look at a maple tree or a squirrel, or inside, at a lampshade or ashtray, Daniel thought she was, in fact, fixing the spot on whatever she at that moment chose. He noted that his father went rigid whenever she paused, as if holding his breath, and he appeared to breathe again only when she continued to move. Evening after evening, he would say, calmly, "Try to sit still." She seemed not to hear him. Then she would suddenly say, "Don't think about me. You've got your work, which I haven't asked you about in a long time, isn't that so? And there's your campaign, you have to think of your campaign. Are you able to think?" He'd say, staring at her as if pleading with her to relieve him of the grim pain, "I must try to." "Yes." "I've got to, I've got to." She would sit and say, "Tell me what you're going to do for the campaign. Tell me. Will it be like the last one, the one in 1938? Tell me." As he told her, in a voice raspy with fatigue, her eyes stared.

One evening, as he advanced towards her from the car she as always went to meet, she saw he was holding his left hand up, and about his index finger was a bloody handkerchief tied like a bundle. She cried out, but drew back. Edmond got out of the driver's seat of the car and said, "He wouldn't see a doctor, he's as stubborn as ever." Jim kissed her and said, "I cut off the tip with a buzz saw."

The blood drained from her face, and she felt weak. She didn't want to look at it, but he was holding it up. The handkerchief was soaked with blood.

"It'll be all right," he said.

She followed behind him as they walked slowly up to the

house. In the bathroom, she unbuttoned his shirt and carefully drew the left sleeve, the cuff stained with blood, over his hand. He winced. She untied the knot in the handkerchief and gently unwound it. The gauze was oozing with blood, and she now winced as she unwrapped it. He asked, quietly, as if speaking out loud would add unnecessarily to the pain, "Could you boil me some hot water?" She ran to the kitchen, Daniel and Julien stood motionless just outside the bathroom door. Blood flowed down the father's wrist and down his arm. He waited, as motionless as the boys, until his wife rushed back into the bathroom with a steaming kettle. She rinsed the basin with the boiling water, plugged it, then poured. The steam rose up about her and her husband, and, in the steam, she turned to look at the exposed finger for the first time, and shouted, "Jim!"

He said, "You'd better go out of the bathroom."

"No," she said, but her eyes narrowed as she tried to look.

"I've cut off the tip and some of the nail."

"Oh!"

He reached his index finger out as if he were going to touch something and submerged it in the water. He drew in his breath with a slight hiss through his teeth. He agitated his finger.

"But will that do any good?" Reena asked. "How do you know?"

"Could you get more hot water for me?" he asked.

He was up all night, alone in the kitchen at the table, his finger raised. He wiped the running blood from his hand and waited for it to clot about the wound. Often, Reena came downstairs and found him, his elbow on the table, his bloody finger pointing upwards, his head sloughed forward, his bathrobe slipped from his shoulders. He raised his head each time she came in and said, "Go to sleep," and she drew the bathrobe around him before she left. With dawn, the finger began to throb. The aching throb reassured him. He walked about, his hand, as always, up, and after a couple of hours more, by the time Edmond came down, he lowered it.

189

His wife said, "But you won't go to work today," he said, "I'll be all right." She had to help him dress.

Daniel, reading, sensed all day that there was something behind his reading which he had forgotten, and which his reading tried to make him remember. He would fall out of his reading from time to time, fall out the back of it, not on to the screened porch with the scalloped edges of its green awnings flapping, but on to something beyond the book, something to which the book kept giving way. He put down the book. He thought: it wasn't anything he could remember, or wasn't anything he'd forgotten, because he hadn't seen it: his father at work. Not only could Daniel not visualize him having the accident, he could not visualize him at his work. He tried to imagine his father, now, unable to work with his left hand, holding it up and away from his work. He couldn't imagine him, but the sense, the deep sense of him working in a deep dimension, deeper than anything Daniel was in contact with in his book, stayed with him all day, and he could only think of that sense, abstractly, as a sense of loss. Behind the book, behind the screens, behind the trees, behind the lake and the sky, he thought as he walked about outside, there was some great emptiness, and his father, out there, was working in it.

He walked with Julien the twisting length of the dirt road to meet his father returning from work with Edmond. They reached the paved country road, where there were battered mailboxes nailed to posts and on the other side of the road an apple orchard. They waited for the car and, in case Edmond might have driven right past them, hailed it with outstretched arms. Edmond stopped and they got into the back seat. The father said nothing to them, and when Daniel asked, "How is your finger?" he simply held it up, wrapped in a gauze bandage that was spotted at the top with a red black stain.

Daniel felt something go dark in him when his father said, to no one in particular, "In five more days we go back to the city."

190

Daniel got out of the car and walked away before his mother came to it. He walked by the lake. He saw, where he hadn't seen anything of it before, bits of broken glass along the drive, rusty tin cans, and coils of rusted wire in the bushes, and bald bicycle tires half sunk in the lake mud. He went to the island and there went from tree to tree, in brightness or in darkness, with a sick feeling. He pressed his chest against a pine tree, and leaned a little to the side and gently hit the trunk of the tree with both hands clenched into fists. Resin stuck to his chest when he pulled away from the tree.

He avoided his father over the next days, and he avoided his mother too, and Julien and Edmond.

They left on Saturday afternoon, the two densely loaded cars swaying with the ruts in the road.

IX

JIM FRANCOEUR was leaving the house, his face clean-shaven, dressed in a dark suit and dark overcoat, his fedora perfectly shaped (the crown tucked in about the top, then pinched at the front to form a peak, two hollows, like the hollows of large temples, on either side of the peak, the brim raised in the back and lowered to the level of the eyes in front and shadowing his face: a millinery style so complex it was explained only in part by settling the hat on or removing it by the conveniently pre-pinched peak), his wide tie knotted in a very small knot high up between the stiff wings of his white collar, his shoes polished black, on his way to a political meeting.

André saw his father open the kitchen door, and suddenly, with a twang in his voice, said, "Dad, how about me coming with you?" The father said from a remoteness, "If you want." The father sat in the rocking chair, his overcoat and hat on, not rocking, nervously, repeatedly separating his lips to wait for André to get dressed. The mother watched him waiting, and knew he didn't want his son to go with him to an abandoned grocery shop near the river in an Italian neighbourhood, rented at a very low rent, which they called their party headquarters. On leaving for the meeting, the father didn't kiss the mother, who stood at the door wishing she could make a sign to André which he would understand was meant to keep him back, saying, perhaps, he'd forgotten there was a radio broadcast he had to hear.

About three hours later, the mother, while reading the

newspaper spread open on the kitchen table, heard André's voice in the back entry, high-pitched as though he had been talking without stop since they'd left the meeting. The father came into the kitchen first, André behind, still talking, saying, "And the very first thing that ought to be done is that that place should be cleaned up a little, it's so dirty, and repainted a little, it's so dilapidated," while the father, nodding his head slightly, took off his hat and overcoat, and went into his room. He perhaps expected that when he got back into the kitchen, he would find André had become involved in his music, but André was all set to continue to say what he had to say, reprimanding with an unrelenting high pitch not the father but the organization, and the father had to sit and, his face set in a permanent wince, listen. "It's not that no one said anything intelligent," André said, "or that what was said was fatuous," (the father would not have understood that word) "it was that no one seemed to have anything to say at all, and I kept wondering, sitting in my broken chair, well, now, what's the point of this meeting? What's the point of it?" André paused.

The father stared at André, then said, "You're asking me what the point of the meeting is. Well, you know, I'm a Republican. You know, when anyone asks me why I'm a Republican, I say, it has nothing to do with me. I used to think, not long ago, I used to think that if I could work for myself, and not work for anybody, not be an employee, and, too, not have anyone work for me, not be an employer, I would be able to work, really work. I've had ideas of tools I wanted to make. I thought, once, that I'd have a shop of my own to make those tools. My father once invented a tool with a glass blade, and with it he could join two boards together in a skirting, the skirting of a semi-circular bow-window alcove, could join them so smoothly no one could tell where the join was. I don't say anything about this at the meetings, about work. The old curé is right in one respect, you know: work is holy. No, not any more. I want a rally to take place in a mill, an abandoned mill—"

"The mills were prisons, though, Dad, and no one can regret a prison closing down—"

The father didn't say any more; his jaw set.

"And who says the Republican Party is particularly devoted to the holiness of work? They're more dedicated to the holiness of capital, because without that you can't work—"

The father said, "Well, tsi gars, it's late," and, perhaps thinking that, though he had explained himself clearly, he hadn't been understood, he went to bed.

The mother said to André, "You shouldn't have gone."

André said, "I wanted to see what it was all about."

The mother quickly said, "You don't understand."

"Oh, he's intelligent, more intelligent than any of his sons," André said.

"Yes," the mother said.

"You know," André said, "I found out something about my father this evening I'd never before seen—"

The mother was a little worried. "What?"

"Well, you know, I'm a rather practical person, after all—"

The mother waited.

"But he's not practical. I used to think his greatest strength was his sense of practicality. In fact, he's more extravagant than I ever was at my moment of greatest enthusiasm in wanting to be an opera singer. What does Dad want?"

The mother raised her hand, fingers separated, to her mouth.

As she walked home from grocery-shopping in the rain, she saw multiple images of her husband all about her on handouts and small posters, saw the eyes of her husband stare at her from a curb, from a puddle, from the base of a tree trunk, from among a pile of sodden leaves, from the street under the bumper of a parked car, from a telephone pole, and the eyes disoriented her. They demanded that she vote for ARSACE (JIM) FRANCOEUR FOR REPUBLICAN DISTRICT

194

REPRESENTATIVE, vote for him FOR GOOD CLEAN GOVERN-
MENT. She could hardly expect that the man who would
come home from work later, who would kiss her, who would
sit at the table, would be the same man as the one in the
littered photographs; and yet of course they were the
same, and the private man she knew made public embarrassed her, and the strange public man made private (talking
at supper with a measured grandiloquence, telephoning
people the wife did not know, coming home late) made her
uneasy.

After the rain stopped, and while she, in the wet sunlight,
was hanging sheets on the sagging line in the back yard, her
brother Lawrence came, stepping through the weeds that
had grown high during the summer. Lawrence was State
Inspector of Insurance, was a Democrat, and worked under
the white dome of the State House. His hair was parted in a
very straight line just slightly to the left of the middle of his
head, and it was cut so close round the sides his skull showed,
and on top was combed flat.

She believed what her brother Lawrence told her because
she understood him without having, really, to understand
him, understood, that is, his tone of voice, a clear even tone
that she recalled was her father's tone of voice. (Like Lawrence, her father had above all always been reasonable. He
had said to her when she announced to him, to him first,
then to her mother, that she had accepted a proposal from
Jim Francoeur, "Now let's talk about this, let's talk about
this," and she'd listened to him talk. He had been against
her marrying Jim—or, as he called him, James—and he
explained why he was against the marriage: not that James
was not a good man, a good worker, an attractive man, but
that he thought in a different way from the way she was
used to. She had not understood then; she'd said she felt
safe with him. Her father'd tried to explain; he didn't act,
James, by thinking everything out first. But, she'd said, she
wasn't intelligent, wasn't herself capable of being very
reasonable. Her father had said, "Well, just consider this:

195

you and I are talking, in a calm way, about your marriage, we're trying to understand it, we're trying to be reasonable about it, aren't we?" She nodded. He continued, "And do you think he, James, is having the same conversation with either of his parents? No, he isn't. I know them, I know what they're like. It wouldn't occur to James to talk about his marriage with his parents, or even talk to himself about it. He wants to marry you on—" "What?" Aricie asked. Her father shook his head. She had understood, without quite being able to understand, her father, whose voice she heard as she listened to Lawrence.) Lawrence said, calmly, a little sadly, as she stretched the sheets across the line, "He doesn't understand, Reena, and has never understood." Aricie asked, "Did you come to tell me this?" He said, "I don't want you to get hurt, you're my sister." Aricie said, "He's my husband." "Well, protect him. Don't let him get his hopes up too high. After what happened to him at the file shop, he must be putting a lot of hope into winning this election, and, you know, there's no chance that he'll win." "Oh, I know," she said, "a French Canadian immigrant with a grammar-school diploma. He says to everyone: in *those* days a grammar-school diploma was something." "Think of his competition." Aricie smiled and said, "He wants so much."

So much, she thought, in the back entry taking off her rubbers, and none of it comprehensible to her. She might have understood if he thought politics would get him into, say, her younger brother Lawrence's world, a world geographically located across the river, on the East Side of Providence, on a steep hill where white colonial houses with black shutters lined the narrow streets, where old brick Brown University was situated, where the expensive doctors had their offices; but she was more aware of the East Side as a separate world than her husband, if he was aware of it at all, and if he was aware, he might have thought there was nothing there that interested him.

On the kitchen table was a neat pile of handouts. She

196

picked one up. He was smiling in the picture. His jaw was square. His hair was grey at the temples. His ear lobes were long, his eyes were black. Staring at the photo, she half expected to see his expression change, as it changed often, the flesh of his face drawn back as if all at once pulled at the back of his head, from a smile to taut expressionlessness.

At the lunch break at La Salle Academy Daniel sat by himself in the high-school dining room, at the end of a long table. At the other end, close together, were five classmates, who held bananas so they curved up, then quickly turned them over so they curved down, then up again. They were laughing. One student held two small oranges in one hand and the banana in the other, and stood the end of the banana between the oranges and shook it. The others laughed, but not too loudly. Daniel watched them.

After lunch, he put on his coat and walked about the school grounds. The large evergreen shrubs blew in the wind. He walked to the tennis courts, then to the baseball pitch where the white chalk diamond had been almost obliterated by rain. He looked out over the puddle-filled field until he heard the bell for the end of lunch break, and he turned back to the school. He saw the group of classmates who had been playing with the bananas and oranges in the dining room now standing behind a big evergreen bush. They were jumping up and down, laughing. They hit one another's shoulders. They didn't seem to have heard the bell. Daniel paused for a moment to look at them. One of them saw him watching them, and they all looked round, then disbanded.

Daniel joined the students gathering at the back entrance of the school. He studied them. He wondered how he would approach a couple, the two brightest in the class, who were talking to one another, or three leaning towards one another to see a photograph one of them held up. On the edge of the paved area, turned away, a classmate was standing alone. Daniel went to the edge of the pavement and looked over the scruffy lawn, where all students were forbidden to step. He glanced at the boy standing near him. He had many tiny pimples that studded his face, and many more blackheads, and sometimes yellow pus wriggled out of the pimples; his stiff hair was greasy black and plastered to his head; his tie was always dirty and the underarms of his shirts were always yellow. He was Italian, and no one ever spoke to him, and Daniel was aware that he was approaching him now just because no one ever spoke to him. Daniel said, "I wish the grass were water, and it were hot, and I could dive into it," and the boy, at first startled, frowned as Daniel said directly to him, "I'd race you to the other side and back," then the boy, with difficulty, it appeared, opening his huge mouth and large teeth, said, "Fuck off," and Daniel simply stared at him for a moment before he turned and left. He went immediately to the three students who were looking at a photograph and asked if he too could see it. The photograph was handed to him. It was of the three students in bathing suits, at the edge of the lake. Daniel handed it back. They were waiting for him to say something, but he left them.

In history class, half listening to Brother Aloysius describe the qualities of an ancient Roman, he wondered what the qualities were which his schoolmates shared, which someone in the future might describe as the qualities of a La Salle boy, and why he, who most likely wouldn't have been able to get along with the ancient Romans either, did not have those qualities which would have made it possible for him to get along with the boys? Why did he, in a very clear way, stand outside them? *Why* wasn't he interested in cars, in baseball and football, in blow jobs, in smoking, in beer?

He couldn't talk to his classmates about new car models or about the scores of big-league teams or who blew what guy in the locker room or ask for or offer a cigarette or say what his favourite brand of beer was, and that he couldn't all at once amazed him. He could only wonder how it had happened that he should be completely apart. He knew he was, in the most basic way, utterly uncultured, for he had no interests at all.

When he got out of school, it was drizzling, and he walked the long way home slowly, up hill, as La Salle Academy was outside the parish. Near his house, he saw a handout announcing his father's candidacy in a heap of red leaves raked together in a gutter. He picked it up and continued walking, his books under one arm and the publicity photograph of his father in the other hand to study it.

His mother was standing at the kitchen table, she too studying a handout, as he came in with the one he had picked up from the street.

She said, "My brother Lawrence said he won't win."

But when he saw his father, one Saturday morning in the hardware shop (Daniel and Julien went with him to buy glass to replace a pane broken on one of the storm windows), talking to the owner behind the counter and three other men who had come in to buy screws and nails, a flash came to Daniel, like a camera flash, of his father as a politician. His father was talking about the mills closing down and the reasons, but it wasn't what the father was talking about that revealed him to Daniel all at once as a politician, it was the way he talked: standing at a centre formed by the other men, both hands raised, palms open and outward, in a gesture of complete openness and honesty, and also a gesture to keep them there motionless, and talking rapidly. The two who had little bags of nails or screws wanted to leave, Daniel saw, and the man who had come in after the father had begun to speak wanted to buy what he'd come for, and the owner of the hardware shop wanted to sell him what he'd come for. But the father kept them where they were, and the father, by talking to them when it was obvious that they didn't want to listen, was doing just the opposite to what he no doubt intended; instead of getting them to agree with him, he was causing them to disagree with him—Daniel saw this in their expressions, in the way they shifted their bodies impatiently from one foot to the other—even if they might have agreed with him. Daniel wanted to stop him each time he saw two of the men glance at one another, or one of the men raise his finger and open his mouth, and say, "Mr Lambert and Mr Dandeneau have to go," or "You should give Mr Laplante a chance to say what he wants to say." Daniel worked himself up to the point of saying his mother would be waiting, and this happened: he saw the men become attentive, saw their faces and bodies become motionless, as though one word the father said had transfixed them, and Daniel became aware of their stances in relation to the stance of his father, became aware of their feet, of the knee-bulges of their trousers, of their set bodies, their arms to their sides, their eyes turned to his father, whose feet were planted one before the other, whose body appeared to be in torsion, whose eyes went from one to the other, who pointed to the floor, to the ceiling, out the large window of the store where there were galvanized garbage cans, rakes, snow shovels, and whose voice was now low, monotonous, like a motor which, once started, turned over and over on its own, would go on and on, taking the listeners with it. To Daniel it seemed a very long distance that his father took the men, but then he realized it was only the length of a moment, and again the men began to shift, to glance around, and the one who had come in to buy a pair of pliers turned away completely, then the others turned away. Arsace said goodbye to each one by his first name and they, now facing the counter, looked over their shoulders and raised their hands and said, "Take care, Jim."

He went early to a rally, so his place at the supper table was empty.

The mother said, "I couldn't see myself there with all those people, even though I know that I should have gone, that he wanted me to go."

Whereas the mother knew she would be uncomfortable at the rally—she had been, in 1938, to two—either because she wouldn't know anyone there or because communication with the two or three she would know wouldn't be in private terms but in the public terms of the rally which, like an overriding principle of government, made everyone there "people", and she could never be comfortable among "people", she knew her husband was at ease there, and he was at ease just because of the abstract, overriding principle, to which he was dedicated.

Edmond said, "Well, I've been campaigning for him. I said to everyone at the ice-cream parlour, I said they should vote for my father."

"What did they say?" Julien asked.

"They said they would, sure thing."

"They said the same to me," the mother said, "and I don't believe it."

"Believe what?" Daniel asked.

"I don't know."

"That he'll win?" Edmond asked. "Sure he'll win. You wait and see. He'll be going down there to Washington, shaking hands with the President himself, down there."

"You know," the mother said, "he's not a popular man, your father. You've got to be popular to win. He's in a false position, trying to act on a popularity he doesn't have. My brother Lawrence told me that. He also said the Republican Party is using him to get a few French Canadian votes, there are no French Canadians who ever try to get into politics, he said, and that makes your father an exception, I suppose, but he's not a popular exception, he's a strange exception, and everybody knows that when he tries to be popular he's being false."

"False?" Daniel asked.

"I wouldn't want to see him at the rally."

"Why?" Daniel asked.

She said, "He doesn't know how to act in a natural way."

"Yes," Daniel said, a sudden blush rising throughout him as if he too had just been caught acting, though all he was doing was mashing his potatoes flat with his fork.

"Well," the mother said, "he says I don't support him. Well, should I act too?"

"Mr Lévêque said to me," Edmond said, "he said to me, 'Edmond, your father is the kind of man we need, strong, I'm going to vote for him.'"

When the father came into the living room the mother turned the radio off, and he, standing above them, said, "The Republican candidate for mayor attended to hear, and he said to me after my speech, 'We'll win'—"

"Did he understand the French?" the mother asked.

"I gave the speech in English."

"We never speak French any more," the mother said.

Daniel thought: their French had fallen away, as if it had happened in a moment. He went to his bedroom to sit at the little table at which he studied. He thought how his mother used to say, just as one of them was about to cry, "Il va broyer du noir!", or when she was complimented by a son on a pretty housedress, "C'est une vieille guenille," the double "ll" pronounced as a hard "g"; and to say that something Daniel or Julien wanted was too expensive, the father used to say, "I don't have that many piastres," or he said to a son, "You've got to get your hairs cut"; and the sons used the verb "puer" as an English verb, "I pue, you pue, he pues"; and everyone in the family, in writing, gave many words, especially verbs, final "e"s, as "controle", "develope", "considere".

Religion was French, Jésus Christ was a French name. Whenever he heard the name in English, even when spoken by the Irish Christian Brothers at La Salle, who made faces at the few freshmen from the French parish who did not know their prayers in English, Jesus Christ in English always sounded to him, no matter how pious the intention, like blasphemy.

French was a private language, the language of his religion. English was the public language in which he would have to work, and religion and work, like Church and State, were separate. No one in the English State, for which he would have to work, for which he would have to fight wars, would care what he felt in French.

He went into the living room where his parents were listening to the Republican candidate for mayor make a brief paid political broadcast on the radio. The mother said, looking up from the radio which she had been watching with a blank look, "Daniel, your father and I have been talking, we're going to get together, all of us, to support him." Daniel cringed. She added, "After all, shouldn't his word be law?"

When Albert, on a hop from his Stateside base, came home on a short leave to vote, the father didn't rise from his chair to shake his hand.

Albert asked, "How's it going, Dad?"

"All right." The father stood. Albert stepped towards him. The father looked at his watch and said, "I've got to get ready to go to a meeting."

Albert sat with his mother at the kitchen table. He looked about the kitchen, then back at his mother. He said, "I've got some jokes for you, Momma."

He used words the at-home family had never heard—nebulous, ubiquitous—and it was obvious that, away from home, he not only spoke with great sophistication, he swore. At home, he didn't. His father didn't even use the words "hell" and "damn", though the mother would. Albert used the words "shit" and "fart", as if he knew, though they were never used by anyone else in the house, they were allowed by him to tell jokes to his mother.

The mother laughed as she hadn't laughed in months. It was as though Albert had come all the way home to tell his mother the jokes. He didn't speak of anything else, didn't even ask about the house in the country. Albert leaned towards his mother and at times—when he wanted to tell a punch line he thought the boys shouldn't hear—he whispered, and the whisper was transformed into a saliva-shattering burst of laughter from the mother. The mother was aware that she was listening to and laughing at his jokes at a risk, but she wouldn't, she didn't want to, guard herself by drawing away from Albert. Her laughter increased with each joke. All his recent experiences were, it seemed, contained in these jokes.

The humour—that awareness of a delicately sustained load of shit above them, both of them excited by the danger of it collapsing on them—continued after the father returned and they sat down to supper, though, at supper, Albert didn't tell any jokes, as he knew his father wouldn't approve; but the spirit of the jokes had got into their most commonplace talk, and all Albert would have to say was "Something smells" for the mother to blurt out a more than half-stifled laugh. Edmond, from his end of the table, kept saying, "Geez, you two," and would try to laugh. The boys, not quite understanding, looked at their mother, then the father, who ate with his head lowered. The mother shook her head as if to shake out of her whatever was in her that made her laugh, and said, "Now that's enough." There was a strained silence. She tapped the end of her nose and said, "Hey, Al." Albert looked at her and again they both burst out laughing. The mother said, "All I was doing was tapping the tip of my nose. What's so funny about that?" Another strained silence. She lightly scratched the side of her nose. Another burst of laughter. "What's so funny?" she asked, as if amazed herself that she should be laughing. The spirit of the humour had become so rarefied all she had to do now was to sniff loud, for her and Albert, and Edmond and the boys too, to break out laughing. She had taken over completely from Albert. She said to him, "I dare you to look at my nose without laughing." Albert tried. The mother laughed before he did, her eyes watering, then, drawing her laughter back as with her breath, she said, "Let's stop this. We've gone far enough. Your father doesn't like it," but, half glancing at him first, she covered the half of her face towards her husband with a splayed-out hand and pointed with the other hand at him, hunched over and dumb-mouthed, "He doesn't like me to joke, but he can't see me," and the father, looking at her for a long time, his eyes narrowed, suddenly, lightly smiled as at a girl who, for a long while darkly dispirited, had all at once recovered her health. It was Albert who said, "Come on, that's enough." The mother lowered her hand.

The father said, tilting his head to the side, "I know a joke."

"What?" Reena said.

The father said, "Why is it unnecessary that a man should ever go hungry as long as he has feet?"

The family frowned.

The mother said, "Well, he can walk to a shop."

"No," the father said, "he doesn't have any money."

"He can steal and run," Daniel said.

"He would never do that."

"He can run a grocery," Albert said.

"No," the father answered quickly, perhaps not understanding, and answered, "He can always eat his corns."

With a unanimous disgust they wouldn't have expressed at the fart and shit jokes, the family said, "Ugh."

The father smiled broadly.

The mother remained high-spirited, as though supporting her husband in his election campaign were itself something of a joke, which was what he wanted from her; her way of supporting him, she knew, was entirely in her attitude, not towards his politics, but towards him, for she knew that whenever she was in a low grey state he became low and grey as well, and when she was light-spirited, even joky, he was sure that everything was all right. Her laughter reassured him, her saying, "When your father becomes District Representative, we'll put a big chandelier in the bathroom," made him confident.

On Election Day, he, his wife, Albert, Edmond, and Daniel and Julien went early to the polling station, in a classroom in a public high school. Daniel and Julien couldn't go further than a man and woman sitting just inside the classroom at tables with large registers in which they checked off names, but they were able to see into the room. The classroom was stark, the backboard washed and matt black, the desks pushed to the back wall, and at the front of the classroom, where the teacher's desk should have been, was a voting booth.

The mother went in first. The curtain of the booth, with a little jerk, closed, but her feet showed. In a moment the curtain jerked open, and she stepped out smiling, her look that of someone who had done something inside which no one outside would have suspected.

The father went in with a businesslike brusqueness, and yet with the solemnity of knowing that this most private act behind a curtain would have vast consequences, and the most immediate consequence would be that he himself would change from being a private person into a public person; his vote, if no others, would win him the election. The curtain shut with a clank. Behind it, simply by pressing the lever, something would happen and he would come out different from when he went in, so everyone would look, stunned, at him; what in him had been most private, what in him had been most secret, would, revealed, make public his dark body. The curtain opened as soon as it shut, and the father was already turned round to step out, but he seemed to hesitate in the shadow of the booth.

Daniel, with a kind of panic that came over him as he stared at his father, thought: No, no, I don't want him to win, I don't want him to win. And then, suddenly, some other feeling, deeper than his panic, took him over, and he thought with a greater sense of urgency, as if someone's life or death depended on it: yes, his father must win, yes, he must. He loved his father, he loved his large, strong, public father stepping out of the voting booth.

He came out of his bedroom the next morning to find his father taking from the open drawers of his desk in the living room papers, envelopes, leaflets, and he followed him to the cellar furnace, beside which was a pile of more papers, thin notebooks of his punctuationless 1938 speeches, yellowed newspapers, old handouts, stacks of printed envelopes, rolled up and flattened posters, a couple of telegrams, incidental additions like a catalogue of ball bearings or a manual on repairing old radios, a book called *Famous Speeches*, and he opened the furnace door and threw in a sheaf of papers.

Daniel pulled out political comic books from the pile to read them while his father threw the papers into the furnace; on the front of one was a drawing of a soldier in a foxhole, his helmet shading his face, his carbine raised ready, and the foxhole was in the middle of a well-kept lawn in front of a clapboard house, a small house with a hedge, and the caption read A FOXHOLE IN YOUR FRONT YARD. Another was captioned FROM YALTA TO KOREA. He threw the comics into the furnace, on to a heap of papers curling black at their edges; they remained intact for a moment, then, noiseless bombs, they exploded into flames.

Albert came downstairs. He stood for a while by the furnace and looked in as the father threw in batch after batch.

Albert said, "You know, Dad—"

His father stood up straight and looked at him.

Albert said, "What you are can't be altered by your losing an election, not for us. You probably thought, off and on, that we didn't take much interest in your campaign—Philip and André not coming home to vote, not sending telegrams or telephoning—but, in fact, we all know you're above winning or losing."

The father threw into the flames the batch of papers he was holding. "When are you leaving?" he asked.

"Today."

"I wanted to show you the accounts I've been keeping of the payments on the mortgage," the father said.

At the ice-cream parlour on Sunday afternoon, Mr Lévêque asked Edmond how his father was, and Edmond said, "Oh, fine." A very tall and fat young man with a baseball cap on and, though it was a bright day, rubbers on his enormous feet, asked, "Hey, Edmond, is it true about your father?" Edmond was friendly with everyone; he said,

"What's that, Bill?" Bill's feet were pointed in opposite directions, and his long lower legs slanted outwards as though his knees were jointed to bend sideways; he moved his feet further apart and smiled, his fat lips swelling. "Is he going to run for ass-wiper to the Republican Party in the next election?" There were five other people in the ice-cream parlour, standing at, some leaning on, the fountain; they all laughed, Mr Lévêque too, and after a moment Edmond did also. "I don't know, Bill," he said. "You should ask him." "Well," Bill said, "he wouldn't win." Edmond looked at the ice-cream parlour owner, unshaven, his apron tied high about his waist, his arms crossed, then he looked at those near him; he said, "Hell, I knew he wasn't going to win." "He didn't have a chance," Mr Lévêque said. "Twenty-two votes." "I knew that," Edmond said, his black eyes large. Bill said, "Have an ice-cream soda on me, Ed, and we'll celebrate." Edmond leaned an elbow on the fountain. "Make mine vanilla," he said. The owner prepared the ice-cream soda. Edmond reached for it, his fingers and nails black with printer's ink; he mixed the ice cream and the soda with the long spoon, but stopped and looked at Bill. "Aren't you having one?" he asked. Bill laughed, his heavy bare jowls, like a woman's soft ass, went up and down, and he said, "No one asked me if I wanted one." Edmond stared at his ice-cream soda; he didn't know what to do with it. He said, "Well, here, have this one," and handed it to Bill, who took it and drank it down, taking the melting lump of ice cream in one mouthful. He handed the empty glass, in its metal container, back to Edmond, and said, "That was yours, now where's mine?" Edmond said to the owner, "Give him what he wants." "Make it strawberry," Bill said. He drank it down, his lower legs splayed farther apart. Everyone looked at him, then looked at Edmond fumbling in his pocket for change to pay for the ice-cream sodas. He said he had to go.

At home, his mother got him alone in the pantry where he had gone for a glass of water and asked him, "Why've you come back so soon?" He shook his head, swallowed, and said, "Oh, there wasn't anyone there." "What were they saying?" Edmond said, with a passionate burst, "I told them, I said, if my father had won that election, they'd know about it, he'd do what none of them, not one of them, had the guts to do. I got real angry." "You didn't," the mother said. Edmond looked away. "I wanted to," he said.

The father spent all Sunday afternoon at his desk, his eyeglasses splattered with paint, his hands nicked, carefully studying the checks received from his sons before he added them up and subtracted the sums from the mortgage owed.

Part Two

X

THE WINDOWS OF the high house, closed up, reflected the winter sun setting over the frozen lake. While Edmond, inside, turned on the steam heat so the house would be warm when, two days later, the family all came to the country, Daniel and Julien walked by the lake. Near the shore they saw black water lapping under clear ice; they walked out on to the frozen lake, to where the ice was blue-grey and crackled and crumbled in long rifts. They walked out far enough to look back at the house with its burning windows, and all about, but for the tall green pines, were trees apparently burned black and brown by an immense cold fire. It was very strange to stand where for summer after summer they had swum. The wind blew dry oak leaves across the ice, leaves which months before had made the trees familiar. The only season the country had for Daniel was summer; nothing happened in the country during those summers which he was not unaware of, which he didn't in some way control: not a leaf turning in the morning breeze, not a fish breaking water in the evening. They walked over the ice to the bridge, crouched to walk under the planks of the bridge, walked along the side of the island. He had so often walked the length of the island and looked out at the lake; now, walking on the solid lake, he looked in at the island, through the bare bushes spotted with red berries to stone outcroppings and bare fallen tree trunks. A fine longing passed across his chest, up the back of his neck.

Julien said, "I'm going back to the car."

Daniel walked on alone for a while, not stepping, really, but shuffling his boots across the smooth ice, until a blast of wind forced him to turn his back against it, and he returned to the car. Julien wasn't in it. He went to the house, in through the garage, and found Edmond in the boiler room, standing by the oil burner and staring at it.

Edmond said, "Albert writes that we should all spend Thanksgiving at the lake, but who has to prepare everything for everyone? Me. Dad wouldn't."

"Dad said he'd come."

"That's because Albert said he would. If I said that to Dad, he wouldn't do it."

"Where's Julien?"

"I don't know. I think he's gone upstairs."

The frozen air in the house was thick and dark. The floors creaked. Daniel found Julien in his bedroom, asleep on the bare mattress, his overcoat, cap, gloves, boots on. A beam of late sunlight from between the edge of the drawn blind and the window frame streaked diagonally across the floor, across Julien, and up the wall opposite where it flamed in a mirror. Daniel looked at his brother asleep. His mouth was open, his head bent to the side as if his neck was broken, his eyes were a little open. Daniel left the room to find a blanket in a hall closet, then came back to cover his brother. As he was covering him, Julien woke.

Daniel said, "I thought you might be cold."

"No," Julien said, "no," and he got up.

As they drove back into the city the evening darkened.

André telephoned from the train station in Providence to ask Edmond if he'd come downtown to pick him up. Edmond half shouted, "Oh, sure thing, my brother, sure thing!" but when he hung up he said, generally, "They expect me to do everything. They go off, they do what they want, but when they come home who has to go and pick them up, who has to do everything for them? Me."

Daniel and Julien went downtown with Edmond. André, who hadn't been home since he left business administration and joined the Navy, was standing in the light of a street lamp outside the railway station, wearing a dark Navy over-coat and a white cap. He raised both hands high in greetings and laughed.

And when, the day before Thanksgiving, the father and mother, Edmond, André and the boys were eating supper in the dining room of the still-chilly lake house, the telephone rang, the father rose from the table and answered, and Philip said he was in the house in the city where he'd expected them to be, had let himself in with his key when he found the house locked, and he asked if Ed could come down to the city for him; the father hung up and said to Edmond, "Philip is waiting for you to pick him up," and Edmond drew his lips deep into his cheeks and released his breath through his teeth. His mother said, "They're grateful, Edmond, we're all grateful for what you do."

André said, running his hand through his short hair as if he still had the wave, "Ed, you're a great guy, a really great, a really really great guy."

The father said, "I'll go too."

Edmond knew that even though his father said he'd go and could himself drive, Edmond couldn't ask him to pick up Philip.

"I want to have a look at the house in the city," the father said.

"But we left it just a couple of hours ago," the mother said.

"I want to have another look."

They found Philip sitting in the kitchen rocker in the dim yellow glow of the ceiling light. His Air Force bag was beside him. He immediately rose, pulled down the jacket of his lieutenant's uniform flat against his chest, and, his cap wedged under his left arm, he held out his right hand to shake his father's hand, and held it while both men smiled at one another. The father said, "You're welcome back." "Thanks," Philip said. Edmond clasped his brother's hand in both his and shook it, not up and down, but from side to side, and said, "Gee whiz, gee whiz, my younger brother," and tears rose to his eyes.

The father left them to go from room to room, opening and closing closet doors, looking in the front entry, raising blinds to look out, as if the dark outside, seen from the inside, were an extension of the inside he must check. Edmond and Philip waited.

In the car, Edmond said, "So you'll finally be seeing the house in the country."

"Right," Philip said.

"You'll see what your money's been buying."

Philip said, "I didn't send my last contribution, I brought it to give it in person."

The father nodded.

Edmond said, "My contribution is to be the family errand boy, that's my work in the family—"

"You do a lot," Philip said.

"Oh, I do what I can. But you guys—you, Al, André, even Richard, all of you who're sending money to Dad every month—you do a lot too, and you're hardly ever here to enjoy what you do in the family. Look at me, I don't pay anything, and I'm at the house all summer long. You all, you should stay at home, you should enjoy what you're paying for."

"As long as the family's enjoying it," Philip said.

"Oh, we enjoy it, I'll tell you." Edmond began a long inventory of all the enjoyments they had had over the past summers, enjoyments which, he was sure, Philip was very much interested to hear about, as though the life of the family was to Philip naturally more important than his own life over the past years: one day Julien caught fifty bluegills, put them all in a bucket, then threw them back in; a duck laid two eggs in a nest under the dock; a squirrel got down the fireplace chimney one night and scared them all; they now had a motor boat—

Philip, half listening, half smiled.

His mother drew a chair out for him from the dining table

216

where she had set a place for him to eat, and where André and the two boys were already seated to be with him. His father said, "Don't you want to see the house first?" Philip looked at his mother, who said, "Go with your father."

She heard them walking about the house, heard her husband talk. They came into the kitchen finally, where she was, and the father and son stood facing one another.

"Oh yes," the father said, "I've got many a plan." (Daniel, also in the kitchen, wondered where his father had learned that "a plan".) "I'll redo the place. You'll hardly recognize it for what I'll do to it."

"You'll put so much work into it?" Philip asked.

"I want to. I want to make it really great, a really really great house. I know how to work on a house."

"Yes," Philip said.

The mother thought: her husband didn't care at all about Philip, wasn't even aware that it was Philip standing before him; Philip might have been any of the other sons, for his father's attitude towards him was the same towards them all, was to treat them all as one son.

His father finally let him go, went into the living room to read his papers, and Philip sat with the rest of his family. The mother said, "I want to know everything you didn't write in your letters."

She sat on the edge of his bed in his room while he unpacked. She noted that he had folded his clothes neatly in his bag, and that he placed them neatly in the drawers of the bureau. She thought: it was difficult to say how he stood apart from the other boys—perhaps, simply, he was neater than any of the others. He spoke of Texas, where he was stationed, in a neat self-contained way. His body, when he took off his shirt and trousers to change, was neat. There was a look on his face of concentration meant to keep his talk, his actions, his body neat.

He lay on the couch in the living room and, silent, listened to the others, about the fire, talk. His father too just listened, then in a little while went to bed. A cold draught blew across the floor, and the outside country darkness penetrated the walls, so the lamplight seemed to shine in outside darkness. The brothers went to bed. The mother sat by the fireplace in her robe and pinned up her hair and watched Philip, who she thought was asleep until she saw that his eyes were open. She approached the couch to say goodnight to him, and she surprised him, she imagined, by being someone he hadn't expected to speak to him. He was somewhere else, he was with someone else.

She asked, "What are you thinking?"

"Oh—," he said.

"I don't want to know anything that isn't my business." He smiled.

She said, "I only want to be sure you're not worried about anything."

"Do I look as if I'm worried?"

"I don't know."

He laughed a little. "No," he said, "I'm not worried."

"I'll go to bed," she said.

He said, "This house—Dad's very proud of it, isn't he?"

"He thinks a lot about it."

"Yes," Philip said.

As Richard stopped outside the house in his family-crowded station wagon on Thanksgiving morning and the doors flew open and children ran out in all directions, snow began to fall. Richard carried a large cardboard carton in his arms, and his wife Chuckie, followed by a child, carried a bundled baby, the last of seven children. Daniel and Julien went out to help empty the car of paper bags of apples and bananas, a big battered pot of soup with its cover tied on with twine, waxpaper-wrapped pumpkin pies, a mixing bowl of jellied cranberry sauce. The voices of the older children resounded by the lake.

The mother and Chuckie cooked, and the men wandered in and out of the kitchen. They stood at the steamed-up windows and looked out at the grey-white land, the grey-white lake, the bare grey-white trees. From time to time a child ran past a window, shouting, but the outside appeared empty and silent in its grey whiteness. The men left the kitchen to stand for a while in the living room, at the large steamed-up window there, through which the landscape was wan. They did not know how to settle into the house. Shoes and boots were piled in the corners of the living room and dining room, clothes were thrown over the backs of chairs, over the hall banister. And they did not know how to settle with one another, and talked to one another for a moment or two, at the foot of the stairs, crossing the living room, at a doorway, outside an occupied bathroom, before they relentlessly separated.

Edmond stood by the stove in the kitchen. "I want to eat at twelve o'clock," he said.

The mother said, "We can't eat before Albert arrives."

"I don't care, we always eat at twelve o'clock, and that's when I'm going to eat. They go, they come when they like. There're rules in this house, dinner at twelve o'clock. They can do what they want outside, but in here they've got to keep the rules."

André, at a kitchen window, said, "There's a taxi coming up the driveway."

The children were running after it. It stopped, and out of the back door stepped Albert, as on to a city sidewalk.

Edmond said, his voice heavy with offence, "But why didn't you telephone me? I'd have gone downtown to pick you up."

Albert said, "I wanted to get here by twelve o'clock, when I knew you'd want to have dinner."

They had to extend the dining room table at each end with card tables. The mother tried to make a whole table by spreading over the uneven tables two tablecloths, one with a flower print, the other a trellis pattern, which overlapped in the middle. They—the mother and father, the seven sons, the sister-in-law, the six children, and the baby in a collapsible high chair—sat down to: big gallon bottles of milk, saucers of radishes, glasses of celery stalks, saucers of small green pimento-stuffed olives, a mixing bowl of cranberry sauce, great bowls of heaped-up mashed potatoes and turnips, a bowl of turkey meat stuffing, the immense turkey on a platter, soup bowls of green beans and yellow wax beans, a plate piled high with slices of white bread, a stick of margarine on a saucer, big salt and pepper shakers, a sugar bowl. There were glasses of milk at the children's places, cups of tea with tea bags by the plates of the adults. Each one's shoulders were pressed against those on either side.

Albert said, just as the standing father was about to cut into the turkey, "I think we should say grace."

The mother, squeezed among the children at the card table, said,

"You do it, Albert."

"Oh no. Dad, you say grace."

The father frowned. "How about one of you boys doing it?"

"Richard, you're the oldest son, you do it," Albert said to his brother.

Richard drew away from the table. "No, no," he said, "no, I'm not the one for that."

"Come on," Albert said.

The two brothers looked at one another, and a sudden little smile, like a twinge in his mouth, his cheeks, about his eyes, passed across Richard's face. He continued to look at his brother. Another slight smile momentarily twisted his features. "All right," he said. He lowered his head. The others lowered their heads. Richard said, "Good drink, good meat, good God, let's eat." When they raised their heads, he was smiling broadly, and he smiled especially at Albert, uncertain, it seemed, of him, but Albert smiled.

The fireplace smoked. Edmond swung open and closed, open and closed, the door to the screened-in porch, trying to cause a draught, while André tried to pile the logs so they would burn clean. Philip told Edmond he was freezing them out, and Richard took the fire tongs from André and pushed the birch logs to the back of the bent andirons. The children, at floor level, read comic books spread out on the rug or banged toys against the floor boards. The father sat apart, at the end of the room opposite the fireplace, by the window, the small panes of which were piling with snow. Albert said to him, "Why don't you join us, Dad?" The father rose, as if stiff, and sat in a platform rocker by the fireplace, now burning clear.

Albert asked him, "Do you have any new ideas for the house?"

"Yes, yes, I do."

"What's that?"

The father clasped his hands against his waist. "I was thinking I'd make this living room larger by knocking down the wall between it and the porch to make them both into one big room—"

"You've given up the idea of converting the garage into a rumpus room for the kids?"

"Well, that's always a possibility. There's so much I want to do."

André, who was sitting on a hassock before the fire screen, said, "You've got all the time in the world to make it the best house in the world."

The father nodded.

"And even if you don't do anything to it," Richard said, "it's pretty good as it is."

"Oh yes."

"And a solid investment," André said.

"Yes, it is."

"Would you ever think of selling it?" Philip asked.

They all looked at him.

"Well, it's yours to sell, to do with as you want."

"Sell?"

"I mean, if you needed the money, needed a little capital. A bit of the mortgage has been paid off, hasn't it, enough to give you a few thousand dollars if you needed it for capital."

"For what?"

"Well, you always said you'd like to open a small hardware store in the parish."

The father looked at the fireplace. "There's a lot more of the mortgage to be paid off first."

"It'll be paid off sooner than you think," Albert said.

Edmond said, "I painted the boathouse last summer. That's more than anyone has done to the house. The whole place needs painting, if you ask me. And there's a leak in the roof."

Philip got up from his chair and stepped over the children to the couch where he lay down, a throw pillow under his head, and closed his eyes. The room filled with wood smoke.

Daniel said, "I'm going out for a walk."

Philip opened his eyes, "Where?"

"Up the Orchard Farm."

"I'll come with you," Philip said.

They walked along the snow-covered country road, under white branches; the grey-white ground was the same grey-white as the sky, and the thin snow seemed both to fall and to drift up through the grey-white air. It was not only the unfamiliar season in the country which made Daniel feel displaced, it was being with his brother, who inhabited, in himself, an unfamiliar season, the strange season of someone who lived away.

Philip said, "You all like being here, don't you?"

"Yes," Daniel said.

"And Dad, does he, really?"

Daniel said, with the sensation of a sudden physical risk, "No, he doesn't, he doesn't like being here."

Philip said nothing.

"We come up in the summer as late as possible. He's always postponing our coming. And whenever we have a storm and there's no electricity for a couple of days, he says we have to move back to the city. At the end of the summer, he always wants to leave a week before school starts."

Philip said, "We bought it for him. We bought it because

we thought, after everything he lost, he'd at least be able to say to himself, well, my sons think of me."

Daniel said, "Oh, he's proud of it."

Philip blinked as the snowflakes fell into his eyes.

They reached the paved country road where a car had passed, and they walked in the wheel ruts to the farm on a low hill, to a great fieldstone barn with bushel baskets of apples outside it in the snow. An old man, wearing a lumber jacket and a visored cap with ear flaps down, was sitting just inside the doorway, a kerosene stove by him.

Daniel said, "That's Mr Leveret. He used to own the land our house is on."

Mr Leveret stood, as if to prevent them from coming into the barn.

"You want apples?" he said.

"Yes, all right," Philip said.

Mr Leveret kicked a basket. "That's a good winesap."

Philip picked up an apple and bit into it.

Daniel stood by the kerosene stove. He asked, "Mr Leveret, were there ever Indians around here?"

"Who else could've been here?" he said.

"Do you know who they were?"

"I know there was a sagamore, named Tocomus, Tocomo, something like that, who sold eight, nine square miles of land to some one of my people, for fishhooks. He made the oldest son lie flat on the ground and put his mark on his back, and his other sons had to sign one another's backs, that was the deed."

"And where did they go?"

Mr Leveret made a gesture in the air.

The two brothers carried the basket each by a wire handle, the wire cut into their hands, and sometimes the basket jogged and apples fell out into the snow. Small wind currents through the woods whirled the snow into ghosts that ran wildly among the dark trees; in the deep silence the sound of the blown ghosts was a faint *wish*.

Richard, Chuckie, the children were throwing everything

223

—empty bowls, pans, comic books, toys, boots—into card-board boxes, preparing to leave, when Philip and Daniel got back to the house. Dusk was falling, pulled down by the continuing snow, when they drove off.

Albert, André, Philip went to their rooms to nap.

Daniel stood at the living room window to watch the snow, grey-blue. He saw, across the covered lawn, through the bent birch trees, a tall figure and a short figure walking down the drive to the bridge; he made out Edmond, in a large old Army coat and knitted cap, and a boy who he thought at first might be a nephew left behind. He said to his mother, sitting near him with her eyes closed, "Who's that with Edmond?" The mother got up to look. Edmond and the boy were standing on the bridge. The boy had a scarf wrapped about the lower part of his face and his cap was pulled low. Edmond motioned to him to follow him on to the island. The mother suddenly broke away from the window, opened the large front door in the living room, and shouted through the frozen screen door, "Edmond! Edmond!" Daniel, at the window, saw Edmond seem to throw a pebble or pinecone, but it was a gesture of annoyance Edmond always made. "Edmond!" his mother called. Edmond left the boy on the bridge and came slowly up to the house; he hadn't buckled his boots, so they flopped. The mother held the screen door and large door open as he took off his boots to come inside, then she shut them hard. "Where were you going?" she asked. "I was just going to show Billy the island." "Who is he? Who is Billy?" "He's the son of a farmer." "Well, he knows the island then, he doesn't need you to show it to him."

Daniel said, "Ed, you should stick to people your own age."

Edmond threw his cap on the floor. "Oh yeah, oh yeah! Well, you go off, you have your friends, what friends do I have here? I stay at home, I do what I can, I take care of Mom and Dad. You'll be going off to college, too, and then Julien will go. I'll be left. I'll be left to do everything you don't want to do!"

Daniel shouted, "No one's forcing you to stay. Go, go, if you want."

Edmond pointed at him. "You just wait till you go to college. Try telephoning me from the station and asking me to go down and pick you up, you'll see what I'll do, I'll slam the phone in your face. You think you're so smart—"

"Oh, shut up," Daniel said.

"No, I won't shut up. I'm not stupid. I know you all think I am. I'm not. I'm sick of being the errand boy for the family, I'm sick of being the family chauffeur. Stupid Edmond. That's me."

"All right, that's enough, the both of you," the mother said, then said to their father, "Tell them to stop."

The father, by the fireplace, said, "That'll do."

Julien didn't look up from a comic book.

In the silence of the house the mother sat in a platform rocker across from her husband by the fire. She was used to not knowing what he was thinking, but she was not used to not knowing what her sons were thinking. Edmond, sprawled on the couch, was reading the comic book Julien had finished. The others came into the room, one at a time, from their naps: Albert rubbing round the skull edges of his eyesockets, André running his hands through his crew-cut hair.

While they had tea and slices of pie in the living room, Daniel went quietly to his room.

He passed Philip's open door and saw Philip, on his bed, holding up a photograph. Philip held the photograph to the side to glance at Daniel and, as if he had expected to see him there, said, "Hey, Dan." Daniel waited. Philip looked at him for a moment, then looked back at the photograph, lowered it to his chest, and crossed his wrists.

Daniel lay on his bed, his eyes open, and tried to visualize the face and body of his brother Philip in the air.

At supper, the mother said to Philip, "I think that the next time you come home, if you want to come again, you won't be alone."

He stared at her. "What?"

"Oh, I feel—"

Philip smiled a little.

"Am I right?" she asked.

Edmond lowered his fork, on it stuck a big piece of cold turkey.

"Right about what?"

The mother said, "And is it serious?"

"Yes," Philip said.

"Where is she?" the mother said.

"She's in Texas."

"She's Texan?"

"Yes."

"How did you meet her?"

"I went to stay with a fellow lieutenant, a guy named Jack Hantz, at his family house in Texas, near the Gulf. His father has a cotton plantation. Jenny is his sister."

"Jenny."

"Yes."

The mother looked at the father, who looked hard at Philip.

Philip said, "You know, I didn't think she even saw me when I first went there. She and her brother Jack and I went to a football game at her college. She's a sophomore. When we were leaving the stadium, she took my hand. Would you like to see her picture?"

Edmond's eyes dilated enormously. "We would!"

Philip took from his wallet the photograph and handed it to his mother.

"Oh, she's pretty."

She passed the photograph to the father whose head bent up and down as he looked at it as if the girl were before him and he were looking at her from head to toe to head again.

The mother's brow furrowed when she asked, "Is she French?"

Philip said, "Her name is Jenny Hantz."

"Come on," André said, "you can't expect us to marry girls from the parish."

"It would have been nice," the mother said.

The father passed the photo to Albert. "Her father has a cotton plantation, does he?"

"About five hundred acres, I reckon."

"Oh ho!" Edmond said. "Do I hear that ole Southern 'I reckon' already?"

"Is she a Catholic?" the mother asked.

"No," Philip said.

The mother held out her hands as though she had just released a bird to fly from them and looked first, not at her husband, but at her son Albert, who was looking at his father; he too, she saw when she turned to him, was looking at Albert.

Standing alone by the mother as she washed the dishes, Philip asked her, "Does it matter very much to you and Dad that she's not Catholic?" The mother wrung out a dishrag as if she were wringing out her mind, then said, "You know, when we were kids, we were told by the nuns not to pass in front of the Protestant church, but to cross the street and pass on the opposite side, because the devil was in the Protestant church. You must try to understand that. Your father and I would never go to a wedding in a Protestant church, even if two Protestants were getting married. You see, they wouldn't be getting married, not really, because only the Catholic marriage is valid, and if we went to a Protestant marriage we'd be condoning sin." "I'd never be married in a Protestant church," Philip said. The mother looked at him, her face slightly twisted. "I know, I know. I know you wouldn't commit sin." "What did Dad say?" he asked. "He didn't say anything." "Does his silence mean he doesn't approve? I should know." "I don't know what it means." "Would he be against my getting married?" "Oh, your father never says anything. He leaves everything that has to be said up to me." "If you said it was all right, would he follow what you say?" She said, "I'll pray. I'll pray for what's best." Philip smiled. He grabbed his mother and hugged her close, pressing his face into her neck. "Don't worry," he said, "don't worry. I won't commit sin. We'll all be in heaven together, just as you want, and my wife, who-ever she is, will be there too." The mother let her arms hang and said while he held her, "We can't expect you to stay in the parish. We know that. We can't even expect you to stay in Providence. Oh, but Philip, don't leave the Church." He let her go. "You're intelligent, the most intelligent of us. I've saved your report cards from La Salle. And you've met people you'd never meet here, and I think you'd never bring them here. Albert has gone far from us, farther than anyone, and yet, when he comes back, it's as if he'd always been home. But it seems to me that when you're home, you're here for the first time. I only worry sometimes that you've gone too far. I mean, don't go out of the Church. Please don't. Because you can't be saved outside the Church." She pressed her hands against the base of her throat.

They sat in the living room in the late evening. It had stopped snowing, and in the soft wind that blew about the house they could hear the pine branches over the house creak. While Albert taught Julien to play chess, both crouched over the coffee table, and Edmond continued to read or reread the comic book he had been reading all after-noon, and Daniel read, ". . . ideas—conceptions such as *these*—unthought-like thoughts—soul-reveries rather than conclusions or even considerations of the intellect. . . ," and the mother and father rocked on either side of the dying fire, and André wrote in the notebook, Philip, at the collective centre of all their awareness, sat on a hassock by the fire.

Philip said after a silence, "I want to buy her a gift."

"To take back to her in Texas?" the mother said.

"Yes, I want to buy her something in Providence."

"Perfume," André said.

"Oh, something more lasting—"

Snow released by a branch thudded on to the roof.

Philip said, his head lowered, "Maybe I should buy her a rosary."

228

The mother brightened, as though Philip had solved a problem she knew had to be solved before they could go to bed and sleep. "Oh, Phil, that would be so nice."

Albert slammed his palm down on the coffee table. The chess pieces jumped. "For God's sake," he said, "don't force our religion on her!" He was staring at the mother.

"Oh, I—" she exclaimed, her body suddenly rigid.

"Don't you know you can't *force* a person to do what he doesn't want to do! Don't you know you can't *force* anything on anyone."

No one spoke, then the mother said, her voice as rigid as her face and body, "Well, what do you do in war if you don't force other people to do what you want them to do?"

"You don't understand, woman."

"Well, I want to understand. You all seem so strange to me sometimes. I don't understand what you're thinking."

Albert said, "We fight wars, woman, to give people the chance to choose what they want for themselves, we fight wars to give them freedom—"

"Oh, but—" she said.

"That's enough now," her husband said to her.

Albert said to Philip, "We'll go downtown together. We'll choose something special for her."

"Thanks," Philip said.

"She must be a very special girl," Albert said.

Julien said, "What's so special about a girl?"

The brothers and the father too laughed. The mother looked at the fireplace and andirons, which were black iron owls.

The father put down his cup on a pile of newspapers and said, "Well, I think it's time for me to go to bed." He said to his wife, "What do you think, ma p'tite fille?"

André said, "Stay with us a little bit longer, Dad. It's nice to see you among us all, enjoying your house with us."

"Well, it's not mine fully until the last payment is made," the father said, his hands pressing against the arms of the platform rocker, rising.

229

Philip said, "Of course if I get married I won't be able to send any more payments."

The father remained half risen from the rocker.

Albert said quickly, "We'll take care of all that—"

The father rose to his feet. He continued to look at Philip. He said flatly, "But you made a commitment."

Philip looked away.

After a moment, during which everyone but Philip looked at the father, he said to the mother, "We'll go to bed now."

She rose.

He said, "And we'll go back to the city tomorrow."

Edmond said, "But we came to spend the whole weekend."

"You boys stay. Your mother and I will go back to the city tomorrow."

"Why?" Daniel asked.

The flesh on the father's face became taut; his ears moved. "Because I want to," he said.

He went out. The mother looked silently from son to son, then followed their father.

Albert held his hands up. "Everything's going to be all right," he said.

Daniel said, "I think I'll go out for a walk."

He walked down to the lake, to the little beach. The only light came from the window of the living room, a wide pale beam over him and out into the darkness of the lake, from where he heard distant booms. He stepped out on to the snow-covered ice, and stood for a moment trying to make himself walk further out, then he stepped back on to the land.

He saw through the large window that the living room was empty. A floor lamp by the side of the fireplace was lit. He opened the screen door to the porch, and the ice about it cracked, then he opened the large door quietly. He heard his mother say, "Oh," and when he closed the door he saw her, in her bathrobe, standing at the side of the fireplace opposite the floor lamp.

230

She said, "I thought you had gone to bed, I thought I was the only one up."

He took off his boots on the mat before the door.

"I went for a walk."

"In this cold?"

"I like it."

She didn't move.

He asked, "Is something wrong?"

"I didn't want to disturb your father. I was tossing a little."

"You couldn't sleep."

"I came down to read the paper."

He took off his coat and scarf. He said, "Shall we sit on the couch?"

"I'd like that," she said.

They sat at either end of the couch. She rocked her body back and forth. She said, "I guess you're looking forward to going away, to going to college."

"That won't be for a while."

"It won't be like here—"

"No," he said.

"Maybe you'll like it more."

"I don't know."

"It won't be easy for you. You know, you have your own way at home. All of you do. You do as you like. Your father and I, we've always given you your own ways. You'll find, though, that you can't have your own way when you're outside. You remember when you wanted a bicycle, you said you wanted one, and I said—I don't know, I suppose I shouldn't have joked about it—'I'll give you two, one for weekdays, one for Sunday,' and you threw your glasses on the floor and broke them, glasses your father worked hard to buy for you so you could read without any trouble, and I said, 'You won't get a bike, not after this,' and yet you did, you got it, we bought it for you. You and Julien, the youngest of the family, you've had it much easier than your elder brothers. No one asks anything of you here. You'll find it's a lot different outside. You won't be able to have your own way in everything. Look at your father. He wanted his own way. He couldn't have it. You'll have to do many things you don't want to do. Your father always wanted everything his own way. Well, you see what happened."

"Am I like Dad, then?"

"I don't know. Maybe. Like him, you think you can have what you want. You'll always be disappointed if you think that, as your father has been. You won't get what you want."

"What did Dad want?"

She rubbed the back of one hand with the tips of the fingers of the other. "He just wanted his own way."

"And he couldn't have it?"

"No."

"And you think I want my own way and won't get it?"

"I wish you would get it. As your mother, I hope you will get it."

Snow slid off the roof and fell by the window to the ground.

The mother said, "I wonder what will happen."

"I don't know," he said.

She leaned slightly, silently.

He asked, "Shall we go to bed?"

"No," she said, "it's all right here," then added, "But maybe you want me to leave you alone."

"No, no," he said.

She seemed to take a deep breath and said, as though in one released breath, "Oh Daniel, oh Daniel, there's so much I feel I want to say. Why can't I say it? You're the only one who listens to me try to say it. Things go round and round my mind, not thoughts, because if they were thoughts I could think them, couldn't I, then say them; but I can't think them, not clearly, and I can't say them. Your father's a good man, such a good man. He says just what he thinks. Where would I be without him? His thinking is so clear. He doesn't understand. And if I say to him, 'Jim,' he just looks at me. You're not becoming impatient with me, are you?"

"No," Daniel said.

"I think you are."

"No," he said, turning sharply to her, "no, I'm not."

"Don't be impatient with me."

He thought: there was, there had to be, in his mother, some small floating globe, some free-floating centre, to which all her talk was connected, or which itself sent off, wave after wave, the drifts of her talk; he wanted to locate that centre, wanted her, in one sentence, in one word, to reveal it, and he would know what she was talking about.

She said, "I sometimes wonder if one of my miscarriages might have been a daughter. I hoped you'd be a daughter. Your name was going to be Janine Marie. I had your father paint your crib pink, I put pink ribbons on it, I was so sure. After you, I had a miscarriage, then Julien, then another miscarriage. Your father wrapped the embryos in newspaper and burned them in the furnace. It's only because of your father that you and Julien were born. After André was born I developed—well, I can tell you, you're old enough—a lapsed womb. The doctor, Dr Dalande, said I should have my womb removed. But you know how your father is. He wouldn't let me be operated on. He made up his mind, and that's all there is to it. He said, 'My wife's not going to be subjected to the knife.' Dr Dalande said, 'If she becomes pregnant, she could die.' I think that's what he said. Well, I should have had the operation, but your father said no. You know we wouldn't use birth control or anything like that. But your father insisted that we should sleep in the same bed. You understand, don't you? My life depended on his self-control. It was hard on him. We lived like that for seven years. I got sick. I made up my mind, this isn't life, we've got to live, I'll risk having a baby. I decided it. I didn't care about myself. I honestly didn't care if I died as long as we had peace in the house. I made up my mind. You were born. You see, if your father had listened to the

233

doctor, if he'd allowed me to have my womb cut out, you wouldn't be here. You owe that to your father. But I thought you'd be a girl. Then I had a miscarriage. It was a little thing with gills. Your father burned it. Then Julien was born. I knew he would be a boy. And I had another miscarriage after."

Daniel sank back against the couch and closed his eyes.

She said, "I'm boring you, I know."

He couldn't open his eyes. He said, "No, no."

She said, "There are things a son, no matter how kind, can't understand."

Behind his closed eyes, he sensed he was not a body but a large space. He said, "No." He felt the couch move a little with the constant rocking of the mother.

The rocking suddenly stopped. She said, in a lower voice, "Daniel, promise me something."

He opened his eyes. She was looking at him.

"Please, please, promise me you'll be patient with me."

"Patient?"

"Please, please, don't get impatient with me, ever. It's asking a lot from you, I know. It's asking for more than I have a right to ask."

It took him a long while to say, "I'll be patient," but as he said it a shock of restlessness passed through him.

"Oh," she said.

He reached out to take her hand. It was as if he were forcing himself to step forward when he longed to fall backward. He said, "You think I wouldn't understand, but I would."

"No," she said, "no, you wouldn't, not even a daughter would."

"I would."

"You want to go."

"No, I don't."

She began to rock again. "I think of you all, all you boys, so often. I know if I asked you, you'd be patient with me. I think of you all when you were babies. When I can't sleep,

I think of you in your cribs, when you took your first steps, when you first spoke. I know you wouldn't ever disappoint me, none of you."

Daniel listened to her talk about the family. He kept biting the backs of his hands.

"Richard, il était un vrai diable, but, oh, everyone loved him, with his blond light long curls and his blue eyes always wide open. He used to lift women's skirts from behind to look under. He dropped his teddy bear in the chowder. Your father ate it, I couldn't. He shouted at passers-by from the piazza, 'Je vois tes fesses,' and I had to hope they didn't understand. Once he threw a potato into Albert's crib. Your father got angry. He hit him on the head. I said, 'No, no, not on the head, don't hit him on the head.' He never, your father never hit any one of you again. You don't remember him ever hitting you, do you? Albert was dark. He had a Dutch cut. He was always quiet. He never wanted to go out. We took him and Richard to a movie at the Castle when they were old enough. There was a film about a snake and a mongoose fighting. The mongoose won. Albert had nightmares about it, would wake up shouting. Edmond was dark too. He was always coming to me to tell me, 'They're picking on me.' I'd say, 'Well, defend yourself.' He once came to me and said, 'They think they're so smart, but I'm smarter, I told them, I said, you're not so smart, and I gave it to them, I beat them up so much I think I broke their bones.' I said, 'Ed, you didn't.' He cried. 'Well, I wanted to.' Philip could throw such fits of anger. Edmond never really got angry, but Philip did. He'd be shouting and thrashing around, and I'd have the older boys take him into the bathroom and hold him while he struggled and I'd wet a face cloth till it was sopping with cold water and I'd wipe his face. He'd shout, 'You're drowning me,' and I'd say, 'Keep quiet and you'll be all right,' and he'd become quiet, and I'd dry him and comb his hair. We never hit you. The most we'd do is show you your father's razor strop and say, you'd better be good or else. André never gave any trouble.

He was always involved in doing something by himself, in his room. And you, you didn't give us any trouble either. Well, not one of you gave us any trouble. You'd play for hours with rags from the boxes in my closet, you'd take out the rags from the boxes and arrange them by colour and pattern all over my bed. I said to your father, 'He'll be a rag man.' Because you had blue eyes, like Richard, I thought he should be your godfather. Julien never gave us trouble as a baby either, but he was so silent we wondered for a while if he was deaf. He never spoke much even when he did learn to speak, and he was stubborn in his silence. I took him downtown shopping one day, and we stopped at an ice-cream fountain, and I asked him what he wanted, and he said, after a long silence, 'Water.' I thought I couldn't have an ice-cream soda with my little son next to me at the fountain drinking water. I tried to tempt him with flavour after flavour, but he kept saying, 'Water, water.' Well I wanted an ice-cream soda, so I ordered one for myself, and I had to say, loud to the waitress, 'He only wants a glass of water.'"

She stopped rocking, and was very still.

She said, "I'll try to go to sleep now."

"Yes," he said. "I'll shut off the lights."

Before leaving she said, "Don't tell your father we were talking."

"No," he said.

He locked the doors. On the seat of the chair under the floor lamp was a newspaper. He picked it up and saw, carefully written in pencil in her clear, even handwriting: Richard A. Francoeur, Albert B. Francoeur, Edmond R. Francoeur, Philip P. Francoeur, André J. Francoeur, Daniel R. Francoeur, Julien E. Francoeur, Richard A. Francoeur, Albert B. Francoeur, Edmond—

XI

ALONE, EVERY THOUGHT that the mother had—that the windows needed washing, that there was one less person in the house, that the clock was slow—made her wince; every slight feeling—that she was cold, that she didn't feel like talking to Edmond when he got out of the bathroom in the morning, that she felt she didn't want to wake Julien from his bed—made her wince. Over the long morning, she was struck painfully by the sight of a book left on a table, the sensation of hot water in the dishpan, the sound of the steam pipes banging. She stared at the book, swirled her hands round and round in the water, listened to the banging pipes without knowing why they all hurt her so. Whatever was wrong, she thought, could easily, very easily be put right—as easily as putting the book away in the desk, adding cold water to the hot, releasing steam from the boiler. She had worried thoughts about a crack in the ceiling, anxious feelings that she might fall out when she leaned out a window to hang out her laundry, and among these thoughts and feelings occurred and reoccurred, as worried or anxious as the thought of cracks or the feeling that she might fall, the thought, the feeling that she would lose her home.

She loved her sons, but she did not want, ever, to be dependent upon them—and now she couldn't think of anything else she could do but appeal to them to help, because after all she was, her husband and she were, dependent upon them. She hadn't wanted that, she hadn't wanted that. Was it her fault, then? She hadn't wanted that, what had happened. It wasn't Philip's fault, it was her fault; she didn't blame Philip. Her thoughts went round and round. If only she could think what to do. It was all her fault, so she must think what to do. She was sure that with the right thinking she could easily, very easily, set everything right.

She went to the front entry, and picked up a letter from the floor. It was from Albert. She read it in the cold entry. She went to her room afterwards to lie quietly on hers and her husband's bed.

She gave Albert's letter to her husband after he had changed into his slippers. He handed it back to her when he'd read it. She held it and looked at him. He pointed to the letter with the stunted finger.

"That doesn't change anything," he said.

"But it does," she said.

"No."

"Albert will take care of everything. He'll take over the whole mortgage, he said, from Richard and André as well. He can afford it."

"Another twelve hundred dollars a year."

"He says he can."

"He'll be left with nothing."

"He says he wants to."

"It's not right of Philip, of any of us, to expect Albert to take care of everything."

"You wouldn't have said that a few months ago."

"I say it now."

"But Albert wants to."

"He's being forced by his brothers."

"Forced? No. Albert would never do that. *He's* doing what he knows is right—"

"I thought he was more devout than now he turns out to be."

"But he is devout. It's exactly because he is devout that he's making such sacrifices to keep us a peaceful family."

"Well, his sacrifices are for nothing, because we're not a peaceful family."

238

"But who is that up to now?"

"You know."

"You want Philip to give up his marriage?"

"I want him to do what he said he would do."

"But not even Albert, who is so strict about honour, demands that. Philip and Jenny are marrying in the Church. He's not committing a sin."

"He is. Philip made a commitment."

"Why do you insist?"

"Because I do. I spent all day today washing ceilings. Now I'm tired."

"They would never hurt you."

The father looked towards Julien's door, from behind which music sounded as from a tightly shut-up house.

"I'll knock on his door and tell him to turn down the phonograph," Reena said.

"No," Jim said darkly, "let him be."

The father spent the evening at his desk composing a letter to Philip. He showed it to his wife. It briefly stated, without punctuation, that if Philip married he would no longer be able to consider the family house his home and would next see his father, if he saw him ever, in a pine box.

Reena asked, "Do you want to know what I think about it?"

"No," he said, "I just wanted you to see it before I send it."

The mother walked about her house as if it were a city which, once native to her, no longer belonged to her, and at a signal she would be told to leave it. It was not her husband who had brought in the troops, she knew, nor was it he who commanded them; they had come in because of some great war which had nothing to do with her husband or her, and neither her husband or she had an idea who commanded.

When a letter arrived from Philip, addressed to his father, the mother studied Philip's handwriting, as clean and careful and rounded as her own, then placed it on the kitchen table.

Jim saw the letter as he was taking off his jacket, but didn't reach for it until he had hung up his jacket and put on his slippers. His wife left the kitchen while he read it. She knew it would be, not a letter from Philip, but orders from the head of the occupation forces that they must leave their house. When she returned to the kitchen she found her husband rocking in his rocking chair and looking out of the window. On the kitchen table were the letter and envelope torn in many pieces and, beside the torn-up letter, the photograph of all the sons taken at Philip's graduation from M.I.T. cut in three sections, Richard, Albert, Edmond in one section, Philip, in cap and gown, in the narrow central section, André, Daniel and Julien in the third section, and the sections were separated, so Philip stood alone; the scissors were also on the table. Reena immediately left the kitchen to sit in the living room.

Daniel didn't know, when he arrived at the house on the corner which appeared closed up and deserted under the low and purple evening sky, if he should just go in or if he should ring the bell. He tried the door; it was locked. It was only locked if no one was inside. He wondered when his parents and Edmond and Julien might be in on Friday evening; he took his key from his pocket and opened the back door. He was returning from his long distance, he thought, to an empty house. As he opened the kitchen door, he heard a voice from inside dimness ask, "Who's there?" and he saw his father sitting in his rocker.

Daniel put down his bag. His father rose, and Daniel shook his hand. "Where're the others?" Daniel asked. "Julien's gone to his friend's, Edmond to the ice-cream parlour, your mother is in her room." "Is she all right?" "She's gone to bed early." Daniel thought: he shouldn't have expected them to celebrate his coming home. His father didn't ask him how his first two weeks at college had been, but perhaps Daniel wouldn't have been able to say; the father sat again. Daniel stood in the middle of the dim kitchen, the windows livid pink squares in the dimness, and asked, "Why was the door locked?" "Your mother wants it kept locked." "Oh," Daniel said, then asked, "Well, what room should I use?"

He slept in Julien's bed. He woke from time to time and listened to his brother breathe heavily. He didn't know his brother when he was awake any more than when he was asleep, he thought. Half awake and half asleep, he was both conscious that he was hearing his brother breathe and dreamed that he heard his roommate breathe in their small dormitory room. He was in two places at once.

He recalled, when he woke in the morning, that he had dreamed at college of waking to the sounds he now heard about him in the house: the toilet flushing, water running, a kettle clanking, and the low voices of his parents.

When, long after Julien got up, he got up, he found his mother ironing in the kitchen. The kitchen smelled of warm clean sheets and pillowcases. "I hope we didn't wake you," she said. "I wanted you to sleep and sleep." He went to her and held her, but when he stepped back he didn't know what to say. "Where are the others?" he asked. "Your father's working in the cellar. Edmond and Julien are out." "There seems to be only one person at a time in the house," he said. She didn't understand; she said, "There's so much I want to ask." He sat at the table with a cup of tea, he felt dizzy. "Are you well?" she asked. She frowned as though to concentrate hard on what she said. "It's strange," he said, "there I dream that I'm here, and here I dream that I'm there." "What did you dream?" "I'm not sure." "Tell me," she said. "Did you dream of your roommate?" "Yes, I did. I dreamt of him brushing his teeth. In the bathroom that's for our floor there's a row of wash-basins and we brush our teeth standing next to one another. He usually stays on and talks, and I go back to the room and get into bed and wait for him to come back. I can hear his voice, and I know he'll be coming back when I hear him tap his toothbrush against the wash-basin." "Do you get along with him?" "Yes. But I don't see him much, you know. In the evenings, after supper, when we have to be in our rooms studying, often he's not in our room, but in some other guy's room, talking. He likes to talk. He's very sociable." "Does he have a lot of friends?" "He's already got hundreds of friends. He carries a little address book around with him and copies down the address of everybody he speaks to, even for five minutes. He says that everyone in Oak Park carries around an address book. He's going to run for president of the freshman class. He's already campaigning." "You must have a lot in common." Daniel didn't answer. "And do you like the Jesuits?" the mother asked. She was trying to form questions out of the thin grey air in the kitchen. He thought: she's not interested. "It's such a different way of thinking," he said, "their way of thinking." She stood the iron upright and spread a pillowcase over the board. "I should have done this last Tuesday," she said. "I didn't, somehow I couldn't. And today we've got to do the shopping. I'll ask your father to go with Edmond. I don't feel like going. I can't think of food." She slid the hot iron over the damp pillowcase; steam rose. "Never mind that," she said; "tell me more about college." He couldn't think of any more to tell her. "Did you think of us?" she asked. "Of course." She hadn't finished the ironing, but she stood the iron on its end as if she couldn't push it any more. Her voice all at once rose. "Daniel, do you remember my favour in your prayers?" "Yes, yes," he said. "Do you? Do you?" "My roommate says his prayers on his knees at the bedside before he gets in to go to sleep, and I do the same now, and each night I say a special prayer for you." "You say your prayers on your knees?" "Yes, as he does. His father doesn't believe in God." "His father doesn't believe in God?" "No, but his mother does. He prays for his father." "Oh Daniel, please don't forget. I pray too, but my prayers aren't strong enough. I don't know what's going to happen. I told myself, I said again and again to myself, that I would make your homecoming pleasant, that I wouldn't speak to you as I am now. You'll resent me, you'll get impatient. Daniel, I must tell you; I

242

can't go on. I can't. My stomach is twisted up, all my muscles are twisted up, I have a buzzing in my ears, I hear it now, a constant buzzing." Daniel stared at her. "You'll want to go back to college right away. You won't want to stay here. You shouldn't have come home. For your own sake, you shouldn't have come home." He continued to stare at her, then asked, "But what's wrong?" "Oh, don't tell your father I'm talking to you like this. He'll get angry with me." "What's wrong?" Daniel asked again.

He followed her to her bedroom, where she opened the bottom drawer of her bureau, and from under slips and underwear took out an envelope, and emptied the contents of the envelope on to the top of the bureau: torn bits of paper and the photograph of the sons, cut in three and taped together at the back.

"That's a letter from Philip to your father," she said. "I've tried to put it together to read it. I can't. What does picayune mean?"

"I don't know," Daniel said.

"Philip wrote on one bit that his father's action in writing his letter to him was picayune. You know Philip's anger. Will you look it up for me?"

"What did Dad write?"

"He wrote to Philip that the next time Philip sees him he'll be in a pine box." She bit her lower lip to keep herself, it seemed, from smiling.

Daniel laughed. "A pine box?"

Still biting her lip, the mother too laughed. "He wrote that."

"Dad doesn't mean it."

"Oh, he does. And Philip wrote this letter back. He shouldn't have. Your father tore it up. He took the photograph of you all from his wallet and cut Philip out. He left it and the torn-up letter on the kitchen table. When he went to bed, I taped the photograph together. I didn't tell him that I had kept everything. He didn't ask. He wouldn't ask. Philip doesn't exist any more. He's taken his photograph from the living room wall. You can go and see. There's a gap. There's nothing displayed around the house that has anything to do with Philip—the M.I.T. pennant, the fraternity mug, everything that had to do with Philip has been put away. It's as if he burned it all up, and that's the end of Philip."

Daniel smiled at his mother as if what she spoke about was not really important. His mother looked down. He said, "I'll go and look up the word 'picayune' for you."

He wasn't able to give her the definition, as the father had come up from the cellar and was sitting in the kitchen and watching his wife, who, at the table, was writing out a shopping list. She was drawing circles on the paper. She said, "I can't think." "If you put your mind to it," Jim said, "you would be able to do it in five minutes." "Can't you do it?" she asked. He clenched his teeth and his jaw, as his mother's did, stuck out. "You've always done it," he said. "I can't think of food. Please, you do it." He breathed in and out heavily. "You can write down what I say," he said. "Yes, all right." He started, "Five pounds of potatoes—" She threw down the pencil. "I can't. Please don't force me to do what I can't do." "You can do it if you make up your mind to it." "I can't." "All right," he said, "I'll do it. I'll do the shopping." "Edmond will go with you." "All right. I'll ask Edmond to go with me."

While the father and Edmond were shopping, Daniel sat with his mother in the living room; she sat next to him on the couch, then got up and went to an armchair, then to a straight chair, then to the couch again. She said, "Tell me about college. Tell me something that will get my mind off myself. I can't stand thinking about myself. All I think about is myself. It's terrible, thinking about yourself. It's the worst thing in the world. In hell, people must think about themselves all the time. I pray to God to help me to stop thinking about myself. I can't sleep. I lie awake thinking about myself. You think and think, and think you can exhaust your thinking by thinking, but you can't. When I lie awake, I try at least to concentrate my thinking. I go through the house. Are you listening? Does this bore you?" "No," Daniel said, "no." "I think of my father and mother's house on Sheridan Street, I think of all the rooms. It was a big house, with a big yard. It used to belong to people with money. My mother had all kinds of flowers growing in the yard—nasturtiums, zinnias, bachelor's buttons, marigolds. She used to tie strings from the ground to the railings for morning glories to climb up. She used to sew. She made all our clothes. And knit. I don't do any of those things. And she had twelve children. She was so sad when my father died. She said, 'Oh, Reena, you'll never know what it's like to be without your husband until it happens.' He was proud of the house. He was proud of the house, he was proud of his car. He used to wash it with a toothbrush. He learned to drive at a late age. We used to say, 'Pa, we'll bury you in your car,' and he'd laugh. 'Reena,' he said, 'Edmond will be a driver. I'll tell you, he will.' He died when my mother was sixty. I'll be sixty in five years. She didn't know what to do. She signed her house over to my brother Claud because Claud lived with her, she thought Claud would live with her until she died, an old bachelor. And then he got married, he got married to that old nurse, and my mother lived in her son and daughter-in-law's house, not hers any more. And when she fell and broke her hip they wouldn't take care of her, they couldn't, they said. I took her in. Do you remember her, my mother, in our house? She gave me all her furniture, the furniture was still hers. I didn't know what to do with it. I put it in the cellar, some in the attic. I tried, I did my best to help her. I had to take care of her and to take care of my family. My family suffered. I had to think of my family. When she'd mess her bed, she'd say, 'I'm like a baby again,' and I'd say, 'That's all right, Ma,' but she knew it wasn't all right. She'd call for her bedpan at night, I'd get up from bed and slip it under her, and after half an hour she'd say she didn't need it, but after I removed it and went to bed she'd call me because she messed herself. And I had so much else

245

to do, too, with your father, with all you boys. How could I have kept her? Before we took her to the nursing home she gave me a box filled with the clothes she wanted to be laid out in, her underwear, her long purple silk stockings. She said, 'Promise me you'll take my rosary from my hands before they close the coffin lid.' I said, 'Yes, I promise.' I visited her every day, every day. You remember that, don't you? You remember coming with me. She kept telling me, over and over: 'Keep your house, Reena. Don't ever lose your house. You're nothing without your house.' I should have kept her with me. She died in that nursing home, without any home. I so often think of her home, think of it when it was mine too, when I lived there. I think of so many things. On Good Friday, we kids would keep silent for three hours, pressing our lips together, but grunting, pointing, and writing on the ground with sticks. Then we made pinny poppy shows. Let me talk. I talk so much to your father. He listens. He's good. He listens to me talk and talk. You take a picture, a picture of a tomato off a tin can or a flower from a packet of seeds, and you dig a shallow hole and you place the picture in it and cover it with a piece of broken glass, then you sift sand over the glass. 'How much does it cost to see your pinny poppy show?' your friends asked. 'Two pins,' you'd say. They'd run home to ask their mothers for the common pins, and once they paid you'd push the sand covering the glass to one side to show the picture. That's what I called your private parts when you were little boys. 'Don't touch your pinny poppy.' Do you remember? Just before he died, my father said, staring up, 'Le chemin est si beau. Regardez les belles fleurs.' We cried and cried. So many in the family have died. I think of them, I pray to them and ask them for help. My sister Agnes died in the last influenza epidemic. She had the last white casket in Providence. One time, when we were all about the big dining room table stringing popcorn for the Christmas tree, the piano in the living room began to play, just by itself. My mother was frightened. Agnes said, 'It's just mice running about inside.' She died not long after. She was older. She was so beautiful and so intelligent. She taught me how to tease my hair and to make cootie traps on the sides. Once, she called me in to do the dishes, it was my turn, but I was playing baseball with my brothers. It was Lawrence's turn to bat. 'I want my last turn,' I said. 'I want my last turn,' he said. 'I can't stay,' I said. So he picked up a big mickey and hit me on the head. The boys used to throw stones at the outhouse when Louis'd go in. Claud once put pieces of coal in our Christmas stockings. I remember my brothers coming home and telling my parents they and their friends had thrown stones at a man who was exposing himself in an alley. I didn't know what that meant. I didn't know anything about sex until I got married. When I was very young, a boy put a cigar ring on my finger and kissed me and I ran in to my mother and asked, 'Ma, am I married?' Later, someone asked me if I would marry him. 'Wait a minute,' I said, 'I'll go ask my mother and father.' I said to my mother, 'He wants to marry me,' she said, 'Es-tu folle?' I went back to him and said, 'They won't let me.' There was a Swede I liked. He wore a red hat with a pompom when he skated. My heart went thumpety-thump when I saw that hat when I went down to the flats to skate. He took me out. Once, when he took me home, we were standing in the entry and I saw that he was trembling. 'Are you cold?' I asked him. He said, 'I want to kiss you.' I let him. He just pecked me on the cheek. He died. My father didn't want me to marry your father. My mother didn't think I should marry anyone. She said I wasn't strong enough. We had good times when I was little, living at home. We pounded stones to a fine powder, and my mother used that as her Dutch cleanser. She paid us each a penny. With five cents we took a Sunday walk to Onlyville, and stopped at Sansouci for candy, a big bag of jelly beans, then went home again and Agnes played the piano while we stood around and sang, though I never sang well. I never did anything well. My mother said that. Well, I knew it. I know it now. I've never done anything.

I'm not a cook, don't sew or knit, I'm not a good house-keeper. My mother said to me, 'Well, how do you expect to be a wife and mother when you can't do anything?' I couldn't. I can't. Only one thing I've done, the only right thing in my life, is to have seven sons."

"Don't say that."

"It's true. It's true." She all at once wailed; it was frightening. "Oh, I can't do anything. I can't. Please don't make me do what I can't do! Please don't make me!"

"No one's making you do anything you can't do, Momma."

"It's just that I can't. You know, I can't."

Daniel's muscles tightened with the impulse to move, but he held himself still. "I can't," she said, "I can't." She was sitting on the edge of an armchair; she said over and over, "I can't," and rocked back and forth each time she said, "I can't, I can't." She became suddenly still and rigid when she heard the door open. The father came in. He looked from his wife to Daniel, from Daniel to his wife.

During the night, the mother screamed. Julien sat up. Daniel lay still. He heard Edmond go out of his room towards the parents' room. The mother continued to scream, high abrupt screams. Daniel heard them through the wall at his head, then the parents' bedroom door was opened and he heard the screams more clearly. He got up, put on a bathrobe, and went out. Julien remained sitting up in bed. Edmond was standing at the open door of their parents' bedroom. The light was lit. The father, in his underwear, was standing by the bed, holding the calf of one of his wife's legs which stuck out from beneath the bedclothes; she was twisting her body from side to side and screaming, "Ah! Ah! Ah! Ah!" The father pressed her calf. He said, "It's only a cramp, it'll go away in a minute." She screamed, "Oh, Jim! Oh, Jim! Make it stop! Make it stop!" The father's eyes were wide.

Daniel wrote to Albert. He knew that what made him write to Albert was not to communicate to him what was happening so much as to express his sudden, strange excitement at what was happening. He wrote the letter on Sunday while he pretended to have a nap before leaving for college. His excitement—his activated fascination—grew as he wrote: he was more and more excited, he realized, by the very fact of writing about what was happening, and all the while he did write he thought, no, he shouldn't be writing, it was wrong to be writing about his mother, and his writing to Albert about her was simply an excuse to write about her. "I'm writing this letter surreptitiously. Momma wouldn't want me to write it for fear of worrying you, but I think you should know, and think you would want to know, that she is not well. She woke up screaming last night. She had pains in her left leg. She said this morning that it was a blood clot which will go to her heart and kill her. She couldn't go to Mass, and yet she couldn't stay in bed. She's frightened to walk around because she thinks moving will make the blood clot move, but she can't keep still. She wouldn't get dressed. Dad kept telling her she should do that, only that, wash her face, comb her hair, dress, and he would do everything else, prepare dinner, make the beds. Julien and I helped. She did finally dress, but she said she had to force herself. She said she couldn't eat, but she's worried that if she doesn't eat she'll get too thin and weak. At dinner, she burst out crying and said she hoped the blood clot would go to her heart and kill her. Dad said, 'Stop it, now, stop it.' The worst is she can't stop herself from crying, can't stop her restlessness, can't stop herself from thinking. I look at her and I think: why can't she stop, why can't she simply stop? It is as if some inside body had taken over, and that body is completely out of the control of her own body, and controls her body, makes her cry when she doesn't want to cry and has no reason to cry, makes her shift from chair to chair when she wants to sit still, makes her think and think when she wants to be calm. I don't know what to do. I stay with her as much as possible, I listen to her talk on and on, because she talks as much as she thinks, and I try to reassure

249

her: she'll be all right, she'll be all right. I watched her this afternoon tearing up newspaper pages into long strips, and I wondered, not knowing at all the answer: what can I do?"

On the train he did the studying he should have done at home. He studied a page of short arguments in a textbook on logic to reduce them, as an exercise, to simple categorical syllogisms which would then demonstrate the validity or invalidity of the argument:

1. He is obviously a Communist, since he's always screaming about the evils of capitalism, and that's exactly what the Communists are always screaming about.

2. All true democracies have respect for the dignity of the human person; hence, since Vatican City has respect for the human person, it must be a true democracy.

3. Americans will never tolerate tyranny. From their earliest days they have been accustomed to freedom of opportunity and to freedom of thought and expression. No nation with such a background will ever submit to an arbitrary and self-seeking despot.

4. All true democracies have respect for the dignity of the human person; hence, since Vatican City is not a true democracy, it does not have respect for the dignity of the human person.

5. He thinks that labour unions should be abolished. The reason he gives is that they cause strikes and, according to his way of thinking, whatever causes strikes must be done away with.

6. No dogs are cats, because no cats are spaniels, and all spaniels are dogs.

7. Everyone who hates his brother is a murderer. And you know that no murderer has eternal life abiding in him. Hence, you see that none who hates his brother has eternal life in him. (John 3:15)

8. Whatever encourages tenants already in possession to use space wastefully at low rents brings about the appearance of a housing shortage. Many tenants would move if it

were legal to demand of them the amount of rent that their apartments are worth. Hence rent control has itself brought about an appearance of a housing shortage.

The train carriage was almost empty, and the lights were dim. It comforted him to isolate in his mind a function, high and dispassionate, which reduced all problems to subject, predicate, conclusions; he was not so interested in doing his exercise as in thinking about that function of his mind, so recently revealed to him by a Jesuit in a classroom with gothic arched windows and a bare plank floor. He knew it was curious that he did not want to use the function to think about anything—to think, if he could clearly, about his mother and father or about himself—but he simply wanted, on the rattling train, to think about it in itself, or maybe think on it, as though the function were not a centre of active consideration, but a centre of some totally inactive contemplation. He wished the train would never arrive at Back Bay.

Albert, in his officer's uniform, sat with his mother and father at the kitchen table. The father's forearms were on the table, and his hands were crossed. He leaned a little over the table and looked at Albert. The mother sat away from the table. Her hands hung down below the seat of her chair. She stared so at Albert her focal point seemed to be at the middle of his brain.

Albert spoke calmly to them. "You're both under great strain, I think, and I wouldn't want the strain to become too much."

His parents were tense; they knew that Albert would never say anything to either one which they might take as a judgement on them, because Albert would never, would not ever allow himself to judge his parents; and yet he knew they were listening to him with the attention of working-class people listening to a bureaucrat who could, at any moment, by a slight alteration in his voice, shift from a man of large calm tolerance to a man who told them they were wrong in everything.

Albert said to his mother, "You look tired. Do you sleep well?"

"Yes," she said.

The father raised his folded hands a little and lowered them, raised them and lowered them.

"If I have trouble sleeping, I say my prayers. Isn't that right? I pray for us all to sleep well. Isn't it good that I pray, Albert?"

"Yes," he said.

The father again raised and lowered his folded hands; they were spotted with white paint.

With the same large calm tolerance he'd used to ask them about themselves—a large calm tolerance which was nevertheless tense with the deliberateness with which it was held large and calm—Albert said, "Philip was married this morning in Virginia, where he's stationed. André went to the wedding. I couldn't go, so I wrote to ask if he could get a few days' leave to go, as he's just back from the Fleet's Mediterranean cruise. It was a quiet wedding, I think. In any case, André will tell us. He'll be coming home this weekend."

"André is coming here too?" the mother asked.

"Yes, just for the weekend. I thought you might want to hear about the wedding, Mom." He didn't look at his father.

"I didn't know he was back in the States," the father said quietly. "The last we heard of him was a postcard from Barcelona."

"He'll be here," Albert said.

The mother's eyes, which had all along been focused on or in Albert, focused in the same way on her husband. Then she sat back. She said suddenly, "Well, when André does come we'll have a good discussion."

"What?" Albert asked.

"We'll discuss everything—"

"Discuss—"

She opened her hands and tried to speak with a clear impersonality. "I don't blame anyone for what's happened. I don't blame anyone at all. But, don't you think, we've got to decide something, we've got to decide something and act on it—" She indicated a round table with her hands. "A round-table discussion, you and André and Edmond too, and Richard if he comes down, and Daniel too, and Julien too, and your father. And if you decide your father is right, well, I'll go along with that. But I want him to say that if the discussion reaches a decision that he's not right, he'll go along with that. Isn't that right? Isn't that using your mind? Isn't that the way to have peace?" She turned to her husband. "Isn't that so, Jim?"

He didn't move, and neither did Albert, who looked at his father. The mother made a sudden startled movement when she heard the back entry door open. The kitchen door opened and Daniel came in. The mother went to him and put her arms around him. Daniel looked at Albert, then his father, over his mother's shoulder.

The father interrupted Daniel while he was reading, late in the evening after the mother had gone to bed, by handing him a postcard and announcing, "It's from Barcelona." That a postcard from Barcelona, Spain, had reached their house in Providence, Rhode Island, seemed to be for the father a personal accomplishment. His knowledge of geography was to a large extent determined by where his sons had been, and though he could not have situated Barcelona on a world map any more than he could have situated Miami, he could refer to those places where André had been with a possessiveness which in itself made them major capitals of a world he was in control of. Daniel's possessiveness (and, as a matter of fact, his uncertainty of geography) was greater; he didn't know where anything was, really, but he would himself possess the whole globe. He studied the postcard. The picture showed the arches of an arcaded

253

sidewalk, and there were small tables and chairs on the sidewalk and a few people sitting at the tables, and beyond the arches palm trees, and beyond the palm trees the windows of the buildings across the square. The picture looked as if it had been taken twenty years before, and it was coloured in pale washes of pink, blue, green and the people at the tables floated in little bright clouds of red and yellow.

He tried to visualize himself sitting at a table by a café entrance. He wondered if André had sat there. The postcard was of the Plaza Real/Place Réal/Royal Square. He tried to visualize himself, in a small cloud of shining blue, walking past the arches, past the palm trees, and out of sight, but he couldn't.

André let himself in with his key. He found his father at his desk, papers with columns of numbers spread over the top, and on a chair to the side Albert was sitting to study the papers with his father; his mother was lying motionless on the couch, her eyes open, her mouth open and a little twisted; Daniel in a chair, his legs over the bolstered arm, was studying a picture in a movie magazine; Edmond and Julien were watching the television, on which grey roller skaters raced round and round a grey racing rink.

Before André could salute them, the father rose, quickly went to him, took his right hand in both his and shook it so André's entire body shook. He said again and again how happy they were to have him home, and André, to confirm his appreciation of the welcome, grasped his father's hands in both his and shook them more than the father shook his. The mother, as if she had been asleep and was half woken, rose with difficulty, and searched the room to see who had come in, then said, "Oh." André went to her with a light bound and held her tightly to him. He kissed her cheek, her earlobe, the side of her neck; he pressed his face into the side of her neck, which she craned to the side, away from him. He drew back from her and turned to his brothers, whose hands he shook gravely. He sat on the couch. They, standing, watched him.

He said, "Oh, it's marvellous to be home again. Mon cher père et ma chère mère, let me tell you—" he shook his finger, as if admonishing them, and his voice went nasal—"let me tell you something seriously, something I realized during the long hours at sea as clearly as, more clearly than, I've ever realized anything: that you both, père et mère, mère et père—and I assure you I'm very serious—have made the ideal home, and I'll tell you why it's ideal—" He compressed his lips for a moment. "It's because you've made it together." Albert frowned. "You've always done everything together, every decision has been made together, and that's why, when I come home, I feel what I never ever feel when I'm away from home: a wonderful harmony. It's a rare, rare, rare quality." No one spoke. "You know," he said, "I thought up a few words to live by while I was at sea. I typed them out. I thought so many things. I saw others looking up at and thinking about the stars, and I thought: think beyond, contemplate what's beyond, wonder how many universes there are. But the most important thought I had—and if I've come back to pass this thought on to you so you'll believe it, both of you, I'll have done everything, really everything, a son who loves his parents could ever aspire to do—was this: how two people can, by their harmony, set the chords of harmony humming throughout the world, throughout the universe, through universe after universe, on and on and on." He sat back.

After a humming pause, the father asked, "And did you—?"

André said, "No, wait, I've brought you some gifts."

He hurried into the kitchen and came back carrying two canvas suitcases. "I brought gifts you could all enjoy, they're gifts to the family. Jule, come and help me." From tissue paper Julien helped him unfold and hold up, like the train of the fantastic wedding gown of an invisible bride, an immensely long, heavy, lace tablecloth. André lowered his end so it trailed on the carpet, and unwrapped from more tissue twelve large napkins with deep margins of lace. He held one up by pinching the centre, and the lace fell in long deep folds. He said, "It's for a twelve-place setting." The father said, "Look at that, Reena, look at that!" The mother placed her hands together as if praying and said, with a quiet alarm, "Oh!" "What a meal we'd have on that!" the father said. "Yes," she said, "but we eat at the kitchen table." The father said over her, "Beautiful, really beautiful!" He wanted to elaborate the tablecloth and napkins— these accoutrements of a very very rich ceremony—into a general activity that would, he perhaps hoped, engage them all, engage his wife especially, as in a rich bright ceremony, and exclude, as uninvited, the thin dark people he knew stood just outside and might at any moment force their way in.

The mother said, "Yes, yes." She sat.

André looked over the tablecloth spread on the floor.

Albert said, "And the wedding?"

There was a sudden tense silence, but André took up the silence as though it were a dramatic pause before he, with a shift in expression from high-pitched, overly emphatic enthusiasm to an enthusiasm made more emphatic by its low pitch, said, raising and lowering his head, raising and lowering his eyebrows with each sentence, "It was beautiful! It was beautiful!" There was another tense pause. The sons did not look at the father or mother.

Albert, with a vast disinterest he took for granted in others as much as in himself, asked, "Tell us about it."

The father left the room.

Albert said, "Tell us about it."

André said, "It was exactly what you'd expect Phil's wedding to be: very simple, and just because very simple, very beautiful. Oh, and Jenny! Oh, she's marvellous, marvellous, a really marvellous girl. And her folks. They're terrific people. They came from Texas to Virginia for the wedding. They said that they didn't mind that the wedding hadn't taken place in Texas. They weren't sure about their daughter marrying a Catholic. They thought it was better that she was getting married elsewhere. Oh, they're terrific

256

people. You can see how much they like Philip. They treat him just like a son. Jenny's mother said to me, 'We knew from the first time he came to our house with our son Jack that he was good, and that he must have come from a good home.'"

The door to the cellar closed, and they heard the sound of the father's steps going down. The mother was looking away from André and her sons.

"Go on," Albert said.

The mother got up, walked to the open double doorway between the living room and the dining room, stopped and stood there, her back to her sons. She walked on to the doorway between the dining room and the kitchen, again stopped, and after a moment turned round and grasped the jamb on either side of her. As with a small thrust forward, she walked quickly through the dining room, into the living room again, and to the doorway to her bedroom. She went into her room but immediately came out and rushed through the living room and dining room to the kitchen. Albert made a step to follow her. She reappeared at the doorway between the kitchen and dining room and stood there and again held the jambs for a moment and again thrust herself forward, through the dining room, into the living room, all the way to one end, then turned, rushed to a corner, rushed to her bedroom doorway, stopped before going in, turned round and looked about the living room, then rushed towards the dining room again. Albert reached out to grasp her by the arm, her body jerked back, and she tried to pull away. He reached his other arm around her and drew her to him and held her, her back pressed against his chest, so she stared out from him. She didn't move. He let go of her and she sat.

André, Edmond, Daniel and Julien stayed with her while Albert went down to the cellar to the father.

Albert said, "She's been through this before. I wasn't so young that I can't remember it. Something's got to be done—"

257

The father said nothing.

"I'm going to telephone Dr Dalande," Albert said, "and take her to him."

The father's head was lowered; he shook it a little.

"What do you say?" Albert asked.

"I don't say anything."

Albert went back upstairs. He said to her, "Stand up," and she stood up. He said, "Put your coat on," and held her coat open for her so she could slip her arms into the sleeves. He said, "André has your hat," and she took it from André and put it on. He said, "Button your coat," and she did. "Let's go," he said, and she walked between them.

A long time after they had gone, the father came upstairs. He walked about the house. Edmond switched on the television set and sat close to it. Two large grey men, who appeared greased, were clenched in a wrestling match. The shouting behind sounded very far from them. Edmond answered the telephone when it rang. It was Albert. Edmond handed the receiver to his father and returned to the wrestling match. Albert said, "Dad, we're taking Momma to a sanitarium." The father said nothing. "Dad." "Yes," the father said. Albert said, "You must remember, more than I, the previous times. Neither of you can go through anything like that again. Do we have your permission?" "But she doesn't have a toothbrush or nightgown or clean underwear for tomorrow—" "She'll be all right for one night. We'll take her whatever she needs tomorrow. Do you agree?" "Yes," the father said. Edmond turned up the volume to hear the referee. The father said, "I agree." He put the receiver down and went to sit before the television set. Edmond moved so he could see. He got up after a minute to go into his bedroom.

When he heard Albert come into the house, he rose heavily, his body rigid as with the rigor mortis of a death he'd been condemned to, and went into the kitchen. He stood before Albert, who had been congratulating Daniel and Julien on their presence of mind in preparing supper, and who, at the appearance of his father—the condemned man come back to declare by his very appearance the injustice of his condemnation—said, "Look, Dad, she had to get out of this house, it's a house of death," and the father appeared all at once to decompose. Perhaps it was true that his father would suffer her absence more than she suffered his presence, but Albert, now, saw the decomposition of his father as a kind of morbid magician's trick to awe his spectators, and the moment the spectators gasped and pleaded with him to stop the magician would reconstitute himself in his pride at having done what he wanted to do. Albert remained stark.

"I shouldn't have given my permission to let her go," the father said.

"Did you want to keep her here and kill her?" Albert asked.

The father looked at André, who smiled.

"She'll be her old self in a couple of days," André said, "you'll see."

The father said, "She won't be my wife any longer when she comes back."

"Come on, Dad," André said.

"No, she won't. They'll change her. She won't be what she was."

"She will be as she was, as she was at her best, a happy, laughing woman who loves her husband and her family."

"She won't be as she was, and I won't be. You think I keep her here to kill her. *I'm* dead without her."

"Dad, you're being a little dramatic," André said.

"No, I'm not. I'll be dead when she comes back. She knows that." His face was white.

Albert said, "She didn't want to stay. We left her weeping. She wanted to come back here, to you. We made her stay. We made her stay for the good of you both. You can't kill one another."

The father said nothing.

Albert said, "I want to tell you this, Dad: no one is condemning you to death by taking Mom away from you for anything you've done. No one, no one at all, thinks that you've done anything wrong. You've done as you felt you had to do, as you've always done. We admire you for it. We admire you for holding to what you hold to. We haven't taken sides. We won't take sides. It'd be wrong of us to take sides, and we all know that. If you think we've done wrong in taking Mom away, in separating you—and maybe we have—all you have to do is say to me, 'I want my wife back,' and I'll go right away and get her. Your word holds, not ours. It holds even against Mom's word. If there's any condemning to be done, you're the one to do it, not us. You can condemn us, you can condemn Mom. I swear to you that we do not, not one of us, and least of all Mom, condemn you." Albert all at once bared his crooked teeth, and it was as though he were violently swearing. "I'd fight, I'd fight any of my brothers, I'd fight Mom herself, to keep it the way it is."

The father looked to the side.

"Do you want me to go get her?" Albert asked.

"No," the father said.

During the night, Albert woke up to the creaking sound of the rocker in the kitchen, and he got out of bed, put on his Japanese robe, and went out; he sat across from his father, who, in his robe, continued to rock in the blue darkness.

"You should try to sleep," Albert said.

"I can't help thinking what they're doing to her," the father said.

"They're no doubt calming her down."

"I don't know. I can't imagine what they're doing."

"You'll see tomorrow."

"No, I don't think I'll go tomorrow."

"You don't want to see?"

"No, I don't."

"You don't think she's better off there than when, in the past, she raved, and you didn't know what to do?"

"We somehow got through it."

"She's all right, Dad."

"I don't know."

"Why don't you pray?"

"I was praying. I was praying to my mother."

"Did you ask Matante Oenone to pray?"

"I will."

"Do you want to pray together?"

"Yes, I do," the father said.

"Do you have your rosary?"

The father raised it from his lap.

"I'll get mine." Albert went back to the room he shared with Edmond and reached under the pillow of the studio couch he used as a bed to pull out his rosary; he returned to the kitchen.

"You say the mysteries and lead," he said, "and I'll answer."

Richard arrived the next morning as his brothers and the father were leaving for Mass. He joined them. They all sat in one pew at the back and left quickly as the curé was leaving the chancel in procession with the altar boys. The father and Julien drove home in the Dodge. The five brothers went out in the opposite direction in Richard's car.

Albert directed Richard. He told him to turn off into a gap in brown-grey woods. The dirt drive was like the drive to their country house. Branches scraped the sides of the car. Suddenly there was an opening, a large white clapboard house with glassed-in porch, gables and turrets; it had many wide windows which were opaque with reflections of the flat blue sky and passing clouds. They got out of the car into wind.

Richard, Edmond, Daniel waited outside. Albert and André went in. Around the square of lawn was a square gravelled drive, and along the edges, under the bare trees of the surrounding woods, were wooden benches. On the bench nearest Richard was an old man in a big overcoat sitting with his arms crossed over one another, his left hand on his right knee, his right hand on his left knee; he looked down, motionless. Richard turned away from him. He nervously walked about the small, indefinite and yet definite area they stood in. He said, "I'd like to get out of this place." André came out. He carried his Navy lieutenant's cap. He said, "She's coming home. The doctor hasn't okayed her leaving, but she insists."

In the car, wedged between Richard and Albert in the front seat, she talked as if, inside, she hadn't been allowed to talk in months, and, released, the very activity of talking excited her. "When you left me yesterday, some women came to me to ask me what was wrong, and instead told me, all together, what was wrong with them. Nerves, nerves. I couldn't stand listening to them. I kept thinking, why don't they do something about themselves? I couldn't stand the word nerves. 'My nerves, my nerves.' And then when I went in to see the doctor he said, 'We're going to give you shock treatment,' and I asked, 'Is it painful?' and he said, 'Mrs Francoeur, you'll feel as though you're dying,' and I said, 'No, no, I won't have it.' I said I wanted to get out, I didn't want to stay there. He said, 'Well, we'll prescribe tranquillizers, but we think you shouldn't go.' I said, 'You've got to let me out of here, I've got to get out, I want to go back to my husband.' I slept in my slip. They gave me pills. I don't think I slept, but my mind wasn't going round and round. I could hear the other women around me, breathing, and I wondered if they were sleeping, or if they were awake, thinking. I waited all morning for you to come. I'll be all right. You'll see. I'm going to get over this. You can tell your father I'm determined. Tell me how he is. Will he have a long face when I get back? That's the only thing that worries me, that he'll have a long face because I left him against his will. Will he?"

"Dad'll be so happy you're back," André said. "Everything is going to be fine. You believe that, Momma, and everything will be fine. I've learned that."

"I will, I will," she said.

She was euphoric. André was, Daniel thought, more euphoric. He from the back seat, she from the front, talked about how fine life was if you simply opened your eyes and ears to a real appreciation of it, and it seemed to Daniel that for them both—for the mother now, and for André always—life was a bright dense expanding gas, a euphoric gas, and the mother was now breathing it in deep breaths ("Open the window, I'd like the clean fresh air—oh, fresh air") while André never breathed any other air ("Ah oui," he said, "ah oui, respirez bien l'air"). André and the mother were able to communicate through a kind of overexcited appreciation of life. The others remained silent.

André helped her, as she was a little unsteady, up the stoop to the back door of the house. The door suddenly opened, and the father stood there. The mother stopped, her body lightly jerked back, but as she looked up at her husband a soft warm brightness spread over her face and she said, smiling, "Oh, Jim," and reached an arm. He came out on to the stoop, his arms too reaching out, and as André stepped away he held her, and helped her into the house.

"Oh," she said.

The father held her. She pressed herself a little away from him with her hands against his chest, and said, "Now I want to say something, Jim, I want to say something that I made up my mind about last night, and I want our sons to hear it. The sons go away, do what they have to do. I can't live for them." She looked at her husband; her eyes were a little unfocused, and one side of her mouth was slack. "Isn't that so, Jim? The boys should know this, all of them: that you and I, we're living for one another."

Daniel arrived home in the middle of the week. His parents, Edmond, Julien were at the supper table. Edmond shouted, "Hey, this is a surprise!" and got up to shake his hand. Daniel shook Julien's hand, and Julien, who stood too, said nothing, and Daniel said, "You're taller than I am." The father got up quickly and he said, both his hands about Daniel's, "Oh, it's good to see you, oh." Daniel smiled

at his father. He said, "We've been given a little holiday."
He didn't look at his mother, who remained seated.

The furniture in the dining room and living room was in
the middle of the rooms, piled up and covered in drop cloths.
The walls were stripped to the plaster. Daniel followed his
father around the newspaper-covered margin, around lad-
ders, over scrapers and wetting brushes and pails, to see the
work he had done. The father took a roll of wallpaper from
a neat pile on the floor, and unrolled it as if he were going
to give an oration on its pattern; it was for Daniel to see.
"Beautiful," Daniel said. "Do you like it, really?" the
mother asked. She was standing behind him. He studied the
pattern of maroon plumes in blue vases on a pale green
background. "Yes," he said, "it's beautiful." The father
laughed. "I chose it," he said; "your mother left it up to
me." "Yes, yes," Daniel said, "it's very beautiful." "I'm
glad you like it," he heard his mother say. He could not turn
to look at her.

He got up in the morning as soon as he heard Julien, the
last to leave, slam the door. He couldn't look at his mother
when he spoke to her; he looked down or to the side.

"How are you?" he asked.

"You won't believe me if I say I'm well, but I am."

"You made up your mind to change?"

"I just let whatever happens happen. I'm getting along.
We're getting along."

He looked at her. "Philip and Jenny are in Providence."

She extended an arm to touch Daniel's shoulder, he
thought for support, but she smiled.

"Philip wrote to me to say they'd be here. That's why I
came down. I cut classes. We can telephone them at their
hotel."

The mother opened the storm door to a tall fair woman
wrapped in winter clothes and surrounded by the steam of
her own breath who reached out to embrace her. The mother,
standing inside, clung to her outside. Philip, behind his wife,
reached his right arm over her shoulder and grasped his

264

mother's soft shoulder in his large gloved hand. Jenny embraced Daniel, she held him down, he felt, with her mittened hands and pressed her cheek to his, then Philip shook his hand.

Jenny said, "I'm so pleased." She had a Southern accent.

The mother said, "The house is all upside-down."

"Come on, Jen," Philip said. "I'll show you where I was born and grew up."

Philip took her about the house. The mother and Daniel followed close behind. They went in and out of rooms, Philip opened and closed closet doors, studied the furniture, the lamps, the photographs on the wall. "Look, that's a photo of Albert," he said, or, "Is Ed so devoted still to l'enfant Jésus—he seems to have hundreds more holy pictures on his bureau," or "Look, Julien's trigonometry book is exactly the one I used when I was at La Salle." Jenny smiled.

What was so strange to Daniel was that Philip should be treating Jenny familiarly; he'd somehow expected that Philip would treat his wife with the same startled unfamiliarity with which he, Daniel, or the mother treated her; he'd expected Philip to see her as from a distance even though they were standing near her, with the same awe.

"While away," Philip said, "I reduced everyone and everything here to still pictures, to the photographs I have of you all, of the house. It seemed to me you all, the house, existed entirely in pictures. And now—" He smiled at his mother.

The mother made tea in large white cups.

Philip said, "I've been trying to teach Jen French, Ma."

The mother looked at Jenny with slight surprise and asked, "You don't know French?"

"No."

"None at all?"

"No." Jenny smiled brightly, but she blushed, and her eyelashes flickered. "I'll try to learn."

"Make her say something in French," Philip said to his mother.

"Oh—"

"Go on," Philip said.

The mother laughed lightly. "Well now, this is the test, say *reçu*."

"What?"

"*Reçu*," the mother pronounced carefully.

"Raysou," Jenny pronounced just as carefully.

They all laughed, Jenny too, but her blush deepened and her eyelashes flickered more.

Philip said, "I sometimes use our special French endearment when I'm feeling particularly affectionate towards her. Don't I, Jen?"

Jenny said, "Yes, but he won't tell me what it is."

Philip kissed her on the cheek. "Ma petite crotte noire."

"Oh, Philip," the mother said, and laughed loud.

"What does it mean?" Jenny asked, her voice an octave higher.

"I can't tell you," the mother said, and put her hands to her mouth.

"Go on, tell her, Momma, tell her just how affectionate the French Canadians can be."

The mother whispered, leaning towards her, "My little black snot."

Jenny howled, "No."

The mother's face beamed.

When they were leaving, the mother asked, "Will you stay in Providence?"

"No," Philip said, "in a small town outside Boston where I have a good job." He put his arm around Jenny. "I may not be able to make her a French Canadian, but I'm going to make her a Northerner."

The father hung his cap and coat in the closet. He looked about as though he knew the house had been altered, but he couldn't detect what the alteration was, perhaps that the colour had changed, that the walls, floor, ceiling, had a faint blue tone. His wife asked, "What did you do today?" He didn't answer her. He frowned. He went into the other rooms, then came back into the kitchen.

He said, "They were here—"

The house did seem to go a deep blue.

"They were in my house," he said.

"Jim!"

"You saw them. You saw them here in my house."

The muscles of the mother's face twisted; she tightened her hands into fists and hit the air. "He's my son! My son and his wife!"

The father opened the kitchen door to go down to the cellar. He held it open. He looked at his wife. He said calmly, but his voice cracked, "Not in my house."

. The mother's face softened; she unclenched her hands and lowered them.

Daniel, alone, wandered from room to room. The rooms seemed to him very small. He went into his parents' bedroom, which was almost entirely taken up with the bedroom suite. He opened his father's armoire, in which he kept his best clothes and hundreds of ties; he found, in a drawer, an old money belt heavy with old foreign coins, many Chinese coins with square holes in the middle, a hernia truss, bits of mineral samples from the mine he had invested in before he got married, a gold pocket watch. He looked in the cedar chest, an engagement gift, he knew, from his father to his mother, which was alongside the bed, and fingered white flannel trousers and blue blazers, long underwear, a swath of pure Chinese silk, bits of wedding veil.

Over the cedar chest was hung a long narrow framed picture of a man and woman, he in thirties tuxedo, she with a white short clinging dress that revealed the outlines of her low breasts, the couple in the midst of roses on an arbour, she standing with her back to him but leaning against him, he with his big brown hand on her white arm, his cheek next to hers. The picture came from an advertisement for soap which, when she had seen it in a pharmacy shortly after she was married, had struck Reena enough that she had asked for it, and framed it, and hung it in hers and her husband's bedroom.

He lay on his parents' bed. He felt weak, and he got up from the bed with an effort when he heard his parents come into the house.

He left while his mother was asleep. His father said he would say goodbye to her for him. The train was crowded, and he had to sit in an aisle seat with upholstery so dirty he didn't lean his head back. He took from a notebook a piece of paper and wrote her a letter. It took him the whole trip to Boston to write it.

"I wish I was at home. I wish, now, we were together. I wish we were drinking tea and talking. I often think now of our drinking tea and talking, either both of us sitting at the kitchen table, or you at the ironing board and me in the rocking chair. I wish for it now. I miss the smell of the clothes being ironed, miss the sight of piles of folded linen in the laundry basket. More than anything I miss the cups of tea, I miss our talk. I used to think those silk-fringed pillowcases which Richard and Albert and Edmond sent to you with Army or Marine Corps insignias on the side and poems to Mother on the other side were embarrassing. I didn't understand that what was embarrassing to me was embarrassing because I hadn't ever experienced it. I miss you because I love you—"

He stopped. He wouldn't be able to send a letter solely to his mother, without including his father. He was about to tear the letter up, but put it among the pages of his notebook.

In the chill morning, the mother woke Julien by shaking his feet through the bedclothes. He raised his head, and she whispered, "It's time." Dressed, he sat at the table in the kitchen, but didn't eat. The mother with a distant voice asked, "What's the matter?" He answered, "Nothing." She studied his dark face, which was a little lowered. She said, "You don't want to go to school this morning?" "No," he said. "You've got to go," she said. "I don't want to," he said. She didn't want him to go; she didn't want to be alone in the house. She said, "But you've got to." He bit his upper lip. She said, "I'll go with you. Do you want me to go with you?" Julien released his upper lip and bit his lower lip. "All right," the mother said, "I'll get a kerchief and my coat."

They took the bus. Julien sat next to her, silent, and looked out of the window. The bus descended Mount Pleasant to where, in a neighbourhood of bricks and clapboard houses on wide lawns and surrounded by shrubs, La Salle Academy sat on its own lawn, among its own shrubs. When she and Julien got off the bus, she said, "I'll stay here, you go." "All right," Julien said. She turned away so none of the boys collected about the main entrance would see her, and she crossed the avenue; from the opposite side, at the bus stop, she looked back to see Julien approach a group of boys, one raised his arm to greet him, and Julien disappeared among them. She had to wipe her eyes to see the bus number.

When Daniel next went home, his father said, "Your mother's in bed. She hasn't washed and dressed in three days." Daniel went in. She wore the father's bathrobe over her nightgown. She was half raised on pillows. Daniel sat on a chair by the side of the bed. His mother looked away from him, but he saw that she was crying. The father came in and said, "Now stop that, stop acting up." She said, "I know, I know, I promised you I'd be all right once Daniel got back, I promised you we'd have a nice holiday, but I can't, I can't." "You *can*," he said. He looked very tired. Daniel said, "Dad, let me stay a little with her." "She'll cry." "I can't help it," she screamed. "I can't take it," the father said. "I'll go up to my sister Oenone's." "Yes," the mother said, "go, go, poor thing, go get some relief from me, you deserve it. He does so much for me, Daniel, he feeds me, does everything, and I can't do anything to repay him—" Daniel said to his father, "Go to Matante Oenone. I'll stay with Momma."

The father left. The mother began to rock back and forth against the pillows. She spoke through her clenched teeth. "Has he gone?" "Yes." "I wish I'd die so he'd have peace," she said. "No, no," Daniel said. "Oh yes." "He'd die if you died." She rocked back and forth. "What am I going to do? What am I going to do? Oh, Daniel, dear Daniel, Daniel. Does it get you when I keep calling you Daniel? Oh, Daniel, dear Daniel, what am I going to do? What will I do?" "Do you want to get out of bed?" "No. Oh, no, no. I can't. I can't relax out of bed and I can't relax in bed. Look, it's that knotting in my stomach, knotting there, and the bzz-bzz in my ears, there all the time, and all the parts of my body are tingling. And what are we going to do for supper? What are we going to have for your father and Ed when they come home from work? I think that every day. I can't look at it. The look of food is enough to make me want to vomit. And your father gets mad at me if I don't eat. But I can't eat. What will I do, Daniel, what will I do? I'll end up in the insane asylum. They have to come and put me away. That's all there is to it. And think of the disgrace to the family. Think. Oh, Daniel, dear Daniel, I don't want to disgrace the family."

"But there's no disgrace. You're being silly."

"Oh but there is," she cried. "Oh, Daniel."

He wiped the tears from beneath her glasses with a tissue and put his arms around her. A smell came off her, a faint smell of body and talcum powder, enveloped in the smell of the father's thick bathrobe.

"What will I do? What will I do?"

"Do you want a tranquillizer?"

"No, no. I had one before, and anyway they don't do any good, not any more." She shouted through her clenched teeth, "Oh, Daniel, oh dear Daniel, oh dear, dear Daniel, oh I love you."

He drew back from her and sat a little way from her.

"I'll spoil your vacation," she said.

"Of course not."

"You'll wish you were back at college. You'll want to go back right away."

"No. No. Of course not. Don't be silly."

"Oh, honest, Daniel, honest."

"Of course."

"Oh thank you. Oh thank you so much. Thank you."

He leaned towards her and kissed her.

"I'm so tired," she said. "I'm so tired. I'm so tired. All the parts of my body are tired and I can't relax." She shouted, "Jim, Jim."

"Now you know Dad can't do anything."

"Yes, I know, but I wish he were here. He would hold me and rock me like he does."

"All right, Momma, that's enough."

"Oh, Daniel, dear Daniel, what will I do, what will I do?" She reached out for his hand. Her hand was moist. She squeezed his hand in her moist hand for a moment, then rubbed the top of it with her other hand, rubbed the knuckles, rubbed the wrist. He pulled a little against his held hand as if he could pull away from it and leave it. "I love you, Daniel," she said, "I love you, I love you like a mother loves her son. I can remember when you were a boy, I dressed you in a blue knit suit with a white beret, I remember, and Edmond took you out in the stroller and everyone said how beautiful you were. And I had you. To think I carried you, to think I carried you nine months under my heart, and your body came out of my body."

His hand sweated. She squeezed it in one hand and rubbed his wrist with the other.

"Oh, it was a privilege."

Daniel tried to pull away. "No."

She held his hand. "Yes, yes. It was a privilege. It was a privilege to carry you."

Daniel pulled his hand hard out of hers and got up.

She stared at him. "What's the matter?"

He sat. He said nothing.

"Oh, Daniel," she said.

She went to Mass with them Sunday morning. She was hardly able to hold herself in sitting, standing, kneeling positions; her lips moved very very rapidly while praying. Daniel too had to hold himself still. He kept looking at his mother. There were lines, he noted, radiating from her lips and from the corners of her eyes; the pores were large on her nose; a black hair curled from under her soft chin. His entire body strained to keep from moving away from her.

The mother walked out of and into and out of and into the kitchen. She opened the kitchen door to the back entry, and the father, who had said nothing to her as she walked in and out of the kitchen, said, "You're not going outside, are you?" She said, "No, I'm going down to the cellar." She slammed the door. They heard banging from the cellar. "Go down and see what she's doing," the father said to Daniel. He went down. He saw his mother hitting a post with two long pieces of wood, one held in each hand; she hit with the wood in her left hand, then hit with the wood in her right hand.

Edmond said he would drive them up to the lake for apples. It was a clear, cool day. The mother said she couldn't go. The father said, "Try, you like being in the country." "No," she said. "Please, for me," he said, and his voice broke a little.

In the car she held tightly to the hand strap in the back seat as if she were holding her body in some tense, frightened suspension. The lake was bright, and calm. The mother said she couldn't go for apples; she wanted to walk around their land a little. The father asked Daniel, "Keep an eye on her, will you?" and he, Edmond and Julien went for the apples in the car. The mother slowly walked to the lake and out on to the dock. Daniel watched her from above. The water below her sparkled; the sparkles flashed and died, flashed and died. He saw her staring into the water. He felt all his muscles go slack suddenly, and he thought: Go on, Momma, go on. She stayed at the end of the dock till her husband and sons came back.

His father was sitting in the rocker by the kitchen window. Whenever a car passed in the street, going in either direction, he turned his head quickly to see if it would stop. Julien was on one side of the kitchen table, Daniel on the other. Daniel was rubbing Albert's Japanese ink stick in a little water on a lacquer tray to make ink, and Julien was practising calligraphy with Albert's brush by supporting his right wrist in his left hand and swinging the right brush-holding hand to make loose wet downward strokes that ended with short, abruptly reversed upstrokes. The brothers were silent. A car passed, seemed to slow down. The father jerked his head to the side to look and, at the same time, was about to rise; but, though the car did stop, it was an unfamiliar car which stopped across the street, and from it someone went into the house across the street where the Italians lived. The father continued to rock. The floorboards under the linoleum where he rocked creaked; the rocking seemed to make the house creak in other rooms. The father folded and unfolded his hands as he rocked. A car stopped outside. Its windshield reflected the cold grey late morning light. The father jumped up, quickly opened the kitchen door, went into the entry. The boys heard the outside doors being opened. The doors were left open. A gelid draught blew in. The boys heard car doors thump. Julien and Daniel stared at the kitchen door. Albert came in first, backwards, reaching down and holding up one of his mother's arms. Richard was close behind her, holding her other arm. She could hardly walk. They got her into the kitchen and held her on either side. Her head lolled. The father came in behind. The two eldest sons held her without moving for a moment, as if all the air had become solid. The mother's hands dangled, and her forearms moved loosely; she swung her head up, and her eyes appeared blind. Albert said, "All right, let's go to your room," and he and Richard helped her forward. The sons slowly moved her across the kitchen floor and to the door to the dining room. The father followed behind and he looked at his wife as if she were dead. He stopped at the dining room door and

273

looked at Albert and Richard taking her through the dining room, into the living room, into her and his bedroom.

After a moment, Albert, his overcoat and scarf on still, came into the kitchen. "Look, Dad," he said, "she's going to have to go to the hospital to stay for more treatments." The father stared at him.

When Richard and Albert visited her in the hospital, she asked, "Where is your father?" "He won't come," Albert said. Richard leaned over and hugged her, but she didn't put her arms around him.

The next day Albert and Richard and Daniel visited her, and she said to them, "I'm coming home." Richard said, "I'm glad." Albert said, "But you know it'll all be as bad as before, if not worse." "No," she said, "I swear I'll be all right." Richard looked at Albert over the bed. Daniel stood at the foot of the bed. "Can you promise me," Albert asked his mother, "that you'll continue to have the treatments?" "Yes," she said, "I'll have them, I promise." "You can't want them, we know, but you must continue, not only for your sake but for Dad's sake, and for the family. You're making a promise to us all, all your sons," Albert said. "Yes, all right, I promise you all." "Everything will really be destroyed if you give them up," he insisted. She frowned. "I won't give them up," she said, "I won't." Daniel said, "It's because of Dad that you're coming home." She looked at him. "If it weren't for Dad you'd stay here and continue the treatments," Daniel went on. Albert said, "Dad will try to make you give them up, you know, and that'll be a disaster. He'll try to make you give them up because he thinks they'll change you, because he thinks you'll no longer be his wife. He doesn't know they'll make you better." "I've promised you," the mother said, "I won't give them up." She looked at Daniel.

Her husband was at work. In her bedroom, she found the top of her bureau bare; he had taken all the perfume bottles on a mirror tray and boxes of powder and brushes and combs and doilies off it and put them in drawers.

Richard asked, "Do you want me to put everything back as it was?"

"No," the mother said. She put her hand on the bare top.

Richard said, "He took everything off because he wanted us to feel bad for taking you away and because he knew you'd be back sooner or later, and he wanted you to see it to make you feel worse for going. Do you think he would have done it if there was no one to see it done?"

"He's a fake," Daniel said.

When he came in only a sudden frown showed that he saw his wife in his rocker. She got up, went to him, and put her hand on his elbow. "Hello, Jim," she said. He pulled his elbow away. "Don't talk to me," he said. He put his cap and coat in his closet behind the rocker.

Richard, Albert, Daniel, Julien watched their parents.

The mother asked, "You don't care for me?"

"No," he said, "now leave me alone."

"But what did I do? I'm back from the hospital. Are you mad at me because I'm having the treatments? Is that it?"

"I gave you my signature."

"But you said to the doctor on the phone that you were all for them. I heard you myself. Yes, Doctor, yes, Doctor, certainly, Doctor. What happened?"

"I told you I gave you my signature."

"Jim, how do you expect me to get better?"

"Go back to the hospital."

"The treatments won't help me any if you're like this. Don't you care if I don't get better? Jim, don't you? I'm your wife. Don't you care for me?"

"I did care. I cared for you when you were still my wife."

Daniel shouted, and his parents and brothers, jolted, turned towards him: "You're killing her!"

The father said, his eyes red and watering as from a cold, "No, you're killing my wife. You're electrocuting my wife."

He went into the bedroom and closed the door.

She said, "I couldn't stand it at the hospital. I kept

looking at the door. When I saw Richard and Albert come in without your dad, my heart split. The woman in the same room with me asked me if your father was dead. She said, 'He hasn't been in, your husband, he isn't dead, is he?' My heart split in two because he wouldn't come to see me and hold me. And now I can't stand it here." She was in the middle of the kitchen floor. She looked at her sons in silence for a moment, then said, "When I was young and my mother and father had their ins and outs, I couldn't stand it. They kept it up for a long time. It didn't seem to bother my brothers and sisters, but I couldn't stand it. And now I think it must bother you." Her voice was calm.

Albert and Richard were going out as Edmond came in from work. He had an ink stain on his nose. He slammed his lunch box on the kitchen table when he saw his mother. "I said if you left the hospital this time—" Albert said, "Ed, go wash your nose." The two eldest brothers left the house.

While Daniel and Julien peeled potatoes in the pantry the mother walked round and round the kitchen table. She suddenly went to the bedroom and opened the door. Her husband was lying on the bed in the dark and smoking. "Jim," she said, "Jim, I can't stand this. If there's anything I've done that's wrong, can't you forgive me? You say your Notre Père. You say, 'Pardonnez-nous nos offenses,' and you won't forgive me."

Daniel heard her from the pantry. He went to the dining room door. "Momma!" he shouted. "Momma!" He couldn't see her. He shouted as if she were far from him, and he knew she wouldn't hear him even when he shouted. "You didn't do anything! Can't you understand? Why should he forgive you? He has nothing to forgive! He should be asking you to forgive him! You know it!"

"Jim," she said, "Jim, why don't you talk to me?"

"Momma!"

"Jim."

"Momma!" He was terrified, all at once, that she would go into the bedroom and close the door behind her.

She said, "I'll give up the treatments. Even if the boys don't like it, I'll give them up."

He jumped up and ran to the bedroom door. He saw his father, by the light from the living room, lying on the bed; the dark room was filled with smoke. Daniel stood on the threshold, at his mother's side. He shouted at her, "No, you won't! You won't!"

His screams made her wince, but she didn't look at him; it was as if he wasn't there, and he screamed to make her know that he was there. His strained sore voice suddenly lapsed into a screech that shocked him; he imagined he heard the screech from an immense distance, and he wondered what it was.

"No, no, no. You won't! You won't!"

"Jim, please, please!"

Daniel screeched, "He's winning! He's winning! Can't you see he's winning!"

She finally looked at Daniel, but again as from a great distance. "But I want peace. All I want is peace in the house."

The father said, "I gave my signature. Go to the hospital. Go to the hospital and have a shock. Go get a shock."

"Jim! What did I do?"

"You've got a choice. Me or the shocks."

"I'll give up the shocks."

Daniel screeched, "No, you won't!"

The look she gave him brought him from his great distance to close to her; her eyes were wide. "Leave me alone." She stepped past him into the room.

He stood in front of her. "Get out of this room!" His screeches made him tremble. "Get out of this room! You're getting those treatments!"

"But I want peace."

"Get out of the room!"

Edmond screamed from the kitchen. "Can't we ever have peace in this goddamn house? What's the matter? What's the matter anyway?"

Daniel heard Julien close the door to his bedroom.

"Get out of this room!"

"No," she said. She stood halfway between the door and the bed.

"Get out of this room!" His screech suddenly cracked like an adolescent's voice; he continued to shout with a voice that wasn't his, "Get out! Get out!" She stepped away from him. "Get out! Get out! Get out!" She cringed a little. He saw she was frightened of his screaming. She backed out of the room. Without looking round at his father lying on the bed, Daniel slammed the door. It hurt his throat when he spoke. "Don't you know what he's doing? Don't you know?"

"But all I want is peace," she cried. "That's all I want, is our family to be peaceful."

Daniel sat with her in the living room. He wanted to leave her, but he thought that if he did she would go back to his father.

She said, "If I could just fall asleep and not wake up. I want to die. I want to die. Promise me you'll pray that I'll die. Promise me."

"No, no," he said impatiently. "I can't, I can't promise that."

"You're mean then. I never thought you'd be mean to your mother, Daniel. I never thought it."

Richard and Albert came in with bundles, which they put, wrapped, on a bed. Daniel and Julien set the table. The mother sat on a chair by the kitchen door like an uncomfortable, ignored visitor who might at any moment get up and leave. The older sons sat on other kitchen chairs; they discussed her and the father as if she were someone they didn't know who would not know what they were talking about.

"Of course he wants his wife with him," Albert said.

"Yes," Richard said.

"Wants?" Edmond said. "He can't stand it when she's away. Well, when she went to Massachusetts to stay with those old friends, didn't he say she could go? But while she was away he wouldn't eat or talk to us. And when Momma came back he was lying on the floor in front of the stove. And when she went to stay with her mother, because she couldn't take the house and us kids any more, went for just three days, he told his mother that his wife had up and left him and the children, had deserted him—"

Richard held his hand up to stop him. "All right, Ed, all right—"

"But it's the truth."

Richard shook his head. "Yes, yes."

Edmond raised his voice. "Never mind, all right. It's not all right. We never talk about what's happening. Why did he cut off Philip? Why did he? I know why. Goddamn it, I know why."

"What is it?" Richard asked.

Edmond compressed his lips.

"I know why," the mother said.

The sons turned to her.

"It's because of the money," she said, her hands in her lap, "that's all."

They said nothing; Edmond too looked away.

She said, "Julien, go tell your father it's time to eat."

The father served himself, ate, and rose when he had finished. The others continued to eat silently. The father went to his closet to take out his coat and cap. He put the coat on.

The mother asked, "Where are you going?"

"I'm going up to my sister Oenone's."

"Now? It's late."

"I'll stay there."

"Stay?"

He isolated his wife from the midst of their sons by talking to her as though they were not there. "You won't see me again."

His wife's body silently sank.

"You're all against me," he said. "All right. I'm leaving. I'll call up a lawyer tomorrow and I'll make arrangements for a divorce." He hit his finger hard against his chest. "No one is going to pull the wool over my eyes. I know what's happening. You're all trying to get rid of me. Well, that's all right. You never wanted me." He spoke directly to his wife. "Since you all say I'm the cause of the condition, I'll cut out the cause." He suddenly shouted, "Go get shocked, go get shocked, go get shocked!"

Albert said, "Dad, no one has accused you of anything."

The father looked at him.

"Are you afraid of the treatments?" Albert continued.

"Yes," the father said, "I'm afraid of them."

"And you want her to stop them?"

Edmond jumped up and pointed to his mother. "Didn't I tell you when you went into hospital that if you left I wouldn't have anything more to do with you? Didn't I? Well, I don't give a damn what happens to you. Stop the treatments! Go ahead, stop them! I'm through with you. I'll go away."

"Where would you go, Ed?" the mother asked.

"Sit down, Ed," Albert said.

Edmond sat.

Albert said to his father, "She can't stop the treatments."

The father put on his cap; he pulled the peak down over his forehead. He said to his wife, "You can have all the money except the eighteen hundred dollars my mother left me. And I'm going to try and keep this house. I don't care about the other house. This will be my house."

The mother suddenly got up. She stared at the father as she stepped towards him. Richard, who had been sitting next to her at the table, also rose, and reached out when he thought his mother was falling. His arms remained reaching towards her as she, on her knees, rocked back and forth. All her sons rose.

Albert stood above her. His mouth twisted up to one side. The sinews of his neck stood out. He shouted, as no one in the house had ever heard him shout, "Stand up! Stand up! Stand up! Get off your knees and stand on your own two feet like the mother of a Marine! Your husband is sick! Do something about it! Stand on your feet and do something to help him, woman, your husband is sick! Get up on your feet! Get up!"

No one moved. She stopped keening, but her breathing heaved her body. They watched her get up. She stared at her husband. She said, hardly moving her mouth, "Don't go. Stay. Please stay. Stay. You're breaking up our home. Stay for Julien."

He stared at her with the same fixed look. After a moment he removed his cap. He said, "All right, I'll stay. You win."

Daniel, standing, was holding a glass of milk. He threw it against the wall. He saw everyone instinctively turn his face from it. He shouted, "Win? Win? Win? *You've* won, Momma? No. No. No. It's he who's won! *He* hasn't given in! *You've* given in! *You* have! He thinks he's making a sacrifice, he thinks he's the martyr! Oh no, oh no! *You're* sacrificing everything! *You're* the martyr!"

Richard put his hand on Daniel's shoulder. "All right, all right, try to control yourself."

"Oh no. He can't win!"

Richard's voice was soft. "I know. I know. He worked it out. He worked it all out."

Daniel wiped his eyes and turned away. He heard Richard scream. He turned back to see Richard standing before the father with his fists clenched tight. There was a look of frightened surprise on the father's face.

"Is this another part of your plan?" Richard shouted. "Is it? Is this another part of your plan?"

Albert came up to him. He took his older brother in his arms when Richard began to sob. Richard drew back.

"Thanks," Richard said, and sat.

The father put his cap back on and left.

The mother and her sons sat on the chairs that were pulled out from the table.

The mother said to Julien, "You want your father, don't

you? Go up to your Aunt Oenone's and tell him we need him. Please, Julien."

"No," Julien said.

"You used to get along so well. Won't you miss him?"

"I won't miss him."

They were still sitting when the father came back. He took off his coat and cap and put them in the closet. He said to his wife, "It's time to go to bed." She got up and followed him. The brothers remained sitting.

Albert said, Christmas morning, "Dad, try your overcoat to see if it fits." The father put the overcoat on. "Stand in the middle of the floor so we can see." The father stood in the middle of the floor. "The collar should be pulled up," the mother said. Daniel pulled the collar up and smoothed the shoulders flat. "Does it fit?" Albert asked. The father's face was stark, but he said, "Yes, it fits."

The day darkened rapidly. Daniel looked out. The long late light lengthened on the black deserted street. The father and mother spent most of the long afternoon in their bedroom.

When the parents woke, Albert prepared tea. The kitchen was dark and they were silent. Out of the dimness and silence, the mother finally said, "I've got to tell you, I'm going to break my promise, I won't have any more shocks."

Albert put his cup down. "You must do what you think is best," he said.

Daniel drove Albert to the small military airport outside Providence. Gusts of wet wind blew old leaves against the windshield.

Daniel said, "You know, I don't think I've ever thanked you for what you're doing for me."

"What's that?" Albert said.

"We don't ever thank one another in our family for anything." He paused. "For paying for my tuition and room and board at Boston College."

"I'm not sending you to college for yourself alone, lad, I'm doing it for all of us."

"Yes," Daniel said. He paused again. "But I must get a job to help pay. I've been notified that room and board will be eight hundred and fifty dollars next year, a hundred and fifty more than this year."

"I can manage that, I think."

"No, don't say that. I can't allow myself to expect you to pay for me. I've got to get a job."

Albert said, "To prove you're independent?"

Daniel said, "I'm not independent." A leaf slurred across the windshield. "In fact, I don't want to work. I come from a working family, and yet you know when I tell myself, you've got to work, I ask myself: work? work? I don't know what it means. Has Dad ever really worked? Am I crazy? I wonder: what did he work for? Yes, I am crazy. These questions are horrible. He worked because he had to work, and I'll work because I have to work. And yet— You know, I'll always have little, I know that, and that doesn't worry me. I may not even have all the essentials, and that doesn't worry me. But working terrifies me."

"You could work for God," Albert said.

"Yes," Daniel said.

When, alone with his mother in the house the long, slack days following the New Year, Daniel heard her come into the kitchen where he was, he went into his room, and when he went into the living room where she was she went into her room. He felt that the tendons throughout his body were loose, and when he reached he couldn't quite control his arm and hand, which swung out further than he intended and knocked over a glass. In the silent house, he tried to study. The space between the words, between the letters, seemed to stretch; it took him hours to read a paragraph. The silence was so deep he got up to see, as if it were a constant deep sound, where it came from. He looked into the living room. He saw his mother standing in the middle of the floor, her back to him. She didn't move for the long time he stood and watched her. Standing still himself, he felt the tendons of his body tighten. He went to his mother. She looked round at him.

"Are you all right?" he asked.

"Yes."

"I don't think you are."

"Yes, I am."

"You're not better, and you're going to get worse than you were."

"No, Daniel, I won't."

His body jerked. "You should have continued with the treatments."

She said nothing; she appeared rigidly calm.

"You should have." He had no idea why: tears began to form in his eyes and drip down the sides of his face.

"I couldn't," she said.

"It isn't too late."

"It is."

"Yes, you're right, it is."

"Daniel."

He looked at his mother's face. It flashed through his mind that she should have died.

"Oh," he wept.

"Stop it," she said.

"All right."

"I couldn't have continued. It would have destroyed me, it would have destroyed the family."

"I don't care," he said.

She looked past him. He turned to see his father at the door. There was a streak of black paint across his right cheek. He came into the living room.

"You don't want your mother to get better?" he said.

Daniel was a little frightened. He felt his body step back into silence while, at the same time, it stepped forward and the body that stepped forward said, "I do."

The father's voice was dark, but calm. "You're wrong. You're all wrong. I do care."

"Then—"

"He gave his support, then he took it away, and you all take his side." While he spoke he reached out and put his hand on his wife's shoulder.

That body of Daniel which had stepped back watched, from its distance, the body that had stepped forward reach out and pull his father's arm, so his hand slipped from the mother's shoulder. His mother stepped closer to her husband.

Daniel shouted, "I know what you want!"

The mother said, "No."

"I know! I know! I know what you want to do! I know! Then do it! Do it! Do it!" He wondered, from behind himself, who the person screaming was, or what he was screaming about.

He saw his mother looking at the body before him as from above it, but her eyes were not really focused on it. He heard her say down to that body, "Your father did a lot for you. You've easily forgotten how much he's done. If it weren't for him—"

"Yes," he said through his teeth. "If it weren't for him, I wouldn't be here, but I don't want to be here."

He saw her eyes focus, saw her arm swing up and down. She smashed him on the face with the side of her hand.

He stood still for a moment. He saw, behind his mother, his father; his father had his hands over his face. Daniel tried to find his way out of the living room, which seemed to him to be the living room of a house he'd never before been in.

He went immediately to pack. He phoned the train station for the next train to Boston. It was in four hours. He sat in Julien's room.

His mother came in. "You're leaving," she said.

"I'm going a week early."

She left him alone. He heard Edmond come in, and he went out into the kitchen, looking at no one else, to ask him if he would drive him to the station. Edmond made a face. "Never mind," Daniel said, "I'll take the bus." "I'll take

285

you," Edmond said. Daniel got angry. "No," he said, "I'll take the bus." He shouted, "I don't *want* you to take me!" Edmond said, "I'll go start the car."

Daniel put on his overcoat, scarf and gloves in the bedroom and walked through the kitchen with his suitcase. He opened the kitchen door and went down the steps into the entry. He heard his mother say, "Are you going without saying goodbye?" Daniel turned. His mother was standing at the top of the entry stairs. Behind her, his father was sitting at the kitchen table playing solitaire. Daniel's face seemed to swell.

"You're leaving without saying goodbye?" the mother repeated.

Daniel saw that his father, though playing solitaire, was crying.

His father said, not looking up, "That's all right, Daniel."

"You come in here and shake hands with your father before you leave. If you leave like this," the mother said, "you'll be sorry. You won't have a home here any more. Come up and shake hands with your father."

"This isn't a home any more. It can't be. I'm not happy here."

"It was your home for seventeen years."

He took off his gloves, climbed the entry stairs, entered the kitchen, and went up to his father. His father pushed his chair back and stood. His father held his hand for a long while. He said, "If I did anything to hurt you, Dad, I'm sorry."

His father's eyes were red. "If you don't have to leave tonight, stay. Why don't you stay and leave tomorrow?"

"I can't."

"Why can't you?" the mother said.

"I can't. I have studies." He thought, no. He said again, "I've got to go."

"All right," his mother said, "goodbye," and tried to kiss him, but he drew away.

Edmond lit the headlights as he got into the car. He saw

the blind go up from the kitchen window, and saw his mother lean close to the window, her hands extended on either side of her face to block the reflections from inside to see out. Edmond started the car. Daniel didn't look to the side but he knew his mother was waving.

He said to Edmond, "Never mind, I'm not going." Edmond shut the engine off. They sat in the darkness for a while. "No, I'll go," Daniel said.

XII

HE FOUND A birthday card in his mail box. It was signed, in the mother's writing, "Dad and Momma." On the back the mother had written this note:

Now, you're eighteen, and you're near to being independent. I'm sure you want to be independent, and you are right, to want to be. We would like to see you. When you can, please come home. I must tell you that I'm not 100% well, but I am well. We haven't heard from you, in a long time. We hope you're well.

It was a cool note, and it was cool, he knew, with her respect for his independence. As he concentrated on the handwriting, it seemed to him his brain all at once moved, all the inner perspectives of time and space—which were not, he knew, focused at a point on the back of his brain, but converged at one point now, another point a moment later, if they converged at all—shifted, and he was no longer at Boston College in March 1958, as his mother was not in Providence, Rhode Island; he didn't know where he was, but he knew he was looking at the handwriting of someone very far in space, very far in time, as if she had died. He was startled. He had not been home in a month and a half, perhaps to show that he was independent. Now, suddenly, his independence, which he had forced on himself all the time he was away, detached him not only from his family, his mother and father, his brothers, but detached him from the

288

time and place he was in. He felt that he had been so cut off from his mother he would never be able to see or speak or write to her again. He needed to get in touch with her right away. He wanted to reassure her that he wasn't independent, and didn't want to be independent. Though he had a class that was to begin in five minutes, he hurried to a public telephone to phone her. He shouted: "Momma."

Her voice sounded very far away. "Oh, Daniel."

"I'll come home."

"Oh," she said again.

His mother's birthday was four days after his; he imagined that she was born after him, was as young as he, and he was as old as she.

On the train to Providence, Daniel sat next to the dirty window, on which when the train suddenly, jerkily shifted direction he saw his face, then, when the train shifted again, through which he saw the Boston South End slums, boys running down an alley, a torn poster, a shattered window, the smokestacks of a factory. The train passed through intermittent countryside, through spindly winter-bare woods, passed a deserted clapboard house in an overgrown field surrounded by a fieldstone wall, passed a huge junk yard filled with the chassis of old cars and enormous piles of battered oil drums, and a bare tree in the middle of the junk yard was hung all over with old tires. The sun set. The train passed brick towns with neon signs flashing against the brick walls, and the sky still purple above. Some people in the train were reading newspapers, some had their eyes closed.

He slept in his seat finally but woke often with the startling sensation that the train had reversed itself and was going backwards.

He felt, too, that he was walking not forward down the street to the house but backward, and when he saw the house on the street corner, in the bluish light of the street lamp, all its windows dark except the kitchen windows, where, through drawn shades, there was a pale yellow light, he imagined he had come to it by a reversal of his senses of space and time. He stopped for a moment to look at the house. For the moment, he thought: I can't go in. He thought it not only because he did not want to go in and his body stopped short of it, but because it seemed to him his body couldn't cross the space and time that separated him from the house. He slowly walked up the stoop and stairs, opened the storm door, took out his key and opened the back entry door. In the back entry he paused for a moment.

The door to the kitchen opened with a widening margin of yellow light, and in the light, leaning to see, was his father.

Daniel said, "It's me, Dad."

"I thought I heard someone," the father said. He still held the door open and leaned beyond to look at Daniel.

"I came for Momma's birthday," Daniel said.

"I'm glad," the father said. He appeared older than Daniel remembered; like his own mother, his eyes were sinking into their sockets and his cheekbones stuck out. He opened the door. Daniel passed into the kitchen and put his bag down. Julien was sitting at the table.

"How are you?" Daniel asked him.

"I'm all right."

Daniel turned to his father, and as he did his father suddenly grabbed his shoulders. He held him. His face was stark. He said, "Your mother will be glad. Your mother will be so glad."

"Where is she?" Daniel asked.

The father looked at him for a long time, then released him.

"She's in her bedroom."

"Is she sleeping?"

"I don't think so."

"Does she want to see me?"

"Oh yes."

Daniel took off his overcoat. He stood in the middle of

the kitchen. He didn't want to go into his mother's room.

The father asked, "Have you heard from the others?"

"I got a letter from Albert. He sent me some pyjamas for my birthday and a small check to buy whatever I want."

"What did he say?"

"He didn't say anything."

"And Richard and André?"

"No, I haven't heard from them."

The father took a step back. "You couldn't get in touch with them and ask them to drop a line?"

Daniel frowned.

The father said, "We understand you all think it's best if we're left to ourselves. That's all right, Albert sends the checks each month, for the mortgage and for you at college, but it would make a difference if there were a letter."

"Yes," Daniel said.

"It'd make a big difference to your mother."

Daniel, too, stepped back. "I'll go see her," he said.

"Go on."

But he asked Julien, "Why don't you come with me?"

"No," he said.

He knocked at his mother's door. He heard "Yes," and he went into the dim room. She was sitting in bed. Her hair was uncombed, and her skin shone in the yellow light from the lamp by her. She closed her husband's robe round her neck when Daniel stepped towards her.

He stepped towards her as if about to fall; he sat on the chair at the side of the bed.

She spoke through her clenched teeth. "You shouldn't have come."

"I wanted to see you on your birthday."

"You should have stayed away. You were right to stay away. You should have stayed away like the others."

"You knew I'd come back."

She raised her hands, held palms outward, to her face.

"Don't look at me."

He leaned his heavy body forward to take her in his arms.

"Oh, Momma!"

"No, don't come near me. I smell. I haven't washed in four days. I can't."

He put the tips of his fingers to his forehead.

She said, "I want to die."

"Oh, no," he said.

"I do."

"I won't let you."

He looked down at her; she looked up at him, but she said nothing. He pressed his knees against the side of the bed and leaned a little over her.

He said, "Momma—"

She said, "Go back to college."

He shook his head violently. "I won't go. I won't. I won't go."

"You said that because you've stayed away so long, you feel I'm like this because you, because you all, stayed away. After two days you'd want to go again. And you'd be right. I'm like this not because of you or any of the others or your father. I'm like this because of me."

"No," he said.

"Yes."

His voice was very dry. "I'll stay. I'll stay. You'll see."

"There's nothing you can do, Daniel. Your father has been out of work for two weeks now, taking care of me. He'll lose his job. He does everything he can, everything. He loves me. I know he loves me. And I love him, but I want to die."

His body leaned more over the bed, and he felt he'd fall on it, across her legs. He pressed his knees hard against the side of the mattress and shook his body a little.

"Momma—"

He felt all throughout him, his whole body given in to it, a dark flow, felt the flow fill him, fill him and overflow him.

He said, "I love you." He shook himself. He said, "I love you. I love you."

She said, "Don't, Daniel."

He didn't look at her. He went out of the room.

His father was lying on the couch in the living room. He was on his back, his body at an angle, so his feet extended stiffly over the edge. His hands were bent at the wrists and pressed together on his chest. His head was back, his mouth open, his eyelids open to white slits.

Daniel was trembling a little. He went into the kitchen, where Julien was sitting as before at the table. Daniel sat at the table also.

"How can you bear it, day after day?" Daniel asked.

"I listen to music," Julien said.

"You should come up to visit me at college. You can stay in the dorm."

"I'll be all right here."

Edmond came in. He grunted when he said to Daniel, "So you came back."

"Yes." From time to time his body jerked; he felt light-headed.

"So now you can take over. I've had enough."

"You could leave," Julien said.

Edmond turned to him, his eyes straining out.

The mother screamed from her room, "Jim! Jim! Jim! Jim!"

Through the doorways of the kitchen and the dining room, Daniel saw his father, in the front room, jump up from the couch, then fall back in a half-sitting, half-lying position, his shoes thumping the floor. He got his balance, and quickly went into his wife's room. Daniel could hear his voice, low, saying, "Yes, yes, yes," while his mother continued to call as if he were far: "Jim! Jim! Jim!"

Edmond shouted, "Oh, for crying out loud, you're not going to start up again."

The mother screamed, "Darling, darling, darling, I don't want to do anything wrong. I know it's a sin, darling, I don't

293

want to disgrace the family, but I'm afraid I'll become desperate. Jim, Jim, do something. Do something! I don't want to go to hell."

Edmond went to the door and bellowed through it: "Stop it! Stop it! No one can help you! You've got to do it yourself!"

She howled, "I can't, I can't."

Julien said, "Edmond." Edmond stepped back from the door, looked about the kitchen and sat. He raised his hand. "I—" But he stopped when Julien got up. Daniel watched him go to the doorway of his parents' room, where he stood just outside, and looked in.

Julien said, "Momma."

"What?" the mother asked.

Julien didn't say anything.

"What can I do?" she asked.

He said, "Get up, wash, dress, put on some make-up."

After a while, she said, "All right."

The four men waited in the kitchen for her to come out of the bathroom. They didn't speak. She came out wearing a flowered housedress, and her hair was combed, her face clear and powdered, and she had reddened her lips. She moved slowly. She sat.

The father said, "It's Julien, isn't it? You did it for Julien?"

"Yes," she said, "my last born."

"Is there anything I can do for you, Momma?" Daniel asked.

She couldn't look at him. "No."

"Can I make you a cup of tea?"

"No."

He said, "I've brought you a present."

He opened his bag, which was still by the kitchen door, and he took out a long flat package wrapped with white paper and tied with string. He gave it to his mother. She held it in her lap and tried to untie the string.

"Wait," the father said, excited, "I'll get scissors." He cut the string.

The mother raised the open box; in it were six knives, the blades held upright by slits in the cardboard.

She said, "They're nice." She put the box on the table.

"We should celebrate," Daniel said.

The father said, "I didn't have a chance to—"

She shook her head.

"Well, this is the best celebration we could ever have," the father said, "seeing you here with us."

She tried to smile.

"And it's all because of Julien," the father went on. "Now if that doesn't show his special power—"

"Yes," she said.

"And doesn't it show, too, what power you have? You can change, you can be a new woman, if you just make up your mind to. You could do it," the father said, "you could. You *can*. I know you can. You just have to want to."

She shook her head a little. "No," she said, "I want to die."

Daniel's head went dark, and in the large darkness he heard his voice, as if he himself, infinitely small, were standing in that darkness behind his forehead, call, "I love you, I love you—" She looked at him for a moment, then got up and went into the living room.

He watched his mother, who was lying flat on the couch. She was still. The father was sitting across from her. He was also still. Daniel watched him raise a hand to his forehead and he imagined that if he touched his father's arm he would knock it away and his father would fall over. Edmond was watching television, Julien, sitting at the other end of the living room, was turned away from them.

Daniel thought that the house about him seemed to have many rooms, many more than it had, so if he left the living room he would find doors upon doors leading into rooms upon rooms, and he, in his chair, had no idea what was happening to them. He heard faint sounds from them, a dull distant thump, a low whine, and, perhaps, voices.

A sudden desire came over him to get out of his house into

the outside and at the same time he wanted to close the door to the living room, to close all the open doors, against what would come in.

He jumped a little when a door opened in another part of the house. They all turned their heads. Edmond got up and went towards the kitchen door as Richard entered. The father smiled when he saw Richard. Behind Richard was Albert, and the father stood. Behind Albert Philip came in, and the father's flesh appeared to fall slackly away from the bone. Behind Philip was André.

Philip said, "Hello, Dad."

Albert stood by Philip. "I brought him down," he said.

André said, "We came to celebrate Momma's birthday."

Philip held out his hand. The father managed to reach out his hand, but shaking Philip's he looked away.

When the father let go of Philip's hand Richard went up to him and held him by his arms. The father continued to look away. The mother went suddenly to her husband, and Richard stepped to the side.

She said to Philip, "You shouldn't have come back."

"It was time to," he said.

"Jim," she said.

She walked to the end of the room. She stopped, her back to them, and shook her head, again and again.

"Momma," André said.

She turned round to them, still shaking her head.

Albert said to his father, "I did what I thought was best for us all."

She went to her husband again and took one of his hands, held it up, and stepped close to him, bending his arm and pressing it against her as she put her arms about him.

"You'd better go," she said. "You'd better go away, all of you."

Albert made a small gesture towards his father.

"Go away," she said. "Go away, leave us alone, leave us alone."

"Momma," Albert said.

Her lower lip stretched, the skin on her chin puckered, her jaw jutted, and she shook her head, back and forth, back and forth. "We love each other." She turned her head away and pressed her face into her husband's shoulder, at his armpit. He held her. Philip stepped back, and as he did raised his hand to his brother's to indicate he was quietly, quickly leaving.

Albert asked, "Shall we go, Dad? Shall we?"

The father shook his head a little, "No. No, no," the father said.

Daniel, alone awake in the sleeping house, walked from the living room to the dining room, to the kitchen, back through the dining room to the living room. He touched the furniture. He sat, he stood. He moved about. He turned the slats of the Venetian blinds to look out at the street light. A car passed. He turned the slats down again. In the dim light inside he studied the long gilt-framed mirror that had been a wedding present to his father and mother, then a bowl of paper flowers, then the books in the shelves of the glass-fronted desk. He opened a glass door. He took out *High School Self-Taught*, which his father had been reading for years and years, leafed through it, put it back. He opened the desk flap. Some pigeonholes were empty, others stuffed with papers and envelopes. He pulled out a small stack of old envelopes bound by elastic and removed the elastic to separate the seven envelopes. Each one was inscribed, in the mother's writing, with the name of a son, Richard A., Albert B., Edmond R., Philip P., André J., Daniel R., Julien E., and inside was a clipping of hair from the first haircut the father had given each son. He lifted the hair out of each envelope and slipped it back; fine blond hair, massy curly hair, straight dark hair. Daniel's sight blurred a little. He replaced the envelopes and reinserted the stack in the pigeonhole. He took out another stack. These were old letters. He stood at the desk and read one of them in the silence of the house.

297

Sgt. Albert Francoeur USMC
V.M.S.B. 342 M.C.A.T.
Newport, Ark.
Oct. 3, 1944

Dear Mom and Dad,

I went up on a dive bombing hop this morning and saw one of the most beautiful sights I have ever seen. When we took off the sun wasn't shining because there was a thick blanket of clouds at 5000 feet, but we climbed up through the clouds into the warm sunshine and all around as far as I could see was a great white country with huge mountains, narrow valleys, hills, dales, and wide bright prairies. We zoomed around the base of one of the mountains and hedgehopped through the valleys and over the hills and prairies. The nicest thing about it was that we couldn't see the ground and I felt as though we were in another world. I was happy up there.

While looking through the *Reader's Digest* today, Mom and Dad, I came across an article titled "A Catholic Mother Looks at Planned Parenthood". Now I'm proud of a certain man and his wife who live at 128 June Street, Providence, Rhode Island. I read the article to find out the opinions of a modern woman about married life and compare those opinions with the old-fashioned laws by which the above-mentioned man and wife allow themselves to be governed. After reading the article, I immediately came to the conclusion that you, Mom and Dad, are indeed the two most wonderful people I have ever or will ever know. The utter unselfishness you displayed in putting aside a life of ease which you could have had for years of pain, heartache, worry, misery and hard work just to follow the will of God makes me so *proud* to call you my beloved parents. My heart almost bursts with pride, love and admiration for such splendid people. Oh, how you rise above the seething mass of sinners, like a King and Queen! You are the wondrous ones who have seen your duty to God and perform it. I promise you that my brothers and I shall do our utmost to see that you taste some of the bliss of which Heaven is so full that upon this earth some *does* overflow. God bless you, Mom and Dad, I'm the proudest man in the world to be your son, and I say that straight from the heart and soul. I only wish I could perform my duty in the Marine Corps as well as you have to God.

Kiss Julien and Daniel for me.

Love,
AL

P.S. I signed my payroll last Saturday and will draw $90 on the fifth. You can expect a money order for $70 in the near future.

Daniel opened his mouth to try to release his sobs noiselessly. His eyes and nose ran. He put the letters away, closed the desk, sat on the couch. He had to catch his breath between sobs. He couldn't stop. He opened his mouth wide, he tensed his body against its shaking. It was as if he were vomiting with nothing to vomit up.

The door to his parents' room opened. He was in darkness, and he saw his father lean out into the dim light beaming from the kitchen. His father looked towards him.

"Tsi gars?"

"Yes," Daniel said.

"What's the matter?"

Daniel sobbed. "I don't know."

His father came towards him. In the presence of his father, he felt all his constraint give way, and his body shook. His father put a hand on his shoulder, by the side of his neck. A kind of howling broke from Daniel.

"Tais-toi, tais-toi, tais-toi," his father said.

Daniel shook his head.

His father put his other hand at the back of Daniel's head and pulled him towards him, so Daniel's body was leaning forward, his face pressed into his father's bathrobe just below his chest.

Daniel drew back. His face was wet. His father pulled a handkerchief from the pocket of the bathrobe and handed it to him. Daniel wiped his face, blew his nose. He gave the handkerchief back to his father, who held it and looked down at him.

His mother called from the dark bedroom, "Jim."

The father turned.

"Go tell her I'm all right," Daniel said.

His father put the handkerchief in his pocket, "You tell her."

Daniel rose and walked a little unsteadily to the bedroom door, where he paused; he couldn't see inside. He said, "Momma."

"Yes," her voice said.

The father passed him, went into the bedroom and closed the door. Daniel stood looking at the closed door. Then he went to the window at the far end of the living room. His thoughts lightly rose and swelled. He hadn't wept, he felt, someone outside had wept. He inserted a finger between the slats of the blind and raised one to look out at the deserted street.

He thought: Pray to God the Father

    To the Holy Spirit

    To the Son

    To the Virgin Mother

    To all these, in their strange high country, in their large bright house, pray for the small dark house in this low country

    Pray that that love they have for one another, which light is reflected one to the other, be extended beyond them in grace to us, that we may love one another as they there, that we may reflect their love for one another to one another here

    Pray for the illuminating grace, pray for the transfiguring grace

Pray for what they know, and what we do not know, what they see and we cannot see, what they hear and we cannot hear, what they touch and we cannot touch, what they smell and taste and we cannot

Pray for the awareness of their movements above us, that we may move as they move

O Holy Father

O Holy Spirit

O Blessed Son

O Blessed Mother

That we may move as they move, that we may meet, may part as they, may move in their grace

Pray for the house, pray for the holy house